THE SMUGGLERS
AND
MADAME GIN SLING

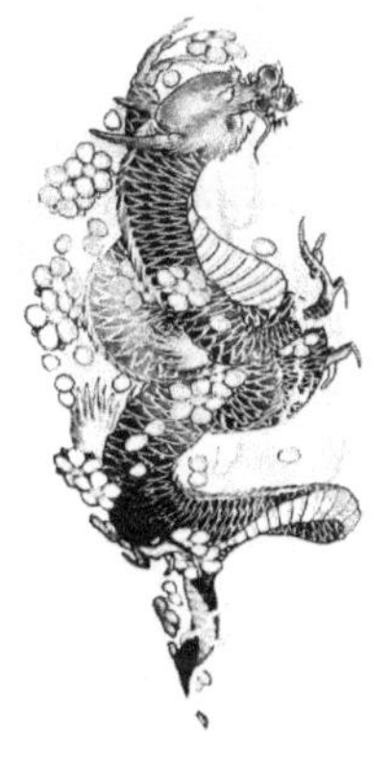

By
Jay Alt

KCM PUBLISHING

A DIVISION OF KCM DIGITAL MEDIA, LLC

CREDITS

The Smugglers and Madame Gin Sling by Jay Alt

ISBN-13: 978-1-939961-49-5
ISBN-10: 1-939961-49-1

First Edition

Publisher: Michael Fabiano
KCM Publishing
www.kcmpublishing.com

For Easy

Acknowledgements

This book would not have been possible without the help and suggestions of several people. First of course, I must thank my wife Polly, who is a great editor and proof-reader. My agent Lois De La Haba, whose encouragement and sage guidance proved invaluable. Michael Fabiano, the publisher whose vision made this book a reality.

The Smugglers
and
Madame Gin Sling

Jay Alt

Contents

1

Pete Smith leaned back against the headboard of his bed as the maid took away his breakfast tray. His wife's hairdryer howled in the background as he reflected on the last two years of his life. If someone had told him on the day he retired from the army, a confirmed bachelor, that in two years he would be living in a mansion in Santa Barbara, with a maid, and a cook, he would have called them crazy. But, meeting Sophie in Macau was definitely a life-changing experience. Marriage, children, a home in Santa Barbara . . . none of it had been in his plans.

The noise in Sophie's bathroom stopped, and she came into their bedroom using her crutches. She was wearing a bra and panties and sat on the other side of their bed to put on her peg leg. Sophie had lost her left leg a few inches above the knee at the age of five, during the fall of Saigon. At first she used the peg leg a la Captain Ahab, out of financial necessity. But it quickly became her trademark as she built her empire of casinos and whorehouses in Asia and became known as Madame Gin Sling. Now she had the peg leg fashioned in a variety of materials and lengths to coordinate with what she was wearing.

Dressing for a day at home, Sophie decided to wear a wraparound denim skirt and a sleeveless blouse. When everything was tucked in she came around to her husband's side of the bed and sat down. "Do you need anything else before I go down-stairs?" she asked.

He gave her his best thirty-two tooth grin.

"I am still too sore, but I am healing fast," she said, having given birth to twin boys only two weeks before. "But, speaking of that, have you given any more thought to getting a vasectomy?"

"Yes."

"And?" she asked.

"No."

"Why not?" she wanted to know.

"As I explained to you once before, no one is getting near my nuts with a scalpel."

"One night with a bag of frozen peas for pain and swelling, and voila, end of problem," she said.

"I have spoken," he said in his deepest basso voice.

"Listen, I really don't want to get pregnant again. The twins were very tough on me."

"Well, I thought you were the lady who couldn't get pregnant. Besides, you can get your tubes tied or use the Pill if you're so worried about getting pregnant."

Sophie flashed an involuntary quick glance at her peg leg and then said, "I'm afraid of doctors. My experience with them hasn't always been the best."

"Things are appreciably different now," he pointed out.

"I suppose so," she said, rising to leave.

When Sophie had initially learned she was pregnant with their first child, she was totally shocked. Long ago her doctor had told her it would be a miracle if that ever happened, considering the scaring in her uterus caused by back alley abortions.

She didn't know Pete very long yet they had fallen for each other quickly. Given that she was going to have a child, Sophie "convinced" Pete that they should marry, and unilaterally decided to move with him to the States to make sure their child was born in the US.

While Sophie sold her businesses in Asia, Pete was responsible for finding a suitable mansion where they would live. He had done that with a great deal of trepidation, spending twenty-five million dollars of his wife's money on a house she had never seen. On top of that, the eight-bedroom, ten-bath Hollywood colonial needed considerable updating and renovation so he spent the next six months overseeing the renovation and another two million dollars making the house livable. Throwing that kind of money around wasn't something Pete normally did – unless it was to outfit a Special Forces unit and then Uncle Sam's bottomless pockets were picking up the tab.

He slid down under the covers and dozed off. Active all his life, he had never enjoyed enforced idleness. It was almost noon when he awoke. Boredom had set in and he decided to get up and take a shower. Three weeks of bed rest was all he could stand. He had been shot the abdomen three weeks before while taking down some terrorists who were trying to release poison gas in San Francisco. He shaved before showering. Fifteen minutes later he walked downstairs wearing blue jeans and a t-shirt. He found Sophie in the small dining room feeding their one-year-old daughter, Alexis.

"Should you be out of bed?" Sophie asked.

"I feel pretty good, the bullet wound is healing nicely and the doctor thinks I should start moving around. I must be getting better because I'm hungry. Could Jean Claude fix some French onion soup for me? In fact, maybe I should go to Paris for a week or two for a taste of the real thing. You know French onions are decidedly more flavorful than American onions. Can I get you to come with me?" The hotel complex Sophie had owned in Macau had had a French restaurant. Jean Claude had been the chef until Sophie had brought him to the United States with her. Now he took care of cooking lunch and dinner for the family and ordering all the food from a grocery store that delivered, although occasionally he would shop himself.

"I know Paris is your refuge. Well, perhaps refuge is not the right word, but where you go to recharge your batteries. I also think it is a little premature for you to think about going to Paris. Before you go anywhere mister, you are going to get a clearance from the doctor."

"Listen, I am just fine. I'm not too big on sawbones myself."

"I'm dead serious about this. You haven't seen me have a real tantrum yet, but if you leave here without a doctor's clearance I will perform that vasectomy myself."

"Do you plan on using anesthetic?"

"No!"

"Sounds painful."

Ignoring his last remark, Sophie said, "However, if you do go, would you do me a favor?" she asked.

"Sure."

"Buy a condo. I have a feeling this won't be your last trip there. Get something big enough for the whole family."

"Condos in Paris are very expensive," Pete said.

"Real estate is always a good investment. Your last trip cost about a hundred grand," Sophie said.

"Why don't you come with me?"

"Between breast feeding the twins and taking care of Alexis, it would be just too complicated. I would love to go, though. I am French, you know." Alexis was their one-year-old daughter. Sophie had been born in Saigon to a Vietnamese mother and a French father. Her father had registered her birth with the French counsel which conferred French citizenship on her. According to Sophie, that was the only thing her father had ever done for her, except split.

After lunch, Sophie took Alexis upstairs for a diaper change and a nap. Soo Ling, their amah, took the twins for their nap. Sophie had also brought Soo Ling with her from Macau. Pete went outside on the terrace. Sophie's reaction to his proposed Paris trip worried him. He loved his wife dearly but she had two faults: she was insanely jealous and had a volcanic temper. His last trip to Paris had brought both of these flaws to the fore.

When Pete was honest about it, he would admit he occasionally pushed her buttons deliberately. Even though she knew he was doing it, she could not stop herself from reacting.

When Sophie walked out on the terrace, he indicated he wanted a kiss. She went over to him, he took her by the waist, and spun her onto his lap.

"Should I be sitting here?" she asked.

"Oh sure, you're on my thighs not my stomach."

He kissed her and said, "I want to tell you how much I love our life together. I never in a million years would have thought marriage would be so wonderful. But I must say that is, largely because of your loving and caring nature."

"Well, I think you are very special, too," she said blushing at his unexpected remark.

***

Ten days later, Pete and Sophie invited two other couples for dinner. First to arrive were Mike and Diane. Mike and Pete had served in the army together. Mike was the finest soldier Pete had ever known. His wife, Dianne, was a beautiful former topless dancer who was covered with tattoos; she now worked in a small hotel Sophie had bought. Sophie decided she needed to keep herself busy, as if a husband and children were not enough. Pete thought it represented business withdrawal.

Jack and his wife Carol arrived a few of minutes later. Pete and Sophie had meet Jack and Carol while renovating the house. Jack, a former Marine and a genius with wood, had worked on the house during the renovation. Carol taught in the local school system. She and Sophie had become best friends, lunching and shopping together as often as Carol's schedule would permit. Their son, Jack Jr., had been born five days after Alexis.

Mike and Jack had joined Pete in the jungles of Laos going after a drug dealer/arms merchant who was threatening to kill Sophie. They had assisted with the recovery of the poison gas.

As they were waiting for dessert to be served, Sophie said to Carol, by way of idle conversation, "Pete is going to go to Paris in a couple of weeks."

"Lucky him!" Carol said.

By this time, everyone at the table was listening as Sophie said, "Why don't you all go with him? He's taking the plane. There's plenty of room, you know."

"I don't think I could find a babysitter for two weeks," Carol said.

"That's not a problem," Sophie said. "I'll take care of little Jack for you. Between Soo Ling, Mrs. Chou, and me, we shouldn't have any trouble."

"Jack, what do you think?" Carol asked.

"Sounds good to me," Jack replied. Jack, a freelance carpenter, had no problem taking time off, especially for a free trip to Paris. Carol's summer vacation was about to start.

"Dianne?" Sophie asked.

"Will you give me the time off?"

"I think we can get along without you for a few days," Sophie replied.

Looking directly at Mike, she said, "We're going." Mike just shrugged; there was nothing left for him to say. He was also retired army and not working at the present time.

***

Later that evening as they were getting into bed, Pete said, "Madame Gin Sling strikes again." He always used her Asian alias when he thought she was manipulating things.

"Don't call me that!" Then she innocently asked, "Whatever do you mean?"

"You know exactly what I mean. You're not as sly as you think," Pete replied.

"Moi?"

"Oui, toi. You just ever so subtly orchestrated my trip arranging for me to have four chaperones in Paris," he said.

"I thought you would enjoy having friends with you in Paris," she said, still feigning innocence.

"Oh please, this is ol' Pete, who has lived with you for the last two years and seen you in action on numerous occasions. How about having a little faith in me?"

"All right, what do you want me to say?"

"Just fess up," he said.

"Yes, I want you to have someone go with you. You know I have a problem with jealousy. I'm always worried that another woman will come between us."

"I have on several different occasions offered to help you with your jealousy problem."

"How do you propose doing that?"

"I could have dinner with Giselle."

That brought a derisive snort from his wife as she took off her glasses and turned off the light on the bedside table.

The following Saturday everyone returned to Pete and Sophie's for what Sophie referred to as a Barbecue. That really meant that Jean Claude would cook on the outdoor grill and they would eat on the patio. The topic around the table was the upcoming trip to Paris. Sophie had spoken to the pilots and they had told her the approximate flying times. It would take five and a half hours to get to the East Coast and an additional eight hours to get to Paris. As far as the arrival time went, just add thirteen hours to the departure time from the East Coast.

The consensus was to spend the night in Boston and leave early the next morning so they could have a decent dinner in Paris their first night. Although not going, Sophie insisted that Pete have two more weeks to recuperate prior to leaving, and his doctor's blessing.

As the departure date approached, and as much as he loved Paris, Pete suddenly realized he did not want to leave his wife and family. He was going to go, however, rather than risk disappointing everyone else.

***

On the Wednesday before they were supposed to depart, a man knocked on the front door of Pete and Sophie's house. Toy answered the door. A Latino man of about thirty-five stood there wearing a floral print shirt and blue jeans. "May I help you?" Toy asked.

"Yeah, I wanna speak to Madame Gin Sling," he said.

"Wait here. I'll see if she is receiving," Toy said, closing the door.

The man was indignant. If the Chinese guy at the door hadn't been the size of a semi-truck he would have barged into the house.

Toy went looking for Pete. "There is someone at the front door who wants to speak to Madame Gin Sling," he told Pete.

"That sounds like trouble. See if you can find Chou, I'll look for Sophie," Pete said. Sophie had brought Toy and Chou, her bodyguards, with her from Macau. As Toy and Chou strode down the hall toward the front door together, Sophie and Pete came down the stairs. "You guys take him into Sophie's office, we'll be in in a few minutes. Check to be sure this guy isn't armed," Pete said.

"He was carrying this," Toy said, holding up a Glock 9mm by the barrel when Sophie and Pete walked into the room through the side door five minutes later.

Sophie walked behind her desk and looking down at the man seated in front of her said, "I am Madame Gin Sling. Who are you and what do you want?"

"I am Raphael Arroyo, and I work for Don Roberto Alessio."

Looking at Pete with a quizzical look on her face, she turned back toward the guy and said, "Who is Don what's-his-name? Am I supposed to know this guy?"

"Don Alessio controls most of the import trade into the United States from northwestern Mexico, if you know what I mean. He thinks you owe him five million dollars. You or your men blew up his tunnel that led into Calexico from Mexicali. And that is the price he has placed on it." They had indeed blown up a tunnel, which was at the time being used by Arab terrorists to smuggle Sarin gas into the United States.

"And what are you instructed to tell me if I choose not to pay?"

"Don Alessio said to say, 'You and everyone associated with you will be very, very sorry,'" he replied with a smug look on his face.

Sophie had heard enough. "Toy, Chou tape him to the chair," she said. Pete was stunned by the speed of her reaction and wondered about the severity of it.

Immobilized by Toy and Chou the guy stopped struggling and started screaming threats.

"Tape his mouth," Sophie said, when they had finished taping him to the chair. "I doubt this guy came alone. Find who came with him and bring him or them to me," she said to Toy and Chou.

Pete had heard of his wife's reputation as a formidable woman who was dangerous when crossed. She commanded the room. Her attitude clearly indicated she intended to "take no prisoners." The expression on the face of the guy taped to the chair indicated he knew he was in trouble, big trouble.

Toy and Chou returned ten minutes later with another Latin-looking man of about thirty, wearing faded jeans and a dark green t-shirt. They each had one of the guy's arms, his feet touched the ground only occasionally. When they brought him into the office, Sophie said, "Tape him to a chair, too. Then take him to the garage. Come back for this one. Start with the toes and soften him up a little. I'll be along in a few minutes."

Normally, in a situation like this Sophie would have spoken Chinese with Toy and Chou. But Pete then realized that she wanted these guys to know what she had said. After Toy and Chou had taken both men to the garage, Pete asked Sophie, "What are you going to do with these guys?"

"I'm going to find out everything these guys know about this Don Alessio. Are you coming?"

"I think I'm going to give Mike and Jack a call. They need to be aware of this since they were involved in blowing up the tunnel as well. How long do you think it'll take you to pump these guys dry?"

"Not long," Sophie replied. "They don't look very tough to me."

"I'll be along in a couple of minutes."

Pete spoke with both Jack and Mike. They decided to get together at seven that evening. After hanging up with Jack, Pete walked out to the garage. Pete heard a scream as he neared the side door. He entered the garage and standing in front of him was his wife looking at the guy who had come to the front door. His right foot sat in a puddle of his own blood. It was clear his toes had been hit with a hammer. Sophie stood there coolly, and totally immune to the gore in front of her, smoking a cigarette. "This guy is tougher than I thought," Sophie said to Pete. Then she looked at the guy in the chair in front of her and asked him, "Are you ready to talk yet?"

"No."

"Well, you think about it. In fifteen minutes Toy is going to start on the other foot. Everyone talks sooner or later. If you don't want to leave here a hopeless cripple, you'll start talking, now." Having said that, Sophie looked at her watch.

"No sense in me hanging around here; you seem to have the situation well in hand," Pete said, turning to leave. As Pete walked back toward the house he thought about his wife, Sophie, who had been raised in Saigon. She learned early that in Asia life was cheap. Sophie had at one time operated two hundred forty-seven whorehouses, gambling joints, and a major hotel/casino. She had had to defend her turf many times. Once she had established her willingness to do so, she had been more or less left alone.

Fifteen minutes passed and she signaled Toy to hit him again. The guy let out an ear shattering scream. Luckily the garage was far enough away from the neighbors that with the doors shut the screams would not be heard. Sophie thought for a moment he was going to pass out, but he didn't. Instead, once he had regained a minimum of composure, he spit on her.

Sophie leaned into the apparent leader of this gang of two and said, "If you spit at me one more time I am going to introduce you to real pain." As she stood, she said, "I will hook your balls to the light plug and turn on the power. Everybody talks then. Everybody. Now you will tell me what I want know or is it necessary to get rough with you?" she asked.

"I'll talk," he mumbled in a barely audible voice, Sophie's threat had broken him.

Forty-five minutes later, Sophie went to work on the other one confirming what the first guy had told her. Satisfied she looked at Toy and said, "Finish them off and then get rid of them."

"Where?"

"What kind of car did they come in?" Sophie asked.

"Some beat up old Ford," Toy answered.

"Put them in the trunk of their car. They should both fit in the trunk of an old Ford. Park it at LAX in the public lot. Can you get back by 7:00?"

Toy looked at his watch and said, "I think so."

2

By five minutes of seven, everyone had assembled in the large dining room of Pete and Sophie's house. Jack and his wife Carol and Mike and his wife Dianne were there. Toy and Chou sat at the table as well. Everyone who could be expected to be a target of this Don Alessio, except the police officer who had helped them with the recovery of the poison gas cylinders in the Bay Area, were at the table.

"Let me recap what happened today just to be sure everyone is on the same page of music. Two guys were sent up here from Mexico to demand five million dollars from Sophie for blowing up the drug dealer's tunnel. This messenger said that everyone involved would be very sorry if the funds were not paid. Obviously Sophie is not going to let five million dollars be extorted from her," Pete said. He went on, "Sophie questioned them at some length with Toy and Chou's help. Sophie would you tell us what you learned?"

"There is apparently a Don Alessio. His principle residence is about twenty miles east of Hermosillo, Mexico. His messengers kindly provided directions. This guy is really serious. If he isn't paid, he is going to have everyone involved killed for destroying his tunnel. To be honest I'm not sure which names he knows."

"Do you think he can and will do it, Sophie?" asked Carol.

"Well, I don't know if he can do it, but I believe he will try," she replied.

"As I see it there are three choices. One, pay him; two, do nothing, and see what happens; or three, go after him," Pete said.

"If Sophie pays him, does he go away or what?" asked Mike.

"Open question, whether he will decide to extort the rest of you or not. Also, he may come after Sophie again for more money at some later date," replied Pete.

"Doesn't seem to me as if there is much of a choice. We have to go after him," Mike said, expressing the feeling of everyone in the room.

"I hate all this violence," Carol said.

"Sometimes it is necessary," Sophie observed.

"I know, but that doesn't make it any more palatable," Carol responded.

"Is that unanimous?" Pete asked.

Mike looked around the table, and said "Unanimous."

"All right," Pete said, "the first step is recon. Tomorrow I'll fly down to Mexico and get some photos of this guy's layout. Mike will you call General Lane and get him to use his contacts at the DEA to get everything he can on this Alessio guy?" Pete and Mike had both served with the general in Special Forces. Upon leaving the Army, the general had been hired by the CIA.

"You keep that general out of this!" Sophie with some degree of vehemence.

"Will you calm down?" Pete asked. He understood his wife's feelings about the general; she thought he kept putting her husband in constant danger.

"I'll take care of it," Mike said. Then he added, "I think we should get a hold of that cop in the Bay Area who helped us. He may also be affected by this guy's threats."

"Why don't you do that. Let's plan on getting back together the day after tomorrow at the same time."

***

After everyone had left, Pete asked Sophie if he could use her Gulfstream 550 to go down to Hermosillo. She agreed immediately saying, "You don't need to ask, just call the pilots and tell them what you want to do."

"You sure? I know that airplane is your pride and joy." Pete really didn't like using his wife's wealth, it gave him a semi gigolo feeling.

"Of course, I'm sure. You take the plane whenever you want. You don't need to ask me. But let's make an effort to avoid conflicts, not that I ever go anywhere without you," she answered.

"Right. I'm going to go call the pilots and set it up," Pete told her. After talking with the pilots, he passed along the plan for the next day. They would fly to Tucson where they would rent a small plane and fly it down to Hermosillo. They'd refuel there, take their pictures, and then return to Tucson.

"Why not just take the jet to Hermosillo?" she asked.

"It stands out too much. We don't want to alert this guy that we're coming after him."

The next morning as Pete boarded his wife's Gulfstream 550, the co-pilot, Sam Davis, stopped and told him the weather was good and that he had made arrangements to rent a Cessna 172 for the trip into Mexico. They landed at Tucson International and taxied to the private aircraft facilities. Sam told him that they needed to take a cab to an outlying airport to rent the Cessna. When they arrived at the rental company, they were informed that Sam needed a "checkout." Forty–five minutes later, they were getting ready to leave when the person at counter advised them they needed a deposit of a thousand dollars for rentals into Mexico. Pete had planned to pay cash everywhere they went, so he had enough cash to pay the deposit demanded. He wanted to leave as little a paper trail behind as possible.

Pete had only told the pilots that he wanted to go to Hermosillo in a high-wing airplane. But once they were airborne, Pete gave Sam all the particulars of what he hoped to accomplish. Sam told Pete they might be able to make the trip without refueling but the safest course of action would be to refuel in Hermosillo and then take their pictures, proceeding back to Tucson without stopping. Pete readily agreed; when it came to airplanes he liked the safest course of action.

The directions they had were a bit on the vague side: east of Hermosillo, about twenty miles, right on the paved road for about ten miles, then left on the dirt road. They groped around a bit backtracking several times before spotting what they thought was the hacienda of Don Alessio. They made a low pass around the mesa that the Don owned. Then they climbed the aircraft to 4,000 feet. Pete took pictures from every angle as the plane circled the mesa. Pete said, "Let's go back," after taking about fifty pictures.

Back in the Gulfstream, as the lights of LA started to appear, he realized how hungry he was. If he was hungry the pilots must be, too. He walked into the cockpit and asked, "Is anyone else hungry?"

Both pilots nodded their heads vigorously. "Are you guys meeting girlfriends tonight (he knew they were both single) when we return?" Pete asked. They both nodded again. So he asked, "Can I set you up with dinner this evening when we get in?" They both nodded and grinned. "All right, give me a minute."

Three minutes later he came back into the cockpit and said, "You're setup for a table for four at the Santa Barbara Inn. Have whatever you want, get a couple bottles of good wine, too."

"My girlfriend will certainly be impressed," the co-pilot said.

***

When Pete arrived home, Sophie was waiting in the doorway for him. "I was a little worried," she confessed. "I'm afraid of little planes."

"I appreciate your worry, but it's really not necessary."

"I'm sorry but I've never been in love before and I'm still adjusting."

"Well, I hope it won't take a whole lot of adjusting. Just out of curiosity, how long 'til you are fully adjusted?"

"A lifetime. Caring for somebody else is a new experience for me. For almost forty years there was no one else in my life."

"Well, what did you learn?" she finally asked.

"It's difficult to say until I've some time to study the photographs. What's for dinner?"

"I don't know. Not knowing when you were going to be back, I sent everyone home early."

"I didn't know you could cook," he said.

"I can't! But, I can make reservations."

"Well, let's see what we can find in the kitchen." He wrapped his arm around her shoulder and they started off for the kitchen. After a bit of searching, Pete found some white bread, cheese, and a can of Campbell's tomato soup. Soup and a sandwich had been a favorite of his since boyhood. As Sophie looked on with interest, Pete heated the soup and made grilled cheese sandwiches.

He set a plate down in front of Sophie saying, "Careful, the soup is very hot." As they ate, he questioned her about her day and how the kids were doing. She queried him about the trip.

Finally, she asked him when he intended to print the pictures he had taken of the hacienda.

"Tomorrow," he replied. "But I want to buy a new printer first because I want to able to print documents and pictures bigger than eight and a half by eleven. I want to go to at least eleven by seventeen."

"I guess the bigger size makes it easier to see detail," she said.

"That's it exactly." Their meal finished, he stood and said, "I cooked so you can wash." A soup spoon came flying across the table at him just missing his shoulder. "Or not," he added.

"You can be so infuriating," she said, rising.

He cleared the table and loaded the dishwasher. Then he went up to their bedroom. Sophie, already in bed, asked, "Have you got dishpan hands, yet?" Pete, having just taken off his shirt, threw it at her. They both started laughing.

As he crawled into bed he realized Sophie still wore her leg. She usually did when they made love because she liked to use the bathroom afterward, and hated using crutches. Pete momentarily reflected on their love life together. They were like two teenagers, who had just discovered sex. They couldn't get enough of each other.

They made fiery and tempestuous love and afterward lay in each other's arms. After a few minutes Sophie went into the bathroom, emerging five minutes later. She took off her leg, and got back in bed, propping herself up against the headboard. Then she reached over and grabbed a pack of cigarettes from the bedside table, and lit one with practiced ease.

"I wish you would quit that shit," Pete said.

Ignoring him, Sophie said, "I've been thinking about getting a new tattoo."

"That might just be the worst idea you have ever had," he responded without hesitation.

"Why?"

"Think of it like makeup, some enhances a woman's appearance but too much makes her look cheap."

"I only have two, you know," Sophie said.

"The perfect number."

"I'm thinking about flowers on my tummy, right here," she said, indicating the area between her hip bones.

"Don't do it."

"I'll give that some thought," she said crushing out her cigarette after only a few puffs. She turned out the light on her bedside table. Sliding down into bed, she wiggled over toward him, as he simultaneously moved toward her. He put his arm over her.

"I hope you like sleeping this way. I never asked before," he said.

"Sleeping like this is the only time in my life that I really feel safe." With that he brought his head forward and kissed her on the cheek. Damn, he loved his wife.

***

The next morning Pete returned from the computer store with a printer capable of printing eleven by seventeen sheets. A very frustrating hour ensued as he tried unsuccessfully to print his pictures on the larger paper. The installation instructions assumed that you knew more than he actually did. They had clearly been written by some egghead who couldn't believe anyone was that dumb in the first place. On a couple of occasions the printer had come very close to being pitched out the window. But after an hour, the printer whirred away spitting out the pictures he had taken yesterday.

Scott Woods rang the doorbell shortly after four-thirty. He doubted he was in the right place. Pete and the others had tracked terrorists from Calexico to the Bay area. Scott, a traffic cop, had come upon them as they were setting up to prevent the terrorists from leaving their safe house. Scott helped stop the terrorists from leaving. The mansion in front of him astounded him. The word gorgeous did not do the place justice. But when Toy opened the front door, they instantly recognized one another. "I'm early for the five o'clock meeting, but I wasn't sure I had the address right," he said to Toy. Then he added, "It's good to see you. How have you been?"

"Fine. Come on in. I'll show you to the formal dining room where everyone is supposed to meet."

The entry intimidated him. A twenty-five-foot-high ceiling and a staircase to the second floor on each side of a thirty-foot-wide entry hall impressed him no end. When they reached the dining room Toy said, "I'll tell the Boss you're here."

"Ah . . . Who lives here?" he asked.

Toy looked at him as if he was crazy and answered, "Madame Gin Sling and the Boss."

"I was invited here by someone named Mike Jar something or other, to talk about the events in the Bay Area a couple of months ago. Other than that, I really don't know anything."

"I'll get the Boss for you. I'm sure he will explain everything," Toy said.

Scott looked around the large dining room as he waited. The table seated twenty-four. Two sideboards, one on each side of the entry door, contained what looked like Limoges china and crystal glassware. Looking through the doorway into the rear of the house, he saw the biggest swimming pool he had ever seen, a patio, and what looked like a pool house. Nice pile of bricks, he thought. Three minutes later, Pete walked into the room. He walked up to Scott with his hand extended.

"Nice to see you again," Pete said as they shook hands. "Our first meeting was not under the best of circumstances," he said, referring to the events in the Bay Area when he had been shot by Arab terrorists.

"Yes, sir," Scott said while shaking hands. "I'm not sure why I'm here. Although, getting to see this house was certainly worth the drive."

Pete smiled and said, "A situation has arisen that may affect you, but let's wait for everyone to get here before we delve into things." First to arrive were Jack and Carol. As soon as they were introduced to Scott, Carol wandered off to find Sophie. After Mike and his wife Dianne arrived, Pete asked Toy to tell the others that everyone was here and they needed to start.

When Sophie entered the room, she immediately went to Scott with hand extended and said, "I'm Sophie Smith and you must be Scott."

"Yes, ma'am," Scott responded, absolutely stunned by the woman standing in front of him. This Eurasian woman was drop-dead gorgeous, poised, and charming. Sophie sat about as far from the head of the table as she could, while her husband stood at the head of the table, conveying the impression that she was deferring to her husband. Scott noticed that the two Chinese guys were also at the table.

"For everyone's benefit, I am going to recap what has transpired in the last few days," Pete began. "Two days ago, a man came to the front door claiming to have been sent by Don Roberto Alessio, who, as it turns out, is a major drug dealer and smuggler. Don Alessio owned the tunnel we blew up in Mexico, when we grabbed some of the Sarin gas. He believes Sophie owes him five million dollars for the loss of his tunnel. After some interrogation, the messenger provided the location of this Don Alessio. I flew down there and took some aerial photos of his operation. Mike also called the general and asked him to supply whatever he could about the activities of Don Alessio. He was very forthcoming. The file in the center of the table contains the information he furnished us. Alessio is a very violent man and is responsible for several hundred killings in the drug wars currently going on in Mexico.

"If Sophie doesn't pay him the five million dollars, he's going to kill her and all those involved in the operation. Now, why don't you all take a look at that file and photos before we try to assess the situation?"

Forty-five minutes later, Pete said, "Scott, as you can see, I'm not sure whether this will affect you or not. You had nothing to do with the destruction of the tunnel, but you did participate in the take down of the terrorists. I think this Don Alessio got our names from the newspaper stories covering the Arab take down in your area. He was able to find Sophie and this house, so he may also have some connections inside the government. What is about to be said here the military would classify as top secret. I'm offering you the opportunity to walk away now, no regrets. If, however, you chose to stay, you will be required to keep your mouth shut forever about what you hear tonight."

"I'm in. I'm off tomorrow and can arrange for some vacation after that, if need be," he said simply.

"Are you sure you understand the implications of this?" Pete asked.

"Yes."

"Jack, thoughts and ideas," Pete said redirecting the discussion.

'Well, first off, there is no doubt in my mind that this guy is for real and will follow through on his threat. And as I said before, I think we have to take him out."

"Mike?" Pete queried.

"I agree. He won't stop until we're all dead. He'll keep sending people until one gets lucky. The only thing to do is stop it before it gets started. Through the General's DEA contact, I've confirmed that this guy is extremely violent and responsible for hundreds of murders."

"I see no other alternative," Pete said. "All right, let's talk about how to do it." Pete looked around the table. Carol had paled and was visibly unhappy with the situation; Dianne looked unsure, but open-minded; Sophie, Toy, and Chou were inscrutable; and he really couldn't read Scott.

"Let me tell you what we know about this thing. Toy, Chou, Sophie feel free to jump in any time. Alessio's house sits on the top of a thousand foot high mesa. Its only access is a road that was apparently carved from the side of the mesa itself. From what we can see in the photographs and what the general supplied, there is a guard shack manned by two men at the bottom of the road and another at the top manned by four men. The guard house at the bottom is probably there to warn the guards at the top since neither guard can see more than fifty yards of the road because of the curve as it goes around the mesa. All are armed with AK-47s. The Don's house itself is rectangular, a swimming pool patio area sits in front of the house, and a second swimming pool is in the center of the rectangle. The living room has access to the patio and pool area in the front of the house. To the right side of the living room there appears to be a dining room and kitchen. There are bedrooms on each side of the rectangle. On the left side there is a six-car garage under the bedrooms. On the right side is the office. As you look at the house from the front there is a wall which starts on the right mesa and runs to the left side of the house where it takes a right turn and is attached to the left wall of the house. The wall creates a courtyard in front of the house that is about ten feet wide. Once you enter through a door in the wall you have a choice to proceed straight ahead and go to the front door of the house, or turn to the right toward the office. The office door opens onto a reception area and the Don's office is to the left of that. The office itself has an additional door that opens into the house.

"There are two additional guards on the other end of the mesa. As a vehicle enters through the guarded gate at the top of the mesa, it can make a sharp left and go into the garage, or proceed straight ahead to a circular drive in front of the house or it can veer off to the right and park in front of what appears to be a bunk house. The bunk house has about twenty tiny rooms, judging from the number of windows. It is probably for the off-duty guards. Opposite the bunk house is a helopad. Yesterday there was a helicopter sitting on the pad."

Jack said, "This house sits close enough to the edge of the Mesa that maybe we can blow the bottom of the hill and drop the house into the valley below."

"How would we do it?" Pete asked,

"We drill holes into the side of the mesa using a well auger," Jack said.

"How much explosive do you think we would need?" Pete asked.

"A couple hundred pounds of military grade C-4 should be enough to shatter the face of the mesa and bring the whole thing down," Jack replied.

Sophie left the room at that point. When she returned she had a ruler in her hand and an abacus. They were discussing the feasibility of using a well auger to bore the holes. She sat quietly for a few minutes figuring something. Pete watched her with a wary eye knowing something was coming.

"Do you think the general will give us the explosives?" Jack asked.

"Don't bother asking," Sophie said. "Just get a firecracker because you're going to get the same result."

Pete looked at her and signaled for her to continue.

"You're trying to move several hundred thousand cubic yards of earth. Six holes are not going to do it. You are going to have to move at least the first two hundred fifty feet of the mesa face in order to be sure you move the house. With twenty-foot-deep holes you have no chance of moving that much dirt."

"She's right," Mike said, "I don't know why I didn't see it before."

"Do you have a suggestion?" Pete asked Mike.

"Take him when he comes down the road," Mike responded.

"You can't count on that because of the helicopter," Jack injected.

"I think I saw something in the file that said this guy has a condo or villa in Mexico City and another in Acapulco. Maybe we can get him in one of those places," Mike suggested.

"We can't count on him going there any time soon," Pete said.

"Force him down the road," Sophie said. "Then you can blow the road."

"How?" Pete asked.

"Attack his house with rockets from the air. You're Special Forces, you figure it out," Sophie replied.

"We could shoot rocket-propelled grenades from the door of a Huey if we had one," Mike said.

"I wonder where we can get one?" Pete queried.

Scott spoke for the first time, "Do you have a computer I can use? I may be able to find one for sale on the internet."

"Toy, would you show Scott the computer in the library?" Pete asked.

Fifteen minutes later Scott returned to the dining room, "There is a Huey for sale in Montana. I took the liberty of using your phone and called the guy. It's still for sale. It sounds like a pretty good bird on the phone but you never know. You need to see it, fly it, and have an inspection done by a good mechanic to be sure."

"Where do we get a pilot?" Jack asked.

"Look no further," Scott said.

"What exactly is your background?" Pete asked.

"I bummed around for a couple of years after high school and then joined the army. After basic I went to Ranger School but I realized the army was not a long-term career for me. So I went to flight training and flew helicopters for three years before going through fixed wing transition. I have sort of set my sights on flying for the airlines. Being a cop is a fill-in job until I can get enough fixed wing hours to apply to the airlines."

"I'm a retired army colonel, Delta Force; Mike is a retired Delta Force sergeant major; and Jack a former marine, Force Recon," Pete offered.

"I think we need to order some dinner. What does every-body want?" Sophie asked changing the subject.

They went around the table ordering diner. Toy wrote down everyone's request. Scott asked, "What are the choices?" when it became his turn.

"Just order whatever you would like and if Jean Jacques doesn't have it, we'll let you know, and you can choose some-thing else," Sophie said.

He was beginning to realize just how rich these people were, and it was intimidating. It led to all kinds of questions in his mind. He decided to remain silent and see what developed. His concern was that all this cash was coming from a drug busi-ness. If that turned out to be the case, he wondered how the hell he would get out of this mess.

"Scott, how long would you need to get that helo, assum-ing it is worth buying, from Montana to the Tucson area?" Pete asked.

"I'm not sure. I need to look at a map. You can't go in a straight line because it won't overfly the Rockies. If you'll give me a few minutes I'll figure it out. I have my flight bag in my car," Scott answered. Pete nodded, and Scott left the room.

The conversation had turned to acquiring the RPGs as Scott reentered the room. He sat down and took out what Sophie thought were very strange maps. She watched him as he carefully studied them and then started adding what she thought were distances. Her curiosity was peaked. "What kind of a map is that?" she asked. "There are no cities or roads on it."

"Aviation charts show radio stations. An airplane basically flies from radio station to radio station," he answered. Before she could inquire further, Jean Jacques started serving diner.

Scott had taken only three bites when he realized he was eating the best meal he had ever had. He looked at Sophie and said, "This is absolutely delicious."

She smiled saying, "I'm glad you're enjoying it."

When the plates had been cleared, Pete looked at Scott and asked, "How long would it take to get the Huey into the Tucson area?"

"Total time?"

"Yes."

"Assuming I could get there tomorrow, a couple hours to inspect the helo and fly it, then probably three or four days to schedule an inspection, and two to two and a half days to fly it there. So a week maybe eight days," Scott answered.

"Today is Thursday, so if you got there say by eleven o'clock tomorrow you could conceivably be under way by two and into Tucson some time Sunday, if you skipped the inspection. Is that correct?" Pete asked.

"Yes, but I wouldn't skip the inspection," replied Scott.

"As long as the thing is airworthy, let me worry about the inspection," Pete said. "Now we need a plan of how we're going to do this."

"There is one more thing you need to know before you start planning," Sophie said, interrupting. "This guy has a safe in his house. It's over six feet high and about five feet wide. I don't know how deep it is. I'm tired of paying for all this stuff. This time we steal the safe. Reimburse me for the expenses and divvy the contents equally among you."

Dianne perked up. "How much is in the safe?" she wanted to know.

Sophie replied, "I don't know, but two days ago it was full of hundred dollar bills, at least according to the guy he sent up here. My guess is, considerable."

"That's the perfect cover for this operation. It will look like someone took down the Don for the contents of the safe," Mike said.

"How much does a safe like that weigh?" Scott wanted to know.

"I don't know, tough to tell," Pete said, "it depends on the safe."

"The helo may not be able to carry that much weight," Scott said.

"Not a problem," Sophie interjected. "Just push it onto a hydraulic dolly, dump it over the edge, and we'll pick it up at the bottom."

"How do we pick it up at the bottom?" Pete asked.

"Simple, use one of those hand operated hydraulic fork lifts," Sophie replied.

"Those things don't roll very well on dirt, you know."

"I know. You put some sheets of steel down and roll the fork lift on the steel. Then you back a truck up to the fork lift. You lift it up and use a block and tackle or something to get it into the back of the truck," Sophie said.

"Then what?" Pete asked his wife, who had obviously given the matter some thought.

"The truck goes to a house we've rented. We use one of those super powerful torches to cut the top off. Then we put the contents into suitcases, and I fly it to Zurich. It goes into a bank there."

"Aren't Swiss banks pretty strict about the providence of funds deposited?" Scott asked.

"I can get it done. I'll tell the banker that it is the cage cash from the sale of my casino and show him the sale documents," Sophie replied, confidently.

"With some minor refinements that should work," Mike said.

"First thing, who is in the helo with Scott?" Pete asked.

"I am," Jack answered quickly, "I've shot RPGs before."

"Okay, then what is the first target?"

"The guard shack at the bottom of the hill first, then the guard shack at the top of the hill. As you come around, put one in the swimming pool, the Don's helo, and the barracks building," Mike suggested, "after that, targets of opportunity."

"Finish your thoughts," Pete said to Mike.

"You and I climb the back side of the mesa away from the house. When the first RPG goes off we take out the guards on that end of the property. As the helo comes around, some of the guards are going to start shooting at it. We take them down, too. The Don will try to run. We let them go down the road. Sophie and Dianne pull the trigger on the explosives we've planted there. They then check to make sure everyone is dead. Meanwhile, the helo lands and the four of us get the safe over the side of the hill. Toy and Chou load it into the truck and depart for the safe house. The rest of us climb in the helo and depart for the safe house."

"Good basics," Pete said, "anyone have anything else to add?"

"Yea," Scott said. "What happens to the helo after landing?"

"We burn it," Pete answered simply.

"That isn't going to do much to hide ownership. Those things are covered with serial numbers. The feds will be able to trace it," Scott said.

"You have any suggestions?"

"Yes, as a matter of fact I do," Scott replied. "I think the way to fly this mission is to leave from Arizona early and go directly to the Don's house. Once we are ready to leave the Don's, we go to the safe house and refuel, then fly to a place in northern Arizona where we have prepositioned some fuel. I will then continue to a little airport owned by a friend of mine in western Colorado, and tuck the thing into his hanger. In a year or so you can sell it."

"Tell me about your friend," Mike said just as Pete was about to ask the same question.

"We served in the army together. He and I became best of friends. He knows how to keep his mouth shut, and I trust him completely. I've visited his place. When he got out of the army, he bought an old army air field left over from the Second World War. He has a large hangar, which is in the process of falling down. He runs a flight school, does repairs, and crop dusts. He's single so that cuts down on the number of people who know about the helo."

"How do we preposition the fuel?" Pete asked.

"Get an old pickup truck and drive it to a secluded spot that is relatively flat and get the GPS coordinates. When I leave the safe house, I'll take Jack with me. He helps me refuel, then he drives the pickup into Phoenix and parks it in the rough section of town with the keys in it."

"Okay, I think we have the makings of a pretty good plan. Scott do you have a place to stay tonight?" Pete asked.

"No."

Pete saw Sophie nod, imperceptible to anyone but him, and said, "Toy would you show Scott to the guest house when we're done?"

"Sure, Boss," came the reply.

"Sophie, can you make the arrangements for Scott to use the jet tomorrow?"

"Okay," she said getting up to do so.

"Mike will you work us up an equipment wish list I can give to the general?" Pete asked.

"Sure, I should have it to you by ten tomorrow morning. Jack, I'd like you to give it a quick look-see as well. Is it okay to give you a call early tomorrow and plan to get together then?"

"You bet."

Sophie returned to the room and said, "Scott is all set for tomorrow. I've got you set up to depart at 7:15. You should plan to leave here by 7:00."

"What do I… I mean what happens if this thing is okay?"

"You call here and we'll take it from there. It's late. Let's plan to meet back together tomorrow afternoon around 5:30," Pete said.

After everyone had left except Toy, who was waiting to show Scott to the guest house, Scott asked Pete, "Where is all the money coming from? I'm a little concerned that this is drug money."

"Not to worry, Sophie is one of the richest women in the world. She owned casinos and whorehouses throughout Asia. She has since sold all that."

"Her? That sweet woman? Whorehouses?"

"Two hundred and forty-seven of them."

"Egads! I wouldn't have believed it if you hadn't told me!"

"Imagine how I felt when I found out about it after we were married."

"Must have been a shocker."

"Oh, yeah. Surprisingly enough though, she is a genuinely nice person. She's also the smartest person I have ever met."

"Quite a bundle," Scott said. "You're a lucky guy."

"I know." With that, they all left the room, Pete heading upstairs to the bedroom and Scott following Toy to the guest house.

When Pete entered the bedroom, Sophie was still in the bathroom getting ready for bed. Pete brushed his teeth and climbed into bed.

Sophie came out of the bathroom on her crutches. She leaned them against the wall before joining Pete in bed. "I don't like this plan."

"Why not?" he asked.

"I don't like the idea of you climbing up the side of a mountain at night with two armed men guarding it. One little sound and they spray the side of the mountain with bullets."

"This isn't the first time I've done this; believe me this is really no big deal."

"You saying that doesn't make me feel any better about this."

"Well, if you have a better idea I'm all ears."

"If I did you would have already heard it. What do you think of this guy Scott?" she asked, changing the subject.

"I think he's pretty good. If it wasn't for him, I would probably be dead now. When we got in the shootout with the Arabs in San Francisco, he took a few shots that settled the whole thing, and allowed them to start giving me first aid."

***

That resolved things for Sophie. Anyone who saved her husband's life walked on water as far as she was concerned. "The co-pilot gave two weeks-notice today. So when I talked to the captain tonight, I asked him if he would let Scott fly a little and then let me know how he did. You know, sort of an informal evaluation."

Sophie wasn't wearing her leg, so Pete knew she didn't want to make love. He thought he might be able to persuade her, but then decided to let it go.

The next morning, Pete met Scott in the small dining room where he was eating. "Here's a cell phone for you to use until we finish with this mission. I'm speed dial 'one'. Call me if the thing checks out okay. I'll get the money into the guy's account asap. When you stop for the night, call me and let me know where you are," Pete said. "Oh, be sure to destroy, and I mean destroy, the cell phone when you are done with it. Pay cash for everything. Here's ten thousand dollars. Make an effort to leave no trail behind. Wear a hat and sunglasses to make it hard to identify you later should anyone try."

"Do you think there will be a serious manhunt after this goes down?"

"No. I think the FBI will pay lip service to the Mexican government with some sort of half-assed investigation. Remember we're doing the world a favor in getting rid of this guy. He's a stone-cold killer and everyone knows it."

"Whenever you're ready, Toy will take you to the airport. The car is out front now, but don't rush," Pete said to Scott the next morning as he was finishing his breakfast.

Scott found the front door, after wandering around, bewildered, for a minute or two. After opening the door, he found Toy standing beside a limo, clearly waiting for him. Toy opened the rear door as he approached the vehicle. "If you don't mind I think I would rather ride in front with you," Scott. "I'm not used to such luxury," he offered by way of explanation.

"Not at all," Toy answered.

"Have you worked for the Smiths a long time?" Scott asked, after they had pulled out of the driveway.

"Chou and I have been with Mrs. Smith since the very beginning, over twenty years ago," Toy answered simply.

"How did all this happen? I know I must sound awfully nosey, but I'm curious."

Toy hesitated for a moment, "I guess I might as well tell you the whole story. You'll hear it sooner or later anyway. Sophie lost her leg at the age of five during the fall of Saigon. A bullet wound became infected and there were no drugs to treat the infection. She was sold into prostitution at age fourteen by a "kindly" uncle. At fifteen and a half, she broke free and started her own whorehouse. She kept opening houses all over Asia.

"Then she discovered the gambling business. She bought all the machine rooms she could get her hands on. A machine room is one of those places that are full of gambling machines, and it usually has a mahjong parlor in the back. That led her to build a hotel casino complex.

"How big was the hotel?" Scott asked, interrupting.

"Eight hundred rooms but she has since sold everything in Asia and moved to the United States. Her plan was to live quietly and raise her family." They reached the airport as Toy finished his account. Toy pulled out onto the ramp and stopped in front of a G550, the largest private jet made.

"I'm going in that?" Toy nodded. "Whoa, baby. Let's go!" Scott hooted.

The normally inscrutable Toy could not resist grinning at Scott's enthusiasm. Toy waited until the plane became airborne before returning to the house.

"Did he get off okay?" Pete asked when Toy entered the house.

Toy gave Pete a thumbs up as his answer.

The group reconvened later that afternoon. Preliminary chit chat finished, and Pete got to the point by asking, "Mike, can I see the equipment list you and Jack worked up?" He studied it for a few minutes before saying, "I think we need at least seventy-five pounds of C4 and six .22 pistols with silencers. Why don't you call this in to the general? Oh, and ask him if we can pick this stuff up at the Marine Base in Yuma tomorrow."

"What did he say?" Pete asked, when Mike returned.

"He said he is always happy to help out those doing public service work, and Yuma is not problem. There will be a package waiting for us at base ops." That drew a round of smiles from the group.

"I've worked up a tentative plan. Let's go over it. I'm sure we'll find many things that need to be refined."

"Tomorrow Toy, you, and Chou will go to LA and buy a truck with a tail gate lift sufficient for 10,000 pounds. Take the little white car. You will also need to buy twelve fifty-five gallon drums. Chou, you will continue on to Phoenix in the truck. Toy, you follow him to Phoenix in the little white car. Toy, Chou, do you have any questions?"

"No, Boss," Toy said.

"Jack, you buy an older pickup truck and rendezvous with Toy and Chou in Phoenix. Transfer all the barrels to the pickup. Then late on Saturday evening, Jack, go to any small airport where they sell jet fuel and fill the barrels. I am confident that someone will ask you why you are buying so much fuel. The answer is: it's for a crop dusting service sixty miles west and you want to be sure to have fuel on Sunday. It'll be a young kid working the pumps, so offer him a little extra for helping you out. Toy, you, and Chou do the same thing filling the barrels in the back of your truck. We'll use those four barrels to top off the helo at the safe house."

"How much do you think I should offer?" Jack asked.

"You are going to have to play that one by ear. If you offer too much you'll make them suspicious."

"Once the barrels are full, Chou, you follow Jack in the white car to the place I've marked on this map. It looks to be flat but it's difficult to tell. Leave the pickup there but cover it with a camouflage net. I have one in the garage. Be sure to write down the lat./long. from the GPS read-out so we can find it again. Then the two of you proceed to Nogales and hook up with everyone else. Oh, and Toy? When you buy the barrels, buy a hand-operated transfer pump, too."

"Dianne, you and Sophie drive the van we got from the CIA to Nogales. Mike and I will find a decent motel there, which hopefully will have enough rooms for everyone. We'll send you an email with the name and location of the motel. We'll leave the equipment that Jack and Scott are going to need in one of the rooms after six o'clock. It should be safe from the maids at that hour.

"Mike and I will then head down to Hermosillo and rent a house somewhere well outside of town. We will then scout the 'Don's place'. Questions and or comments?"

"Dianne, do we still have all the listening equipment that came in that van?"

"Oh yea, it's still there, and it worked the last time I tested it," she replied.

"I doubt we'll need it, but to have it and not need it is better than to need it and not have it," Pete said.

"Sophie, do we have enough cash for all this?"

"Yes, I went to the bank today thinking that having cash on hand would be helpful," she replied.

"Sophie, will you arm Mike and Jack with about $15,000 each and about $20,000 for Toy?"

She did not reply but merely left the room.

"What about the torch to cut the safe open?" Toy asked.

"Mike and I will pick that up in LA tomorrow," Pete answered.

"One more thing," Mike said. "Suppose the helo needs fuel in Mexico. What then?"

"Good point," Pete said. "Chou, you follow Jack and Toy until they get the barrels filled. Leave four barrels in the truck. We'll refuel the helo in Hermosillo at the safe house after the mission."

"Let's get back together at seven tomorrow morning to finalize our plans and be sure we're all on the same sheet of music," Pete said as Sophie reentered the room with two envelopes in her hand. "There is one last thing we need to resolve. Carol, I think you should take all the children to the hotel Sophie owns, including Chou's children, along with the amah and Mrs. Chou. We don't know when this guy is going to act, but if he does while we are gone, I don't want him to have an easy target. By going to an address different than this one we add a layer of protection."

"One last question before we go," Mike said. "Have we heard from Scott yet?"

"He called and said the helo was okay. We wired the funds but have heard nothing since then. I expect him to check in at any time with an update," Pete responded.

Later that evening, when they had just settled into bed, Pete said to Sophie, "I am a little worried about being able to be traced through the ownership of the jet."

"Don't worry about that. I've been assured by some of the highest-priced legal talent in the world that it's untraceable."

"Is it legally registered?"

"I think so. It's insured so it must be registered somewhere," Sophie replied.

"One would think," Pete responded, grudgingly.

***

At seven o'clock the next morning they reassembled. Pete advised them that he had heard from Scott and he expected to arrive in the Nogales area Sunday night. They agreed the attack should take place Tuesday morning. Email was to be the method of communication for assembly points. Scott had found a small airport near Nogales. Pete and Mike would rent some rooms in the adjoining town and email the address to everyone. Pete cautioned everyone to use internet cafes, which were still common in Mexico, and alternate email addresses in order not to leave "fingerprints" behind.

"Sophie, there is one thing I didn't think of yesterday. I think we should have the jet fly into Hermosillo Tuesday morning. He needs to top off and file a flight plan for a fuel stop in Goose Bay. He should be ready for an eight-thirty departure. That way, as soon as the cash is bagged, you can be off to Zurich. Don't let the pilot stop in the U.S., that way we don't run afoul of any currency restrictions in this country."

"Also," Pete continued, turning to Jack, "Mike and I will leave everything you will need for the helo in the motel rooms."

Mike and Pete arrived in Nogales about six o'clock that evening. They rented six rooms and left the address on the internet. They crossed the Mexican border eating Big Macs. They rented a pair of rooms in Hermosillo, and retired for the evening.

The next morning at breakfast, Mike said, "I think we're going to have trouble finding a real estate agent to rent us a house on Sunday."

"The same thought hit me last night so I talked to the hotel manager about it. As it happens, he has a friend who is a real estate agent. He agreed to meet with us this morning. We'll see if we can't rent something today."

Pete had just finished his croissant when the manager and another man approached their table. Pete rose as the manager introduced Carlos Esteban, a local real estate agent. As the manager excused himself, Pete asked Senor Esteban to have a seat. "We're looking to rent a house, probably to the east of town. We would like it very secluded and very luxurious. We would like it for two months minimum and will pay cash in advance."

"Surprisingly, I think I have exactly what you want. When would you like to take possession?"

"Immediately."

"Let me make a phone call and see if it is still available."

Returning to the table five minutes later he said, "It is still available, but it is very expensive."

"How much are we talking about?" Pete asked.

"Eight thousand a month," Esteban responded.

"Let's go see it," Pete said.

***

Pete and Mike left an email message for the others describing the location of the house and then went to put eyeballs on the Don's hacienda. It didn't appear that planting the charges to bring down the entry road would pose a problem. Then they went around to the other side of the mesa to be sure they would be able to scale the cliff and take out the guards Tuesday morning. That also did not appear to be a problem.

The others had arrived by the time they returned to the house. After an early dinner, Pete and Mike left to start planting the charges to bring down the Don's access road. Planting the charges turned out to be slow going, and at three in the morning they had only completed about three hundred and fifty feet of the road. Their thinking had been that they needed to plant charges under at least eight hundred feet of the road to be certain the explosion would bring down as many as three cars.

He tried not to wake Sophie when he crawled into bed, but was unsuccessful.

"I'm sorry to wake you," he said.

"I wasn't asleep," she replied, adding, "I can never sleep when you are in danger."

"I wasn't in any danger."

"I consider sneaking around under the noses of men armed with automatic weapons dangerous. How did you do?" she finally asked.

"Not real good, can we talk about it in the morning? I am exhausted." Having said that, she felt her husband's breathing change and knew he was asleep; she fell asleep shortly thereafter.

***

Pete and Mike briefed Sophie, Dianne, Chou, and Toy on their limited progress in mining the road. They would be going back to try to finish that night, although they were not sure how much progress they would make. They pointed out to Sophie and Dianne how the charges were wired to two different detonators and that they would have to understand exactly which one was going to explode what. Then Pete said, "You ladies are going to have to go and examine your handy work after the blast to be sure everyone is dead. It would probably be best if you just shot everyone in the head. That way you'll make sure they're all dead. If any of these guys live to tell the tale, you can be assured they'll come after us." Sophie remained stoic after Pete's statement, but Dianne shuttered involuntarily.

Later that morning, Mike and Pete took Toy and Chou around to show them how to access the base of the bluff. As they walked toward the base of the bluff, all four realized that the ground was not hard enough to support the weight of the truck. After a hasty conference, it was decided to go to Tucson and buy a Jeep with wide tires and enough chain to be able to tow the safe to the road. Mike and Pete also took Dianne and Sophie to their observation point and then showed them how to access the base of the mesa.

That night Pete and Mike finished wiring the Don's access road. All was in readiness for the attack Tuesday morning.

Pete and Mike left the house at four o'clock the next morning. They donned their ghillie suits and started to climb the side of the mesa. They were in position by six o'clock as planned, their thinking being that the less movement after sunrise on that side of the mesa, the less chance to alert the guards on that end of the Don's property. They had split up so each would be in position to take down one of the guards the moment the attack began. They had talked about using knives on the guards, but decided against it because they were not certain they could get close enough without being heard or seen. The silenced .22 pistols became the default weapon of choice.

They heard the unmistakable sound of an approaching helicopter at one minute of eight. Pete and Mike scaled the last few yards of the cliff. Pete reached the edge first. The sound of the helicopter became louder. As soon as Mike was in position, Pete shot the guard on his side of the mesa. The other guard, distracted by the ever increasing noise of the arriving helicopter, didn't realize the other guard had been shot. He died unaware of that fact.

Generally, when the first shot is fired, the battle plan goes out the window, but in this instance things proceeded according to plan. Jack opened up on the guard shack at the bottom of the hill precisely on time with the RPGs the general had supplied. With both of those guards dead, Jack's next RPG shot went into the guard shack at the top of the entry road. Then he put a round into the swimming pool. As their helo came around the side of the mesa, someone started to run for the Don's helo, probably the pilot. It exploded before the pilot reached it as Jack put his fourth shot into the Don's helo. Jack then went to work on the guards sleeping quarters. After four additional RPGs, it had been reduced to rubble. Scott brought the helo back to a point where Jack had a good shot at the house itself. Just as Jack put a RPG into the living room area, two black Cadillac escalades came roaring out of the garage and turned down the hill.

Pete and Mike had been ready with sniper rifles to take out any guard bold enough to start shooting, but none were. Jack shot another RPG into the front of the house. As Scott brought the helicopter around to the front of the house for landing, they heard the blast as Sophie and Dianne blew the hillside. Scott and Jack got out of the helicopter bringing two long steel pry bars with them. Toy had found the pry bars in Nogales the day before and thought they might be useful.

Approaching the house cautiously, Pete said, "Jack, you and Scott get ready to blow the wall behind the safe while Mike and I clear the rest of the house. We don't want any surprises."

Sophie and Dianne approached the two SUVs slowly, fearing that someone might be alive inside one of them, and prepared to shoot. One of the SUVs was lying on its side and the other had come to rest right side up except there were no wheels. Sophie said to Dianne, "I'll take the first one and you take the other. Check to be sure the Don is in one of them."

Dianne walked over to the one on its side and, standing on tip toes, looked into the SUVs and said, "I think these guys are all dead." It was then she heard the "Phsst" of Sophie's silenced .22.

"Shoot 'em all in the head," Sophie said. "We need to make sure they're all dead."

"I don't think I can," Dianne replied.

Sophie fired again. "Look at it this way, if they're dead they won't feel a thing, if one of them recovers, he'll try to kill you." Dianne closed her eyes and fired. When she opened them again, there was a neat round hole in the head of her target. Dianne reluctantly shot the other two men, taking solace from the fact that they were probably already dead.

"Dianne," Sophie called, "come over here would you? Look at this one. I think he's the Don. What do you think?"

"I think you're right, he looks like the picture in the file we got from the general," Dianne replied. "We should take some pictures."

They took a half a dozen pictures with Sophie's cell phone camera. Sophie and Dianne went back to their car and headed for the safe house.

Pete and Mike finished their room-by-room sweep of the house, finding only two maids cowering in the kitchen. "Let's blow this thing," Jack said to Scott indicating the huge safe as Pete and Mike rounded the corner to enter the Don's office. They all backed out of the office and around the corner into the reception area. "Fire in the hole," Jack said as he pushed the detonate button.

Even before the dust had settled, they ran into the office. There was indeed a safe-sized hole in the wall. They pushed the safe through the hole in the wall. It fell onto the hydraulic dolly on its back as it landed. "Not as heavy as it looks," Scott said. No one responded. Jack started to pull the dolly and said, "Let's get this thing over the edge." Moving the safe required all their strength, but finally they got it over the edge of the mesa. Pete watched as the safe tumbled down the hill. The others ran for the helo. He wanted to make sure the safe reached the bottom. It did. In fact it rolled almost to the jeep and it had Toy and Chou running to get out of the way. He rejoined the others as the turbine engine in the helo was coming up to speed. Scott lifted off as Pete climbed into the helo.

As expected, they arrived at the safe house first. Jack and Scott immediately went to work on refueling the helo with the hand pump. Pete and Mike set up the cutting torch. Sophie and Dianne arrived a few minutes later. They all were starting to wonder what happened to Toy and Chou when the truck finally arrived. Toy backed the truck in behind the house to ensure privacy as they went to work unloading the safe.

As soon as the safe was unloaded, Pete handed Toy and Chou shovels saying, "Go about a hundred yards away and dig a hole eight feet by four feet by four feet or as deep as you can get it."

"What for, Boss?" Toy wanted to know.

"As soon as we get this thing unloaded we are going to cut it into small pieces and bury it." Pete went over to Dianne and Sophie and said, "Ladies, it's time for you do another job. First you need to vacuum the floors, take the dust bag out, place it slowly into a plastic garbage bag and put it in the Jeep. There are bleach and paper towels on the counter. I want you to wipe everything in this house down with bleach. Every surface, do you understand?"

"Why?" Sophie asked, as Dianne was opening her mouth to ask the same question.

"I don't want to leave any trace of our DNA around if I can help it."

Sophie and Dianne went to work wiping down the house. It took only about five minutes to cut the top off the safe; however, when they finished, the sides of the safe were too hot to touch. Finally, they turned the garden hose on the safe to cool it faster. It took twenty minutes to empty the safe which was full of hundred dollar bills. Pete and Jack carried all the money into the living room.

Sophie peered into the living room just as Jack asked Pete, "What do you want to do with this crap?" He was referring to all the papers that the safe had contained.

"Pack it separately and give it to me," Sophie interjected.

It took seven large trash bags to hold all the money. As they filled each bag they loaded it into the van for transport to the airport.

Pete went into the back yard to see how Mike was doing on cutting up the safe. He watched for a couple of minutes as Mike finished the last cut. Toy and Chou returned just as Mike finished work on the safe.

"Get the garden hose and cool those pieces down, then carry them to the hole and fill it in," Pete said. He then went inside to check on Sophie and Dianne's progress. "How much longer?" he asked.

"About ten minutes," Dianne answered.

Jack and Scott had finished fueling the helo. Jack came into the house and told Sophie and Dianne they were ready to leave. But Pete said, "Even though we're away from everything I want the helo to be the last to leave. When the helo leaves it is going to attract attention, and I want to have everyone gone in case someone comes snooping around."

"Okay," Jack said. "I'll tell Scott."

Pete went into the back yard and watched as the last piece of the safe was hauled out into the desert for burial. Toy came back into the yard from the direction where the safe was buried.

"I want you and Chou to take the truck and ditch it in Tucson somewhere where it is sure to get stolen," Pete said to Toy.

"No boss. I am going with Mrs. Smith. Her safety is my job and with all that money, she could be a target."

"You're right, but I think it would be better if Chou went with Sophie. You speak English better than he does; if there are any problems at the border, you'll have a better chance of re-solving them than he would."

Toy, grudgingly, said, "Okay."

"Dianne and Mike can take Sophie and Chou to the airport," Pete said, adding, "They can leave right now if they want."

As Mike, Dianne, Chou, and Sophie were going out to the van, Mike said to Pete, "Dianne and I are going to take a couple of days getting home so don't worry about us." Moments later Toy followed in the truck. Pete took one last look around, shrugged, and climbed into the Jeep, heading for the border. A minute later the helo left.

Pete had been home for five days when one morning he found a message on his cell phone. Sophie had sent it in the middle of the night saying she had encountered some problems and would be home in four or five days. She didn't say what the problems were, and it worried him. He was concerned, and cursed himself for not knowing where she was or how to get in touch with her. She wasn't answering her cell phone. A day later Dianne called him, wondering if Sophie was back yet. The fact that Sophie wasn't back yet worried Dianne, and her worry increased his own anxieties. He started to imagine all sorts of unpleasant possibilities. He alternated between worrying that something had happened and anger that she hadn't called. He felt that he was going slightly crazy as his emotions vacillated wildly.

***

Four days later, Sophie called Toy from the jet. She told him that she would like him to pick her up in two hours, but not to tell Pete. Toy complied with this request.

Pete was staring idly out the den window at one o'clock when the limo pulled into the driveway. He had not known it was being used. It stopped with the back door by the entry walkway. Sophie hopped out of the rear door. He breathed a huge sigh of relief that she had finally gotten home. As he did so, his anger mounted. He'd been frantic for eight days.

"Not even one lousy phone call," he said as she walked through the door. "Do you know how worried I have been?"

"I forgot the charger for my cell phone. How about a welcome home kiss?" she said walking toward him with her arms open wide. The kiss, lasting at least thirty seconds, clearly became the promise of things to come in the very near future. He picked her up and easily carried her up the stairs and into the bedroom saying, "Your room didn't have a phone in it? Were you staying in a flop house? You haven't heard the last of this."

"Oh yes I have," she said kissing him again.

***

A few minutes later, Pete said, "I think we should call everyone and get together this evening. They've been calling to find out what happened in Zurich."

"Why don't you tell Jean Jacques to throw a steak on the fire or something?" Sophie asked.

"Okay. Is there something special you would like to eat? You know, something that makes you want to pick up the phone and talk?"

"Enough!"

"My talker is just fine, and I'm not through yet," Pete retorted.

"Well, get through!"

"That may take years."

"It better not take twenty minutes."

"Oh, is that a threat?"

"I think we can discuss that the next time you mosey down to the Blue Fox," the Blue Fox being the topless place where Pete and his golfing buddies liked to stop after eighteen holes for a beer. Sophie, an extremely jealous wife, had threatened to have the Blue Fox burned down once. Calling the Blue Fox a sore subject with Sophie would be like calling The Great Chicago Fire a weeny roast.

"I am going to take a shower," Sophie told Pete.

Everyone sat chatting in the large dining room waiting for Sophie. Finally, she entered and sat at the head of the table. Jack, Carol, Toy and Chou sat to her left, and Pete, Mike, and Dianne to her right. Sophie extended the drama of her entrance by lighting a cigarette before speaking.

"All right, drum roll, let's get to what everyone wants to know," Pete said. Then he added, "I got a hold of Scott but he had to work."

"Well," she started, in a most deliberate fashion, "the safe contained $47,657,150 dollars. I was…"

She was interrupted by Dianne who was yelling, "Yahoo!"

"Calm down," Mike said to his wife.

"Normally, you must prove the providence of cash before the bank will accept it," Sophie continued. When I sold my casino in Macau, as part of the deal, I kept all the cash on hand. I used those documents to deposit the cash. As I said, "The safe contained $47,657,150 dollars. After deducting the million I kept for expenses, I deposited the sum of $5,832,143 into an account in each of your respective names."

"Now as you will recall, the safe contained some paperwork. I went through that on the way to Zurich on the plane. One document had a list of bank accounts and passwords. I started to investigate those accounts. They were, for the most part, still open and they were full of money. So much, in fact, it scared me. With the help of some friends, I started to empty those accounts. Then I divided the money into smaller amounts and sent it to other accounts. I went to Geneva and sent the money around the world a couple more times. I changed cites again, this time going to Paris and sent the money around world a couple more times. Finally, I sent the money to an account in Lichtenstein owned by a company I used to own that hadn't been used in years. After all the expenses incurred, this brought the total to $229,151,600 dollars. So I deposited $28,643,950 dollars…"

"Yahoo!" Dianne hollered, leaping into the air with both arms extended over her head like a cheerleader. Dianne's enthusiasm was contagious. Even the normally stoic Toy and Chou were grinning. "As I was saying, this brought the total in each of your respective accounts to $34,476,093 dollars."

Sophie continued, "Here are files for each of you with your personal bank records. But you each need to think about what you are going to do tax-wise."

"What are our choices?" Dianne wanted to know.

"You can each leave the money in Europe. Never pay taxes on it and only spend it when you are out of the country. You can move to a state that has no state income tax, declare the money and pay thirty-five percent in federal tax. If you chose to stay in California you will pay an additional ten percent in state income tax."

Dianne looked at Mike and said, "Start packing. Las Vegas here we come!"

Jack asked Mike, "Do you think we can get a package deal on a moving van?"

Pete couldn't help but laugh. Sophie was grinning as well. At that point Jean Jacques arrived with a magnum of champagne. "Well, when are you all going to Paris?" Sophie asked.

"Gee, I hadn't even thought about that," Carol said. Continuing she added, "I guess it had better be soon since we are apparently moving to Las Vegas."

"What about this weekend?" Jack suggested.

"What does everyone think about that?" Dianne asked.

"Look," Mike said, "if we really want to move to Las Vegas, shouldn't we get started on that little project first?" Mike asked the group.

"Mike is right," Jack said. "However we can't move to Vegas until we have some place to move to, if you follow me. So what I suggest is that we stop in Vegas on the way to Paris. Rent or buy something and continue on." Then looking at Sophie he asked, "Can we do that with your airplane?"

"Oh sure," she answered.

***

Sophie and Pete made love again that night. Sophie, not thinking that they would make love again, had taken off her leg. After they finished, she put on a night gown that went down to mid-calf. "Why do you always put a night gown on when you go to the bathroom using crutches but never when wearing your leg?" Sophie just shrugged. "Is it to hide your stump?" Pete continued.

"Yes, if you must know."

"I've seen it before you know," Pete replied.

"It's so ugly."

"Sweetheart, I love you just the way you are, stump and all."

When Sophie had crawled back into bed, she said, "I'm still thinking about getting a new tattoo. What do you think about that?"

"Please don't do it. You're going to turn yourself into a freak with so much tattooing."

"You don't even want to know what I am thinking about getting?" Sophie asked.

"No."

"I think I am going to get flowers on my tummy.

"Oh."

"Boy, are you a wet blanket."

"Look," Pete said, "if one tattoo is good that doesn't mean more are better." Pete thought about it for a second and said, "If you have to tattoo something, do your stump, at least that won't show."

"I like the idea of flowers on my tummy better."

"Well, if you must tattoo your tummy, put a small sign about this size," he said holding index fingers together with his thumbs down. "It should say, 'BEWARE, all ye who enter here', and it should be surrounded by flowers."

***

The next morning Pete sat behind his desk in the library reviewing the household account when Sophie entered.

"If I tattoo my stump, what do you think I should get?"

Without saying a word Pete walked over to the book case and took out a thin volume of the English romantic poets. After searching the index he opened it to "Ode on a Grecian Urn." "Read this," he said, simply handing the book to Sophie.

"I get it; the best part of life is the chase."

"You got it. Do a little research on Chinese urns, they have beautiful designs around the top and the bottom."

"You know I wouldn't be able to wear my leg for a couple of weeks while the tattoo healed."

"Then don't do it. In fact, don't get any more tattoos at all."

"Humph," she snorted leaving the room.

3

On their first night in Paris, Pete took the group to the café Les Deux Magots in the center of St. Germain des Pres.

When they were seated at their table, Carol asked, "Okay, why here for our first night in Paris?"

"This is old Paris," Pete answered. "This restaurant has been here since the 1890's. In the twenties Ernest Hemingway, Scott Fitzgerald, John Dos Passos, Pablo Picasso, Claude Monet, and Cole Porter, among others, hung out here. It is one of the many places where we can actually touch some history. And, maybe most important of all, the food is very good."

"Do you have a plan for tomorrow?" Carol asked.

"I thought I would take you on a mini-tour of Paris," Pete answered.

"What will we see?" Dianne asked.

"I thought we would go to Montmartre, the Eiffel Tower, and Versailles, followed by dinner. That will take most of the day. And that will be the last semi-organized event," Pete said.

"Where is the best shopping in Paris?" Dianne wanted to know.

"Rue St. Honore," Pete answered. "Just go out the front door of the hotel and turn right. It's two blocks down."

When they finished their meal, everyone agreed the food was indeed excellent.

The following day Pete introduced them to the Metro. They went from Montmartre to the Eiffel tower by Metro. Having seen the Eiffel Tower, the Trocadero, and the Champ de Mars, they got back on the Metro and continued to Versailles.

Returning to the hotel, Pete said, "I have a dinner planned for tonight, but after that you all are on your own."

He took them to the Tour d'Argent, allegedly Paris' finest restaurant. They dined that evening in style on wonderful haute cuisine. The restaurant exceeded their expectations. Pete grabbed the check and the expression 'sticker shock' came to mind as he put his credit card into the small leather folder for the waiter, ryely thinking it must have been the third bottle of wine that drove the bill into the ionosphere.

The next morning, as Pete ambled through the lobby, he saw Mike picking up a complimentary copy of the Herald Tribune. "Where's Dianne?" he asked.

"She and Carol hit the shopping trail about nine-thirty. I haven't seen Jack."

"I'm going to wander over to St. Germain and grab a little something to eat. Wanna come?"

"Sure," Mike answered.

They found Jack, with an empty coffee cup in front of him, in the first café they passed. "We're going to St. Germain in search of nourishment. Would you like to join us?" Mike asked.

"Love to," Jack replied.

Pete stopped and looked at property for sale advertised in the window of every real estate office they came upon. "Are you just window shopping?" Mike finally asked.

"Not really, Sophie told me to buy something here and be sure it was big enough for the whole family," Pete said.

"Really?"

"Apparently when she was in Paris ten days ago, she fell in love with the city. She knows I love this city and wants to be able to come with me and bring the family," Pete said.

"Must be nice to be married to a woman who can afford an apartment in Paris," Jack interjected.

"It is, but you are, too, my friend," Pete responded.

"Oh, yea, I forgot. Lost my head there for a moment."

They found an interesting little sidewalk café on Boulevard St. Germain and sat down. Mike sat across from Pete, Jack sat next to Mike facing the street.

After they had been there for about a half hour, Mike looked at Pete and lowered his voice saying, "Don't look, but I believe we've seen the man sitting behind us and next to the wall on the other side of the room before."

"I need to use the rest room; I'll be back in a minute," Pete.

"You're right; he was in the hotel in Hermosillo," Pete said, sitting back down. After a moments pause, Pete said, "I bet he was trying to hook up with that smuggler."

"He was also at the drug factory in Laos shepherding those gas bottles," Jack added, referring to their operation in Laos.

"You're right, Jack. When I saw him in Hermosillo, I knew I had seen him before, but I couldn't put my finger on where," Mike said. He continued, "I wonder what he's trying to smuggle this time."

"Something to kill a million Americans, no doubt, guaranteeing his entry into Paradise in spite of what it says in the Koran," Jack said.

"Jack, see if you can get a picture of this guy with your cell without him knowing it," Mike said.

"Okay," Jack responded.

"Pete," Mike continued, "I think we should follow this guy. And we should email the photo to the general."

"Jack, you follow him when he leaves the restaurant - about a half a block back should be fine. We will be on the other side of the street. As soon as you see one of us drop in you turn off and head back to the hotel," Pete instructed. "Mike, let's get in position."

***

"Where did he go?" Jack wanted to know, when they had reassembled at the hotel.

"The Arab cultural center," Mike answered.

"That's bad news," Pete said. "We've seen this guy escorting a very deadly gas. He tried to use a drug dealer to smuggle it into the country for him, then we see him in close proximity to another smuggler in Hermosillo. He must have another cargo he wants to move into the United States in a clandestine fashion."

"Well, let's call the general. This is definitely the bailiwick of the CIA. If it turns out to be Homeland security, the general can pass it along," Jack said.

"Agreed," both Mike and Pete said at the same time.

***

That night Pete left the group and went to have dinner with his friend, Giselle. He had just been seated when his cell rang. Pete looked at the number and knew it was Sophie.

"Your wife again?" Giselle asked.

"Yes," Pete said turning off his cell phone.

***

The phone was ringing when Pete entered his room. He calmly unplugged the phone, climbed into the already turned down bed and went to sleep. The next morning he awoke to the sound of someone knocking on his door. A bellman stood in front of him and handed him a message, saying, "This is very urgent." He tipped the bell man and opened the small envelope. The message simply read, "Call home."

He went into the bath, showered, and shaved. He finally decided to plug the phone back into the wall. It rang immediately. He picked up the phone and said, "Hello, Sophie."

"I've wanted to talk to you for the last day," she said.

"Well, I haven't eaten any talking food recently."

"You asshole!" she hollered and hung up.

He thought she would call right back but she didn't. Forty-five minutes later someone knocked on his door, again. Opening the door, he saw the entire staff of room service, along with four trollies full of food. "Where would you like this, sir?" one of them asked.

"Put it on the dining room table," he said laughing. The phone rang again an hour later, it was Sophie.

"Have you had your talking food now?"

"Sophie, I know why you're calling."

"Why?"

"Because I had dinner last night with Giselle," he answered.

"I don't like it when you dine alone with other women, you know that, and you do it deliberately."

"Listen Madame Gin Sling, I have several friends who are women, although I haven't seen them lately, and I intend to dine with them whenever I want. Had you been here I would have invited you to join us."

"I still don't like it."

"Speaking of things I don't like, I don't like being followed everywhere I go. If it continues, I am going to lose whomever you have doing it which will really drive you nuts."

"All right, I'll stop . . . probably. I also gave it some thought and decided to apologize for not calling when I was in Europe."

"Apology accepted."

"Have you found a place to buy yet?"

"I canvassed the agents yesterday and found a couple of interesting things but I haven't seen them yet. Before I buy anything, I'll call you."

"I feel better now that we've spoken," Sophie said.

"How are the kids?"

"They're fine."

"Some people are here, I gotta run."

"Talk to you later," he said.

"Love you," she said, hanging up.

Pete spent about an hour on the internet looking for apartments in the areas of Paris that interested him. He called two real estate agents and made appointments with both of them to see units that seemed to fit his requirements. Walking to keep his appointment with the first real estate agent, he passed the small café where he and Mike had found Jack yesterday. Mike and Jack were both there this time, and he asked them if they wanted to go look at apartments. They both decided to come along, having nothing better to do. Their ladies had decided a second day of shopping was necessary to complete their wardrobes.

They walked across the Seine and found the real estate office. The broker, an effusive little man named Pierre, had decided to show the apartment himself. He suggested they walk. The apartment was in an older building, although it appeared to be well maintained. The asking price of two and a half million euros seemed high to Pete. The apartment itself was not in tip top condition and while it was advertised as a four bedroom, it was not. The fourth bedroom appeared to be a large broom closet. There was no way Sophie would buy off on this place.

On the sidewalk they thanked the agent and went looking for some lunch. They walked over to the second real estate agent's office after lunch. The broker's delight at seeing someone who had an interest in a seven million euro apartment was evident. Again, they walked to the property. The apartment itself was also in an older building. The apartment had recently been redone. It contained all new appliances. Hardwood floors ran throughout. The furniture, likewise, appeared brand new and very tasteful. The four bedrooms were all generously sized, and there was a fifth room that was currently unfurnished. Pete took a dozen or so pictures and emailed them to Sophie. "This place looks like someone completely remodeled it and never moved in," Pete said to Jack and Mike. Then in French he asked the real estate broker the story behind the apartment.

"This is really two apartments that were put together and then remodeled. It belonged to the son of a very rich Saudi, and it was he who commissioned the remodel. But before he ever spent a night in it, he blew himself up making a bomb in Iraq. His father does not want it, and it is he who is selling it," recounted the agent.

Before he had finished going through the apartment for a second time, he received a text from Sophie that read, "Go for it."

"Offer him five million, ten percent down on signing, and the rest in cash at closing, and be sure the offer includes the furniture," Pete said to the real estate agent.

"I will need that in writing," the agent replied.

"Fine, I'll be at the bar in the Ritz. Bring the paperwork by when you have it prepared."

They said good-bye to the real estate agent on the sidewalk. Mike, Jack, and Pete headed in the opposite direction to the hotel. Pete turned to the others as they walked along and said, "I suppose I should give Sophie a call and tell her I made an offer."

"Nah, what for?" Jack said.

"I did tell her I would call her before I actually bought something," Pete answered. "But it can definitely wait until I have a cold one in front of me," he added.

"That's the ol' Pete I know," said Mike.

***

"Well, here goes nothing," Pete said sitting at the Ritz bar, taking a sip on his beer with one hand and opening his cell phone with the other.

Toy answered the phone and went to find Sophie for him. Two minutes later Sophie came on the line and without any preliminaries said, "Well?"

"I made an offer on a beautiful apartment here." He went on to describe it in detail.

"The pictures look good, I can't wait to see it," Sophie said. "Damn."

"What?" Pete asked.

"I hear tears. I gotta run. Another crisis to solve. I'll talk to you soon. Bye," and with that she was gone.

"I notice your wife didn't even ask the price," Mike observed.

"I hadn't noticed, I guess I'm finally adapting to being married to a billionaire, albeit somewhat slowly."

Carol and Dianne looked into the bar to see if the husbands happened to be there and, seeing them, they came into the bar, their arms full of packages. "Will you ladies join us?" Mike asked.

"Just let us get rid of today's purchases and we will," Carol answered.

"Give them to the bell man and save yourself a trip," Pete said.

"I'd say you're adapting beautifully," Mike said. The three men started to laugh to the bewilderment of Carol and Dianne.

"I'll tell you a short story about Sophie. Right after we got married I asked Sophie why she had decided to make such a dramatic change in her life, I mean she was sitting on an empire and making money hand over fist. She said, 'I looked at the future. On the one hand I could wind up an eighty year old crippled half-caste with five billion dollars in the bank, or I could marry the man I love, move to the States, raise a family, and enjoy spending what I had already earned.' And that is the way she operates."

"I think I would have made the same choice," Mike said.

"What's the plan for dinner tonight?" Carol asked, upon returning from the bell stand.

"Well, I thought I would go to Harry's New York Bar for a drink, then look for a good restaurant. You're certainly welcome to join me if you'd like," Pete answered.

Carol looked at Jack who just nodded, and said, "What time shall we meet in the lobby?"

"Six-thirty, okay?"

Pete signed the bill and they all rode the elevator to their respective floors.

***

Later that evening when they were all seated in Harry's, Dianne asked, "What do you see in this place?"

"It's like the Deux Magots, old Paris. It is also the home of the Side Car."

"You mean like the thing for a motorcycle?" Dianne asked.

"No, the cocktail," Pete responded.

"Never heard of it," Dianne said. The next time the waiter passed, Dianne ordered a side car. "Not bad," she declared after sipping it. She passed it around, and everyone had a taste.

They walked to Montorgueil Street, about three quarters of a mile away. Montorgueil Street is one of the few streets in Paris where walking in the center of the street is the norm. It is a street designed to please the gourmet in us all. There are pastry shops, bakeries, cheese shops, fish shops, and restaurants featuring virtually every specialty food imaginable. They chose an Italian restaurant near the end of the street. The food definitely exceeded their expectations.

The following morning, the real estate agent advised Pete that his offer had been accepted on the apartment. There was no counteroffer, which Pete had expected. Apparently, the owner just wanted out. The real estate agent said he have would have paperwork for him to sign prior to his departure, but he need not be in Paris for the closing.

The following two days were spent sightseeing, but at last the day of their departure arrived. Pete was ready to be home, he had missed his family more than he thought possible. They left the hotel at seven o'clock in the morning for an eight o'clock departure. As the pilot poured the power to the engines during the takeoff roll, Pete realized how much he enjoyed the luxury of a private jet.

When they were about an hour from landing, the captain came back into the cabin and told Pete that they had made unusually speedy crossing because of a very rare tail wind from east to west. Both he and the copilot felt that continuing on to Santa Barbara presented no safety hazard and would they like do that. After consultation with the rest of the group, it was decided to press on.

Sophie's jet displayed a map giving speed and time to destination on the forward wall of the passenger cabin. With two hours to go, Pete called home. Toy answered the phone. "Toy, we'll be landing in about two hours. Will you pick us up, please?" Pete asked.

"Sure, Boss," Toy said.

"Don't tell Mrs. Smith when we'll be home," Pete ordered.

"Sorry Boss, but Mrs. Smith said you would say that, but if I did not tell her when you were arriving, she go after my manhood with a rusty razor."

"Guess you better let her know when we'll be home," Pete concluded.

"Don't have much choice, Boss," Toy said hanging up.

***

Sophie waited on the door step for him as he got out of the car. She was not wearing her leg, but rather using crutches. He realized instantly that she had had her stump tattooed. In a revelation he also realized that being critical of your wife's new tattoo was a ticket to disaster. She might not be able to get rid of the tattoo, but she could sure get rid of you.

As he approached the front step where Sophie waited she said, "Guess what I did?"

"I already know. You tattooed your stump."

"Want to see?"

"Sure." Sophie pulled up her dress and lifted her stump into the air.

Surprisingly, Pete thought, it does look better. And, he told her so. Then he asked, "Did you also do your tummy?"

Sophie pursed her lips together and nodded yes. "Want to see?"

"Not here, but I have something in mind. You can show it off to me then."

She grinned and said, "Now."

Pete said nothing, just picked her up, and went through the front door and up the stairs to the second floor. Smiling all the while, Sophie finally said, "I guess so."

Pete seemed to Sophie to be inordinately passionate. After she caught her breath, she asked, "What got into you?"

"Must be the new tattoos," he answered.

"I thought you didn't like tattooing on women."

"I never said that. What I said was it can be overdone."

"Changing the subject if I may," Sophie said, "what are you going to do with all your new-found money?"

"Give it to you I guess, to help make a contribution toward running this family."

"I don't want it. You keep it, you earned it," Sophie replied.

"Well then, I guess I'll put it in my brokerage account, pay the taxes and buy stock."

"I didn't know you had a brokerage account."

"I don't know why you didn't know. The monthly statements come here. It's never been a secret. If you want it, you can have it."

"No, you keep it. Just out of curiosity, how much is in there?"

"About seven hundred thousand," he answered.

***

A week later, Sophie came out of the bathroom on her crutches still soaking wet, clearly excited, and said, "Look my tattoos are all healed. The scabs came off in the shower this morning." She held out her stump for Pete to examine. He took it in his hand and carefully looked at it. She had never specifically offered to let him touch it. "And my tummy too," she added.

"Gorgeous," he said pulling her to him. "Let's take them for a test drive."

"Don't, you'll get the bed all wet!"

"So what, the maid can change the sheets."

After twenty frantic minutes, they both expended all their energy. Pete lay on his back with Sophie's shoulder tucked into his underarm, and her still damp head on his chest. He thought about what had just happened. Sophie had become much more at ease with her stump. That would go a long way toward healing the mental scars she obviously still had over the loss of her leg. He had tried to help her heal those wounds, but knew his success had been limited.

***

Four weeks after they returned from Paris, at about five in the afternoon, Pete answered the front doorbell, something he usually did not do. Mike and Dianne had dropped in. "We just came by to say so long, we're leaving tomorrow, making the big move to Las Vegas."

"I am sorry to see you go," Pete said honestly. "Let's go out on the patio."

"How about a beer?" Pete asked when Mike and Dianne were seated.

"Sounds good," Mike said.

"Club soda for me, if you have it," Dianne requested. "Where's Sophie?" Dianne continued.

"She went to the doctor for her final checkup after the birth of the twins."

"Well, we have some news," Mike said.

"There she is now," Pete said looking through the house to the front door. "Excuse me for interrupting."

"I think Sophie will want to hear this as well," Mike said.

Pete looked at Sophie as she came toward them, and said, "Uh oh."

Sophie saw Pete standing on the patio and made a beeline for him. She could not see the seated Mike and Dianne. Sliding the screen door open she hollered, "You son of a bitch!"

"What did I do?"

She came toward him and she neared him, she tried to kick him in the groin with her peg leg. Quick reflexes saved Pete a great deal of pain. She approached him again and he knew she had not given up on her original idea.

As he backpedaled, "What the hell did I do?" he wanted to know.

Sophie kept coming. "I have spoken," she said in a basso voice.

They were at the far end of the pool when Pete said, "For Christ's sake tell me what I did."

"I have spoken," she repeated pursuing him around the far side of the pool. "When I get my hands on you, I am going to kick your ass."

Mike and Dianne, at first appalled, started laughing. After being chased all the way around the pool, Pete passed the seating area. He looked at the laughing Mike and Dianne and said, "This is not funny!"

Sophie stopped in front of Mike and Dianne, finally realizing they were there. She turned to face them and said, "I asked him for one little favor, just one," she said holding up her index finger of her right hand and pumping it back and forth for emphasis. And, "What does he say? 'No.' So, I asked him if he would reconsider and he says, 'Okay.'" A couple months later, I asked him if he had reconsidered. And what does he say? 'I have spoken'," she said in a basso voice passing her right hand in front her chest palm toward Mike and Dianne. "Like he's the fucking oracle of Delphi or something," she continued.

Pete realized what raised Sophie ire to such an extent. He rushed toward her before she could react and picked her up, kissing her on the neck. "Are you pregnant?" he asked.

"Yes."

"What's wonderful!" he said spinning her around.

"I'll never get my figure back," she said as he set her down. "One hundred dresses shot to hell." Pete pulled her on his lap as he sat down, and kissed her again. "You're cut off Buster! Cut off! Do you understand?" she said loudly for emphasis.

"Ah, Sweetie, there's no use locking the barn after the horse has been stolen."

"Ha! You come around tonight, and I'll show you what a locked barn looks like," she said clapping her hands and holding them together.

Sophie looked at Mike and Dianne, whose mouths were still agape and asked, "Did you ever hear the story of how we got married?"

They simply shook their heads, still stunned. So Sophie proceeded to recount the tale. "Colonel Romantic here," Sophie started off, "and I spent three wonderful days together in Macau. Then he goes off touring Asia. Two months later I find out I'm pregnant. I sent Toy, Chou, and some of their associates to Tahiti to bring Pete back to Macau. When we finally sit down together, I tell him I'm pregnant. What does the colonel say? 'I understand my financial obligations and will honor them.' I told him we were being married on Saturday. 'Not me,' he says. I, of course, carefully laid out his options. He had his choice of going into the basement, where Toy and Chou would go to work on his toes with a hammer until he changed his mind, or, he could go to the altar pain free. He choose the later.

"Now listen to him. Three kids aren't enough."

"I freely admit to a brain fart, in that regard. I had no idea the joy that a family would bring into my life." With that he kissed her again. Sophie seemed somewhat mollified.

"Don't think you're going to sweet talk me. You're still cut off." Sophie stood up. "Dianne do you have a cigarette?"

"I quit."

"Really?"

"I, like you, am pregnant."

Pete jumped on that, "Congratulations! See, smoking is bad for the baby."

Sophie just rolled her eyes. "Don't start! You're not on the top of my favorite people list right now." She went off to find a cigarette.

When she returned, she looked at Pete, who had sat back down, and said, "We've been married nineteen months, and I've been pregnant sixteen of them."

"Seventeen, dear."

Sophie turned her head slowly and glared daggers at him. "That is not funny."

If looks could kill, I'd be a dead Pedro right now, he thought.

Pete and Sophie walked Mike and Dianne to their car after dinner. The men shook hands and promised to keep in touch as Sophie and Dianne shared a misty eyed hug.

"I am going to miss them," Pete said to Sophie as they walked back into the house.

"Me, too," Sophie said with a catch in her voice.

Later that evening, Pete locked the front door and they went upstairs. Pete climbed into bed immediately and turned on the television, while Sophie went into her bathroom to get ready for bed. Sophie took off her leg before getting into bed. Generally an indication she did not want to make love. She lay down as Pete pressed the remote button to shut off the television. Sophie snuggled backwards up against Pete's chest into their usual sleeping position, Pete's left arm wrapping around her. She had just closed her eyes when she felt his hand sliding down her tummy. She grabbed his wrist and pulled his hand back to just under her breasts where it was when they slept. Neither said a word. Next, she felt him starting to become hard and protrude through her legs. "You rat," she said reaching for his manhood and rolling to guide him into her.

He remained silent.

***

Two days later Sophie came into the library where Pete was rereading *The Winds of War*, his favorite American novel. She sat down on the couch opposite him and said, "I have to go Las Vegas tomorrow. Would you like to come?"

"I miss them, too, but don't you think it is little early to go visiting?"

"This is business. While you were in Paris, a couple of guys from New York wearing suits paid me a visit. They offered to sell me a casino in Las Vegas."

"What the hell do you want with another casino?"

"Well, after studying the numbers, it looks like I could make a couple of hundred million on this deal in about a year. It's pretty hard to pass up that kind of money."

"Pass it up. We don't need the money."

"I have to admit I like the thrill of making money. Are you sure you don't want to go?"

"Dead bang positive. When will you be home?"

"This should be just a one day visit, although I may be home late."

"What time are you leaving?"

"We want to be airborne no later than seven-thirty."

"We?"

"I'm taking a contractor and an architect with me."

"Sounds like you've already made up your mind."

"Not really. On paper it looks pretty good, but a lot depends on what is actually there."

***

Sophie returned the next evening around nine o'clock and found him reading in the library. She kissed him, and then sat on the sofa facing his seat. "Long day, you look exhausted," he said.

"Longer than I would like, that's for sure."

"Well?"

"I see most of the problems. But I'm just not sure I want to take them on. A lot of it depends on what kind of a deal I can negotiate."

"What kind of terms are you looking for?" he asked.

"Nothing down and never to pay," she replied smiling.

"Glad to hear that."

"Why?"

"Because it isn't going to happen. You have to remember you have a husband and three kids who love you, and you need to be here for them."

"This could be some really easy money. It's hard to walk away from that."

"I guess," he conceded grudgingly.

"I did have lunch with Dianne."

"How are she and Mike?"

"They're fine, although she said Mike is already bored because he has nothing to do all day."

"Takes a little practice, but he'll get used to it."

The next day Sophie spent on the telephone. That evening she found her husband in the library watching TV. "What are you watching?" she asked.

"*Beach Ball* with Mathew somebody and his English tart."

"Why do you refer to her as an English tart?"

"The English all have this superior attitude, and having made a mess of their country, they feel compelled to tell us how to do the same to ours."

"Changing the subject, if I may," Sophie said, "I'm going to Las Vegas tomorrow."

"Again? Just for the day?"

"Yes, I plan to be home late afternoon."

"Well, have fun."

"Sure you don't want to go?"

Absolutely, I hate Las Vegas."

"Why?"

"It's just so garish. Even the advertising slogan offends me. 'What happens in Vegas stays in Vegas.' That's tantamount to saying, 'Come to Vegas, cheat on your wife and no one will tell her.' Great! Total absence of morality!"

"Did someone piss in your corn flakes this morning?" she asked sweetly.

Pete just chuckled at her question, but did not respond.

Is there nothing tasteful in Las Vegas, she wondered? She needed to look at more casinos. But her husband, the rock of Gibraltar in her life, had given her the seed of an idea without even knowing it.

Thirty minutes later when Pete walked into the bedroom Sophie was sitting in a chair with an infant feeding from each breast. It really touched Pete to see Sophie so maternal. "I don't understand how you do it. One minute you're Miss Tuff-As-Nails ready to take on the world. The next you're the sweet, little, diminutive mother with three infants," Pete said.

"After you left Macau, I realized that when I was with you I became a different person. I didn't really like Madame Gin Sling very much. So I really worked at being who I was when I was with you."

"If you get this casino you are not going to revert to being Madame Gin Sling are you?" Pete asked.

"I hope not. I'm sure you will tell me if I start to assume that persona again, won't you?"

"Oh, I think you can count on that!"

4

"**I** have been thinking," Sophie said to the architect just after the airplane lifted off the next morning, "that Las Vegas seems a little garish. I want to create a high roller casino that simply drips class."

"What do you mean a high roller casino?" he asked.

"All casinos have a separate casino for the truly big players; no limit baccarat, that sort of thing. It usually takes a twenty-five thousand dollar account to get into those special rooms."

"What exactly do you have in mind?" he asked.

"I don't know exactly. But I don't want glitz and glitter. I want something tasteful in the extreme, where the attire is a tux for men and evening dress for women, with crystal chandeliers, indirect lighting, that sort of thing. The more I think about it, the more I think you should go to the Peninsula Hotel in Hong Kong and Monte Carlo Casino. Perhaps visit a casino or two in London, you may get some ideas there as well."

"A trip like that will take a lot of time and be very expensive," he said in response.

"Don't worry about the expense. Take your wife with you. I'm sure she would enjoy it."

"And when you look at the Peninsula Hotel, I want high roller suites on the upper floors to look like their suites. Make your own plane reservations, and I will take care of the hotels for you. In Paris, I'm going to put you up at the Ritz. That's the kind of luxury and class I want to see in this hotel, if I buy it."

"I got it."

"I want the high roller casino to smell of Channel Number Five not sun tan oil and perspiration," Sophie said.

***

Pete lay on the red leather couch in the library. *The Winds of War* open on his chest. The kids were all in bed and he had read their daughter a bedtime story. But he was not happy. His wife had been sequestered in her office for the last four days. Simply put, he missed her. They also had not had sex for the last four days either, a fact he found most distressing. Normally, they were like high school kids. They couldn't get enough of one another.

His thoughts were interrupted by his wife entering the room. She came over and sat next to him on the couch. He rolled slightly onto his side to make more room for her and said, "Uh oh."

"What, uh oh?" Sophie asked.

"Every time you sit on the couch with me like this, I know I'm going to hear something I don't want to hear."

"That's not true," she said, kissing him.

"When you get this affectionate, it must really be bad news,"

"How can you say such a thing?" she asked indignantly.

"I am only saying it because it's true. Come on, spit it out."

"I am still waiting on some numbers, but I have tentatively decided to buy the hotel in Las Vegas."

"I was afraid you were going to say that."

"It won't be so bad. I am going to commute for three days a week. It will only be for six to nine months, a year max. I can make us at least two to three hundred million. Think about that!"

"What are we going to do with the money? We have more than we can spend now."

"I don't know. Buy a bigger airplane or how about a chateau in France?"

"Now a chateau does have some appeal," he admitted. "But, I still don't like the idea."

"Why not?"

"Because you have a tendency to be somewhat obsessive, and I'm afraid you'll spend too much time on this project. And, it'll be Madame Gin Sling all over again."

"I won't," she said. She kissed him again, this time much more passionately, her tongue seeking his. He responded by pulling her completely on top of himself and reaching for her left breast, and massaging it slowly. Pete was not normally an affectionate person, but she loved times like these when he was.

"Let's go upstairs," Sophie suggested. He carried her to their bedroom his speed increasing as he got closer to the bedroom. She smiled inwardly, secretly loving it.

The next morning, Sophie asked, "What got into you last night?"

"I had been without for a long time, you know," Pete answered.

"Four days is not a long time, and three times, what's with that?"

"Just catching up."

"Well, you left me bow legged."

He started to reach for his wife and she hopped off the bed saying, "I'm a little sore from last night. You are just going to have to wait 'til tonight."

"Is that a promise?"

Sophie smiled over her shoulder as she went into the bathroom, using her crutches.

***

The next fifteen days passed uneventfully. Mornings and evenings, while Sophie nursed the twins, Pete would feed their daughter, Alexis. After breakfast Sophie would go the boutique hotel she had bought. Pete usually went to the garage where he was restoring an old MG, although occasionally he played golf. The amah looked after the children mornings. They returned home to have lunch with the children.

***

Pete was searching for a book in the library when Sophie entered the room. The previous owner had left an enormous collection of books behind when he moved. "I received the final numbers on the casino I had been waiting for. They looked good, so I signed the offer to purchase the casino today," she said.

"I hope you know what you are doing."

"Me, too."

"Do you think you're going to get it?"

"I'm reasonably sure that I will. I offered exactly what they asked for in our preliminary meetings."

"Is it too late to back out of this deal?" She shrugged and Pete continued, "You know right now we are leading the life you said you wanted. Raising three, soon to be four, children, living in a mansion, and I frankly love it. I have never been happier. I just hope that you don't jeopardize all that we have here."

"This family is the most important thing in my life. I am sure that the amount of time I spend working on the casino will not substantially interfere with our family life. Besides, you have to understand, I am a little girl from the slums of Saigon. I cannot look the other way at two hundred million dollars. I just can't."

"I hope you appreciate that if I think it is interfering with our family I will become very vocal, and you aren't going to like it. I don't believe that a mister mom works. Kids need the influence of their mom."

"Is that a threat?" she asked.

"It's a promise!"

The next afternoon, at about five o'clock, Sophie went looking for her husband. She found him sitting on the terrace, drinking a beer. "I wanted to let you know, I just heard from New York and my offer on the casino has been accepted," she told him.

"Is that good or bad?" he queried.

"Good, I think," she replied.

"Do I hear buyer's remorse creeping into this conversation?"

"Perhaps a little, I hope I have got all the problems figured out."

"What problems do you see?" he asked.

"Well," she said warming to the subject, "the employees are stealing big time, and the place is a dump. It needs to be remodeled desperately. Those are the major ones."

"Will you need to shut down to do the remodel? Generally speaking, remodeling takes longer than estimated."

5

Sophie went to work on her casino deal. She made several trips to Las Vegas and was indeed preoccupied with buying the casino.

One evening, Pete was lying on the couch in the library when Sophie came into the room. He casually asked her how the deal was going. "Not too well," she answered.

"What's the problem?"

"The deal is contingent on me being approved for a gambling license in the State of Nevada. The gaming commission is hung up on who owns the whorehouses I'm fronting for the CIA. How they found about them, I don't know. But anyway, when I agreed to front for the CIA, I also agreed to keep my mouth shut about it. I cannot tell the truth without risking national security, so I'm kind of stuck. I probably won't be approved."

"When is the hearing?" Pete asked.

"Next Wednesday," Sophie replied. They continued to chat about the children and other things of interest to them both.

The next day about noon Pete called General Lane in Washington at CIA headquarters. He explained the problem to him. "I may be able to help, let me look into it."

Pete went to Las Vegas with Sophie to lend moral support the day the hearing was scheduled to start. The hearing on Sophie's application for a license was scheduled to start at ten o'clock.

As Director of Operations at the CIA the general had asked the gaming commission for a private meeting prior to the formal hearing with Sophie and her counsel. The board had agreed. In fact, the CIA had never asked for an audience before with the board. The board members curiosity probably accounted for their granting the request.

After introductions, the chairman of the licensing board said, "General, you asked for this meeting and frankly we're curious as to what the CIA wants us to do."

"First of all, I would like to thank you for meeting with me this morning. What I am about to tell you is classified and I am going to trust your sense of discretion in this matter.

"Before I proceed any further, I feel compelled to tell you that the CIA has looked into each of your backgrounds and we know that each of you has the capacity to keep your mouths shut. As I proceed, you will understand our concern.

"I know that there is some question about the ownership of a number of houses of prostitution in Asia. I am here to tell you that if you look deep enough and penetrated the corporate layers and crooked lawyers, you would find that title to those establishments rests in Mrs. Smith's name."

The board members all had an astonished look on their faces. Normally, no one would admit to such a thing.

"But," the general continued, "she holds title at the request of the CIA. Mrs. Smith owned those whorehouses years ago. When the person to whom Mrs. Smith sold them died, the CIA bought them. We asked Mrs. Smith to take title to those houses. We looked at it as a potential source of intelligence. Mrs. Smith did assume ownership of the houses again, but this time with our people actually operating them. These houses have proven to be a very valuable source of information for us. You may remember the attempted gas attack on San Francisco a couple of years ago. That was thwarted by information we gained from our ownership of those whorehouses. Incidentally, it was Mrs. Smith's husband who actually thwarted the operation in San Francisco."

"General, our concern is not so much ownership as the ties to organized crime that ownership implies."

"I can assure you gentlemen that the CIA in no way participates in organized crime. We do, however, pay the triads one per cent of gross sales because we do not wish to have the houses put out of business by them. It is my understanding that this payment is consistent with what transpired during Mrs. Smith's period of ownership as well."

"So what you're saying is that Mrs. Smith was extorted by organized crime but never benefited in any way from its activities," the chairman said.

"Yes," the general replied simply.

"Do any of you," the chairman said, looking at the others, "have any other questions for the general?"

"Thank you for coming, general."

"I cannot emphasize strongly enough the need to keep the information secret. If it came out, the United States intelligence efforts in Asia would be dealt a serious blow."

In front of the hearing room, waiting for the proceedings to start, Sophie was pacing nervously and chain smoking. "Relax," Pete said to her.

"I can't."

"There's nothing you can do about it now, so just sit back and see what happens."

"Easy for you to say. If this doesn't to go through, I'm going to lose a great deal of money."

"So what. You can afford it."

"I don't like losing money. It usually ruins a whole day for me. But this one might ruin a whole week."

Pete was still chuckling when the general walked past in the corridor. "Good morning, Sophie, Pete," he said continuing on his way. As he passed, he gave Pete a quick wink.

As the general passed, the venomous look on Sophie's face made Pete smile inwardly. Sophie blamed the general for Pete getting shot in San Francisco. She had threatened to kill the general if he ever came near her family again. "I wonder what he is doing here?" Sophie asked.

"Lots of governmental agencies have their offices in this building," Pete replied.

The chairman called the meeting to order. He acknowledged everyone's presence for the record and asked counsel for the State to make an opening statement regarding the pending license application.

The State's attorney had been speaking for about two minutes about the ties between prostitution and organized crime when the chairman held up his hand.

"Counselor, we have been thoroughly briefed on that matter in camera. Is there any other reason why this license should not be granted?"

"No, sir."

"Very well then, the license applied for is hereby granted by unanimous vote of the board. Congratulations Mrs. Smith. This hearing is adjourned."

"That was the most amazing thing I have ever seen in twenty years of practicing law in the State of Nevada," Sophie's lawyer said when they reached the corridor in front of the hearing room.

"Congratulations, you've got your casino," Pete said to his wife.

Sophie was in a daze. Sophie thanked her lawyer, who left immediately to take care of another matter.

"Let's go home," Pete said to his wife.

"I can't. I need to stay until tomorrow," a still stunned Sophie replied.

"Do you care if I take the jet?"

"No. Go ahead, just send it back."

***

The next night Sophie walked into their bedroom about eight o'clock. Pete lay on the bed fully clothed.

"I didn't hear you come in, or I would have come down to greet you," Pete said to her. Looking at the drawn expression on her face, he asked "How are you?"

"Pooped. Between everything that's going on and being pregnant, I'm exhausted. Maybe I have taken on a little too much."

"Don't overdo it. Remember the baby comes first."

"Please don't worry," she said going into the bathroom to get ready for bed.

"I can't help but worry," Pete said sticking his head into Sophie's bathroom on his way to get ready for bed himself. Sophie smiled inwardly. She liked the fact that her husband cared enough about her to worry. The 'shotgun' nature of their wedding had always concerned her, but her husband's actions were slowly allaying the fear that he might not love her.

Pete was already in bed and watching TV when she came out of the bathroom. She took off her leg and crawled in beside him.

"Peter, I would like to know what or how you fixed that hearing yesterday?" Sophie asked.

"I didn't do anything."

"My lawyer told me before the hearing that we were going to lose."

"You ought to get another lawyer," Pete retorted. "An optimist," he added.

"I know you or that damn general did something; now what was it?"

"That, my dear, is something you will never know," he said as he clicked the TV back on.

"Why did you do it?"

"I wanted you to be happy. Although, I have a feeling that I may rue the day."

He set the remote down out of Sophie's reach. "This is a good show."

"I'm pooped! Would you mind turning the light out early tonight?"

He clicked the TV off.

"You're always taking care of me aren't you," she said drifting off to sleep.

"I try," he mumbled as they both drifted off to sleep.

The next morning Pete woke up at five o'clock fully rested. He decided a five mile run would be just the thing to get his day started. He silently slipped out of bed, rummaged around, and found his workout clothes. It was still dark when he left the house. An hour and twenty minutes later, he was having his usual breakfast of a croissant and a hot chocolate at the small table in the kitchen when Sophie came into the room. She had decided that hot chocolate was too fattening some years ago. So she normally drank, what Pete estimated to be, about a gallon of coffee a day. He had made a pot for her.

"So what's the plan now that you can proceed?" he asked.

"Well, I'll be in Las Vegas most of next week. I have the closing and many contracts to let, and the remodel to get started. I also need to work on the operational end of things."

"You'll be leaving Monday morning early and back Friday night, it sounds like to me."

"I hope to be home sooner than that."

"How do you plan to deal with feeding the boys?" Pete asked.

"I'm going to have the amah bottle feed them, I'll breast feed them when I'm home. It is time to start weening them anyway."

And for the next month that is what transpired. Sophie arrived home late Friday, sometimes past midnight, and always left before six o'clock Monday morning. One Saturday morning as Sophie came into the kitchen, Pete said, "I'm unhappy with this whole scenario. You arrive home late and dead tired Friday, sleep for two days, and then go back to Las Vegas. I'm not sure it's good for you, and I know it's not good for the baby. Besides, the kids need a mom and a dad, not a dad and a gambling tsarina."

"I know you're right. This isn't going to last much longer. Just bear with me a little longer."

Finally, Sophie was able to spend more time at home as her delivery date was rapidly approaching. Pete wanted to be there for the delivery and one of them needed to be in Santa Barbara with the kids; he was concerned that Sophie would go into labor in Las Vegas. With three weeks to go he insisted that she stay home. Sophie wanted Pete there, so she acquiesced.

Sophie planned to close the hotel for three months during the major portion of the remodel. As luck would have it, she delivered six pound two ounce Susan Marie Smith one week after shutting the casino for the remodel. The remodel took a little over a month more than originally slated.

Lying in bed one night with her husband, she asked what he thought of renaming the casino.

"I think it is a good idea. You have to change the image of it being a loser," he replied.

"Do you have any suggestions?"

"Yes."

"Well?" After a pause, she added, "You can be so annoying when you want to be."

"Moi?"

"Do you have a suggestion or not?" she said abruptly, her patience expired.

"Madame Gin Sling's Asiana," he said.

"Really?"

"Yes, you made the name famous. Now why not capitalize on it?" he asked.

"As you pointed out one time, Madame has an unpleasant connotation," Sophie said.

"Admittedly, but it will draw people. Every sailor who made a Pacific cruise knows the name. That is a huge advantage, and you shouldn't give it away."

"I need to think about that."

***

Sophie only went to Las Vegas one day a week as the remodel proceeded. When she did she took the baby with her. Pete began to think that this casino thing, as he came to think of it, would not be as bad as he had feared.

Two weeks before the grand reopening, Sophie and the baby left for Las Vegas. He expected her home in two or three days, but that was not to be. The casino was scheduled to re-open on a Friday. Sophie called that Monday and invited Pete and their other children to come to the ceremony. Pete declined saying traveling with three small children would be just too confusing. Besides, he said, "I know you won't have any time for us."

"Hopefully, I will," she said.

"When do you think you'll be home?" he asked.

"Probably Monday," she replied.

"I miss you. I'll see you in a week then."

Three weeks later Sophie and little Susan came through the door of their house in Santa Barbara. "Chou, call the cops. Tell 'em we have an intruder in the house," Pete yelled upon seeing Sophie.

"Ha, ha! I could use a little sympathy. I have had a very tough three weeks."

"Well don't look for it here. I'm plum out. Besides which, your travails are self-inflicted," Pete replied.

"And to think I was looking forward to seeing you, being held, and comforted in my hour of need. Some husband you are."

"Listen, Madame Gin Sling, if you think you're unhappy, think about the rest of us. I've spent the last two weeks waiting for my wife and daughter to show up. The kids need their mother, and she is missing in action, busy making millions, which I will again point out we don't need."

"Perhaps I've made a mistake taking on this thing, but I did it for the best of reasons. I wanted to secure the family's financial future. And you know I don't like it when you call me Madame Gin Sling."

"We cannot go on like this, in spite of your noblest of motives," Pete said simply.

"I know," Sophie acknowledged. "Things will get better."

"I've said my piece for the moment. How did the grand reopening go?"

"We had many of the usual problems. Door keys that didn't work, stove burners that wouldn't light, that sort of thing."

"Make any money?"

"Forty-nine million the first weekend," she said grinning.

"Good God Gerty! . . . That was unexpected, wasn't it?"

"You were right about the name. There were two big players in town from Asia, who were staying at other hotels. When they saw the sign, they came in to see the Asiana. They both decided to play and lost heavily."

"Does that make you think you'll be able to sell the hotel easier, and, hopefully, faster?" he asked.

"It certainly takes a load off my mind, it relieves financial pressure. I had a lot of cash out of pocket after being shut for four months. You have to come see this hotel. I think it's really special."

"I am sure I will one day," Pete replied petulantly.

***

Two months passed before the petulant Pete decided to relent and go to Las Vegas for the weekend. Walking in the front door, the noise of the slot machines assaulted him. He continued into the main casino area. He saw her exactly where he had seen her for the first time, standing in the Black Jack pit talking to one of the pit bosses. He was as taken by her beauty then as he had been the first time he had seen her. She was wearing the same electric blue dress with the high mandarin collar, a white four inch heel on her right foot, and a carved ivory peg leg. Gold hoops and diamond studs were in her ears. Her hair was up with a curl about one inch wide running down her back. He stood and watched the incredible lady he married and counted his blessings. She started to walk away from the pit boss, when she heard something. Walking over to one of the black jack tables, she asked a brown-haired guy sitting in the last seat at the table, "How are you doing?"

"Awful," Pete heard as he moved closer. He knew his wife and from the expression on her face he knew she was up to something. She nudged the dealer away from the table.

"Double your bet," she said to the guy at the end of the table. He did. When everyone else had bet, she dealt the cards. She dealt both of the dealer's cards face up. She had seventeen. The first player had twelve. "You need a card," she said. She gave him a five. Finally she reached the last player, who had sixteen. She asked him if he wanted a card, but without waiting for a response, she dealt him a six. "You're not having a good night."

"Boy, I'll say," responded the guy.

She dealt several more hands in the same way with both of the dealer's cards up.

Pete watched his wife. She was having fun and so was everyone at the table. Sophie drew stares wherever she went, but now she was drawing a crowd. Security moved in to be sure things didn't get unruly. She traded quips with the players at the table, smiling all the while. After ten minutes, she stepped aside. Even with the help she had given him, the player at the end of the table had still lost money.

"Your luck is rotten," she said to him. She turned to the pit boss and said, "Give him a dinner chit, on me." Turning back to the player she asked, "Are you here with your wife?"

"Girlfriend," he answered.

Turning back to the pit boss, she said, "Make that dinner for two."

Facing the player again, she said, "Take your girlfriend to dinner on me, and order anything you want. Come back after dinner, and I'm sure your luck will be better."

"Which restaurant?" the guy asked.

"Any one you want," she replied. As she started to turn away, the crowd started to clap. She faced the crowd, bowed to them, and continued. Pete marveled at his wife's poise. She went into a bar off the side of the casino. Pete realized it had been patterned after one in the casino she had owned in Macau. A rectangular bar in the center, hardwood paneled walls, elevated booths on each wall, and tables between the booths and the bar. He had meet Sophie in that bar in Macau. She had approached him while he sat at the bar. Instead of just joining his wife, he took a seat at the bar and ordered a Heineken.

Sophie saw him and chuckled. She knew exactly what he was doing. She walked over to him and said in Chinese accented English, "Hey sailor want good time?" They both laughed and went back to the booth where Sophie had been sitting.

They chatted for a few minutes between phone calls. "Pete, I did something today which I don't think you are going to like," Sophie finally said.

"Let me guess," he interjected before she could continue. "You bought the joint next door."

Surprised, she asked, "How did you know?"

"I just thought of my worst nightmare."

"It won't take any more time than this one. I promise. If I can turn it around, I can sell the package for even more money."

"Correct me if I am wrong, but I seem to recall someone saying, six months, nine months, max one year and I'm done."

"You're right. What can I say?"

"I'll never do it again is a good start. Let's go eat, I'm hungry."

"Okay. Would you like to eat in the dining room reserved for the high rollers?"

"Sure."

"You have to wear a tux."

With an exasperated look on his face, he said, "I don't own a tux."

"Yes, you do." The surprised look on his face caused her to go on, "Do you remember when you were measured for a suit for our wedding? Well, I took the liberty of ordering a tux for you. It's in the closet upstairs, as we speak."

"You did, eh?"

"Yes, I knew if you thought about it a little you would do the same." Then grinning she said, "I wonder if it still fits? It has been a while, you know."

"How did you know I would order a tux?"

"A wife knows these things," she said sagely.

"All right," he relented, "where do I go?"

She gave directions and said she would meet him in the restaurant.

When he rejoined her, she was on the phone, "Tell whomever it is that you tell, no more phone calls, period," he said with a degree of finality that left no margin for error. He was pissed and she knew it.

"I've been meaning to ask what you've done about birth control. And if you say abstinence, I may throttle you!"

"I gave up on you helping out in that regard. Right after Suzie was born I had a tubal."

Pete intended to stay until Sunday morning, but he left on Saturday instead.

Sophie's second hotel was named Madame Gin Sling's Macau, and it reopened to much acclaim and fanfare. She told Pete a few days later over a quiet dinner at home in Santa Barbara that the Asiana had become more profitable than even she thought possible and that The Macau had made a profit from day one.

The next two years passed with Sophie and Pete stuck in a routine which neither one of the liked. Sophie left for Las Vegas every Monday morning. She returned late Saturday night. Pete ran the house and tended to the children with the help of their amah. Pete had never been one to suffer in silence. His complaints were becoming more and more vocal. Sophie worried that she was doing permanent damage to her marriage. She had loved their life together and wanted to recapture it when she sold the hotels. But her husband was getting madder and madder.

One Sunday morning, she asked. "If I were to acquire the hotel next to the Macau, what would you rename it?"

"I'd redo it in the same style as the Peninsula Hotel in Hong Kong. I would do the lobby in such a fashion that when you check in, you cannot see or hear the casino. I'd keep it subdued, trying to convey that the guest's comfort is the most important thing in the hotel. And I would call it Madame Gin Sling's Hong Kong. Are you going into debt to do all this?" Pete asked.

"No, everything is paid for; that's how the other operators got in trouble, and I was able to get things so cheaply."

"I want to be absolutely certain I understand this. You own three casinos free and clear with no debt whatsoever?"

Sophie reached for a cigarette. Pete knew that she did this whenever she was stalling for time and did'nt want to tell him something. She leaned back and exhaled a lung full of smoke and asked, "Are you ready to explode?"

"Just answer the question."

"Six."

"Six what," he wanted to know.

"Casinos."

"Outright, no debt?"

"Yes."

One Monday morning in September, Sophie didn't leave for Las Vegas at her usual time of six o'clock; instead, they fed the kids together. It was Pete's favorite time of the day, and getting to spend it with his wife was an added bonus. After breakfast he went to his work shop a few miles away in town. His hobby was restoring old cars. He had just about finished his current project, a 1961 MGA. At three-thirty he decided to pack it in for the day. When he arrived at the house there was a large, white Bekins moving van in the driveway. Pandemonium rained inside the house. Boxes and men were everywhere. When he finally found Sophie he asked, in a calm which he did not feel, "What is going on?"

"We're moving to Las Vegas. We took a vote and you lost 5 to 1," she said brightly.

"I don't recall voting."

"You didn't. I voted for you by proxy," she replied.

"I hate Las Vegas."

"You have made that abundantly clear on several different occasions. You have also made it clear you cannot stand our current lifestyle. A move is the only practical solution."

"My children are not going to grow up in a casino, period," he said adamantly.

"I have bought us a nice big house. You'll like it, you'll see. It's a half hour away from the strip. It will be a normal environment for the kids."

"It better be!"

"Everything is scheduled to arrive in Las Vegas tomorrow. We will spend one night in the hotel, that's it."

"All right, I'll give it a try." He knew he should not surrender so easily so he added, with a smile on his face, "There are lots of topless joints in Las Vegas."

The entire family flew to Las Vegas that afternoon. They spent the night in the Asiana, Pete seething slowly the entire time. He fed the baby the next morning in Sophie's suite. Then he took the other three kids to the coffee shop for breakfast. They thought that was awesome. Meanwhile, Sophie left for the new house. Toy found them in the coffee shop and told him the limo was in front whenever they were ready to go to the new house.

Pete's first impression of the new house was that the architect should be de-t-squared or defrocked or whatever they did to architects for designing monstrosities. It did have a lovely front lawn and a really nice back yard where the kids could play. Inside was pandemonium; boxes and men everywhere. He took one look and asked Sophie, who just happened by, if the phone worked.

Pete walked over to the phone, called information and asked for the number of Air France. Air France had a flight leaving for Paris in three hours. He reserved a first class seat one way. Sophie watched slack jawed.

"So you're walking out on me?" she said accusingly.

"Nope, running. This is your mess, Madame Gin Sling, you clean it up!"

"I think you're a real rat for doing this to me," Sophie said.

"Well, you're not on the top of my favorite people list right now either. You ripped me from a life I loved without so much as a by your leave."

"I knew you would never agree, and I wanted my family closer to me. I hate when you call me Madame Gin Sling. Why do you keep doing it?"

"I only do it when you act like a gambling Tsarina unilaterally making every decision affecting your empire and family. I'll be back in a couple of weeks." With that he left. He had started to say something else but thought better of it.

Sophie knew he was really pissed. She also knew she needed him in her life, and he had started to pull away from her. It also created a sense of urgency to sell the hotels. But she was also aware of the old adage that if you have to make a deal today you are going to make a bad deal. She was on the horns of a dilemma and she knew it. She just wished the solution was as easy identifying the problem.

***

On the airplane to Paris, Pete reviewed everything that had transpired in the last two days. Telling Sophie to clean up her own mess was the way you treated a recalcitrant child not a wife. Of course what she had done was also wrong, but then the old adage two wrongs don't make a right came to mind. He had been a complete asshole, but knowing it did not make it easier to accept.

He spent only three days in Paris. He stayed in the apartment they had bought. He decided to pay a quick visit to his parents in Mystic, Connecticut, on this way back to Las Vegas.

His parents were happy to see him. It had been more than six years since he had visited Mystic. He borrowed his Mom's car the second day of his visit to drive around and look at the changes that had occurred in his absence. While driving along the river, he saw a house for sale. It seemed to be on a relatively large piece of land. He thought no more about it until he passed the house next door. It also had a For Sale sign in front. When he had gone no more than fifty yards further, he stopped by the side of the road. "Why not," he thought. He made a quick u-turn. Passing the second time, he noted the names of the different real estate companies. He recognized the name of one company and went directly to their office.

They were surprised that he wanted to make a full price offer without seeing the property, but they accommodated him.

He called the second company and once he got their address, he did the same thing.

That night both real estate agents called his parents' house to say his offer had been accepted.

Pete called Toy at ten o'clock the next morning to get his new address. Then in his mother's car he went to the real estate agents' respective offices. He gave them all the particulars on how to get in touch with him and took down their wire transfer information so he could wire the final payments for closings to them.

Hunger drove him into the local pizza joint. He used his cell phone to get the number of an old high school friend. He had heard through the grapevine that his friend, Steven Dadona, had become an architect. Sure enough, he was listed in the white pages. He phoned Steven's office and discovered he was at lunch, but his secretary made him an appointment for one o'clock.

Steven came into the small waiting room to greet him, and they went back to large rectangular room. There was a drafting table on one end of the room, and a desk with two chairs in front of it. They sat in front of the desk and caught up with each other's lives. Pete was heartened to hear both Steven's parents were alive. Things had gone well for Steven although he said that the last couple of years had been very slow as a result of the economic downturn. At last, he asked Pete what brought him in today.

"Do you have about an hour?" Pete asked. I would like you to design a house for me on some land I just bought."

"Sure, let's go."

"This is it," Pete said, standing in front of the two pieces of property.

"Now, let me tell you what I envision." Pete detailed, at some length, what he had in mind. The explanation took about fifteen minutes. He wanted the existing houses torn down to make room for one large house, and an eight-car detached garage, with a three bedroom apartment above it, and, of course, a large swimming pool. The landscape plan had to keep privacy in mind.

"I think we can do all that on this site, but I need to check on the actual number of square feet in these two lots. There may be coverage problems. This is zoned residential so there is no problem there."

"I am going to send you a plan for the master bathrooms which you are going to find strange. My wife worked out the design years ago. She is missing her left leg a couple of inches above the knee, and this design accommodates her handicap," Pete explained.

They concluded their financial arrangements, and Pete asked, "Do you have a local contractor you can recommend?"

"There are a couple of pretty good ones, but we should put it out for bids and see what we get back before we make a decision."

"I'm in a hurry to have this house completed. What kind of a time frame are we looking at?" Pete asked.

"Probably three months to get permits and six to seven months to build it. Things are slow right now so there should be no problems getting good subs on the job."

Pete left Steven on this final note, "The faster, the better."

The next morning Pete opened a bank account and took care of some other odds and ends. He and his parents went to lunch at a local seaside restaurant. After lunch his parents deposited him at the pickup point for the car service to Newark Airport. Two and a half hours later he arrived at Newark Airport. Pete called Toy from the gate area and asked him to pick him up at the Las Vegas airport at about eight thirty.

6

*H*e found Sophie in bed, propped up watching *CSI Miami*, her favorite show. She turned off the TV as he came into the bedroom. She started to say something, but he held up his hand silencing her. "I owe you an apology; I acted like a complete asshole. You were wrong to do things the way you did, but I had no right to behave as I did either. Two wrongs don't make a right. I know that and just did not think. I was busy having a temper tantrum. I am truly sorry for my behavior."

She took a deep breath and said, "The fault is really mine. I was acting in a way I knew to be contrary to your feelings. I thought not one wit about you, only myself. I apologize as well."

"Apology accepted," he said turning to go into the bathroom. He crawled into bed five minutes later.

"Sophie, I did something in Paris which might make you really unhappy. I looked your father's name up in the phone book and found him, so I called and, after a ten minute conversation, became convinced he is your dad."

"How did you know his name?"

"I saw your birth certificate when you applied for your green card. He would like to see you. Evidently, he did not run out on you as you think. He went to Paris to try to borrow money. He had no luck and when he returned, he spent a year looking for you and your mom before returning to Paris."

"I'll have to give that one some thought," Sophie said.

"Also, when I was in Mystic I bought some land," he said.

"What for?" she asked.

"I am going to build a house on it as a summer place for us when you finally get rid of those casinos. It'll be a rental until then."

"Oh."

"How is that going, by the way?" he asked.

"Not so good right now," she answered.

"Why not?" he said.

"Things are in a very precarious state. We got hit for seventy million last month and I just agreed to buy another hotel in Atlantic City. So another month of big losses and I am in real trouble. I'm trying to arrange a $100,000,000 dollar line of credit in case it goes from bad to worse."

"You can have all my money any time you want it."

"Thank you for the offer. I'm trying to work things out so that will not be necessary; although, I may need to take you up on it."

"Well, maybe you'll make a hundred million next month."

"I only really need about seventy-five million to be truly safe."

"When do you think you will be in a position to sell them?"

"Hard to say," she replied. "I need to get the Atlantic City property turned around first."

"Why are all these casinos in Atlantic City having problems?"

"For the same reasons the casinos here were having problems. They're all carrying a lot of debt which must be serviced. When the economy turns bad, the revenue decreases. The first thing they cut back on is maintenance. The place starts to look like a dump and the few people with money go elsewhere. It's a vicious cycle."

Two weeks later Sophie advised Pete, "I invited my dad to come for a visit."

Pete's reaction surprised her. "I'm glad. I hope you and he can establish some kind of relationship."

***

Ten days later Granddad arrived from Paris for a five-day visit. Granddad's visit was somewhat complicated by the fact that he spoke only French and Vietnamese, so someone was always translating. Sophie took off as much time as she could to spend with her father. Pete thought they seemed to be bridging the forty-year gap pretty well. It annoyed Pete that Sophie was able to spend as much time as she did with her father. She never seemed to be able to do that with their family. Sophie had her dad taken to the Macau every day so they could have lunch together. During his visit, she always came home in time for dinner, which was normally a rarity; however, he said nothing to her.

Granddad finally left for Paris, with everyone going to the airport to see him off.

***

Six weeks later Pete waited up for Sophie. When she came into the bedroom he said, "We need to talk."

"Can it wait until tomorrow? I'm exhausted," Sophie replied.

"Not really. You're not spending any time at all with the kids, and I'm concerned about it. Our children need to spend some quality time with their mother."

"I know you're right. Things should calm down in the next week or two and then I'll have much more time. I have to go to Atlantic City tomorrow. I may be back tomorrow night, but probably not until the day after."

Pete just groaned and turned out the light. She frustrated him beyond belief. He knew she was trying to do something for the family, but it didn't make things any easier to accept.

This theme would be repeated many times during the course of the months to come. But early in May, as spring was coming to the desert, the house in Mystic was almost complete. That was when things came to a head.

Their eldest daughter Alexis was in the back yard playing. Pete and the amah were sitting on the terrace watching her. The amah was making a movie of Alexis with an iPad. Alexis yelled pointing, "Look Daddy, a snake."

"Stand very still, Alexis," Pete said a lot more calmly than he felt.

Until he knew what kind of a snake it was he was taking no chances. He walked slowly toward his daughter. He heard the buzz of a rattlesnake's tail as he came closer. Coming up behind her very slowly, he saw a four foot diamondback rattlesnake coiled three feet from Alexis. "Don't move," he said with authority in his voice, as he reached for the back of her shirt. When he had a good grasp on her shirt, he jerked her straight up, just as the snake struck. The snake missed, but before it could recoil to strike again, Pete pivoted and stepped on it just behind the head. "Come over here, and take Alexis," Pete yelled to the amah. She refused, scared to death by the snake.

Still holding Alexis in one arm he reached down and picked up the snake just behind the head. With Alexis crying in one hand and a four foot rattler in the other, he walked over to the swimming pool. He dropped the snake in the pool.

He got Alexis calmed down with some effort. Then, he said to the amah, "Start packing the kids things: clothes, toys, everything." Finally, with things somewhat sorted out, he went over to the swimming pool. The snake was still swimming. He took the pool net normally used for fishing debris from the pool surface off its hooks on the fence. He caught the snake in the net and proceeded to drown it by forcing it to the bottom of the pool. Then he threw the snake's carcass over the back fence into the undeveloped area behind the house.

Next he called Toy, who he knew was in one of the casinos. "Toy, I need you to bring the limo out to the house to pick up the kids and me."

The tone of Pete's voice left no doubt in Toy's mind that saying no was not an option. "I'm on my way," Toy responded. He wondered what had set Pete off.

When Toy arrived at the house, everyone came out heading for the limo almost before he had shut the engine off. The look on Pete's face told him to ask no questions. The car seats were installed, and the kids finally buckled in and their baggage loaded. "Where are we going, Boss?" Toy finally asked.

"To the Asiana, I guess. Do you know where Sophie is?" he asked.

"She was at the Asiana when I left."

Pete picked up his cell phone. He called the hotel and asked to speak with his wife. He was connected to Sophie's secretary. "I need to speak to my wife, immediately," he said.

"I'm sorry, sir, but she is in a very important meeting, and I cannot disturb her," he was told.

"Well, you pass her a note telling her I am on my way to the hotel. When I arrive, I am going to speak to her no matter what."

As they were pulling up to the main entrance to the hotel, Pete asked Toy, "Can you find a suite or some rooms with connecting doors that's big enough for all of us?"

"Your wife's suite should do. I'll take everyone there and wait for you."

Toy took the amah and children to Sophie's suite. Pete went to the business office looking for his wife, but he found her secretary. "I want to speak to my wife," he said.

"I am sorry, Mr. Smith, but she is still in a very important meeting," the secretary replied.

"You can go in and tell her I want to speak to her right now, or I will, your choice." The reluctant secretary chose the first option.

Sophie came out of the room, clearly mad at the interruption. "What is so important?"

"The kids and I are leaving for Connecticut, tomorrow."

"You're doing the same thing to me I did to you, Colonel, and I don't like it," she hissed vehemently.

"Look at this," Pete said, starting the video on the iPad. Then he added, "It's spring in the desert and this may well happen again."

At first all she saw was Alexis in the back yard. She was about to say something when she realized there had to be something more on the video to alarm Pete. He was generally pretty unflappable. Then she saw Pete lift Alexis milliseconds before the snake struck. "Oh, my God," she gasped, continuing to watch. When it ended, she looked at her secretary and said, "Call the aviation department and tell them to have a plane ready to take my family to Connecticut tomorrow morning."

Then she asked, "Pete, where are the kids now?"

"In your suite," he replied.

"I'll be up in a little while." She turned to leave and then thought better of it and turned back to Pete and asked, "Is tomorrow morning okay?"

"It's fine. See you later."

As soon as Pete left her office, she called Toy in to tell him about the intended move and that she wanted him to go with Pete and her family.

"Mrs. Smith, there is something I have been meaning to talk to you about, and this sort of brings it to a head. I am tentatively planning to get married next month."

"Oh, Toy, that's wonderful! Who is the lucky girl?" Sophie gushed.

"Mai Ling," he answered grinning.

"Do I know her?" Sophie asked, with a somewhat puzzled look on her face.

"You've met her. Her father is the chef in the Chinese restaurant in the Asiana."

"Of course, I remember her now. I want you to know that everything the hotels have to offer is available to you and your bride."

"I need to talk to her about all this. I understand your concern with the move and will go with Pete and the children. I will get together with Mai Ling tonight and advise you what we would like to do."

"Why don't you ask her if she would like to go with you and the family to Mystic?"

"I will let you know in the morning," Toy responded, adding, "That is very kind of you to offer."

Later that evening, after they had put the kids to bed, Sophie and Pete sat on the living room couch. "I want you to know I think you are doing exactly the right thing, taking the kids out of here," Sophie said to her husband.

"I just thank my lucky stars I was there. That snake was big enough that I am not sure Alexis would have survived the bite. A rattlesnake bite can be fatal for the very old or the very young, but even if she had survived, it would have been a very unpleasant experience for her."

"The meeting I was in today was with some people who want to buy the whole casino and hotel package."

"Halleluiah, we're finally rid of those stinking casinos."

"Those stinking casinos, as you so crudely put it, are making this family $700,000,000 a year."

"You're kidding?" She shook her head. So he continued, "How much did you get for the hotels?"

"We haven't arrived at a final figure yet, but it should shake out to be in the neighborhood of ten billion."

"Nice neighborhood! I don't believe for a second that you don't know exactly much you're going to get for them."

"I'm not going to sell them for any less than nine point seven billion. What I don't know is how much cash is going to be in the general account and the respective cages on the date of the closing. There is one thing I do need to talk to you about, though."

"Uh oh."

"Uh oh, what?"

"Every time you talk to me about a business transaction, I know it's something I am not going to like."

"I had to agree to let them use the name Madame Gin Sling and my image for two years after the closing."

"That's not so bad," he said. "And there is something I have wanted to talk to you about for a while now."

"Uh oh," she said parroting him.

He ignored her and continued, "I have been worried for a while now that we're spoiling our kids. They get everything they want. The way we're going they will never learn the value of hard work and money. We are handing them everything on a silver platter. I don't think that's the right thing to do. They'll never be 'well adjusted' enough to live in a normal world. They're being set up to join the idle rich and Hollywood jet set doing nothing with their lives except indulging in self-gratification."

"I have, fleetingly, had similar thoughts, although not as in depth as you apparently. What do you suggest we do to combat the problem?"

"I have tentatively made the decision that when we move to Connecticut, we will live as a normal American family who are well off, but not super rich."

"Yes," Sophie said, "that is probably the best thing for the kids."

"So, we're agreed on that then, and we have a deal?"

Her mind whirled. She knew he was trying to pin her down. Once she agreed, she was committed. He was basically right, of course. But somehow there was a catch in there somewhere. She knew it, but just couldn't see it. Finally, she said, "Yes."

He kissed her on the cheek. She, in turn, kissed him on the lips in a most passionate manner.

Sophie went on to tell him that Toy was going to accompany him to Mystic. She told him, "I want someone around the kids to protect them if something should go wrong. You're only one person and cannot be with them every minute of every day."

"I appreciate your concern but really it isn't necessary. Mystic is a very safe little New England town."

"Humor me," she said.

"Okay."

***

Pete and Sophie were just getting ready for bed, when the phone rang. Sophie answered it. A five minute conversation ensued in Chinese. Hanging up, Sophie looked at her husband and said, "I was going to tell you about this problem."

"No time like the present," Pete said.

"Toy is getting married."

"So?"

"Well his bride and her family live here in Las Vegas and I don't know if she would like Mystic."

"Toy is now a big boy, I'm sure he'll be fine in the long run," Pete replied.

"I invited her to go with you and Toy tomorrow. Toy just told me that she would be going."

"Well, that's good. I think she'll enjoy the jet if nothing else."

Forty-five minutes later, as they were getting ready to turn out the light, the phone rang again. This time Pete answered. It was Toy again, "We're getting married in an hour in the chapel at the Macau," Toy said. Then he asked, "We would like you and Mrs. Smith to attend. It won't be a wedding without you guys."

"We'll be there," Pete answered. "But tell me what's going on."

"Later," Toy said. "Right now I got my hands full."

"We'll see you there."

"What was that about?" Sophie wanted to know.

"In one hour, we will be attending Toy's wedding. You'd better start getting ready."

"Okay," she said somewhat distantly. He knew her gears were going, but he had no idea what she was thinking or planning.

The wedding took place about a half hour later than originally planned. Chou was the best man, and the bride's sister was the maid of honor. Sophie had closed the French restaurant for the wedding. There was finger food available and an open bar, but no one stayed late. Pete and Sophie were back in the suite two hours after they had left it.

In the morning, the amah fed the baby in Sophie's suite, while Pete and Sophie took the other three kids to the coffee shop for breakfast. The kids loved that and were on their best behavior. Back in Sophie's suite, everyone started packing. It took a little doing but finally they were all loaded with their dunnage in one of the hotel limos and on their way to the airport. Sophie kissed each of the children good-bye as they boarded the airplane. To Pete she said, "I should be done here in about six weeks, I hope."

"I can't wait," Pete said, just before kissing her.

Once the aircraft was level in flight, Pete got Toy aside and asked, "Okay tell me what happened last night."

"Well," Toy said smiling, "Mai Ling's father went nuts when he heard she was going to Connecticut with someone who was not her husband. It got really ugly there for a while. The wedding resolved the problem, although Mai Ling is still pissed."

Pete couldn't help but chuckle as he said, "Sort of a Sophie-style temper?"

"Not quite that bad, but close," Toy replied.

Pete asked his parents to meet them at the New London airport. "Did you have any luck getting us motel rooms with connecting doors?" he asked.

"I decided we aren't having our grandchildren sleeping in a motel. We rented two rooms, one for Toy and his wife, and one for Soo Ling. The rest of you are staying at our house. You and the boys can sleep in one room, and the girls can sleep in the other bedroom."

"Correct me if I'm wrong, Mom, but as I recollect there is only one bed in my old room." There were twin beds in the third bedroom.

"We bought air mattresses for the boys. That should work just fine."

Pete asked his parents if they would wait a couple minutes while he rented a car for Toy, Mai Ling, and Soo Ling. They readily agreed.

In military parlance, there had just been a change of command, and he had been relieved. After he had organized the rental car, Pete and his mom and dad loaded the kids into his parents' cars. Car seats had to be organized. Each child had previously laid claim to a car seat and no one else was allowed to sit in "their" seat. It complicated things from day one. Pete knew he had probably overindulged them, but what were fathers for if not that.

The boys thought that it was a great idea to sleep on air mattresses and in the same room with dad. Once everyone's luggage was in the right room, Pete asked his mother if he could borrow a car. She just handed him the keys.

The kids wanted to go, of course, but he made them stay home, saying he had some other things to do after he visited the new house. Only promising to take them to the new house tomorrow would placate them.

When Pete arrived, the contractor had already left for the day. As he walked through the house, it looked as if the only thing that remained to be done was to varnish the first floor. That was really good news. They would be able to move into the house sooner than he thought.

He went to the Cadillac dealer in New London after he left the house. Two hours later, he was the owner of a brand new Cadillac Escalade. It was the only car he could think of that would hold a wife and four kids in car seats, besides a limo, of course, but their days of limos were over, at least for a little while.

The dealer had the new car delivered a half hour after he had arrived at his parents' home. His mom had fed the kids in his absence.

The next morning, the confusion four children were capable of generating was driven home to him yet again. Getting them all into car seats became a major chore. The three oldest children had a running battle over whose car seat was going where. Finally, with his mother in the front seat, they set off. On the way to the house Sophie called him on his cell phone. He brought her up to date on the house and the family. She spoke to most of the children as Grandma leaned into the back holding the cell phone.

New problems arose when they unloaded. They all wanted to go and pick their new rooms. The workmen were sanding the first floor and the kids couldn't enter; no one could enter the house. Other workmen were painting the pool. Grandma took all the kids down to look at the river, while Pete hunted for the contractor. He found him in the apartment above the garage. There were men in the apartment still hanging the drywall. The contractor explained they had neglected the apartment to finish the house as soon as possible. He thought they should be able to live in the house in three days. That was extremely good news, but one set of problems was ending as another set began.

He called the decorator he had hired and told her have the furniture start arriving in four days. She groaned but she thought she could get most of it delivered then.

He had four children to entertain, not an easy task. One day they went to the submarine museum in New London. The boys were a little young to appreciate the museum, and the girls were simply bored.

On another day they went to the whaling museum across the river in Mystic. The kids enjoyed this much more because they had seen the museum's ships from the house. Their favorite was the small playground at the municipal park. Sophie called every morning and spoke to each of them, after Pete updated her on current events.

On the day the furniture was being delivered, Pete arrived at the house at eight o'clock. His mom had agreed to babysit with Soo Ling for the day. Things were hectic all day long with trucks coming and going. In the middle of the afternoon Pete had to go to the hardware store and buy tools to assemble a lot of the furniture. He considered himself fortunate to have Toy there to help. He got back to his parents' house around midnight, exhausted.

He had thought they would be able to move into the house the next day, but he had forgotten about linen. There was none, and the decorator had done nothing in that regard either.

Pete went jogging the next morning, after feeding the kids. As he came into the house, the phone was ringing. He picked it up, he guessed it would be Sophie and sure enough it was.

After exchanging pleasantries, she asked, "Has all the furniture arrived?"

"No, but we have enough to move except for one little thing," He answered.

"What's that?" she asked, concern evident in her voice.

"I completely forgot about linens and dishes and pots and pans. So, today I'm going to spend the day shopping," he said.

"Don't bother," she replied. "I shipped all that stuff from the house in Santa Barbara to you."

"That must have been a monumental chore."

"Not really, most of it was still packed from the move to Las Vegas."

"Well, thank you for saving me again. Do you have any idea when it will arrive?"

"Should be tomorrow or the day after; can I speak with the children?"

"I'm not sure. I don't see them, and I don't hear them," he said. "I just got back from a jog," he explained. "Maybe Grandma took them somewhere. Let me set you down for a minute, and I'll look around." Thirty seconds later he was back on the phone. "Yep, your car is gone so they must have gone somewhere with Grandma."

"I have a new car?"

"Yep, a Cadillac Escalade."

"What color did I pick out for myself?" she asked, clearly annoyed.

"It's kind of a dark red. It's the only car I could think of that will hold four car seats and us. You know you look good in red; that's why I chose it."

At first Sophie found it mildly disconcerting that he knew her so well. She had been guarded her entire life and never let someone get this close. She decided she was pleased and lucky that her husband tried to accommodate her. "Did you consider a limo?" she asked.

"Normal American family, remember?"

Uh oh, she thought, what did I let myself in for? "Well, I should be running," she said to him, after a moment's pause.

Grandma, Grandpa, and the four children returned twenty minutes after Pete got out of the shower. After nap time, Pete took all the kids to the local toy store. He had decided to buy them a swing set. After much debate among themselves, they agreed on the one they wanted. The toy store owner agreed to deliver it after closing time. Then it was back to Grandma and Grandpa's house.

After dropping the children off at his parents' house, Pete went down to the waterfront to look at the boats. He had always loved sailing. He found exactly what he was looking for; it was a thirty-foot day sailor. The boat had a little cuddy cabin, a retractable keel, and a large cockpit. It was on a trailer. He went into the yacht broker's office and asked if the boat was for sale.

"I think so," the broker replied.

"Isn't that like trying to be a little bit pregnant?" he asked.

"A guy ordered it, but I don't think he wants it now. It'll just take a phone call to find out."

"Well, I'd be interested in taking it off his hands if I could get a slip," Pete said.

"The slip shouldn't be a problem. Let me call to be sure."

Pete listened to one side of the conversation, as the broker called the marina where he obviously knew the owner. "No problem with the slip," he said hanging up the phone.

"Well, if he wants to sell it, I'll buy it," Pete said.

Pete's cell phone rang just before dinner. It was the broker, "You bought a boat," he said.

"I'll be by your office to arrange the payment first thing in the morning. Can you work up the final price by then for me?"

Pete thought of the old saying, "The two happiest days in a boat owner's life: the day he buys it and the day he sells it."

That evening the toy store dropped off the swing set.

7

The next morning, with his parents babysitting, Pete started to assemble the swing set. The diagram included proved to be inadequate. The instructions were written in Chinese. After a frustrating thirty minutes, he called Toy. With Toy's help, the some-assembly-required took two hours. As they finished, Pete's cell phone rang. It was the driver of the truck with the things Sophie had shipped from Las Vegas. He said he would be there in a half hour.

An hour later a Bekins van showed up. The van was two-thirds full. It took two hours for Pete, Toy, the driver, and the driver's helper to unload the van. Pete realized almost immediately that everything Sophie had shipped needed to be washed. The boxes were dusty from the trip. Additionally, they would need to store a great deal of what Sophie had shipped. They had thirty-two plates, but only needed ten, for example.

The next day, Mai Ling and Pete's mom departed for the laundromat, while Pete and Toy washed dishes and glassware. They finally finished putting the kitchen together and started carrying the extra things to the basement.

The beds were made, and the bathrooms were all stocked with clean towels. The house was finally ready for occupancy. Pete thought the next morning would be soon enough to make the big move, and that would be the last of it.

No sooner had the family arrived than the boat broker called. Pete needed to sign some more paperwork, and then they could take the boat to its new slip. Frustration started to seep into Pete's psyche: there seemed to be no end in sight to the demands on his time. Pete arranged to meet the broker at his office the following morning and wondered how he had let himself wind up with a full time job. He was, after all, supposed to be retired.

***

The next morning, Pete and the broker motored the boat over to the new slip. They spent an hour together going over the basics, as well as the things that still needed to be purchased for the boat. The broker also made arrangements for Pete to meet with Al McCarthy Saturday morning to have a boat cover made.

Pete got back to the house just as his Mom and Mai Ling were finishing feeding the kids their lunch. Pete spent the rest of his day, and most of his free time in the ensuing days, organizing the house. He was still not finished when Saturday rolled around. He had arranged for his Mother to take charge of the children while he went to the ship's store and met with the guy about having a boat cover made.

Moments after the cover maker left, a man walked down the finger to which Pete's boat was tied. "Nice looking boat," he said.

"Thank you," Pete said.

"This is my little piece of the American dream," the guy said, pointing to the thirty-two sailboat tied to the other side of the same finger. He went on saying, "I'm Al Roca," as he extended his hand.

"Pete Smith," Pete said shaking his hand.

"Is this new?" Al asked

"Brand new," Pete replied.

"How does it handle?" Al asked.

"I don't know," Pete answered. "Would you like to go find out?"

"Sure, I was just going to putter around, but it can wait. Going for a sail beats puttering any day."

"Why don't you standby to cast us off while I get the engine started." The engine fired right up and Pete gave Al a nod indicating it was time to cast off. Al did, and hopped aboard as Pete engaged reverse. "I think it would be best to motor well into the bay before we try raising the sails for the first time."

"Sounds good to me," Al replied.

Once the sails were raised and properly set, Pete tacked back and forth a few times and then offered the helm to Al, who jumped at the chance. They agreed the boat seemed to be very responsive as they headed back to the dock.

Al had a strong New York accent. Pete had early on surmised that Al had probably come into the area to work at the shipyard a couple of towns away. He finally asked, "What do you do?"

"I'm the chief of police here in Groton," Al replied.

"Really," Pete said surprised. "How did you get that job?"

"Well, my wife died five years ago. After twenty-five years in the NYPD I saw an ad, 'Police Chief Wanted'. I applied and here I am."

"I am surprised you would leave New York after having spent your whole life there. What did you do for NYPD?"

"I was a captain in the detective division. As I said, my wife had died and my kids had left the area. So I looked at this as a way out of the rat race. How about you? What are you doing in this area?"

"I grew up here, so I guess you could say I'm returning home," Pete answered.

"What do you do?" Al asked.

"I retired from the army a few years ago, got married, and started a family."

"How many kids do you have?" Al asked.

"Four, two each, the boys are twins. The eldest is five, the boys are four, and the youngest is three."

"What did you do in the army?"

"I spent most of my career in Delta Force," Pete answered. "I think we should drop the sails and motor the rest of the way."

"Good idea."

The boat was very responsive, even at low speed, so the docking was very easy. "How about a beer?" Al asked when the boat was all put away.

"I'd love one," Pete said. They walked up the dock to the small restaurant above the marina office.

After their beers arrived, Pete asked Al, "Where are your kids now?"

"My daughter is twenty-five, lives in LA and is trying to get into the movie business. My son is twenty-seven and works as an engineer for Boeing."

They talked for a while longer as they finished their beers. Pete looked at his watch and said, "I'd love to stay and chat more, but I've got to run. My mother is babysitting, and I'm sure she's wondering what happened to me," Pete said rising. Then he added, "It was a pleasure meeting you."

"Likewise," Al said also rising to leave.

Over the course of the next two weeks Pete's life faded into a normal routine. Pete's mother, and sometimes his dad, came over to assist Soo Ling with the children. Sophie called almost every day and of course spoke to each of the children. He sailed with Al every weekend. At midnight one Tuesday when the phone rang, Pete answered it with a sense of foreboding. It turned out to be Mike.

"Pete, how are you?" he asked.

"Just fine," Pete said. Hearing music in the background, Pete asked, "Where are you?"

"Jack and I are sitting here in the Silver Slip Off, lamenting the fact that we don't like Las Vegas either and are thinking about moving. We thought we would come check out Connecticut."

"Great, come on out. Call Sophie, she always has planes going somewhere to pick up or drop off high rollers."

"Think she would mind?"

"No, actually I think she would be delighted. I'll call and give her a heads up, if you like."

"That would be great," Mike said, "we really appreciate it."

"Look forward to seeing you soon," Pete said signing off.

***

Two days later Jack called from the New London limo drop off point. "Pete, we're in New London. Can you come fetch us?"

"I'll be there in twenty minutes," Pete replied, hanging up the phone.

Pete took Mike and Jack to dinner in town after feeding the kids and cleaning up their dishes. The next morning, Pete lent them the little white car to go off exploring.

That evening after diner, Pete brought up a map on the computer and explained the area much more thoroughly to them. The following day, armed with the knowledge gained from their foray of the preceding day and Pete's detailed explanation, they set off again.

They returned at seven that evening, just as Pete finished cleaning up after the children's dinner. "How did you make out?" he asked.

"While driving around, we both found two houses we wanted to look at. We called the agents and were shown the houses. We've been texting photos to our wives," Mike said.

"Great. Sounds like you are almost there," Pete replied.

Jack and Pete left a week later. Each of their offers had been accepted and they were heading home to start packing.

Pete's life returned to what it had been before the arrival of his friends. He was sure Sophie would be happy to know their friends were in the neighborhood. For the next four weeks, the highlight of Pete's week was his Saturday sailing with Al.

Finally, Sophie called and said, "The sale of the hotels was finalized this afternoon. I'm leaving in the morning. We're going to be landing in Providence."

"Why there?" Pete wanted to know.

"I don't know. But that is what Scott said when I called him to tell them to be ready for an early morning departure. You better bring the van and the limo, I have an awful lot of stuff to take to the house, plus Chou and his family."

"Okay, that I can do."

"I'll call you from the plane when we are about two hours out to give you an accurate ETA."

"Sounds good. See you tomorrow."

8

Pete and Toy waited patiently for Sophie's plane to arrive on the side of the airport reserved for private aircraft. They were both leaning against the hood of the limo when a 757 landed. Instead of turning off the runway and heading for the commercial terminal, it turned toward the private plane area.

That's odd, Pete thought, then it hit him, that was Sophie's plane! "No," he gasped, looking at Toy! "She didn't?"

Toy just grinned.

When the aircraft door opened, there was his wife. She waved him up the stairs. "Look at our new plane," she said, grinning, as he reached the top of the stairs. "Let me show you around," Sophie said, taking his hand.

"Are you crazy? What are you going to do with this thing?" Pete wanted to know.

"I like having my own airplane. Besides which, it was left over from the sale of the hotels."

Pete just groaned inwardly, and took the grand tour as everyone else was disembarking. He decided to leave further discussion for a later date, not wanting to ruin Sophie's homecoming. Sophie had been right. They filled the van and the trunk of the limo with what Sophie had brought with her. Toy drove home in the limo with Chou and his family, while Pete drove the van with Sophie in the front passenger seat.

When they reached the house, they entered through the door on the end of the house closest to the garage and passed through the mud room and laundry area. They passed the two small apartments intended for live- in help and entered the kitchen. The generous kitchen had a butcher block island arrangement. Sophie set her purse on the butcher block, and reached into her purse and pulled out a cigarette. While holding the cigarette between her index and middle fingers and holding her purse open with her thumb and ring finger of the same hand, she continued to rummage around in her purse with her left hand. Pete gently pulled the cigarette from between her fingers and snapped it in half.

"Hey, that was a perfectly good cigarette," she said indignantly.

"There is no such thing," Pete responded. Then he added, "This is a non-smoking house."

"I paid for it; I'm smoking in it."

"You didn't pay for it; I did," Pete replied.

Sophie turned her head, just enough to look at Pete out of the corner of her eye to be sure he was serious. Pete knew exactly what that look was all about and said, "You said you were going to quit smoking."

"Bah!"

"I'll bet you five bucks you said it."

"I'll bet you fifteen, I don't remember!" she fired back. There was no arguing with that; she trumped his hand again.

"Let's go into the living room," Pete suggested.

"Okay."

"This is really nice," Sophie said sitting down.

"I'm glad you like it." Pete heard the clacking of Treena's claws coming through the kitchen. Treena was the German Shepard puppy Pete had bought for the kids. As Treena charged into the living room, she took one look at Sophie's peg leg sticking out in front of her, and evidently thought it was play time. Treena grabbed Sophie's leg and started to shake it.

"Rmghst," came out of Sophie's mouth. Pete wasn't sure what she had said, but he knew there was no vowel in it.

"Treena, no!" Pete said with all the authority he could muster in his voice. Sophie, of course, had a horrified look on her face.

"W-w-what's that?" she said, pointing at Treena.

Treena in the meantime had backed up one step and sat down. The look on Treena's face seemed to say, "Hey pal, what's the deal? We play stick all the time."

Pete lost it and started laughing. "Treena," he managed to get out. His laughter became infectious and Sophie started laughing. Treena got in the act and started barking. Just as things calmed down, Bingo, the kids' Siamese cat, strolled imperially into the room and hopped up on the arm of the chair opposite the couch where Pete and Sophie were sitting.

"And who's that?" Sophie asked.

"Bingo, the kids' cat."

"Are there any more surprises?"

"I don't think so," Pete answered.

They heard the back door open and little feet running toward them. The three oldest jumped right into their mother's lap. Susan brought up the rear and was not yet big enough to jump into Mommy's lap. Sophie reached down and picked her up, giving her a kiss.

"Come on, Mom, come and watch us swing," they all said in unison, pulling on Sophie arms.

"Okay," Sophie said. She stood and started after the children, with Pete following. Seeing everyone grinning, he realized how lucky he was to have such a great family. Sophie had to ooh and aah at the sand box and other outside toys. Then it was inside so Mom could see everyone's new room.

Finally, Sophie asked in a very annoyed tone, "Where is the smoking area?"

"Outside, on the back patio. We even have an ashtray out there for you, just in case you haven't quit." Pete said grinning. This answer drew a look from Sophie which could scorch paint. The humor apparently still eluded Sophie.

Pete sat with Sophie on the screened in porch as she smoked her cigarette. The kids were still playing upstairs under the watchful eye of the amah. At a quarter of six, Pete said, "It's time to start dinner for the kids."

"What about us?" Sophie asked.

"Well, we can go out to dinner or we can eat in. I have a couple of nice steaks in the fridge."

"Let's go out. I would like to see some more of the town."

"Okay."

"What's the cook making for the kids?" Sophie asked.

"The cook is me for the time being."

"You're kidding," Sophie said.

"The typical American family does not have a cook," Pete said. "Normally mom does the cooking," he added.

"I cannot cook!" Sophie said.

"Not to worry, I'll teach you."

"What a dreadful thought," she said rising reluctantly to follow him into the kitchen.

"Hey, this is pretty good," Sophie said after sampling the kid's spaghetti dinner.

"Yea, and it's easy, too," Pete said.

Children went off to play after dinner, while Sophie watched Pete cleanup.

When all the children were bathed and tucked in for the night, Pete finally asked Sophie, "Are you ready to go?"

"Let's do it," she said.

"What do you feel like eating?" Pete asked, as they were pulling out of the driveway.

"The spaghetti put me in the mood for Italian. Is there a good place near here?" Sophie wanted to know.

"Yep, and it's only about five minutes away."

***

"What looks good to you?" Pete asked after they had been seated and given menus.

"I haven't had a pizza in a long time, so I think I'll do that tonight," Sophie answered.

"That sounds good; why don't we split a large?" Pete said.

"Okay."

After they had ordered, Pete asked Sophie, "What do you think of Mystic so far?"

"The area is gorgeous and I love the house; although, I wish it were a little bigger."

"I loved the place we had in Santa Barbara, but it was a little over the top, don't you think?"

"I guess so," Sophie said, "but," she went on, "I really think we need a cook."

"I didn't realize my cooking was so bad."

"It's not. And I really did enjoy feeding the children tonight."

"Yes," Pete agreed, "there is a lot of satisfaction in taking care of the kids. Sometimes it seems like drudgery, but the rewards are far greater."

"What happened to the confirmed bachelor who didn't want to get married?"

"He faded away."

Sophie had taken a few bites of the pizza when she said, "This is really good pizza."

"It is, isn't it?" They finished their meal in silence both concentrating on eating.

Pete parked in front of the house when they reached home. Once they were through the front door, Pete picked Sophie up in his arms and started up the stairs toward their bedroom. "There's something I want to do that I have been thinking about for quite a while now."

"And what would that be Mr. Smith?" Sophie queried.

Pete gave his ear-to-ear grin in response.

"Oh," Sophie said knowingly, grinning herself. Upon reaching the bedroom Pete set Sophie down in front of her bathroom door.

"I'll be right out," she said.

"I'll be waiting," he retorted.

"I'm counting on it," she said over her shoulder.

As she came out of the bathroom and toward the bed, Pete thought, "My God what a beautiful woman. The missing leg was like a chip out of a statue by Leonardo Da Vinci; it doesn't detract from her inner or outer beauty at all."

Pete was already naked in bed and as Sophie climbed into bed, Pete said, "We're going to do something a little different tonight." Pete reached down and unscrewed the wooden portion of Sophie's leg, leaving the plastic piece around her stump. He set the wooden portion on the other side of the bed as he pulled Sophie down to him. Then he started to stroke her tummy with the back of his fingers.

"You don't need to do that," she said. "I'm ready for you." Instead of rolling over on her, he moved his hand lower and started to massage her clitoris. Sophie's body started to move rhythmically, involuntarily. Frustrated, she rolled over on top of him and started to insert him into to her. He rolled her back over and inserted himself into her. They continued in that fashion until she climaxed. Then he slipped off of her, rolled her onto her side with her back to his chest, and entered her again. He put his arm over her hip and gently massaged her clitoris while picking up the pace of his stroke into her. Sophie shuttered as she climaxed again. Pete withdrew and turned Sophie on her tummy. Then he straddled her leg. He entered her vagina from the rear this time, as he reached around to stroke her clitoris again.

Pete was looking at the beautiful, red dragoon tattooed on her back as they climaxed simultaneously. Sophie lay back down on her tummy. Pete rolled her over on her back and said, "This time you're on top, but face my feet." She did. Ten minutes later they both climaxed again.

Pete was still on his back as Sophie climbed off him turning over and sliding her shoulder under his arm, with her head on his chest.

"I don't think I could take another love-making session like that again and live," she finally said.

"If you leave me alone again for two months, it could prove fatal."

Pete awoke the next morning at his usual six-thirty. Pete always slept on his side, but that morning he awoke on his back. Sophie's head was on his chest with her right arm flung across his chest. Her right leg lay across his right leg. He tried to get out of bed without waking her but failed. "What time is it?" Sophie asked.

"Six-thirty, time to feed the kids. Come on, let's go."

"You go ahead. I'll be along in a minute." She added, "If I'm not there, go ahead and start without me."

Pete came out of the bathroom to find that his wife had dozed off. He let her sleep and went to take care of feeding the children.

9

Pete returned to the bedroom forty-five minutes later. Sophie sat up in bed and asked, "What's the plan for today? What should I wear?"

"You should probably wear jeans and an old blouse, which you can get dirty. Bring a sweatshirt or something, too," Pete answered.

"What are we doing?" she wanted to know.

"You'll see," he answered evasively, as he left the bedroom.

"What's for breakfast?" she asked brightly entering the kitchen.

"Cereal," Pete answered. "There's some on the stove; help yourself."

"What is this?" Sophie asked looking into the pot on the stove.

"Oatmeal. Try it, you'll like it."

Sophie spooned some oatmeal into a bowl. She went over to the table with the spoon and sat down. Putting a little on the tip of the spoon, she tasted it. "I don't think this is very good," she said.

Pete looked over and said, "You need to add milk and sugar." After she had Pete asked, "Well?"

"Better," Sophie replied noncommittally.

"It's good for you, too."

Just as Sophie finished her oatmeal, Pete's mother pulled into the driveway. Pete took Sophie's bowl and placed a topsider moccasin on the floor in front of Sophie, saying, "Wear that."

"What is that?" Sophie asked pointing at the shoe.

"That is a topsider moccasin. We're going sailing today."

"I can't go sailing," Sophie said.

"Why not?"

Sophie stood up and pointed at her peg leg and asked, "Do you see that thing sticking out of my left pant cuff?"

"Yes."

"That's why not."

"Nonsense, there have been peg-legged sailors ever since they invented the cannonball." That statement drew a skeptical look from Sophie. Pete continued, "You can at least try it. If you don't like it, or if you get scared or something, I'll turn around and we'll go right back to the dock."

Sophie really didn't want to go, but she knew in the interest of domestic tranquility she had to go. Besides, he said they would come back if she didn't like it. How bad could it be, she asked herself?

***

Pete's mother, Sally, came into the kitchen. She and Sophie exchanged hugs and air kisses. "So, you're going sailing?" Sally asked.

Sophie rolled her eyes and said with great reluctance in her voice, "I guess so."

"There's nothing to worry about, Pete is a very good sailor," Sally said. "He did an awful lot of racing in high school and college."

Sophie brightened somewhat at that and said to Pete, in a direful voice, "Let's go and get this over with."

"You sound like Marie Antoinette on her way to the guillotine," Pete said, giving her a playful little swat on her derriere on the way out the door.

As they were getting into the car, Pete said, "I think you will like sailing."

"We'll see," Sophie said.

After walking three quarters of the way down the marina dock, Pete said, "Here we are."

Sophie looked down at the small little sailboat docked next to the finger where Pete had turned. She was aghast. "We're not going out on that little thing, are we?"

"Yep, that's our boat. I bought it just for us," he said beaming with pride.

"Where's its Mommy?" Sophie wanted to know, looking at the small, thirty foot, mostly open boat.

Pete ignored her question and started taking the boat cover off. He put the boat cover in the little cuddy cabin and started the blower. Reemerging from the cuddy cabin he said to Sophie, "Come over here." She walked down the finger toward the center of the boat. Pete reached over the lifeline and picked Sophie up. He then stepped down from the deck to the cockpit floor, setting Sophie down gently as he did so. She sat down on one of the benches in the cockpit and asked, "What now?"

"I'll take the sail covers off, start the engine, and then we'll be ready for sea."

"What's this we? Do you have a frog in your pocket? I'm not sure I will ever be ready for sea." Sophie's skepticism about this whole venture was continuing to grow.

"I wish you would keep an open mind," Pete said shaking his head. At last, the only thing left to do was untie the dock lines. "All right, here we go," Pete said, untying the bow line and jogging to the other end of the slip to untie the stern line. Sophie meanwhile, had decided domestic tranquility had its limits, and this was definitely above and beyond the call of duty.

They chugged out of the harbor, the railroad bridge opened and they were soon in Long Island Sound. They motored along for five minutes more before Pete raised the mainsail. Then he unfurled the jib and shut off the engine. The wind was light and almost directly behind them, so the boat was not heeling. "Let's go over there," Sophie said pointing to the north.

"Okay," Pete responded. As they changed directions the boat started to heel a little. Sophie got a bit wide-eyed. "It usually is more comfortable if you sit on the weather side of the boat," he said pointing to the seat opposite of where Sophie sat. She shifted across the small cockpit.

"Why do you call this the weather side?" she wanted to know.

"Because the wind is coming from that side of the boat."

"Oh," she said. "What is the other side of the boat called?"

"The leeward side." After a few minutes, Pete said, "Let's go the other way now." With that he tacked the boat changing directions.

"Why didn't we go further?" Sophie wanted to know.

"I don't want to get too far away from the harbor in case this wind dies."

It wasn't very long before Sophie was asking the names of all of the parts of the boat. She had clearly started to enjoy herself. Finally, Pete decided to head back into port and for the first time he came hard up onto the wind, causing the boat to heel even further. He was happy to see Sophie did not react at all. Approaching the harbor entrance Pete started the engine, and took down the sails. They chugged back into the harbor.

With the boat secured in its slip and covered, they walked back up the dock. "Okay," Sophie said, "I was wrong. I enjoyed that a lot!" Pete said nothing. Just as they reached the top of the dock, Sophie realized that all the boats had names painted on their transoms. "What's the name of our boat?" she wanted to know.

"I named it after you," Pete answered.

"The Sophie?"

"No. Ms. Saigon."

"Wasn't that a musical or something?"

"That was Miss Saigon; you no longer qualify as a Miss."

"Oh yea, I guess that's right."

"How come I didn't know that you loved to sail before this?" Sophie asked as they were driving home.

"Probably because we had a three-day courtship and it's the kind of thing one learns a little later on in a relationship."

"We would've had a longer courtship if your name had been Pete instead of Potent."

Pete decided to let that go. He could only dig himself a hole if he didn't. They only knew each other for a few days before he knocked her up and they were soon married.

***

"Well, how did you enjoy your sail?" Pete's mom asked Sophie as they entered the kitchen.

"I loved it! I really didn't think I could go sailing because of my handicap."

"Pete is a very good sailor. Before he left home people were always calling on him to crew on their boats. I'm sure he made it fun for you," Sally said.

"I can see why he was in such demand; he is very good. Thinking back on it now I realize exactly how he brought me along. The boat didn't heel at first, but then it heeled more. At the end we were heeling quite a bit, but I was ready for it and even enjoyed it, very clever your son."

"He can be pretty foxy when he wants to be," Sally agreed. "We were just talking about you. Are your ears burning?" Sally asked Pete as he walked into the kitchen.

"No, should they be?" Pete replied.

"Can we go again tomorrow?" Sophie asked Pete.

"Not tomorrow, we need to put away everything you brought from Las Vegas. Also, we need to go to the bank and get your name on the accounts and order you a credit card."

Sophie had always dealt in cash in Macau. She never had a reason for credit. It was foreign to her

"You know that could wait a day," Sophie said clearly disappointed.

"I put it off one day already, and it really should be done soon. Never put off 'til tomorrow, what you can do today."

"Bah! Then after dinner you can take me to a bookstore where I can buy a book on sailing."

"That I will do happily," Pete replied.

***

Later that evening at the bookstore, Sophie asked, "Which of these books do you recommend?"

"This one is probably as good as any," he said as he wandered off. Pete looked around for his wife a few minutes later and saw her in the checkout line. He moseyed over to see which book Sophie had decided to buy. As he looked at the stack in front of Sophie his eyes widened. He realized she had decided to buy them all. No reason to make a decision when you can just throw money at the problem, and it will just go away, he thought!

"Don't you think that's a little over the top?" Pete asked.

"No, I think I'll be able to learn something from each book."

"If you read all those books you're going to be awfully smart," he said sarcastically.

"I hope so," she replied, ignoring his sarcastic tone.

"Why didn't you buy a bigger one?" Sophie asked, out of the blue, as they were driving home.

"What? The boat?"

"Yes."

"When it comes to boats, bigger is not necessarily better."

"Why is that?" she asked.

"Before you buy a boat you want to know what its mission is going to be. Our boat is just a day sailor, with the possibility of spending a night or two on it. You and I can sail it without any crew," he elaborated.

"You mean you bought a boat just for us?"

"You and I can handle that boat easily, but we could take other people as well if we wanted."

"How big a boat do you think we can handle by ourselves?" she wanted to know.

"How long is a piece of string," he replied. That answer drew an annoyed look from Sophie.

"I'm serious."

"I know you are, but the answer depends on the boat." They pulled into the driveway and he looked at Sophie. He could see the answer placated her, but did not satisfy her. So he said, "I'm sure the answer is in that stack of books somewhere." She glowered at him.

He thought he heard her say, "Smart ass," as he got out of the car, but he wasn't sure, so he let it drop. He knew, however, that she was not going to let it drop. He saw the seed beginning to germinate, and if he wasn't careful they were going to wind up with some enormous boat. He knew, too, that he had never been very successful at reigning in his wife's spending. Of course, she had earned it, but still. . .

***

That night he made veal cutlets for the kids, under Sophie's watchful eye. Once the children were finally in bed, always a struggle, he made veal parmesan for Sophie and himself.

"This is really good," Sophie said half-way through her meal. "I'll never learn to cook as well as you do," she went on.

"Why don't we take a cooking class together?" Pete suggested.

"That's a good idea," she said.

"I'll see what I can find on the internet after dinner," Pete responded. Then added, "Your turn to do the dishes."

"Ugh!"

Pete helped Sophie clear the table. "How do I do this?" Sophie wanted to know.

So Pete gave Sophie a thirty second lecture on rinsing the dishes and loading the dishwasher.

"I am going to see what I can find on the internet in the way of cooking classes." He left the kitchen for the computer in the office. He found a plethora of cooking schools in the local area offering all manner of classes. After an hour, he found exactly what he was looking for. He returned to the kitchen only to discover Sophie was not there.

"I found a cooking class in New London which I think would be perfect," Pete said entering the bedroom. He found Sophie propped up in bed. Her sailing books lay strewn across Pete' side of the bed. Upon further examination, Pete queried, "Any room for me in there?"

"Sure just push those aside," she said, without looking up.

"I think I've created a monster," he groaned.

"You know," Sophie without looking up, "it just occurred to me; I've never had a hobby."

"Really?"

"I've always been devoted to work, and never had the time," she said, finally looking up as she pushed her glasses up the bridge of her nose with her right forefinger.

Sophie's leg lay on the floor next to the bed. "I guess we're not making love tonight," Pete said.

"Can't," she replied distractedly.

"Oh?"

"I am still recovering from last night."

Pete undressed and crawled into bed leaving all Sophie's books between them. "Can I have your undivided attention for a moment?" he asked.

"Certainly, my husband, for you anything," she said her voice dripping with sarcasm.

"I spoke to Toy and Chou today and told them their primary duty would be to watch the children and that I will take care of you. I am worried about kidnapping. I also told them to pay special attention to Chou's children as well. Someone might grab one of Chou's kids thinking it was our child."

"Do you really think there's a risk of kidnapping?"

"When you have as much money as you do?"

"'We' do," Sophie interrupted.

"As we do, there is always a risk of that, although I think it to be extremely unlikely."

"I think that's the right thing to do. That's a problem we don't want to have to try to solve later."

"What do they say? An ounce of prevention is worth a pound of cure? Also, I am sure you have noticed Mai Ling is doing an awful lot around here. I put her on a salary of twenty-five hundred dollars a month since she is helping with the kids and all. Toy thought that was fine, but Mai Ling is going back to school in September. I think we're going to have to find someone to replace her."

"I'll take care of finding someone else. What is she going to study?" Sophie asked.

"I don't know. One last thing we need to think about. I don't know if you noticed when we came home, but a For Sale sign went up on the house across the street. We never bought Toy and Mai Ling a wedding present and that house might be just the ticket. I think we should look at it tomorrow. The location is ideal."

"That's a good idea," Sophie.

"I'll call the agent in the morning," Pete replied. Then he asked, "If we buy the house for Toy will Chou be upset?"

Sophie pensively replied, "I don't think so, but I'll find out."

With that Pete rolled over and turned out the light on his side of the bed with the intention of going to sleep. Normally, Sophie slept on her right side with her back against Pete's chest. "Hey, I don't like that," Sophie said.

"What?" Pete queried.

"You know what. You're sleeping way over there."

"In case you didn't notice, there are a few books someone left on the bed between us."

"All right, I'll move them," Sophie said. And she did, but she continued to read. "I'll snuggle up in a couple of minutes," she said as Pete drifted.

***

The next day they started to settle into what would become their normal morning routine. Feed the kids, light house work, and then off to do a few errands. During naptime, they met the real estate agent for the house across the street. They both liked the house and told the real estate agent to write up an offer but to do it in such a way that they could change how it was titled. They would still need to get inside and inspect the house prior to closing.

About five o'clock that afternoon, the real estate agent called to tell them that their offer had been accepted.

***

Once the children were in bed, she asked Pete, "Can you manage to cook dinner without me while I go talk to Chou?"

"Sure."

"What are we having, by the way?"

"Swordfish, peas, and new potatoes."

***

"Chou understood completely, in fact he was quite happy for Toy," Sophie said, coming back into the kitchen. Her dinner was already on the table, and Pete had already started to eat not knowing when she would return.

"Good. The apartment over the garage was specially designed for Chou and his family. Mrs. Chou also selected all the furniture."

"I didn't know that. How did you work that out?" Sophie asked.

"Over the internet."

"I didn't know that Mrs. Chou was that computer literate."

"She's not, but her kids are," Pete replied.

After a moment's reflection, Sophie asked, "Why didn't I know that?"

"Mundane details, there was no reason to bother you with it. It's not like it was a big secret or something."

"Hmm. . .I like to know what's going on," she remarked, picking up her fork.

"You had your hands full with other things at the time."

"This is really good," Sophie said, swallowing her first bite.

"I'm glad you like it. I'm sure you'll be able to do as well once you are a graduate of the New London Cooking School."

"Ah yes, something to look forward to," Sophie replied.

***

"Your turn to do the dishes," Pete said when they had both finished eating.

"Ugh, I'm not sure I like this arrangement." Then she added, "You know you're going to give me dishpan hands, don't you?"

"Bah! Rinsing a few dishes before you put them into the dishwasher isn't going to give you dishpan hands. Besides, into every life a little rain must fall."

"Have you ever heard of an umbrella?" Sophie mumbled, getting up from the table.

Pete helped Sophie clear the table. "I'm going to go upstairs and read," he said, setting the last of the dishes into the sink.

"Running out on me in my time of need; typical man!"

"There is such a thing as woman's work, you know."

A plastic glass from the dish drainer came flying across the kitchen, narrowly missing him.

Sophie went straight into her bathroom after entering the bedroom. She returned to the bedroom and crawled into bed still wearing her leg.

Pete set his book aside and slid lower into the bed. He reached his hand across to Sophie's tummy, saying, "Ah ha."

Pushing his hand away, Sophie cautioned, "There is no ah ha. Not yet anyway, I want to read a bit." She picked up her sailing book off the bedside table where she had left it.

"I've created a monster."

They did make love, but somewhat later, and it lacked the passion of their reunion.

***

"Who is the woman I saw upstairs in the hall?" Sophie asked Pete as she entered the kitchen the next morning.

"Mrs. Kitchner," Pete answered.

"Who is Mrs. Kitchner?" Sophie asked, clearly annoyed at his evasive answer.

"The cleaning lady. She comes twice a week, Mondays and Thursdays, and does most of the housework."

Sophie walked over to the stove and looked into the pot still sitting there. "I don't think I like oatmeal anymore," she quipped.

"I thought we might go sailing today, if you would like," Pete said ignoring Sophie's remark.

Sophie brightened at that suggestion.

"I'd love to!" she exclaimed, beaming.

***

They had a great sail. The wind blew a bit harder than it had during the last sail, but Sophie enjoyed it more. She spent the first hour and a half going over the parts of the boat with Pete.

Pete realized that she was basically confirming what she had learned from the books she had been reading. Then she wanted Pete to show her the various points of sail. After demonstrating a beam reach, tight reach, downwind, and hard on the wind, Sophie remained quiet for fifteen minutes. Pete knew she was digesting everything she had just had confirmed from her reading.

Next, she wanted to learn how to steer. Pete gave her the helm and he showed her the various things you had to keep in mind to steer well. Sophie concluded she needed more practice at the helm, and that there were certain things you could not learn from a book.

Finally, in unison they breathed a sigh of relief. "Let's go out to dinner," Sophie said after the kids were in bed.

"Good idea." Sophie told the amah they were leaving while Pete pulled the car around to the front of the house.

"What do you feel like eating?" Pete asked Sophie as they pulled out of the driveway.

"You pick; I'm too tired to think," Sophie answered.

"I would like a good steak right about now," Pete said.

"That is so what I want, too," Sophie piped up.

Once they had ordered, Pete asked Sophie, "What do you want to do about the cooking school?"

"You know Jean Jacques is working in a restaurant in Las Vegas. I'm sure he would come back to work for us, if we asked. Cooking school is going to cut into the time we have for sailing."

"But you need to learn how to cook."

"I need to learn how to sail, too," she said.

"Need?"

"Yes, need. We own a boat, you know. Besides, suppose something happened to you when we were out on the water?" She had trumped his hand again.

"You know how to sail; I watched you today," he said, trying for a blazing recovery.

"I need much more practice on the helm. I did terribly today."

"Actually, you did quite well for your first time," Pete said.

"Do you really think so?" she asked, smiling.

"Absolutely." Just then their meals arrived.

Over dinner Sophie suggested that perhaps they could find a one-week cooking class, and Pete could teach her the rest.

"I'll see what I can find on the internet when we get home," Pete said.

***

When they arrived at the house Sophie went upstairs to get ready for bed and Pete went into the office to search the internet.

Sophie closed the book she was reading when Pete entered the bedroom. "I have a question for you," she said.

"I hope I have an answer for you," Pete replied, taking off his shirt.

"Does my leg bother you?"

"Nope, I think it is a very nice leg," he said.

"You can be so annoying when you want to be. I meant, does the fact that I am missing a leg bother you?"

"Nope."

"Not at all?"

"No. Well, maybe I shouldn't say that. It bothers me only to the extent that I know it bothers you, and you know I want you to have everything your heart desires."

"Ha!"

"What do you mean 'Ha'!"

"I mean, Ha!"

He walked over and sat beside her on the bed. He kissed her gently on the forehead. "Okay, what do you want that your mean and nasty husband has denied you?"

"Two maids and a cook," she fired back and then added, "and a massage and a manicure would be nice too."

"The massage and the manicure are definitely doable. Whether you want to admit it or not, you know we are doing the right thing for the kids."

"I know you're right, of course, but I'm a room service kind of gal."

"You'll get over it." He got up and continued to undress.

"One more thing, if I may, would you prefer that I use the latest thing in artificial limbs?"

"You know, I have actually thought about that."

"What did you conclude?"

"I think you should use whatever you want to use. Why all these questions after almost five years of marriage?" Pete wanted to know.

"I don't mind talking about my handicap, but I don't like bringing it up. It is sort of like I'm trading on it, and that I don't like. But, please answer, do you like my using a peg leg?"

"Your peg leg has kind of become a trade mark. It also says I am going to do things my way and I am not trying to hide the fact that I am missing a leg. Sort of like defying convention, and that I do admire, but let me repeat, you do what you want."

"So you do like my peg leg?"

"What I like and do not like in this regard is academic. You do what you want. Now, I have a question for you."

"What's that?"

"Does your stump hurt you at all?"

"For the first ten years or so it felt like the toes on my left foot were on fire. One day I noticed that it had stopped, and now, I never have any pain, although occasionally, I get a little chaffing."

Once fully undressed, Pete crawled into bed. With a large grin on his face Pete said, "There may be only three feet between these two sheets but all the essentials are there."

Sophie rolled over so her chest was on top of him while their hips touched. "I'm so lucky I married you," she said.

"I'm the lucky one."

"Why is that?" she asked.

"I married the most beautiful woman in the world who also happens to be the most intelligent person I have ever met," he answered.

"I didn't know you had kissed the blarney stone," she said reaching for his manhood.

***

Things in the kitchen quieted down after the kids had been fed. Pete and Sophie were enjoying the relative calm and a cup of coffee. "Well, what do you think about the one-week cooking school?" he wanted to know.

"What are the hours?" Sophie asked.

"It starts at eight-thirty and ends at noon. It is extremely doubtful that anyone will enjoy your initial offerings unless you get a little help to start."

"As long as there is no way out of this, I guess you might as well sign us up," she said groaning inwardly. Then she brightened, and said, "You know we could always call a caterer on a nightly basis. We'd have good food, no cook, and no clean up."

"I'll reserve us a spot for next week," he said rising from the table.

"I should have had my head examined before agreeing to this," she mumbled to herself.

"Can we go sailing this afternoon?" Sophie asked.

"We have to see a lawyer about the house across the street. Let's make arrangements for Toy and Mai Ling to see the place because they may not want it."

Sophie said, "I think we should buy it anyway. I just have a feeling that someday we'll need it. We can use it as a rental if Toy and Mai Ling don't take it."

"That's a very good idea," Pete agreed.

When they returned from the lawyer's office, Sophie laid down on the couch in the office. She thought about the property they had just agreed to buy, and she decided buying more property in the area was a good idea. She called the lawyer back and told him to buy all the unimproved buildable land he could find anywhere in town. To keep the price from rising dramatically, she told him to create multiple corporations.

***

That evening, with the children finally in bed, the din that four children can create had subsided. Pete and Sophie reviewed the day. Toy and Mai Ling had liked the house, and Mai Ling had cried when she learned it was going to be her and Toy's wedding present. The visit to the lawyer, while necessary, had proved anticlimactic, just lawyer-created paperwork rig-a-ma-roll.

"Did you ask Mai Ling what she wants to study when she goes back to school?" Pete asked.

"She wants to be a doctor," Sophie replied.

"That bodes an ill wind," Pete observed.

"Why is that?" Sophie wanted to know.

"Well, the only medical school near here, that I am aware of, is Yale, which is very hard to get into. They'll probably have to leave the area for her medical school."

"It's a long way off. Things may change in the next four years," Sophie said.

"Speaking of Mai Ling, what have you done about hiring someone to replace her?"

"I called my father in Paris. He's looking for a French lady for us. I thought it would be good if the children could learn a little French."

"That is a really good idea," Pete said. "I'm glad you thought of it."

"It's easy for them to learn languages now. The more languages they speak, the better off they will be."

"I completely agree. They sure seem to speak Chinese well, I heard Alexis speaking Chinese to Brian the other day. I do think, however, we need to be a bit careful in this regard because they need to learn to speak English well, too."

"You're right. Do you have any ideas how we should go about that?" Sophie asked.

"You speak to them in Chinese," Pete said.

"Yes."

"When I speak to them, I will use only English. They won't start to mix the two that way."

"Okay."

"Tomorrow is Saturday. Can we go sailing?" Sophie asked.

"Sure, we can go sailing any day we want. There's nothing special about Saturday," Pete said.

"I thought it might be too crowded or something."

"No, it's not a problem; we just need to take a little extra care watching for other boats," Pete said.

***

They didn't get to the marina until ten-thirty the next morning. Al Rocca was just coming out of the cabin on his boat as they walked down the finger to their boat.

"Good morning, Al, meet my wife, Sophie. Sophie, meet Al Rocca." Pete said to him.

"It's a pleasure," Al responded.

"We're going sailing. Would you like to come?" Pete asked.

"I was hoping you'd ask. I was getting tired of cleaning the bilge," Al replied.

With the boat and sail covers stowed and the engine running, Al cast off the dock lines. They motored past the railroad bridge and into Long Island Sound. They raised the sails about a half mile out, and shut off the engine.

Pete noticed Sophie watching a group of boats to the South of them intently. "What are those boats doing?" she finally asked.

"Racing," Pete answered.

As they watched, they rounded a buoy and raised their spinnakers. "Those colored sails are spinnakers, right?" Sophie asked.

"Yea," Pete said simply.

"Does our boat have a spinnaker?" Sophie wanted to know.

"It does." Then Pete looked at Al and said, "Sophie is just learning how to sail."

Smiling Al turned to Sophie and said, "It is a lot of fun isn't it?"

"I love it," she said. She stared at the race intently for about five minutes and then asked Pete, "Can we put the spinnaker up?"

Pete knew the determined look on Sophie's face all too well. "Okay," he said, "but we'll have to go way up wind to do it, and it's a lot of trouble." That comment drew him a nasty look from

Sophie. He started the boat upwind and asked Al, "Do you know how to fly a spinnaker?"

"Only in theory," Al answered. "This will be a first for me as well."

"Who wants to steer while I rig it?"

Sophie slid over next to him to take the helm. Pete chuckled inwardly. Pete led all the lines to their proper places, and said, "I need to pack the spinnaker." He went into the little cuddy cabin to do it.

Sophie tried to watch him through the entry door but was unable to see much. Pete brought the spinnaker up and set it on the cockpit deck. "I think we need to go further up wind."

Ten minutes later, Pete said, "I think this is far enough."

First, Pete turned the boat so that the wind was coming from behind them. Then he rigged the spinnaker pole and hooked the bag holding the spinnaker to the deck by the mast stays. Lastly, he hooked the halyard to the spinnaker.

"I think we're ready. Now, Al, take the spinnaker halyard and pull it when I say go. Sophie, you pull on this line," he said handing it to her, until the pole is about four feet away from the head stay." He took one last look at everything, and said "Go!"

Things went better than Pete expected, and with a loud snap, the spinnaker filled with wind. "Now, Al, if you'll take the helm, I'll teach Sophie how to fly a chute." Al came back and took the helm. "Just hold this course, Al." As soon as Pete went forward, he furled the jib. "Now, Sophie, to make this work correctly, you pull this line, called the guy back so the pole is perpendicular to the wind. Then you let this line called the sheet, out until the upper portion of the sail starts to curl. He showed her how it was done and then handed her the sheet. Pete watched Sophie closely. He had never seen her concentrate so fiercely. It took her about five minutes to get the hang of it.

"I think it's about time to jibe. We're getting a little close to the shore. This is how we do it. Al, you go up on the foredeck, take the pole off the mast, and hook it to the sheet. Then you take it off the guy and put that end of the pole into the fitting on the mast. Sophie, as Al is doing that, you let the sheet out and pull in the guy. I'll jibe the main."

"Sophie, the boom is going to come across very fast. Keep your head down because that thing can really ring your bell."

Sophie looked at Pete. She was clearly concerned. "There's nothing to worry about as long as you are aware of what is going to happen and keep your head down."

"Al, if you'll hop up on the foredeck we'll give it a try." When Al was in position, Pete called, "Jibe ho."

The chute collapsed once because Sophie did not get the lines around fast enough.

"I was a little slow," Sophie acknowledged.

"It was pretty good for the first time though," Pete said.

"Let's do it again, and I'll get it right this time," Sophie said.

"In a few minutes," Pete replied. After they had sailed close to shore, Pete asked, "Okay, you guys, are you ready to do it again?"

"You bet," Al said, as Sophie nodded.

"Everybody ready?" After receiving positive responses, he said, "Jibe ho."

This time it went perfectly. Al was faster getting the pole across, and Sophie did a perfect job with the sheet and the guy. "Let's do it again, but this time I want to do the pole."

"No," Pete said. Sophie was Asian enough to know not to argue with her husband in public, but by the look on her face, Pete knew he had not heard the last of this refusal.

"Time to take it down and head for the barn," he said a few minutes later. "Taking it down is fairly easy. Sophie, you grab the sheet and pull the bottom of the sail into the boat. As you're pulling it, I'll let the guy come around. Al, once Sophie has the whole sail or most of it in her arms, you let the halyard go."

"Ready?" he asked. "Okay, let's do it. Sophie, here comes the guy." Al did his job to perfection, and Sophie managed, to get the sail into the boat. "Al, can you unfurl the jib and get it set?"

"I sure can."

"Sophie, unhook the spinnaker. Give the halyard to Al to secure, then stuff the sail into the cabin and we'll sort it out at the dock."

"What do you want to do with the sheet and the guy?" Sophie asked.

"Just hook them together and pull them taunt."

Back at the dock, just as they had finished putting the sail cover on, Al asked, "Would anyone like a cold beer?"

"That sounds great," Pete said.

"Sophie?" Al said. Pete knew that Sophie didn't really like beer, but she accepted just to be sociable. Al disappeared into his boat, and reemerged with three cans of cold Bud.

"That really hits the spot," Pete said taking his long sip.

"Yea, it does," Sophie said, surprised.

"My boat isn't rigged for a spinnaker, so that was my first time sailing with one up," Al said.

"There was not much wind today, so it was fairly easy. They can be quite a handful when it is blowing like stink," Pete said.

"I would imagine," Al said.

"Al, would you like to go sailing with us sometime during the week?" Sophie asked.

"I would love to, but I have to work."

"What do you do?" Sophie asked.

"I'm the local police chief," Al answered.

"We have cooking class next week," Pete reminded Sophie. This caused her nose to wrinkle up.

"How about next Saturday, then?" Sophie proposed.

"It's a date," Al said. Then Al asked, "Would anyone like another beer?" They both accepted his offer.

***

"I had a really good time today. I like Al, and flying the spinnaker was great, too," Sophie said.

"I'm glad you enjoyed the day."

"Oh, by the way, I have a bone to pick with you," Sophie said.

"What bone would that be?" he asked innocently, but knowing full well.

"You told me I couldn't handle the pole while we were jibing the spinnaker."

"Yes."

"Don't be evasive; it is so annoying when you do that. Why couldn't I handle the pole?"

"Well, you are not the strongest of swimmers nor are you the nimblest of people on your feet. If you fell overboard, I might not be able to get back to you before you went down for the last time," Pete explained. Then as an afterthought added, "If you wear a life jacket you can give it a try next weekend."

She didn't try to argue with his reasoning because basically she knew he was right; also an infuriating habit of his. As she drifted off to sleep another thought hit her. No one had really cared about her since mother, over twenty-five years ago.

***

Monday, as they were leaving for their first morning of cooking class, Pete looked at the expression on Sophie's face and said, "You don't look very happy about this."

"I'm not," she replied.

"Come on, it won't be that bad," he said trying to cheer her up.

"I'd rather eat a green snake than do this."

"A green one, eh," he chortled.

***

The following Saturday when Pete and Sophie came down to the dock, Al was already there working on his boat. Al looked up when he heard them and said, "Good morning."

"Hi, Al. Are you ready to go sailing?" Sophie asked brightly.

"I am. How was cooking school?" Al asked with a lilt in his voice and mischievous grin on his face.

"Actually, it was pretty good. I learned a lot," Sophie said.

"She cooked dinner last night, and it was pretty good, too," Pete said praising his wife's expanding skills.

"There are clearly no limits to your talents," Al said good-naturedly.

"Not you, too?" Then nodding at Pete, she said, "I knew he kissed the blarney stone, but until now I wasn't sure about you."

"I'm only saying it because it's true," Al replied.

"Yea, yea," replied Sophie, grinning as well.

All three pitched in to get the boat ready to sail and off they went.

***

Back at the dock with the boat put to bed, Al again offered beers. Both Sophie and Pete accepted his offer. Once everyone had seated themselves in the cockpit, Pete said, "You guys did quite well jibing the spinnaker today. You've turned into a proficient racing crew." Sophie beamed as Al smiled.

They chatted for another fifteen minutes. "What time is it getting to be?" Sophie asked.

"Four fifteen," Al replied, looking at his watch.

"I was planning to do some hamburgers on the grill tonight. If you don't have any plans, we would be happy to have you join us," Pete said to Al.

"I'd be delighted," Al replied. "What time?"

"Five-thirtyish?" Pete said.

"I'll be there," Al replied.

Pete gave him the address.

They finished their beers. Al went back to his boat, and Sophie and Pete walked up the dock.

Pete and Sophie stopped at the grocery store on the way home and bought everything they needed for a barbecue.

Al arrived at five thirty-five, and Pete answered the door. "Come on in," Pete said. "Ready for a beer?"

"I thought you'd never ask," Al said following Pete into the kitchen. Sophie had sliced onions and tomatoes.

"Hi, Al," she said preparing lettuce.

"You have a lovely home," Al observed.

"Pete designed and built it," Sophie said.

"Not exactly correct, the architect designed it. I just gave him a few ideas," Pete elaborated.

"Who was your architect?" Al asked.

"Steven Dadona, I went to high school with him," Pete said. "Let's go outside and light the barbecue," Pete suggested.

Al looked at the art hanging on the various walls and said as they were walking out the side door, "I like your taste in art."

"Thank you."

"What a great view," Al said, as Pete lit the barbeque.

"It is nice."

"Why do you have such a big garage?" he asked after look-ing around a little bit.

"Come on, I'll show you my other hobby."

Al followed Pete to the garage. Pete opened the door on the end of the garage that faced the street. An Austin Healy, in the process of being reassembled, was the first thing Al saw. Look-ing past the work area he saw two Cobras, an Aston Martin, a Rolls Royce, a limo, a van, and the little white car. "My hobby is restoring old cars."

"What a collection," Al said, clearly awed. "I've never seen anything like this outside a museum. No wonder you have an eight car garage. How did you ever get into this anyway?"

"I started when I was in the Army. I fixed up an old MG and sold it. It seemed each time I finished one car, I'd do a little more on the next one. Now I do a 'frame off' on every car I do. When you see the finished product there is a real feeling of satisfaction."

"This is truly amazing."

"There's an apartment on the second floor, and one of the people who works for us and his family live there."

"I am very seldom at a loss for words, but this . . .," Al said waving his hand, "has done it."

"Let's go see how the barbeque is doing." Pete said.

"That is as surprised as I have ever been," Al said.

"I might have a surprise or two left," Pete said chuckling.

The fire seemed to be doing well, so they went into the kitchen to refresh their beers. As they entered the kitchen, the conversation switched from Cantonese to English. Pete intro-duced Al to Toy, Chou, Mai Ling, Soo Ling, Chou's wife, and all seven children.

"What language were you speaking?" Al asked Sophie.

"Cantonese," she replied.

"I noticed even your children were speaking it," Al noted.

"They've been exposed to Cantonese since they were babies," Sophie said.

"Mrs. Chou is teaching her children to read and ours are learning by watching their lessons."

"What languages do you speak Sophie?" Al queried.

"Cantonese, Vietnamese, English, and some Mandarin."

"Pete, do you speak Cantonese as well?" Al asked.

"The only other language I speak is French."

"Can your kids speak French as well?" Al asked.

"No, but Sophie is going to hire a French au pair in the fall when Mai Ling goes back to school." Pete answered.

Everyone went outside to watch Pete throw the first round of burgers on the fire. Soo Wong took the burgers inside to the kitchen when the first batch were done. She, Sophie, and Mai Ling fed the kids as Toy and Chou supervised. It was bedtime for the Smith children almost immediately after dinner so Sophie joined Pete and Al once everyone was tucked in for the night.

"Should I throw our burgers on the fire?" Pete asked.

"I'm starved," Sophie said.

"Me, too," Al added.

Sophie went inside and returned with a tray of condiments and a bowl of potato salad.

Pete set a tray of three burgers on the table. Everyone doctored their burger to suit their own taste.

"This is excellent potato salad Sophie. I can see that cooking school really paid off," Al said.

"I can't take credit for it, I'm afraid. We bought it when we went to the market," Sophie responded.

Sophie cleared the table and took everything inside. She returned with a lit cigarette and an ash tray.

"I gotta ask, what do those two, huge Chinese guys do for you because they sure aren't gardeners."

Sophie flashed Pete an alarmed look. Pete saw Al catch Sophie's look. He decided the truth was in order. "Body guards," he answered simply.

"What do you need body guards for?"

"Have you ever heard of Madame Gin Sling?" Pete asked.

"You mean the Empress of Gambling, the one who owns all those casinos?" Pete nodded. "Of course," Al said.

"She is seated across the table from you."

'Uhhhh... Uhhh," was all that came out of Al's mouth.

"I told you this could be an evening of surprises," Pete said.

"I never thought... Uh,... I would," Al said his voice trailing off. "I can route a police car by here more often if you would like," Al said, getting over his shock.

"I don't think that would be such a good idea. We're trying to keep things as low key as possible, but I appreciate the offer," Pete said.

"You've done that pretty well. I haven't heard a murmur," Al said.

Al looked at the art on the walls as he walked through to the front door intending to leave. "All this art is original, isn't it?"

"Yes," Sophie said, "losers who couldn't pay off. Are we going sailing next weekend?" Sophie asked as Al was going out the front door.

"Absolutely," he said.

10

Their lives morphed into a regular pattern. Sophie assumed more and more of the cooking duties. They shared the cleanup chores. They always sailed with Al on Saturday and usually once or twice during the week. Every night before dinner, they spent at least an hour in the living room playing with their children. They had closed on the house across the street and Toy and Mai Ling had moved into it. Both Sophie and Pete were very content.

The Wednesday before the Memorial Day weekend at about five o'clock, the doorbell rang. Pete answered it, the man standing on the door step said, "I'm Charles Barksdale. I live on the other side of the street at number twenty-three. On Saturday night we're hosting the neighborhood's Memorial Day Weekend party. We would be delighted if you and your wife would attend. It'll give you a chance to meet all your new neighbors."

"We'd love to come. What time does it start?" Pete asked.

"It starts at five o'clock and usually runs until about eight. We supply the food, but it's BYOB."

"Thank you for the invitation, we'll be there," Pete said.

"Who was at the door?" Sophie asked when Pete entered the kitchen.

"One of our new neighbors, we're invited to a neighborhood party Saturday night. I accepted for us."

"That's nice. It's very friendly of them to invite us."

"It's typical of the United States. Neighborhood parties are not unusual," Pete said.

"Speaking of parties," Sophie said, "I'm thinking of having Jack and Carol, and Dianne and Mike over for a barbecue this weekend. What do you think?"

"Good idea," Pete said. Then he asked, "Are you cooking?"

That remark drew an annoyed look from Sophie, but she said nothing. Pete understood immediately she had not agreed to cook and had every intention of passing the cooking duties to him. He knew she liked gabbing with her friends and did not want to be distracted by having to flip burgers. This, of course was fine with him, as he enjoyed cooking. He stuck his head into the refrigerator looking for some peas and he said, "You're not as sly as you think you are."

"Moi?" Sophie said feigning innocence.

"No, Madame Gin Sling." She stuck out her tongue at him.

****

"Don't you hate going to these things where you don't know anybody?" Sophie said as they walked down the street to attend the neighborhood party.

"I have never enjoyed going into a crowded gathering where I didn't know anyone, but in this case, it is a necessity. We need to meet the neighbors," Pete responded.

"I know. That's the only reason I'm going."

They arrived at twenty minutes after five, fashionably late. There were about twenty people in the backyard. Their host, Charles, came to welcome them. He introduced Megan, his wife, as she came up. Charles took the six pack of Bud from

Pete saying, "I'll put this on ice for you. The cooler is right over there, when you want one."

"You have a lovely home," Megan told Sophie as Pete wandered off to mingle, "but I am curious to know why you built so big."

"Thank you," Sophie said, and then she added, "Four kids, we needed something good-sized to hold everyone."

"Excuse me," Megan said, going off to greet another arriving couple. Sophie walked over to the cooler and got herself a beer, popped the top, and took a sip.

Another woman walked up to the cooler and did the same thing. "I'm Mary Johanson. My husband Stan and I live next door."

"Sophie Smith," Sophie said offering her hand, which Mary shook politely. "Pete and I live in the new house just down the street."

"That's a lovely home," Mary replied. More people arrived and Sophie wandered off to find Pete.

"Everyone is very friendly," she said walking up to Pete.

"Yea, it's a nice group."

Charlie had started cooking hamburgers. When the second batch was almost done, Sophie and Pete joined the line waiting. Sophie turned to Pete and said, "At least I don't have to cook."

"Come on, it's not that bad."

"It would be worse than that bad if I had to eat alone and cleanup by myself." Charlie handed them each a paper plate with a burger on it, and they moved away from the barbecue. They ate standing up, and when they finished their meal, Sophie took the plates over to the trash can and deposited them. She stopped at the cooler and pulled another beer out for herself.

She passed two men making hand signals and discussing what sounded like a sailboat race. She stopped to listen. They, of course, noticed her interest immediately. At a break in the conversation, Sophie asked, "Were you racing today?"

"Yes. I'm Stan Hicky," one of the men said, "And you are?"

"Sophie Smith, excuse me for interrupting."

The other man said, "Dave Clark," holding out his hand. "Do you sail?"

"Yes, my husband and I have a small boat," Sophie answered. "What kind of boats were racing today?" she wanted to know.

"Etchells 22s," Dave replied.

"Who won?" Sophie asked.

"Well, it's a five race series. We had three races today and have two tomorrow, but Stan is in first place currently. He had a first and two seconds."

"How did you do?" Sophie asked Dave.

"A second, a third, and a fourth,"

Sophie looked over at Pete who gave her a sign with his head that he was ready to go, but Sophie continued to ask Stan and Dave questions about racing sailboats. Fifteen minutes later, Pete gave Sophie the same sign, but Sophie ignored him, again. This conversation fascinated her.

When she looked over to check on Pete, he was immersed in conversation with a very good-looking blonde. "My lord and master says it's time to go. It was very nice chatting with you. If you ever need a crew, I'd be delighted to go."

"Give me your number, you never know," Stan said, as Dave also pulled out his cell phone, and they programed her number into their phones.

Sophie walked over to where Pete stood talking to the blonde. "This is my wife, Sophie," Pete introduced her. "Sophie, meet Gail Honeycutt now."

"Now?" Sophie queried.

"Pete and I went to high school together and my name then was Griffin."

"It's a pleasure to meet you." Turning to Pete she said, "Are you ready to go?"

"Let's do it," Pete replied.

"Who is that Gail?" Sophie asked as soon as they reached the street.

"An old friend from high school. I haven't seen her in twenty-five years."

"Did you sleep with her?" Sophie wanted to know.

"We're talking high school here," Pete said indignantly. Sophie looked at him skeptically, but let the subject drop.

***

The next morning, at nine-thirty, just as Sophie and Pete finished cleaning up the kitchen, the phone rang. Sophie answered it. Pete listened to her side of the conversation, but was unable to make sense of it until Sophie said, "There have been peg-legged sailors ever since they invented the cannonball."

"What was that about?" Pete asked.

"That was Stan Hickey. He asked me to go sailing this morning. His regular crewman broke his arm in a traffic accident this morning on his way to the yacht club."

"I gather you said you'd do it," Pete said.

"Yes. What should I wear?"

"If I were you, I would wear jeans and an old blouse. You should probably use the leg you have with the hinge in it," Pete suggested.

Sophie scooted upstairs to change. When she came back down, she asked Pete, "Where's the yacht club?" He gave her directions.

Toy was standing in the kitchen as Pete gave Sophie directions. He looked at Toy as Sophie was going through the door to the garage and said, "Follow her, but don't let her see you." Toy smiled, "Okay, Boss."

****

Sophie didn't get home until five o'clock. She found Pete exactly where she had left him, in the kitchen. Pete knew by the look on her face she had had a good time. "I gather you had a good time," he said.

"Look what I won," she said pulling a small silver tray from her purse, and setting it on the counter. "We had a second and a first, and won the regatta."

"Everyone will be here in a half hour. You should grab a quick shower and change," Pete said smiling at her enthusiasm.

"We're joining the yacht club tomorrow," she said turning to go upstairs.

"Not tomorrow we're not," Pete said.

Sophie turned back to face him and asked with an exasperated tone in her voice, "Why not?"

"Tomorrow is a holiday, and the business office will be closed," he said grinning.

"You can be such a pain when you want to be," Sophie replied, turning to go upstairs.

Pete looked down at the six by four silver tray Sophie had left on the counter. It read "Memorial Day Regatta, First Place, Crew." He had the very distinct feeling that that was the most expensive ten dollar trophy he had ever seen.

Jack, Carol, and their two children arrived before Sophie came back downstairs. Sophie was coming down the stairs just as Mike, Dianne, and their son rang the doorbell. "I got it," she yelled toward the kitchen.

The women fed their children, took them upstairs, and put them to bed. The three men had promptly adjourned to the patio each with a beer in his hand. With all the children in bed, the women joined them in a drink. Pete cooked the burgers while Sophie laid out the condiments and side dishes.

By ten-thirty everyone had left, and Pete and Sophie had retired to their bedroom. "Pete, I want to buy an Etchells 22," Sophie said.

"I know."

"How do you know?" Sophie wanted to know.

"I knew the minute you walked in the door with the ear to ear grin on your face."

"I have never had such a good time," Sophie said.

"Never?" Pete said with a grin.

"Okay, never outdoors," she said looking at his lecherous expression.

"Racing sailboats is a lot of fun, especially in a competitive class."

"How do we get started, I mean, where do we go to buy one?" Sophie asked.

"Look them up on the internet, that will be a good place to get started. It's been twenty-five years since I've done any serious sailing," Pete said getting into bed.

As Sophie joined him in bed, she said, "It's hard to believe only going six miles an hour could be so exciting." She turned out the light.

They didn't make love that night for the first time in a long time. Pete knew Sophie's mind would be whirling as she thought about racing sailboats.

***

After the breakfast dishes had been washed, Sophie went into the office to look up Etchells 22 on the internet. Pete headed off to the garage to work on his current restoration project. Sophie came into the garage about an hour later. "Have you got a minute?" she asked.

"Sure."

"I found an Etchells manufacturer in Canada. I think we should order a boat from them. Apparently there are only three manufacturers in the world."

"Sophie, before you plunge into this project, let me give you some advice. There will probably be a consensus of opinion on which combination of mast, sails, and hull is the fastest. That's what you should buy."

"So what you are telling me is, look before you leap."

"Yep."

"Okay, I'm going to get back on the internet," she said turning to leave.

"You might ask Stan and that other guy for their opinions, too."

"Also, a good suggestion," Sophie said before heading back toward the house.

***

That evening when they had both gotten into bed, Pete asked Sophie, "Did you talk to Stan and what's his name. . .?"

"Dave," Sophie interjected.

"What did they think was the best combination?"

"Yes, and I got two different answers."

"What have you decided to do?" Pete asked.

"I'm still researching," Sophie said, as Pete turned out the light on his side of the bed. Then he reached for his wife. "Do you have something in mind?" Sophie asked. Pete chuckled to himself at the ambiguous question. He slid his hand down her tummy. "I can see that you do," Sophie said.

The next morning they went down to the yacht club. Pete's membership to the club had been put on hold while he was in the army, but in order to reinstate his membership he had to bring his dues current from the time of his discharge from the army. After writing a check for five years dues, Pete was back in good graces at the club.

"Why don't we dock our boat here?" Sophie asked.

"Because our boat is closer to home where it is. When I bought our boat I didn't think I'd be doing any racing, and I didn't want to pay the back dues."

"You have got to quit being so cheap."

"Close with a buck, if you please," Pete snapped back.

***

Pete lay on the couch in the office that evening reading while Sophie poured over the internet. "Have you ever heard of a guy named Carl Eichenlaub?" she asked.

"Sure, he was one of the greatest sailors who ever lived. I actually met him at a regatta, probably thirty years ago."

"He is quoted in this article as saying, 'If you want to win sail boat races, get a fast boat.' Do you think that's true?" Sophie wanted to know.

"If Carl Eichenlaub said it, it's gospel. As I said, he was one of the greatest sailors who ever lived," Pete said.

"Yes, but that begs the question, how do you get a fast boat?"

"I thought that was why you were doing research."

"This is very confusing. There are so many different opinions."

"I guess you'll just have to sift through them all to come up with an answer," Pete said.

"You could help, you know."

"This is your project, but please keep me informed," Pete said rising, clearly on his way to bed.

***

Three days later Pete was in bed when Sophie came into the bedroom. "Have you ever heard of Dennis Connor?" she asked.

"Of course, he's one of the most famous sailors in the world."

"Did you know before one of the America's Cup challenges he built three boats to different designs and spent a year racing one against the other to determine which was fastest?"

"Yes, that was when they used to race the America's Cup in twelve meters."

"What's a twelve meter?" Sophie asked. She was still digesting the research.

"It's a sailboat class. They are probably the most beautiful boats ever built."

"I'd like to see one, can you show me one?" Sophie asked.

"There aren't any around here," Pete replied.

"Where are they?"

"I think there are some in Newport," Pete said.

"How long does it take to get to Newport?"

"About an hour," he answered.

"Can we go up and look one day?"

"Sure," he said, and then added, "I think you'll like Newport." As Sophie went into the bathroom Pete dozed off.

"I guess the honeymoon is over," Sophie said to herself coming out of the bathroom to gaze at a snoozing husband.

11

$\mathcal{I}$t wasn't until the end of June that Sophie heard from Stan Hickey again. This time he asked her if she would like to sail in a regatta over the Fourth of July weekend in Greenwich, Connecticut. She, of course, was delighted to accept. He said he had reservations at a local motel for three rooms and asked if she would be using hers. Sophie thought she would talk to Pete about that.

That evening, as they were getting ready for dinner, Sophie asked, "What do you think about me spending the night in Greenwich, and coming home Sunday afternoon? Or do you think I should drive home Saturday night?"

"I suppose it's fine to drive home, if that's you want to do. You can also spend the night. It's up to you."

"Why do you say, 'I suppose'?"

"Sophie," he said slowly, thinking how to carefully phrase his thoughts, "you have many talents, but you are a relatively new driver and have not had that much experience on freeways. I confess, it gives me pause to think of you driving an hour and a half, at night, up the freeway, after a couple of beers. The other potential problem is your leg. Here you have everything you need to fix any problem."

"You don't think I can drive home?" she said, the feminist streak starting to rise.

"Don't put words in my mouth. I didn't say that. I said, 'I don't think it's the best idea I ever heard.' If you want to do it, you certainly can. I told you why I didn't think the idea was so hot."

Sophie didn't really want to spend the night in the No Tell Motel, but if Pete had said "No", she would have been forced to assert her independence. She also knew his reasoning was correct, which was semi-infuriating by itself. She liked being married to Pete, but no man was going to dominate her. After a moment, she asked, "What do you suggest?"

"Why don't you have Toy and Mai Ling drive you to Greenwich? They can have a nice lunch somewhere, do some shopping, and bring you home." Then he thought, but did not say, crisis averted.

"That's actually a very good idea," Sophie said, "but what about Sunday?"

"I'll do the same thing the following day."

"Okay, that's what I'll do," Sophie said, thinking she had been manipulated, but not sure exactly how.

After they made love, Sophie snuggled up next to Pete, her back up against her husband's chest. She replayed their earlier conversation in her mind. It was irritating to think that her husband could manipulate her whenever he wanted. After a few minutes, she realized she hadn't been manipulated, but rather she had been confronted by cold hard logic. Then it occurred to her that being able to reach a consensus was very important in a marriage, not always getting your own way.

Then the realization that she never slept well unless Pete had his arm over her came over her. With that thought in mind, she drifted off to sleep.

***

Drinking a cup of coffee at the kitchen table, Pete asked, "Well, how did you do?"

"We had a first, a second, and a third," she answered.

"That's pretty good," he said.

"Yea, but we have our work cut out for us tomorrow. Some other guy had two firsts and a second," she said.

"Really?"

She just nodded.

"What would you like for dinner?" he asked.

"How about you give me half an hour to take a shower and get ready, and we go out to dinner?"

"You got it."

A half hour proved to be an optimistic estimate, but forty minutes later they pulled out of the driveway. "Are you up for Italian tonight?" Pete asked.

"That sounds really good," Sophie replied.

Over dinner, Sophie just bubbled about the regatta.

"I gather you've decided to buy a boat," Pete said.

Sophie, somewhat taken aback, said, "I thought we had more or less decided to buy a boat to race when you rejoined the yacht club."

"I guess. Have you decided which boat to buy?" Pete asked.

"Well," she said, "as you know there are only three builders licensed by the class to build Etchells 22s. One is in Canada, one in England, and one in Australia. There is also a time lag of between four and eight months from order to delivery, which means we've missed the sailing season for this year."

"Have you considered buying a used boat?"

"Only fleetingly," she replied.

"What are your thoughts about a used boat?"

"If someone is selling it, it's probably a loser."

"Not necessarily, there could be lots of reasons for selling a boat."

Sophie dismissed this observation with a wave of her hand and said. "Did you know that a lot of those guys in Greenwich have tenders?"

"Greenwich is a very wealthy area," Pete observed.

"They carry their extra sails, lunch, tools, and what not on their tenders so they don't have to carry the weight while they are racing."

"I know."

"I think we should get a tender, too," Sophie said.

"Nah, you don't need it," Pete signaling for the check.

***

Pete drove Sophie to Greenwich the next day. He spent a dull day hanging around Greenwich Avenue, and he got back to the yacht club just in time to see the boats return to the dock. He watched from afar as they put the boats on trailers, some for the trip home, others going into the dry storage at the club. He was really proud of Sophie. She pitched in and did everything one could ask of a crew member. She did not trade on her handicap or on being a woman. He deliberately stayed away. This was Sophie's day, after all, and he didn't want to rain on her parade.

He ambled over to them just as they were finishing up and was introduced to Tom Barrett, a guy about twenty-two years old, who was the other crew member on Stan's boat.

"We had a first and a second today, but we finished second," Sophie told him proudly.

"That's great," Pete said.

"Let's go get a beer," Stan said.

"I'm sure ready," Tom said.

They went inside for a beer, and waited for the trophy presentation.

***

As they were driving home, Pete asked, "Have you figured out which boat to buy yet?"

"There doesn't seem to be agreement among the various owners. Everyone seems to like their boat best, and everyone thinks theirs is the fastest."

12

The Monday after the regatta, as Pete and Sophie were having a cup of coffee together, Sophie asked Pete, "I was thinking of going to Paris to see my dad. You wouldn't mind, would you?"

"How long are you going to be gone?"

"I'm thinking a week, maybe ten days. When he came to Las Vegas, I didn't really get a chance to spend much time with him. I didn't even know he was alive until you told me. It's kind of important to me to get to know my father."

"Enjoy yourself, when are you leaving?"

"Tomorrow, I think, unless you have some strenuous objections."

Sophie arrived in Paris at ten o'clock and went directly to their apartment. There was nothing to eat in the apartment, but she wasn't hungry, having eaten on the plane.

Sophie called her dad the next morning and they agreed to meet at a restaurant for lunch. Sophie arrived in a taxi. Her dad had already arrived and came out to greet her. When they entered it was clear he was a regular. He introduced her to practically everyone in the restaurant. They spent two and a half hours over lunch in typical French fashion. Sophie wanted to go to the Rivera to look at boats and she talked her dad into coming with her. At first her father objected to the expense, sounding just like her husband.

Sophie was able to get a two bedroom suite at the Royal Rivera Hotel. She decided to buy a yacht, one hundred and eighty-six feet long. The next day they rented a car and drove around Cap Ferrat. The area was just gorgeous. "Dad, if I bought a villa around here would you use it?" Sophie asked.

"Of course, this is a beautiful place."

"Let's stick around another day and talk to a real estate agent."

They stayed three more days. Sophie bought a six bedroom villa with a view of the bay on Cap Ferrat. She agreed to keep the staff.

Sophie and her father spent three more days together in Paris. On their last night together, over dinner, Sophie said, "Dad, I don't know exactly how to say this but I'm supposed to be one of the wealthiest people in the world. If there is anything you want I would like to buy it for you."

"Sophie, I want for nothing and now that you are back in my life, my life is finally complete. My only real regret is that your mother and I didn't grow old together."

A tear rolled down Sophie's cheek as they left the restaurant.

***

When Sophie returned from Paris, their lives took on the regular pattern, which pleased them both. At least once a week they would get together with their friends Jack and Carol, and Mike and Dianne. They sailed together once or twice during the week and always Saturday with Al. Al was becoming a member of their small circle, often joining them with the other couples.

On the first of August all that changed. Pete and Sophie left at eleven o'clock that morning to go down to the marina to pay their slip fees and grab an early lunch at the marina's little restaurant. No sooner had they sat down than Janet, the very pleasant, young girl who worked in the marina office, asked if she could join them, explaining that she hated to eat alone. Pete and Sophie were happy to have her join them.

After a pleasant lunch, they returned home to feed their children. At three Pete left for the dentist.

He returned home shortly before five o'clock, and noticed Jack and Carol's car in the driveway, and Mike and Dianne's car as well.

He could hear everyone on the porch as he entered. Sophie saw Pete walking through the house and walked toward him. She met him just as he was about to step onto the porch. She gave him a peck on the lips and said, "Disaster, look at that," pointing to the coffee table.

On the cover of *Wealth* magazine was the old photo of Sophie wearing a bikini bottom, a four-inch, white high heel on her right foot, an ivory peg leg, the dragon tattoo on her back on display, as she looked over her shoulder in the classic Betty Grable pose. The caption read, "America's richest woman."

"The cat's out of the bag," Pete said.

"I'm sorry," Sophie said. Then she asked, "What are we going to do?"

"Order pizza," Pete said. With that he pulled out his cell phone, skimmed his contacts, and called a pizza place that delivered. He ordered a couple of large cheese pizzas.

"I'm so upset and you're so blasé about it," Sophie said.

"There's nothing we can do."

"There must be something we can do!" Sophie insisted.

"I'm afraid not, but don't worry, tomorrow it will be yesterday's news," Pete said.

"I hope you're right."

When the pizza man rang the doorbell, Sophie answered it. She paid him, including a generous tip, and handed him an order for four more pizzas. Pandemonium reigned in the kitchen as the four Smith kids, Jack and Carol's two, and Dianne and Mike's one scrambled for pizza.

The doorbell rang again just as the kids finished eating. Once he had been paid, the delivery man asked, "Is it true you are really the richest woman in America?"

"I don't know," Sophie stammered, flabbergasted by his question.

***

Later that evening she repeated the short conversation to Pete. She wasn't sure what his reaction was going to be.

He surprised her by saying, "You gave him exactly the right answer."

"Really, why do you say that?"

"You know how much money you have, but can you say with any accuracy how much other women have?"

"I guess not," Sophie acknowledged.

"By the way, is that story accurate?" Pete asked.

"We have a little over twelve billion, not seventeen as the story claimed. We also owe the taxes on the sale of the casinos. Those are going to be almost a billion and a half."

As he lay down on the bed, Pete wondered what happened. He thought he had married a little lady who worked in the accounting department of a hotel. It turned out that he had married Macau's Gambling Tsarina. When Sophie came out of the bathroom, he shared those thoughts with her as she got into bed.

She left her leg on indicating she wanted to make love. "Are you sorry you married America's richest woman?"

"I'll let you know in about an hour."

As his hand slid down her tummy, between her legs, she said, "Will you stop bragging?"

***

Two days later was Saturday, and they were both looking forward to their weekend sail with Al. This weekend they would be sailing Al's boat. Al saw them coming down the dock, and hopped out of his boat with something under his arm. When they were twenty feet away, he unrolled a red door mat he had bought somewhere. "We got to roll out the red carpet for America's richest lady," he said. Sophie stuck her tongue out at him, and he just laughed.

At the end of the dock there was a huge yacht. Sophie walked over to look at it. As Pete joined her he said, "No."

"No, what?" Sophie asked.

"You are not, repeat not, to spend fifty million on a two-hundred-foot yacht that we don't need."

"But, Peter."

"There is no but Peter about it. If you do I swear I'll take it out and sink it."

They decided to have a beer after they were done sailing and after putting the boat to bed at the little restaurant in the marina. Janet, from the marina office joined them when they were halfway through their first beer.

"Okay, I have to ask . . ." Janet said.

But before she could finish her question, "I don't know if I am the richest woman in America," Sophie said.

"Well, you certainly have become the biggest celebrity in this area," Janet replied.

"I liked things better before that article came out."

They went on to talk about other things. Janet was looking forward to going back to college at the end of the month. She wanted to be a teacher, and she had only one more year left.

Together they fed their children that evening, as usual. Neither one wanted to cook, so they decided to go out to for Italian.

"What are you going to have?" Sophie asked after opening her menu.

"I don't know. I am torn between the veal piccata and the chicken marsala," Pete answered. "What are you having?"

"The veal sounds good."

"Have you noticed an inordinate number of people seem to be staring at us?" Pete asked.

"They are not staring at us. They are staring at my peg leg. It happens fairly frequently to me," Sophie replied.

"I didn't realize, I'm sorry," Pete said.

"There is nothing to apologize for, you didn't do anything wrong."

"I was apologizing for them," Pete said.

"Thank you."

They noticed a ten-year-old girl run out of the restaurant only to return a few minutes later. "That little girl is running around like her hair is on fire," Sophie observed.

A minute later the little girl stood beside their table with a copy of Wealth magazine. "May I have your autograph?" she asked Sophie.

Sophie was shocked at first, no one had ever asked for her autograph. The earnest expression on her face convinced Sophie to sign the cover of the little girl's magazine. "How do you want it signed, Mme Gin Sling or Sophie Smith, which is my real name?" Sophie asked.

A perplexed expression crossed the little girl's face. She brightened and asked, "Would you sign both names?"

"What's your name?" Sophie asked.

"Pam."

Sophie wrote, "To Pam, best wishes, Sophie Smith, Mme Gin Sling."

"Thank you so much," the little girl said skipping back to her table and showing it to her mother.

Before five minutes had passed, Sophie had autographed the back of three placemats and two more copies of the magazine. As they were eating Pete said, "I don't think these people are staring at a lady with a peg leg. They are mesmerized by America's richest women."

"I hope all this folderol goes away soon."

They called for the check and as they waited, the little girl and her mother got up to leave. The mother stopped at the edge of the table and thanked Sophie for autographing the magazine cover for her daughter.

"It was a pleasure. You might tell your daughter that she is the first person ever to ask for my autograph," Sophie said.

"I know she'll be pleased to hear that," replied the girl's mother.

Later Pete stuck his head into Sophie's bathroom as she was getting ready for bed. "You know, the first time someone calls me Mr. Sling, I'm filing for divorce." Sophie turned to face him and saw the grim expression on his face. She walked over to him and put her arms around his neck and said, "I am so sorry. I never thought anything like this would happen."

"You should enjoy your fame, while it lasts," Pete said.

"Suppose this doesn't stop?"

"We'll jump off that bridge when we get there," Pete said.

"Where are we going to jump?" Sophie asked.

"Butte, Montana."

"What a dreadful thought," she replied.

Monday morning the phone started ringing off the hook. Reporters and writers all wanted interviews.

"I wonder how they got this number?" Sophie asked Pete.

"Someone at the phone company probably sold it to them. I doubt you could ever find out."

By two o'clock, Pete had unplugged all the phones. Then the media people started calling their respective cell phones. On wednesday a producer from *The Olivia Winthrop Show* knocked on their front door. Evidently the queen of daytime gab wanted to interview Sophie on the air. Pete answered the door.

"As soon as Mrs. Smith does the first live interview, the pressure from all the other media outlets will back off," he explained to Pete. "It will turn into yesterday's news."

"Give me your card and we'll think about it."

He did and left.

*****

Pete lay in bed reading when Sophie came out of the bathroom wearing her standard too-large tee shirt. She stripped the tee shirt off, and slid under the covers. She was still wearing her leg though.

"I think you should give some consideration to doing this Olivia Winthrop thing," Pete said.

"Why?"

"It may put an end to all this nonsense."

"You think?"

"Maybe," Pete replied. "It's worth a try. I'm not sure how much more of this I can stand."

"I have an idea," Sophie said. "Why don't I go on TV and immediately afterwards you and I will go to Paris for ten days.

I am sure the furor will have died down by then. We can stay in our apartment."

"I knew there was a reason I married you. That's brilliant, let's do it."

"Do you want to ask anyone to join us?" Sophie asked.

"No. Paris is the world's most romantic city, and I want to share it with only you."

Sophie rolled over on top of him and gave him a big kiss, saying, "Thank you for that thought."

Sophie negotiated the terms of the interview with the producer; no references to her family, or where she lived, would be allowed.

Even though they had their amah and Mai Ling, Pete wanted a steady hand on the tiller. Pete's Mom was delighted to take charge of the house and her grandchildren for ten days. They advised their friends of their impending departure. *The Olivia Winthrop Show* advertised Sophie's appearance heavily.

***

Friday morning Sophie and Pete left for Chicago. They arrived at the studio in a timely fashion. Pete hung around while Sophie had her makeup redone. Pete stood in the wings as the studio audience entered and was seated.

The show started with Olivia, the hostess, coming on stage and blowing her own horn, announcing an exclusive interview with the richest lady in the world. Then, on the studio monitors, she showed tape of Sophie's plane arriving. Finally, she announced Sophie. Sophie looked radiant. She came out and shook hands with Olivia. Sophie wore a deep red mandarin dress with a high collar and a very high slit up the right side, a red, four-inch-high heel on her right foot, and one of her carved ivory legs.

"I suppose the question everybody wants to know is, are you the world's richest woman?" Olivia asked.

Sophie chuckled, and answered, "I don't know, but I doubt it."

"Why do you doubt it?"

Sophie replied, "There are some very, very wealthy women in Asia."

"Well then, are you the richest lady in America?"

"Again, I don't know. I know how much I am worth, but I don't know how much everyone else is worth and, frankly, I don't care."

Olivia had a look of mild surprise on her face when she asked, "Why don't you care?"

"My family is adequately provided for. If there are other women richer than I, so what? I never cared about what others have, only what I have."

"The article in *Wealth* magazine estimated your net worth at seventeen billion dollars. Is that accurate?" Olivia wanted to know.

"It is overstated," Sophie replied simply.

"To what do you attribute your success?" Olivia asked.

"I worked sixteen to eighteen hours a day for over twenty years. But some of it was being in the right place at the right time."

Sophie was asked about how she lost her leg and she simply told the truth.

"You must be very bitter about the communist takeover of your country."

"Communism is a false promise of utopia. The Russian Revolution, for example, merely traded tsars for commissars. In the case of Vietnam, we traded the French for commissars.

The only thing that changed for the people was who stole the tax money."

"Isn't that a little cynical?" Olivia asked.

Sophie tapped on the upper portion of her leg and said, "It's reality."

"You've been called the Ray Kroc of bordellos. Is that true?" Olivia asked.

"Who is Ray Kroc?"

"Ray Kroc started McDonald's." Olivia explained.

"McDonalds is worldwide. I was only in Asia."

"How did you get started in the bordello business?"

"I was sold into prostitution when I was fourteen."

"Oh, my God! How awful that must have been for you," Olivia said.

"Worse than you can imagine."

"How did that happen to you?"

"I am a half-cast, not pure Vietnamese, which automatically made me a second class citizen, and crippled to boot. The day after my fourteenth birthday, my uncle sold me into prostitution."

"What happened to you then?" Olivia asked, clearly concerned.

"They put me on a boat. When we arrived in Hong Kong, they gave me to my new owner. I was raped and beaten. About a week after I arrived, I was taped to a table and the dragoon was tattooed on my back."

"That must have been dreadful!" exclaimed Olivia.

"Absolutely ghastly," Sophie said.

"Is that how you got started in the bordello business?"

"I escaped, and met the bouncer coming to work a block and a half from the bordello. We had become friends and he bought me a cup of tea. By that time reality had set in. I was fifteen and a half, in a strange city, and didn't speak the language. The only thing I knew anything about was the bordello business. He asked what I was going to do. As I looked over his shoulder, I saw an empty store. So I said, 'I'm going to rent that store front and turn it into a whorehouse.'" She did not, however, tell Olivia about having robbed the owner before leaving.

The interview turned into mundane chit chat until Olivia asked, "Do you give much to charity?"

"Not really," Sophie replied. She went on to say, "I recently gave $25,000 to St Jude's and $25,000 to the Shriners Burn Hospital for Children."

"What do you do for the poor?" Olivia wanted to know.

"No one in this country is poor. No one in this country even knows what poor is. When I grew up in Saigon, I ate one meal every other day. Here the government gives you food. Poor is a relative term, it means the bottom of the economic ladder. In any system there will always be someone with less."

Olivia did not know what to say to that so she thanked Sophie for coming and concluded the interview.

When Sophie reached Pete's side, she asked, "How did I do?"

"You did great. You handled that with dignity and aplomb."

With that, they were off to Paris.

13

Pete and Sophie had left the little white car at the airport in Providence. They drove themselves home Sunday afternoon on their return from Paris.

"How was Paris?" Pete's Mom asked as Sophie walked into the kitchen.

"We had a wonderful time!" Sophie exclaimed. "How are the children? Everybody okay?"

"Everyone is just fine."

"Where are the kids?" Sophie asked.

"It's still nap time," Sally replied.

"Of course, I sort of lost track of time," Sophie said.

"Where's my shiftless son?" Sally wanted to know, just as Pete came through the door carrying four suitcases.

"Sophie, I think the thing to do is unpack these in the laundry room. Most of the stuff in my suitcases is dirty," Pete said.

"Good idea."

"How's everything here Mom?"

"The phone has been ringing off the hook. If you thought it was bad before you left, it's worse now."

"Why?"

"Apparently, Sophie's interview made such an impression that everyone wants her to endorse their product. There's a list by the phone in your office, but I stopped writing down the names and numbers Tuesday afternoon."

"Egads! I thought this would end after she did the TV interview," Pete said.

"Mom, you and Dad have never been to Europe, have you?"

"No."

"Would you like to go? Sophie has an apartment in Paris you can use."

"Yea," Sophie piped up, "what's the sense of having the world's richest lady for a daughter-in-law if you don't take advantage of it once in a while? The apartment is just sitting there empty."

"I hope you don't think I take advantage of you," Sally said indignantly.

"I said that badly," Sophie said. "What I meant to say is that you should avail yourself of what your family has to offer. You just stayed with our kids for ten days, and we appreciate that very much. It's family helping each other."

"I must admit, I like the idea. I'll talk to Pete's dad when I get home and let you know."

"Pete," Sophie said, "let's order Chinese tonight. I am just too tired to cook."

"Nonsense, I'll stay and at least cook the kid's dinner," Sally said.

"I couldn't let you," Sophie said, "but, why don't you call Tom and ask him to join us. We'll take all the kids to the clam stand just off the main highway for an earlier dinner."

"That's a great idea," Pete said.

***

That evening Pete was already in bed when Sophie came out of her bathroom. She took off her leg saying, "I'm really tired tonight."

"Sophie, I've been meaning to say this for a long time. I cannot tell you how proud I am of you. What you have accomplished is nothing short of amazing. You had the intelligence, the foresight, and the perseverance to carry through when others, myself included, thought you were nuts. And you did it all while you were raising four kids and taking care of a husband. It is truly something."

She yawned and said, "I've only done one smart thing in my life, and that was to marry you."

She was asleep before she heard him say, "Bah."

The next morning, the phone started ringing off the hook at eight o'clock. Pete left for the phone company at ten-thirty. "I'm changing our number," he said, walking through the kitchen toward the side door.

That stopped the phone for the rest of the week. Saturday, though, they went sailing with Al, as usual. While they were sailing, Al asked, "Do you want me to step up the patrols in your neighborhood?"

"I don't think so. I haven't noticed anything out of the ordinary, not even a hint of something criminal," Pete said.

"Just pests," Sophie added.

"I can apply a little bug spray if you like," Al said.

"Thanks for the offer, but I think it best just to keep things low key for the moment," Pete said.

After their sail they decided to have a beer in the marina restaurant. Janet came in after work. She came over to their table, bowed, and said in an Asian accent, "Ah so, Madame Gin Sling, humble servant join fine lady?"

"Ah so, must consult fortune cookie first," Sophie said in the same accent.

"Sit down, Janet," Pete said affably, as everyone laughed.

Janet told them she was starting her last week, and next Saturday would be her last day. "I'll be on my way to Gettysburg next Sunday."

"I'm really looking forward to finishing," Janet said.

The following Saturday, Pete, Sophie, and Al made a special point of stopping by the office to say good-bye to Janet before heading out for their sail.

***

Sunday morning, Treena started whining to go out at six o'clock. Pete got up and went downstairs with Treena following and let the dog out. He had been back in bed only two minutes, when Treena started barking. After two minutes of barking, Sophie said, "Will you shut that damn dog up!"

"All right," Pete groaned as he sat up looking for some pants. Pete went out the side door and saw Treena a couple hundred feet up the river bank, barking at something he couldn't see. "Treena," he called and then whistled. Treena turned around and ran halfway to him. She stopped and started barking again. The she turned and ran toward the river barking again.

Pete decided to follow the dog and see what had her so excited. Thirty feet from the river bank, he saw it. A body was lying on a small mud flat at the edge of the water. He could see it was a woman, and her throat had been cut. He grabbed Treena by the collar and walked back to the house. Pete called 911 and reported the body. He was instructed not to go to near the body, and to advise others to maintain their distance as well. He went upstairs and into the bedroom. "You better get dressed," he said to Sophie. "I found a body down by the river. I already called the cops and they are on their way."

"Cripes," was all Sophie said, horrified.

"Get the kids dressed and keep them away from the windows." Pete said. That drew an incredulous look from Sophie, but she did not say anything. "I know," Pete continued, "there's always something to take the joy out of living. I'm going to go down by the river to keep people away from the body, as instructed."

Pete went no closer than he had earlier to retrieve Treena. It wasn't a minute later when he heard a siren. He knew it was coming to his house, and that all the neighbors would be gathering shortly.

The first officer to arrive walked up to Pete. "Where is this alleged body?" he asked. The officer's name tag identified him as P. Newcomb.

"I'll show you," he said, walked toward the river and pointed. Then, he added, "There is nothing alleged about it."

"How close have you been to it?" the officer asked.

"No closer than we are now."

"Good. Who are you, sir?" the cop asked.

"Pete Smith, I live in this house," Pete said pointing to the house.

"Are you the person who called this in?"

"Yes," Pete replied simply.

An unmarked police car arrived. "That's Detective Baker," the officer said, nodding toward the arriving car. The officer walked over to the detective to confer.

Pete watched as the detective put on paper booties over his shoes and rubber surgical gloves. He carefully walked over to the body. He touched her eyeball. Seeing no reaction, he walked back to where Pete and the officer were standing.

"Are you the person who called in a dead body?" he asked Pete.

"Yes, sir."

"How did you know she was dead?" he asked.

"Unfortunately, I have seen too many dead bodies, and her throat has been cut," Pete answered.

"How's that?"

"Two tours in Iraq and four in Afghanistan."

"What branch of the service were you in?"

"Army," Pete replied, simply.

"I am going to call in the State Police crime scene team." Looking at the officer, the detective said, "Don't let anyone closer to the crime scene than we are right now."

"Yes, sir," the officer answered.

With that he walked over to his car, opened the driver's door, and picked up the mic. Pete couldn't hear what was said.

Pete walked into his house as Sophie was just coming down the stairs. "Well, what's going on?" she asked.

"The cops are calling in the State Police crime scene unit."

"Great, just what we needed. Any idea who it is, or was, I guess?"

"Unfortunately, yes," Pete said. "It's Janet from the marina."

"Ah, shit," Sophie said, tears forming in her eyes, one tear finally dripping down her cheek. Pete was strangely touched by that tear. It had revealed Sophie's humanity. He had seen Sophie in all manner of situations where she had shown herself to be as hard as stainless steel, but he was seeing a new facet of his wife he had not seen before.

Pete gave her a hug. "I should probably go outside and give the police a hand with the crowd control." He went outside just as the first of the neighbors were arriving to see what had caused all the commotion.

Pete patiently explained to each new arrival what had happened. To the extent that he could, he answered questions.

Officer Newcomb knocked on the side door of Pete's house as Sophie tried to calm the kids down and get them fed. The amah opened the door and Officer Newcomb entered the kitch-en through the laundry area. Sophie was surprised to see him.

"I'm going to search your house," he said to Sophie.

"Do you have a warrant?" Sophie asked reasonably.

"I don't need a warrant to search a crime scene," the officer replied.

Sophie looked at Toy and Chou, who had both come into the kitchen as a result of all the commotion outside. "Throw him out," Sophie said to Toy and Chou.

They each grabbed one of the stunned officer's arms and proceeded to the side door. Chou opened the door and Toy gave the officer a good firm shove.

Al Rocca was crossing the lawn on his way to the crime scene when he saw Newcomb backpedaling across the side door stoop. The officer was doing pretty well at keeping his balance until he reached the edge of the stoop, losing his balance and winding up on his back, on the lawn. The officer jumped to his feet, and started to pull his gun.

"Newcomb," Al hollered, "come over here!" When the officer was only a few feet from him, Al asked, "What the hell are you doing?"

"I am going to arrest those two big gooks for . . ."

"Stop right there," Al said. "If I ever hear that word or any-thing similar come out of your mouth again, you are going to spend a week in Hartford going through sensitivity training. Now tell me why you are going to arrest those gentlemen."

"Interfering with a police officer in the performance of his duties."

"What duties?" Al asked in a sarcastic tone.

"I told them I was going to search the house, and this ah… Asian lady asked me if I had a warrant. I explained I didn't need a warrant to search a crime scene." Al's eyes kept getting wider as the officer talked.

"Where is the body?" Al asked.

"Over there, sir," the officer replied.

"So let me see if I have this right. It is your theory that the murder was committed in this house, then the body was carried two hundred feet upstream and left on the river bank?"

"Well, when you put it that way…"

"There is no other way you can put it," Al said, his voice rising. Finally, he said in disgust, "Get out of here, and leave these people alone!"

Pete walked across the lawn to Al. "I swear I am going to fire that guy," Al said to him. After a deep breath, Al asked, "What happened here?"

Pete recounted the story.

"Murder," Al said. "This is the first one in the town since I became chief. I know the town council is going to be all over this, and I want to be prepared to handle all their questions."

As Al turned to walk over to the scene, he causally asked, "Do you know who the victim is?"

The question was asked causally, but Pete knew it was anything but a casual question. "Yep," he replied, "and so do you." That snapped Al's head around.

"Who is it?"

"Janet, from the marina," Pete answered.

"Ah, shit," Al said turning toward the crime scene again.

By noon everyone had gone, and the neighborhood returned to its usual Sunday tranquility.

14

Thursday morning after the children had been fed and the dishes put in the dishwasher, Pete went up to their bedroom to change into his jogging clothes. As he neared their bedroom door, Sophie came out. She wore cream-colored slacks and a deep red blouse, not her usual attire for doing housework.

"Are you going somewhere?" he asked.

"I'm going to see Al, at his office," Sophie answered.

"Why?"

"I want to know if they've caught Janet's killer."

"They haven't. You would have heard, if they had."

"Well, then, I want to know what progress they have made on solving the crime," Sophie said.

Pete watched her go down the hall and turn the corner, starting down the stairs. He wondered exactly what she had in mind. He knew deep down it was more than the simple curiosity she professed. In fact, Sophie did not know herself. She was just incensed at Janet's murder.

When she walked into the police station, she saw a receptionist sitting behind a bulletproof piece of glass. She told the receptionist, through a small speaker inset into the glass, that she wanted to see Al Rocca. The receptionist asked her name and picked up the phone. A short conversation ensued. The receptionist told Sophie to have a seat and the Chief would be out directly.

Somewhat miffed, Sophie took a seat. She hated to be kept waiting. Al appeared in the doorway that led into the recesses of the station a minute later.

"Come on back," Al said to Sophie. Once they were both seated in his office, he asked her, "To what do I owe this unexpected pleasure?"

"I would like to know when you will solve Janet's murder."

"You and everyone else wants to know the answer to that question. It is virtually impossible to say."

"Do you have the reports from the crime lab back yet?"

"I doubt it," Al replied.

"What did the autopsy report show?"

"I haven't seen it," Al confessed.

"Sophie, the State Police and our detective, Alan Baker, are working the case and while I am kept up to date, I don't have the intimate knowledge that they do. We do not talk about details of active police investigations for fear of compromising the prosecution by civilian involvement."

"I could be a big help to you Al. You may not know it, but I am plugged into the Asian telegraph. Asians tend to talk only to other Asians. Information is available to me that may not be available to you."

Al pondered what Sophie had just said, and picked up the phone. "Alan, I am sending Sophie Smith down to you. Open up to her about the Clement investigation. She may be able to help as things progress. Sophie, go down the hall, it's the third door on the left. Our detective is Alan Baker."

"Thanks, Al."

"Alan Baker?" Sophie said, walking into a small room.

"Yes," he answered simply, standing to take Sophie's outstretched hand. Alan Baker proved to be an overweight man, about forty-five years old, with thinning, light brown hair. Appearances meant nothing to Sophie. She learned long ago that appearances were deceptive, but she wondered about his competence.

"The chief says to give you any information that I have, and that you may be able to help," Alan said.

"Perhaps, I hope so. Do you have any suspects yet?"

"Not really," Alan said. "We're looking at a couple of people."

"Who?"

"I hope you understand that this is to be a two-way street," Alan said.

"Of course."

"The guy who lives across the hall from her, Carl Taylor, did three years for rape. He was released on parole fifteen months ago. He says he never saw her Saturday night and that he stayed home that night watching TV. He described the movie he was watching on HBO, and it checked out."

"Have you found her family?"

"We found her mother in New London. Her father died in a car accident when Janet was five.Janet's mother, Marion Clement, told us she had remarried and her second husband, Samuel Luders, had tried to rape Janet twice. She threw him out after the second attempt. She apparently did not know about the first time, but caught him in the act the second time. She says he has a drinking problem. We haven't been able to locate Luders, yet. He is a handyman, and she has no idea where he is now."

"What did the autopsy show?"

"I don't have the official report yet, but I attended the autopsy and the pathologist said the cause of death was blood loss occasioned by having had her throat cut."

"Was she raped?" Sophie asked.

"Not according to the pathologist. There were no signs of recent sexual activity either."

"What was the time of death?"

"Impossible to determine because no one knows how long she was in the river," Al answered.

"Her mother said she had spoken to Janet earlier that day, and she said she was going out with a girlfriend for a final fling before leaving for college Sunday morning. Janet's mother didn't know, or even remember if she was told, who the girlfriend was."

"Have you discovered where she was murdered?" Sophie asked.

"We found her car in front of her apartment with her purse still on the front seat. There was money in the wallet, and nothing appeared to have been taken. Normally, when the throat is cut, there is a great deal of blood, but there was none in the car. We assume she was probably killed on the way to where her body was dumped in the river. We've looked at most of the likely areas, but have come up with nothing."

"What about the crime scene reports?"

"I don't have the official reports yet, but so far there was nothing helpful there."

"You searched her apartment, of course, anything of interest?"

"No, she had no answering machine, no address book, there was nothing to help us. Her cell was in her purse, but the recent calls page on her cell phone showed only a couple of calls to her mother on Saturday. She had a laptop, and the State Police expert is going through that. I haven't heard anything about that yet, either."

"Did you dust the apartment for prints?"

"Yes. We found Janet's, of course, and her roommate's prints were there, but nothing else. The roommate has an airtight alibi.

She left for college in Florida the Thursday before Janet's death. Her mother insisted on driving down with her. The mother flew home Sunday morning, and the roommate drove her mother to the airport."

"Anything else of interest?" Sophie asked.

"Not really," Alan answered.

"Let me give this some thought, and I'll be in touch," Sophie said getting up to leave.

Sophie went directly into the office when she got home. She closed the door and lay down on the couch. She wanted to think things through. Alan Baker, she decided, was reasonably competent. The rapist across the hall had not been thoroughly vetted, since his alibi was still suspect without a good time of death. The answer was to polygraph him. She doubted he would submit to such a test. That meant she would have to have a little "talk" with him. The only place to start to find someone with a portable polygraph machine was the internet.

She got up and went over to the computer and she located a criminologist in Hartford. Sophie called the criminologist, John Sheers. He couldn't come down to Mystic until Monday. She asked him to stand by and to bill her directly. That left the problem of finding the handyman.

Sophie had just laid back down on the couch when Pete entered. He raised his eyebrows. "Yes, sir, there is nothing I like better than watching a human dynamo at work" he said, sarcastically.

"I'm thinking," she said.

"About what?" he asked.

"I had a long conversation with Alan Baker ..."

"Who's he?" Pete interrupted.

"He is the local detective working on Janet's murder. He said they are looking for her stepfather, a handyman, but can't find him."

"Is he still in the area?"

"Janet's mom hasn't seen her ex in years, allegedly," Sophie replied, having apparently picked up the police jargon. "Do you have any idea how to find him?"

"Call property rental companies. They use handymen all the time," Pete suggested.

"That's a good idea." Sophie got up and said, "Were you going to use the computer?"

"I was, but go ahead. What did you decide to do about ordering a boat? Which one did you settle on?"

"Promise you won't get mad until I finish explaining."

"Uh oh," Pete said.

"Promise?"

"Okay," Pete replied.

"I ordered one from each company."

Before she could go any further Pete exploded, "Are you out of your mind?"

"You promised, remember?"

"All right, let me see you explain your way out of this one."

"I've made arrangements with a shipyard near Lyme to store the boats. We'll call them in the morning, and they'll put the boats we want to test in the water, and they'll take them out each evening. Once we have decided which boat is fastest, we will sell the other two boats. No one around here will know we're doing it. There will be no display of wealth for any of our neighbors to see."

"Is that all you ordered?"

"Well, we needed sails and masts, of course," she said in a somewhat evasive tone.

"Nothing else?"

"Not for the boats."

Now he knew he wasn't getting the full story. "You ordered nothing else for this project, is that right?"

"I am having Garmin make special GPSs for us that will read out in hundredths of a knot."

"What's that going to cost?" Pete asked.

"I don't know yet," Sophie answered.

Pete started to turn to leave when a thought hit him. He turned back toward Sophie who was just sitting down at the desk. "You said sails. How many suits of sails did you order?"

"Two for each boat," she said.

"And masts?"

"Two for each boat," she repeated.

Pete hit himself in the forehead with the palm of his hand. Sophie knew he was really pissed. When he got quiet, that was the time to be careful around Pete.

"Let me explain something to you. I grew up in a working class family and we paid attention when we spent our money. We never bought more than we needed. If we had extra, we saved for the unexpected expense. I have a hard time wasting money, which is exactly what you did."

"You don't know the meaning of poor. Trust me on this."

***

Sophie spent the rest of the afternoon on the telephone, but she was unable to find Sam Luders, Janet's one time stepfather.

That evening as they were both sitting in the den, Pete finally said, "You've been usually quiet tonight."

"I keep thinking about Janet's murder. This guy, Sam Luders, seems like a remote possibility, but I cannot find him, and it's frustrating me. I don't like it, being frustrated, that is." Then she smiled and looked up at him and said, "Do you think I'm spoiled?"

"No doubt about it."

"I'm used to picking up the phone and getting an answer. Not being able to do that is driving me to distraction."

"Ah yes, into every life a little rain must fall."

"Thanks for that pearl of wisdom, Plato."

Later that evening as they lay in bed together, Sophie said, "Peter, I know I may have gone a little over the top ordering three boats, but I've never done anything in my life with the intention of being second, and I've never done anything which I enjoyed more than racing sailboats."

"Never," he said with a leering grin on his face.

"Outside, I mean," she said, smiling. Then she went on to say, "I understand your concern about displays of wealth and wasting money, the long-term effect on the children, and I agree with you, it's a valid concern."

"Sophie, we really have to be careful or we are going to raise four spoiled brats."

"I think I camouflaged it well though, don't you? Whatever happened to the guy who agreed to buy a mansion in Santa Barbara?"

"That's a good question, and one which I have pondered as well. We got married in a whirlwind in Macau. Things were coming at me awfully fast. I simply did not think things through to their logical conclusion. I openly confess, becoming a father reinforced my earlier views of life."

***

The next morning Sophie resumed calling property rental companies. It wasn't until eleven-thirty that she found one that used Sam Luders as a handyman. They gave her a phone number for him and recommended him highly. Sophie immediately called the number she had been given, but her call went to voice mail.

She decided not to leave a message, feeling it would be better to hit him cold rather than alert him to what was coming.

Pete and Sophie made peanut butter and jelly sandwiches for the children's lunch, and then washed the children's lunch dishes. "What do you feel like for lunch?" Pete asked Sophie.

"How about a grilled cheese sandwich and a bowl of tomato soup?" she suggested.

"Perfect choice," Pete said, heading for the pantry to find the soup. He had just opened the soup when the phone rang. Sophie, being closer to the phone, answered it.

"This is Sam Luders; you called me earlier. I'm returning your call."

"Thank you for calling me back," Sophie said. "My name is Sophie Smith, and I am working with the police on the murder of Janet Clement..."

"Janet was murdered? When did it happen?" he interjected, before Sophie could finish.

"It was either last Saturday night or early Sunday morning. Your ex-wife told the police you had tried to rape Janet several years ago. Because of that, the police would like to question you."

"I have not seen Janet in at least five years. Where did this happen?" he asked.

"Her body was found in the Mystic River," Sophie answered.

"I haven't been north of New London in at least a year."

"Would you be willing to take a polygraph Monday?" she asked.

"Monday is Labor Day, and I have plans."

"How about Tuesday morning?" Sophie queried.

"Sure, where?"

"We can come to your place, if you like," Sophie said.

"That's fine. Will there be a police officer present?" he wanted to know.

"Yes," Sophie said, then asked, "What's your address?"

He gave it to her.

"Can we make it early, say eight o'clock?" he asked.

"We'll see you then," Sophie said.

She sat down to eat and said to Pete, "Did you realize this was Labor Day weekend?"

"Yes, I did. You forgot that Tuesday is Alexis' first day of kindergarten, didn't you."

"Damn, I did. I guess I'll just have to kiss her goodbye a little early."

"I would also venture to guess you also forgot the new au pair arrives Tuesday, as well. Do you think you might be obsessing a little over Janet's murder?"

"Maybe, probably." When Sophie finished her meal, she said to Pete, "I have to rearrange things. Can you handle the au pair Tuesday for me?"

"Sure," he said. With that Sophie left the table and headed for the office.

She spoke to the criminologist and rearranged the schedule, having him stay all day Tuesday. Finally she called Alan Baker. He wasn't in his office, so she left a message for him. He called back about an hour later. After she explained about the polygraph, he said he did indeed want to be there. Sophie arranged to pick him up in front of the police station at seven fifteen Tuesday morning.

She walked out of the office. Sophie was really looking forward to the weekend. Even though she didn't work, things just seemed to calm down a bit on weekends. Also, there was their ritual sail on Saturday. She found Pete on the floor in the living room playing with all the kids. Sophie sat down in one of the chairs and slid onto the floor. The two boys were wrestling with their dad and Alexis looked left out, so Sophie played Candyland with her. Susan came over and joined the Candyland game as well. These were the moments Sophie loved; her whole family together enjoying each other.

Pete had bought a program on the internet to teach young kids to read. He was teaching the boys to read by making a game of it.

Alexis looked over at Pete and the boys and said to Sophie, "That's for babies." Sophie saw Susan's attention was drawn to the game her dad and her brothers were playing. It didn't take long before Susan went over and sat by her brothers. Pete noticed immediately that her concentration was fierce.

Annoyingly, her husband was right again, as Sophie realized no amount of money could buy the enjoyment her children gave her. Raising great kids took love, time, and attention. The amah stood in the back-ground wisely letting things progress naturally.

"It's almost dinner time," Pete said. He helped Sophie up from the floor and they went off to cook dinner for the children. The children ran off to watch TV with the amah trailing behind them.

***

The next day, it was off to the marina for their Saturday sail with Al. Once they got out of the harbor and raised the sails, Sophie told Al what she had accomplished. She said, "I am going to get the guy across the hall to submit to a polygraph."

"How are you going to convince him?" Al asked.

"Toy and Chou," Sophie answered simply.

"Hang on for a second, Sophie," Al said. "In the eyes of the law you will be considered a police person. If you violate someone's constitutional rights, anything you learn will become inadmissible in court and you may compromise the prosecution."

"You can always take what I learn to develop different evidence."

"That's called fruit of the poisonous tree and is also inadmissible," Al patiently explained.

"How do you ever get a conviction?" Sophie wanted to know.

"It really isn't too hard to develop evidence legally."

"I'll have to give this some thought," Sophie pensively.

15

*T*uesday morning the criminologist, John Sheers, arrived at seven thirty. Sophie invited him in for coffee. If things went well though, she would be picking Alexis up at school. At quarter to eight everyone walked out the door. Sophie kissed Alexis goodbye as Pete got ready to put her in her car seat. Sophie and John Shears then got in the limo as Pete and Alexis left. She had had Toy bring the limo around from the garage. It had not been driven since being shipped to Connecticut. They headed for the police station.

Alan Baker was waiting in front of the police station, and Toy stopped in front of him. At first Alan did not realize it was Sophie. She had to roll down the window and say good morning before he realized the limo was his transport.

"I've never ridden in one of these things," Alan said. Toy followed the GPS's directions and they arrived in front of Sam Luders' apartment a few minutes before eight o'clock. A set of stairs lead to an upstairs garage apartment. "Let me do the talking," Alan said, as they followed a walkway along the side of a house.

"I think I'd better introduce you, since I set up this test," Sophie said, as she climbed the stairs.

"Okay, but let me take it from there."

"You got it," Sophie said, knocking on the door. When Sam Luders opened the door, Sophie said, "Hi. I'm Sophie Smith. I called you last week about a polygraph test."

"Yea, come on in. I'm Sam Luders," he said, opening the door wider. The only word Sophie could think of to describe the small apartment was grungy. It had clearly been furnished at the Salvation Army. She wasn't sure she wanted to sit on any of Al's furniture.

Once inside, Sophie introduced Alan Baker and John Sheers.

Alan Baker entered saying, "I'm the detective assigned to this case by the Groton Police Department. The way this works is I will take you through your statement. We'd like to record the statement. Then John will hook you up to the polygraph and ask you a series of questions. Do you have any questions about the basic procedure?"

"No," Al said, "but, will you tell me the results of the test as soon as it is complete?" he wanted to know.

"I will be able to give you a preliminary answer as soon as we are done," John answered for Alan.

"Can we use your kitchen table there?" Alan asked, nodding at it.

"Sure," Al said going over to it, and taking a seat at the end of the table. Alan took a small, battery-powered tape recorder from his briefcase. Sophie sat on the edge of one seat in order to keep the tip of her peg leg on the floor. John took the remaining seat.

"For the record, I am detective Alan Baker of the Groton Police Department. Also in the room are Sophie Smith and John Shears. I am here to interview Sam Luders about the murder of his former step daughter. Now, Mr. Luders, you understand this is a voluntary statement on your part, but I need to tell you, you have a right to remain silent. Anything you say may be used against you in a court of law. You also have the right to have an attorney present. If you cannot afford an attorney, one will be appointed for you. If at any time you wish an attorney, all you need to do is say so, and this interview will end.

"Do you understand each of these rights as I have explained them to you?"

"Yes."

"If you don't understand a question or are not sure of it, ask and I will either explain it to you or rephrase it. Please don't guess. If you don't know, say so, okay?"

"Yes."

"When was the last time you saw your former stepdaughter Janet Clements?" Alan started.

"About two and a half years ago," Al answered.

"What were the circumstances under which you saw her?"

"She drove by me on Main Street here in town, and I recognized her."

"Did you speak to her on that occasion?"

"No. She was going one way and I was going the other way," Al replied.

"When was the last time you spoke to her?"

"About five years ago."

"How did you learn she had been murdered?"

"Mrs. Smith told me when she phoned me last Friday."

"Where were you a week ago last Saturday?" Alan asked.

"I'm not sure, probably at The Bender. I am a regular there. I generally stop in four or five times a week," Al responded.

"The Bender is a bar?"

"Yes, it's just a couple of blocks down the street."

"Where were you between midnight and four in the morning last Saturday?"

"I don't know, probably in bed."

"When was the last time you were in Groton?"

"It's been at least a year since I was north of New London."

"Did you kill your stepdaughter Janet Clement?"

"No."

"I have nothing further," Alan concluded.

"Mr. Luders, now it is my turn," John Sheers said.

"If you will just sit still, I will hook you up to the machine. I'm going to ask you some questions absolutely unrelated to this case to get a baseline against which I can measure your reactions," John explained as hooked the various wires to different places on Al's body.

"If you're ready, we'll get started."

"Let's get this over with," Al said.

After the preliminary questions, John Sheers took Al back through his statement. He phrased each question so that it could be answered yes or no. It took him twenty minutes before he concluded. As he unhooked Al from the machine, Al asked, "Well?"

"My preliminary reading is that all your answers were truthful."

"Told you so," Al stated in response.

Once they were back in the car, Sophie said to Alan, "That looks like a dead end."

"I think you're right. My read was that he was telling the truth."

"You can lie to me, but not the machine. He told the truth," John interjected.

"That leaves the guy across the hall and the girlfriend no one can find," Sophie said.

"I doubt it's the girlfriend, but she may have information that will give us a good solid lead," Alan said.

"Why do you doubt it's the girlfriend?" Sophie asked.

"The victim had her throat cut. That takes a lot of strength, and it is very messy. Killing in that fashion is not something a woman would do," Alan answered.

They dropped Alan off at the police station. "Will you get me a copy of your final report as soon as you finish it?" Alan asked John.

Sophie dropped John at a hotel. "I'll pick you up at five o'clock," Sophie said.

"I should have the final report done by then," John replied.

Sophie arrived at John's hotel at five o'clock sharp. He was waiting at the lobby entrance. "I notice we've added a second chauffer," he said.

"This one won't be as easy as the last one. Frankly, he may take some persuasion. It may compromise the investigation but eliminating Taylor is worth the risk. Both these gentleman are very good persuaders. I think you should wait in the car until he agrees."

"That sounds like a very sensible idea to me."

Sophie climbed the stairs to Carl Taylor's second story apartment with Toy and Chou following her. It was an older building which had several sets of stairs. Each set of stairs led to a landing with four apartments. Janet had lived in the first apartment on the left at the top of one set of the stairs. Carl Taylor lived in the rear unit on the right off the same landing. She knocked on the door.

"I am Sophie Smith," she said, when a man of about twenty-six opened the door. Before he could respond, she continued, "I'd like to talk to you about Janet Clement's murder."

"Look lady, I've said all I am going to say about that to the police." With that he started to close the door. Sophie anticipated his move and stuck her peg leg into the door preventing it from closing.

"Toy, Chou," she said. Toy lunged at the door which snapped open. Carl went reeling backwards, Sophie entered casually.

"Lady, I don't know who you think . . ."

"Shut up!" Sophie said. "Now listen to me very carefully. When I leave here, I will know the truth. You can take a polygraph or these two gentlemen are going to beat the truth out of you. If you take the polygraph, I will pay you five hundred dollars. Also, I will not give you a Miranda warning, so nothing you say may be used in court. Now make a decision, I don't have all night."

"All right, hook me up."

Sophie nodded to Chou, who immediately left to bring John Sheers to the apartment. Sophie looked around while waiting. It wasn't as bad as Sophie thought it would be. The furniture, while being cheap, was reasonably new, and for a single guy living alone the place was pretty clean. There were no dirty dishes in the sink. The walls were painted an off-white, and there was motel art on the walls, probably supplied by the landlord.

John Sheers came in and set his equipment up on the kitchen table.

"You are Carl Taylor?" Sophie asked.

"Yes."

"Did you know Janet Clement?"

"Yes, but only to see her coming in or going out of her apartment."

"Just so we are clear, that's the front apartment on the other side of the hall?"

"Yes," Carl answered.

"Were you ever in her apartment?"

"No."

"Did you ever have a conversation with her?" Sophie asked.

"The most I ever said to her was, 'Nice day, isn't it?'."

"When was the last time you saw her?"

"I don't know exactly, sometime during the week before she was murdered," he said.

"One last question, did you hear or see anything unusual that Saturday night or early Sunday morning?"

"No."

"John," Sophie said simply.

"Carl," John said, "I am going to ask you base line questions and then specific questions which can be answered yes or no, do you understand?"

"Yes."

As he had in the morning, he went back over the ground Sophie had covered in her questioning. "His answers were truthful," John said.

When John had packed up his equipment and he left the apartment, Sophie said to Carl, "I'm going to get the cops off your back. Here's the five hundred I promised you and an additional five hundred to keep your mouth shut about this entire evening." She left ten one hundred dollar bills on the coffee table. Toy and Chou followed her out.

Back in the car, Sophie said, "We're going to take you to my house, after we stop for Chinese takeout. Your car is still at my house from this morning, and the hotel is paid through tomorrow morning. You can leave tonight or you can use the hotel. You have an open room charge, and I'll take care of the bill in the morning." As an afterthought she asked, "Would you like some Chinese?"

"I think I'll use the room, that way I can finish my report. I'll email it to you as soon as I have it done," John said. "I'll pass on the Chinese food, however."

"The sooner I can get your final report the better," Sophie said.

It was quarter to eight when she walked into the house with an armload of Chinese takeout.

"I wondered how you were going to deal with dinner," Pete said to her as she set a huge bag on the butcher block in the kitchen.

"This just seemed like the easiest solution," she said.

Pete wasted no time in unloading the bag. "It looks like you got all my favorites," he said.

"For you dear, anything," Sophie quipped.

"Well, Sherlock Smith, what did you learn today?" Pete asked, digging into a container of sweet and sour pork.

"Who's Sherlock Smith?" Sophie asked.

"Sherlock Holmes was a famous literary detective, created by Sir Arthur Conan Doyle, and the greatest crime solver in fiction," he replied, with his mouth half full.

Sophie brightened, "I'm glad you are starting to appreciate my talents."

"They are talents that certainly know no bounds."

"Actually, all we managed to do today was to prove two outside possibilities innocent."

"If you keep narrowing the field, you'll find the killer," Pete said.

"The next thing I need to do is learn who the girlfriend is that she went out with that night. I think that's going to be the key. This is much easier in Macau. You can apply a little pressure and nobody really cares, if you get a viable answer."

"That's the ole Marine Corps philosophy! Mission accomplished means more than how it was accomplished, but as a philosophy, it has serious limitations."

"Why?"

"Well," he said, "if you operate on that basis you often run afoul of the law not to mention common decency."

***

Pete went jogging the next morning. Sophie was digging through her purse in the kitchen, a cigarette between her fingers, when he came into the kitchen. She was clearly looking for her lighter. She had chosen to ignore the no smoking prohibition whenever the urge to have a cigarette hit her. Fortunately there was usually someone to "get after her for it."

"Where are you going?" he asked.

"Police station," she said.

"What for?"

"I need to give Alan Baker copies of the written reports from yesterday and I want to find out what is being done about tracking down the mysterious 'girlfriend'."

"I'm going to take a shower. Have fun," he said.

Sophie arrived at the police station only to find Alan Baker wasn't there. However, according to the receptionist, he was due back shortly. She decided not to wait and instead went to the local book store. She bought the complete works of Sir Arthur Conan Doyle.

Alan had returned during her forty-five minute foray to the book store.

She handed copies of John Sheers' reports to Alan once seated in front of the detective's desk. She asked, "What is being done to find the girlfriend?"

"I'm not sure," was his candid reply. He went on, "The state police are handling that."

"I don't understand this. The murder happened in your town, but the state does all the investigation?"

"Frankly, their detectives are more experienced and they have far more resources. We supposedly work together, but in practical fact, they do it all and send me copies of their reports."

"I see," Sophie said, contemplatively.

Sophie called Dianne as soon as she got home. "You understand the bar scene in the United States much better than I do," she said to Dianne after they got pasted the preliminaries.

"Maybe," Dianne said, "but you have sure owned a lot of them. Why are you asking?"

"The girl who was murdered a couple of weeks ago went out with a girlfriend drinking. I need to find the girlfriend," Sophie explained.

"Just start asking bartenders and cocktail waitresses," Dianne.

"Would you go with me?" Sophie asked.

"Sure."

"What time should I pick you up?"

"I can't go tonight. I'm home alone with the kids. Mike's going to a town meeting or something. We can start tomorrow."

"What time do you think we should get started?" Sophie asked.

"Probably about six would be best. No one will have time to talk once it gets busy."

"Okay, I'll pick you up about six tomorrow," Sophie said, signing off.

"See you then. Bye," Dianne said.

It was Pete's turn to clean up the kitchen that evening. He wondered why it always seemed to be his turn. "Probably had something to do with Sophie's manicure," he muttered to himself. He went into the office to check his email and he expected to see Sophie, but she wasn't there. He checked the email, but found nothing interesting or requiring his immediate attention, so he headed upstairs to the bedroom. Sophie was propped up in bed with a book open in front of her. "What are you reading?" he asked.

"Sherlock Holmes."

"Using it as a text book on how to be a detective, are we?"

Sophie looked up briefly, stuck her tongue out at him, pushed her glasses up her nose, and went back to reading.

His climbing into bed had absolutely no effect on her concentration.

"Sophie, I think you should sell that airplane. The expenses are running about fifty thousand a month."

"No."

"Why not?" he asked.

"I like it," she said.

"I like it, too, but fifty thousand a month is a lot of money."

She lowered her book, sensing that this discussion was not over, and said, "We can afford it."

"Yea, that's not the point. Fifty thousand a month is a lot of liking even if you can afford it. If you got a lot of use out of it, it would be different."

"It's a symbol that the little, crippled, Eurasian girl from the slums of Saigon made good. Besides, I have been humiliated by airport security for the last time."

"You know you could buy a nice G-650. They have a couple thousand miles more range."

Picking up her book, she said, "I'll think about it."

Pete knew that Sophie's "I'll think about" deferred saying no. Of course, he did the same thing so he was familiar with the technique.

***

Sophie walked into the kitchen all dressed up. She was wearing beige pants with a deep red blouse. "How come you're so dressy tonight?" Pete asked her.

"I'm going out with Dianne. We're going to try and find out where Janet and her girlfriend went the night she was murdered."

"How late to do you think you will be?"

"Not too late, Dianne says once it gets busy no one will take the time to talk to us."

"Got a stack of twenties with you?"

"Yes, I figured I might have to buy some information."

"Who are you taking with you?" Pete asked.

"No one."

"You should take Toy with you in case any problems arise."

"I don't think that will necessary. We're only going into bars where two young single girls would go." With that, she left.

As soon as she went through the door, Pete speed dialed Toy. He explained what Sophie had in mind and said, "Follow her, but don't let her see you or I'll suffer."

"Okay boss," Toy said.

Sophie came into about nine o'clock. "How did you make out?" Pete asked.

"Not so hot," she replied. "We must have hit twenty different bars. I had no idea there were so many in this area, and we didn't even go north of the river."

"Are you going to try again tomorrow?"

"Yes, we're going to work the north side of the river."

"What happens if you don't find anything tomorrow?"

Sophie contemplated the question for a moment, and answered, "Expand the search area, I guess."

"When do you give up?" Pete wanted to know.

"Never!"

"What has got you so fired up about this case?"

"You don't walk into my town, murder a friend of mine, and expose my children to the body, and think you are going to get away with it." With that she went into the bathroom to get ready for bed.

When she came out of the bathroom, she looked on her bedside table for her volume of Sherlock Holmes. "Have you seen my book?" she asked Pete.

"No,"

It took her a second to realize Pete was reading her Sherlock Holmes book. "You liar, that's my book," she said grabbing for it.

"You keep telling me that everything is 'ours'."

"Yes, that's true, but I never discussed exclusive use arrangements. Besides, Mr. Smarty pants, I didn't know your powers of deduction needed a refresher course."

"They don't, but I am always prepared to expand my repertoire." As Sophie slid into bed, Pete said, "Ah, now we have three feet and a foot long under the covers."

"Will you quit bragging, Stubby."

"I'll show you bragging," he said, reaching for her. Sophie couldn't help but grin in anticipation.

16

At five-fifteen, Sophie walked into the den. She was wearing dark blue slacks and a pale yellow blouse. Her hair was pulled back in a low pony tail.

"Are you wearing pants more often or is it my imagination?" Pete asked her.

"My peg leg is not as obvious in pants as it is in a dress."

"Oh," he said absently. "I thought it didn't bother you that people noticed your leg."

"It doesn't, but ever since that article, everyone recognizes me as Madame Gin Sling. I would prefer to be known as Sophie Smith."

"How come you're leaving so early?"

"I spoke with Dianne on the phone this afternoon, and she suggested that we start in the Stonington borough. Apparently there are only three likely places up there. That will get us back into Mystic earlier."

"Well, I wish you luck." With that Sophie went out the side door to the garage.

As Sophie and Dianne drove into the old section of Stonington, Dianne pointed out the marina to Sophie saying, "One of the places is right in front of that marina. You need to make a left. The road circles around."

"Okay."

The bar in front of the marina proved unsuccessful. No one recalled having seen Janet in there two weeks ago.

They drove into the center of the old section of town. "This is really charming," Sophie said.

"It is, but I'll bet these old houses are maintenance nightmares," Dianne observed.

"The next place is just down there on the left," Dianne said, pointing straight ahead. "Park in the first place you can find."

The place had been built as a retail shop that someone had turned into a restaurant/bar. It had been expanded sometime in the past into the shop next door by cutting a double wide doorway in the common wall. The bar was to the right side of the restaurant. Even at that early hour almost every stool was taken.

They had to wait three or four minutes before the bartender came over to them. "What'll you have?" he asked.

"Did you see this girl in here the Saturday night before Memorial Day weekend?" Sophie asked the bartender. He took the picture from Sophie that Alan Baker had given her, and he held it under the light under the bar.

"I don't think I've seen her before," he answered.

At the end of the bar area, there was a raw bar with four stools in front of it. A guy was bent over an unseen counter, doing something in anticipation of a later rush. He looked to be about twenty-seven years old, wore a dark blue golf shirt with the name of the bar on it, and had long, dark brown hair pulled into a ponytail.

Sophie turned to leave, but Dianne said, "Let's ask him."

"Why not," Sophie said.

Sophie asked him the same question, handing him the picture.

"I think she was in here," he replied.

"Do you know who was with her?"

"Why do you want to know?"

"This girl was murdered sometime that night, I'm working with the police to try and find the killer or killers," Sophie said.

"I heard about a girl getting killed. I didn't realize it was her, though. She was with Samantha Mons. Sam comes in here all the time."

"Did you see her when she left that night?" Sophie asked.

"No," he replied simply. Then he added, "There were all kinds of guys trying to hit on them, but they weren't having any of it."

"Do you know how to find Samantha Mons?"

"No, but her parents live in town here somewhere, they come in all the time."

"Can I get your name? I'm sure the police are going to want to talk to you."

"Charlie Higgins."

Sophie reached for her cell phone, but after searching for several minutes, she realized she had left it at home.

"I can look it up on my phone," said Dianne.

She looked up the name Mons on the internet. While Dianne surfed several mobile phonebook websites, Sophie searched through her purse for a pen and some paper. When Dianne was done reading the number, Sophie asked, "Does it give an address?"

Sophie wrote the address down as Dianne read it aloud. Once on the sidewalk out front, Sophie asked, "Do you think we should call or just go over there?"

"Call," Dianne replied, having already given the matter some thought. "This old bomb," pointing to the little white car that Sophie had bought many years ago in Santa Barbara, "doesn't have a GPS and we don't have a map. My cell phone doesn't have one either. We could be hunting around here all night."

"You're right, but let's do it from the car, quieter."

Sophie dialed the number using Dianne's cell phone and a woman answered the phone. "Mrs. Mons?"

"Yes," the woman responded tentatively.

"I'm Sophie Smith. I am working with the police to try and find who killed Janet Clement. She was murdered two weeks ago and her body found in the river."

"I heard about that," Mrs. Mons interrupted.

"We think that Janet was out with your daughter the evening she was murdered."

"Samantha couldn't possibly have had anything to do with that girl's death," she interrupted, again.

"Actually, Mrs. Mons, I'm sure she did not, but what I would like to know is where Janet went after she left Samantha."

"Sam has gone back to college. She's not here."

"Where does she go to college?"

"Uconn, in Storrs," Mrs. Mons answered simply.

"Could you give me her address there or maybe a cell phone number?"

"Do you have pen?"

"Just a second," moments later Sophie said, "I'm ready." Mrs. Mons gave Sophie both a cell phone number and the address of her dorm.

Sophie thanked Mrs. Mons and hung up. She promptly tried the cell phone number, but it went to voice mail.

"Mission accomplished," Diane said. "I think that calls for a drink."

"Okay," Sophie agreed, "But you drive home."

"Deal."

***

Pete was lying in bed and starting to worry about Sophie. He hadn't had Toy follow her tonight, and he was mentally kicking himself for not doing so. The phone rang. "Hello," he said.

"Come get me," Sophie slurred.

"Where are you?"

"Don't know." Then he heard her ask someone. "Something Frog," she slurred.

"Be out front in twenty minutes," he said.

"Can't stand." Click.

***

The next morning, Pete awoke at his usual six thirty, got out of bed, went into the bathroom, and dressed. Sophie still had not moved. He walked around to her side of the bed and patted lightly on the derriere. "Rise and shine, it's time to feed the kids."

Sophie opened only her left eye. "It won't hurt them to miss a meal." Having made that observation, she pulled the covers over her head.

It was a few minutes before nine when Sophie walked into the kitchen wearing her glasses.

"What's the matter? Couldn't quite hammer the ole contacts in this morning?" Pete asked. Sophie just groaned. "Coffee?" Pete asked brightly, as he rose from the table and put the paper aside. He poured Sophie a cup of coffee as she sat at the table. After a few moments, he asked, "What did you learn last night, other than you like white wine?" Sophie just glared at him and pushed her coffee cup across the table. He got up and refilled it for her.

She rose from the table, took her purse and headed to the porch intending to have a cigarette. "Are you going sailing with Al and me?" Pete asked.

"Maybe," Sophie said over her shoulder.

When she finished her second cup of coffee and second cigarette, she took her purse and went into the office. Sitting behind the desk she picked up the phone and dialed the number she had gotten from Mrs. Mons.

"Samantha Mons?" she queried, when a young girl answered the phone.

"Yes," Samantha said hesitantly.

"I am Sophie Smith and I'm working with the police to solve the murder of Janet Clement. May I ask you a few questions?"

"My mother told me you were going to call. I didn't even know Janet was dead until this morning when my mother told me. Ask away, I'll do anything I can to help catch Janet's killer."

"You and Janet were drinking in the Rusty Toad together the Saturday night before Labor Day weekend, weren't you?"

"Yes," Samantha answered, simply.

"Did you leave together?"

"No. Janet left with Paul Meyers about eleven o'clock. He was supposed to take her to her car. He lives somewhere in Noank, but he's not there. He intended to leave to go back to school the same day I was going to leave..."

"Do you know where he goes to school?"

"Duke, and always makes a big deal out of telling everyone that."

"I'm sure the police will also be getting in touch with you as soon as I pass this information along to them. There's no need to worry. They're going to ask you a lot more questions than I did. Just do the same thing. Answer them fully.

Sophie went back to the porch for another cigarette. Pete found her there forty-five minutes later. "Are you going sailing or not?"

"Yes."

"She speaks," Pete said in a deep basso voice.

***

When they came down the dock, Al already had the sail cover off and stowed, and the engine was running. "Well, Detective Smith how are you this fine morning?" Al asked as they neared.

"Not so hot," Sophie replied.

"Sherlock Smith went drinking last night," Pete supplied.

"Dianne and I were celebrating."

"Pete, if you'll cast off, I'll get us out of here," Al said.

"What were you celebrating last night?" Al asked when they were clear of the dock.

"We solved the case," Sophie said, simply.

That stopped the levity immediately. "You mean you found Janet's killer?" Pete asked.

"Yes."

"Could you give a little more complete recital of the facts than that?" Al requested.

"As you know, Janet and a girlfriend went drinking together that night. The girlfriend's name is Samantha Mons. They went to a place in the borough of Stonington, the name of which escapes me at the moment..."

"The Rusty Toad," Pete supplied.

"Anyway, the guy who runs the raw bar remembered them. He knew Samantha. Samantha's parents live in the borough. I got their number from the internet and called them. Her mother gave me Samantha's cell number, and I spoke to her this morning. She told me Janet left with a guy named Paul Meyers. He's a student at Duke University. Now you have to go arrest him."

"Did you tell all this to Alan Baker?" Al asked.

"I left him a voicemail, but he hasn't returned my call."

"He'll take my call," Al said, his ire obviously rising. "Pete, would you take the helm for a minute?"

"Sure," Pete said.

Al pulled out a cell phone and walked to the bow of the boat. When he returned to the cockpit, he said, "Alan Baker will be at your house at five o'clock."

They raised the sails five minutes later.

Once under sail Pete looked at Sophie and asked, "Do you feel like talking yet?"

"As long as it's not too loud."

"What happened to your leg?"

"What do you mean?" Sophie wanted to know.

"When I showed up to retrieve you last night, the wooden portion of your leg was missing."

"How's that?" Al asked.

Sophie reached down and twisted the wooden portion of her leg to show Al that it unscrewed. "What do you mean it wasn't there?" she asked

"I mean it wasn't there. The plastic cup portion that your stump fits into was there, but the wooden portion was missing."

Looking at Al, Pete said, "She called me and asked me to pick her up last night. I told her to wait out front, and she said she couldn't stand. I thought she meant she'd had too much to drink, but she meant it literally."

Al couldn't restrain himself anymore, and started chuckling.

"So I repeat, what happened to your leg?"

"I don't know," Sophie answered.

Pete pulled his cell phone out of his pocket hit the speed dial for Mike and Dianne's home phone. Mike answered.

"Mike, its Pete. Is Dianne vertical yet?" He listened for a second and then said, "Would you ask her what happened to Sophie's leg last night." As he listened, Pete started laughing and couldn't stop. Finally, saying thanks, he clicked to end the conversation.

"What?" Sophie screeched, holding her head.

It took Pete a little time before he could respond. "You sold it to some guy, evidently. He offered you a hundred dollars for it, and you turned him down. He upped the offer to five hundred if you would autograph it. You took it, and then bought drinks for the house until the five hundred ran out."

"Oh my God," she said, putting her head in her hands. By this time, Al was roaring with laughter as well.

"I had to carry you out over my shoulder," Pete said.

"This just keeps getting worse!" Sophie wailed. "I can never go back there. It was a nice place, too."

***

When they got back to the dock, Al asked Sophie, "Would you mind if I sat in on your meeting this afternoon with Alan?"

"I was going to suggest you do," Sophie said.

"Would anyone like a beer?" Al asked, changing the subject.

"Not me," Sophie said, "and he's taking me home right now."

"We have to help Al put the boat away," Pete said.

As they walked up the dock, Pete suggested to Al, "Why don't you come over to our house now? We can watch the game while we wait for Alan to arrive. I think we have a few cold ones in the fridge."

"I'll be right behind you."

***

Alan Baker arrived promptly at five o'clock. Sophie came down stairs. She was still wearing her glasses.

"Let me bring you up to date on what happened this afternoon," Alan began once they were all seated at the dining room table.

"The State Police are going to track down Samantha Mons and get her statement, as soon as they can find her. I talked to campus police at Duke, and they advised me that Paul Meyers has classes every Monday, Wednesday, and Friday from nine to noon. Tuesday and Thursday he has class from eight to one. The State Police want to send a detective down there to interview him, but they have to get authorization for the expenditure. They will get back to me on when they are going to go. The campus police aren't going to alert Meyers that we want to talk to him until we actually arrive on campus."

"That's nonsense. Let's go Monday, and we'll take our plane. Tell the State Police we're going and invite them to join us if they want."

"Alan, that is not a bad idea," Al said. "Let's see if we can wrap this thing up sooner rather than later."

"Let me see if we can get John Sheers to go with us," Sophie said, rising.

She returned in five minutes and reported, "He's available Monday, but has to be in court Tuesday in Bridgeport."

"I'll call the State Police and invite them to join us," Alan said.

"Our plane is at the Providence airport on the private aircraft side of the airport. I think we should leave by eight o'clock. So, Alan why don't you be here at say seven-twenty? John Sheers is going to meet us at the airport. You can tell the State Police to be there then if they want to come."

17

Monday morning broke clear and cool. Alan Baker arrived on time, and Toy whisked them up the highway in climate controlled comfort.

"I don't like private planes," Alan said after several minutes of silence. I'm as nervous as a long-tailed cat in a room full of rocking chairs."

"Don't worry, the pilots are very experienced."

"Yea, but you're always hearing about another private plane accident."

Sophie just smiled patiently.

They arrived at Providence airport a few minutes before eight. The stairs were down, ready to receive passengers. The two flight attendants waited to welcome everyone aboard at the top of the stairs. John Sheers came out of the private aircraft terminal when he saw the limo pulling onto the tarmac.

"Is anyone from the State Police coming?" Sophie asked as the limo stopped ten feet from the entry stairs.

"This is your plane?" Alan asked, ignoring Sophie's question, as he looked up at the 757.

"Yes, are they coming?"

"I talked to them yesterday, and I was told if they were not here to go without them," Alan replied.

"Would you like coffee or juice, sir?" the flight attendant asked as they entered the aircraft. "We're baking croissants and cinnamon buns now. They should be ready as soon as we're airborne."

The other flight attendant approached Sophie and said, "We're ready to go Mrs. Smith; as soon as you give us the word, ma'am."

"Let's go, we've got everyone." One of the flight attendants retracted the stairs as the other went into the cockpit. They heard the low pitch whine of a jet engine as it started to turn.

The flight attendants offered croissants, coffee, and an assortment of juices a few minutes after takeoff. "Can I get up and look around?" Alan asked.

Sophie motioned to the flight attendant, "Would you give Mr. Baker the tour?" Sophie asked.

"Yes, of course, Mrs. Smith."

The flight was uneventful. They arrived at nine-thirty. A rental car had been arranged before departure by the pilots, it was brought to the foot of the stairs. Sophie signed and initialed. "Would you drive Alan?"

They found the campus police station after some difficulty and were told they would be bringing Paul Meyers to the station after his class ended at eleven o'clock.

At eleven-fifteen a uniformed officer and a lanky young man entered the station. Paul Meyers stood about six feet, had brown eyes and dark brown hair. He already sported a small paunch and, Sophie thought, he is going to have a nasty gut by the time he is thirty, if he doesn't get a smaller fork.

They all went back to a small interrogation room.

As Alan set up his tape recorder, Paul asked, "What's this all about?"

"We'll get to that in a minute," Alan answered.

Alan Baker introduced everyone for the record, then he read Meyers his Miranda rights.

Paul Meyers' early look of concern had given way to a look of outright panic.

"Would you tell me what this is about before you start questioning me?" he requested.

"We are investigating the murder of Janet Clement."

"Who's she?" Meyers asked before Alan could finish his opening remarks.

"Do you recall the Saturday before Labor Day weekend?"

"Vaguely," Meyer replied.

"Do you recall being in the Rusty Toad that evening?" Alan asked.

"Sure, I went there with a couple of friends."

"Do you recall driving someone home that night?"

"Sure, well that's not exactly correct. I dropped this girl off at a parking lot by the Marina," Meyers responded.

"Would you tell us everything you did from the time you left the Rusty Toad to the time you dropped her in the parking lot?"

"There's not much to tell. I drove her to the marina parking lot thinking I might get lucky, but when we got there she kissed me on the cheek with one hand on the door handle and she hopped out. I left and that's all there was to it."

"Did you talk about anything on the way to the marina?"

"I told her I didn't think she should drive home, and I would take her. She said she wasn't going to drive. She was going to sleep on the couch in the marina office," Meyers said.

"That's all?"

"She was drunk enough so there wasn't going to be any conversation. Would you tell me what this is all about?" Meyers asked.

"The girl you dropped off in the parking lot was found in the Mystic River with her throat cut," Al said in response.

"I had nothing to with it, I swear."

Then Al took him back through his statement in detail.

Two hours later, Al looked to Sophie and asked if she had any questions.

"Just one, when you drove into the lot, did you see anything you thought to be perhaps a little odd?"

"Well," Paul said, "there was one thing. There were two white vans parked side-by-side. They were the kind plumbers use, you know?"

"What do you mean, the kind plumbers use?" Sophie asked.

"They have no windows behind the driver's door so they can build shelves in there for their equipment."

"Would you mind showing us the car you drove that night? You said it was in the parking lot." Alan asked.

"Not at all," Meyers replied.

"I am going to tell you something. I believe you. Would you be willing to take a polygraph?"

"Yes, I just want to get this behind me as soon as possible."

John Sheers went to work. He hooked up his machine, and asked Meyers a series of questions. When he was done, he asked Alan to step into the hall. "He's telling the truth."

Paul Meyers then lead them to his car, a nondescript, old, faded red Toyota. Both Alan and John examined it very carefully. "Would you mind if I sprayed a substance called luminal in your trunk?" John asked Meyers.

"Go ahead."

John opened the kit he had been carrying around with him. He sprayed the interior of the trunk with the luminal, then he took out a battery powered light from his kit and shone it into the trunk. He pronounced it 'clean'.

Then Alan said, as much for Paul Meyers, as the campus police officer who had accompanied them all day, "As far as I am concerned, you're in the clear. Thank you for your time."

"Glad to help. I hope you catch the guy."

18

Sophie arrived home at six-thirty, just as Pete was finishing the dishes from the children's dinner. "How did it go?" he asked, as Sophie came into the kitchen.

"We're back to square one."

"Why, what happened?" Pete queried.

"He said he dropped her off in the marina parking lot and left. He passed a polygraph test, and we checked his car thoroughly, no sign of blood," Sophie answered.

"You must be a little disappointed after all the work you did to come up empty-handed."

"The work isn't the issue. Janet's killer is still out there, and that's what bothers me," Sophie said.

"What are you making for dinner?" Pete asked.

"Reservations," Sophie quipped. "No, but seriously, I ate a couple of sandwiches on the plane and I'm not hungry. Would you mind fending for yourself tonight?"

"Not at all," Pete replied.

Sophie went into the office and sat behind the desk. She moved to the couch twenty minutes later, which was where Pete found her. She was staring at the ceiling when Pete entered. "What did you have for dinner?" she asked.

"Peanut butter and jelly sandwich."

"That's not a good dinner."

"I know. What are you so deep in thought about?" he asked, feeling that he probably already knew the answer.

"The case."

"What about it?"

"We're at a dead end I'm afraid."

"Can I give you a little advice, or perhaps more correctly stated, a suggestion?"

"Anything, because frankly I'm stumped, no pun intended."

"Go back and examine your assumptions."

"What do you mean?"

"Well," he started off, "as you try to resolve things you come up with working theories that may lead to an answer."

"Give me an example, be specific."

"Okay. When you learned how she went home you assumed that the guy who dropped her off was the last person to see her alive. Evidently, he was not."

"Think about it and give me a better example, that's just a logical conclusion that proved to be incorrect."

"How about this one. You don't know where she was killed, but you assume she drove her car to her apartment. Maybe she didn't. Perhaps someone else did."

"That's an interesting thought," Sophie said, pondering his observation.

As Pete started to walk out of the room, he said. "Let me leave you with one last thing to consider. You know the sound of two hands clapping. What's the sound of one hand clapping?"

***

After breakfast the next morning, as Sophie walked into the kitchen, Pete looked up from reading the morning paper. She wore cream-colored slacks and a navy blue, short-sleeve blouse. She had braided her hair, and it hung down her back. "You look exceptionally fine this morning. What's on your agenda for today?"

"I'm going down to the marina and then to see Alan Baker."

"Oh, how come?"

"I have some new ideas on how to proceed." As she went out the garage door, she said, "Oh, and one hand clapping makes no sound you can hear."

Forty-five minutes later, she walked through the front door of the police station and asked the receptionist for Alan Baker. She took a seat in the reception area to wait for him.

Five minutes later, she followed Alan back to his desk, she said, "I have an idea on how to proceed."

"Okay," he said, skeptically, "let's hear it."

"Yesterday, Paul Meyers said Janet told him that she was going to sleep on the office couch. I think we should spray luminal in the marina office. I've already spoken to Harry Knight, who owns the marina, and he said it would be okay. I also spoke to John Sheers, and he will be here around four o'clock this afternoon."

"That's actually a pretty good idea. Coincidentally, I had the same idea but haven't gotten approval, yet."

"Why don't we plan on meeting at the marina at four o'clock?"

"I'll see you there. I told my wife and kids all about your plane, and now they all want to go for a ride."

She smiled, and as she was getting up said, "I'll see what I can do about that."

***

Alan Baker arrived punctually at four o'clock. Sophie and John Sheers were waiting for him in the parking lot. Together they walked into the office. "Hi, Harry," said Sophie upon seeing Harry Knight. "Let me introduce you to Alan Baker and John Sheers."

"It is a pleasure to meet you both," Harry said as they shook hands. "The office is right here, so you go ahead and do whatever tests you want."

John sprayed the rug with luminal, but when he turned on his eerie green light, there was no indication of blood. "Nothing," he said. "She was definitely not killed in here," he concluded.

They thanked Harry, and as they were walking to the parking lot Sophie asked, "Does that work outside as well as inside?"

"In theory, but the blood can be degraded to the point where it is unreliable as evidence," John answered.

"Can we try it on the parking lot?"

"Have you had a lot of rain since the murder occurred?"

"Not a lot, a couple of showers only," Alan Baker answered.

"We can give it a try if you like, but it would be better to do it after sunset, since we will be looking for traces. Mrs. Smith, luminal is very expensive."

Sophie waived her hand dismissively. "Let's meet back here then at seven-thirty. John, can you spend the night?"

"I think so, I'll have to check my calendar, but I think so."

***

That evening they all met in the marina parking lot. "Do you have any idea where you want to start?" John Sheers asked.

"According to Paul Meyers her car was parked in this area here," Alan Baker said, walking across the parking lot and spreading his hands to indicate a general area.

John sprayed the area indicated and he turned on his green light. One tiny spot about half the size of a dime turned bright green. "Bingo," he said, "That's blood." He went back to his van and returned with a camera. "Alan would you hold the light while I take a few pictures?"

He finished taking the pictures. Then, he took a clear plastic evidence bag and put the piece of gravel which had brightly lit up in it. Next he asked Alan to hand the light to Sophie. "Alan, I want to take some pictures of you as you scratch the gravel around with your foot."

When they finished, John sprayed the area again and took the light from Sophie and turned it on. "Bingo," he said, as an area about the size of a tee shirt turned bright yellow. "That indicates that there was a lot of blood on the ground. This is probably where Janet was killed. Provided, of course, it's her blood."

He bagged a few more of the stones. "Alan, would you like me to bag some of these for you?" John asked.

"Please," Alan replied.

"I need a sample of Janet's DNA to make a comparison."

"Can we get a sample from the lab?" Sophie asked.

"I doubt that they will release a sample," Alan said, "but we can get the state police lab to run the DNA analysis."

"How long will that take?" Sophie wanted to know.

"Six to eight weeks," Alan answered.

"Unacceptable," Sophie said. Then she looked at John, "Your lab can run DNA, can't it?"

"Yes, we can have a result in two days."

"Can we get into her apartment?" Sophie asked Alan

"No, the State Police released it back to the landlord last week."

"Well, where is the stuff she left inside?"

"I'm not sure, to be honest."

Sophie turned to John and asked, "We can get a valid DNA sample from a hair sample, can't we?"

"Yes, provided it is a hair follicle."

Sophie reached into her purse and took out her cell phone. She dialed Mrs. Clement's number. Al listened to Sophie's side of the conversation.

"Hello, Mrs. Clements?"

"Fine. Do you know what happened to the things that were in Janet's apartment?"

"You did? Great. Was there a hair brush among the things in the bath room?"

"Can I get that from you?"

"I'll see you at eight o'clock tomorrow then." Sophie hung up and said, "We're back in business."

Pete heard Sophie come in at about ten o'clock. He went downstairs to check on her when she did not come upstairs within a few minutes. He found her lying on the couch in the office. "Well, what happened?"

"We found blood in the parking lot."

"Pete, Sherlock Holmes says, 'When you have eliminated the probable, the improbable is the answer.' Do you think that is true?"

"I guess so. Why?" Pete asked.

"No reason, really," Sophie said as she got up. "Let's go to bed. I have a lot to do in the morning."

***

"It's your turn to clean up," Pete said, as Sophie breezed out the kitchen door, grabbing a croissant.

"I'll owe you," she said over her shoulder.

Using gloves and a plastic bag, she picked up Janet's hair brush from Mrs. Clement and called John Sheers. "I got the hair brush, and I am on my way, but I'm going to stop at the marina first. Something occurred to me last night."

Harry Knight stood behind the small counter when she entered the marina office. "Good morning, Harry, Sophie said, brightly.

"Sophie, how are you this morning?"

"Just fine, I have a question for you."

"Fire away," he said.

"When did that big, dark blue boat leave? The one that was on the end of "A" dock?"

"Let me see," he said, starting to type something on the computer. "They were paid up until the thirty-first of the month but left on the twenty-fourth."

"What was the name of that boat?" Sophie asked.

"The Angelique, registered in Dubai."

"Thanks." She turned to leave, but before she got half way to the door turned back to Harry. "If someone wants to rent a car, do you always recommend the same rental company?"

"Uncle Harry's Car Rental, I own it."

"Do you rent vans there?" Sophie asked.

"We have two. People rent them for local moves, that sort of thing."

"Are they available for rent now?"

"I'll call over and check." He made the call. And with the phone still to his ear said, "One of them is available."

"Has it been rented since it was returned in August?"

After a short pause, he said, "No."

"Who was the last person to rent it?" Harry asked the same question of the person he was talking to on the phone.

"It wasn't rented to a person. It was rented to a guy with a company credit card. They are looking for the original paperwork to get the driver's name now. If the vehicle comes back without any problems we only save the original contract for about a month."

"Do they know who returned it?"

"No, they picked it up here. The computer shows a pick up charge," Harry answered.

"I'll take it. Tell them not to touch it or move it."

She called John Sheers and asked him to meet her at the rental car location. Next she called Alan Baker and told him what she had in mind. He said not to start until he got there. She lit a cigarette thinking it was nice to have a cigarette without somebody pinging on her.

She arrived before the others and paid for a one day rental. She was walking out of the office when John Sheers arrived. They went into the storage yard behind the office and were looking at the van when Alan Baker arrived.

As he walked over to them he said, "I think we should dust this thing for prints first." He looked at Sophie and said, "I think we may be chasing wild geese again."

Sophie shrugged as John got out his fingerprint dusting equipment. Looking at John as he put on latex surgical gloves and got started Sophie thought, he's a real find.

"I've found some prints on the wheel," he said as he started to lift them. After about an hour John said, "But this thing has been wiped."

"How can you tell?" Sophie asked.

"There are a few prints on the wheel, but nothing anywhere else in the driver and passenger's area. Normally you would expect to find some prints. The thing I need to do is to print the guy or gal who brought this thing back here."

John came around to the back of the van and dusted the area around the rear door handle. Finding nothing, he opened the door. The inside of the van seemed in pretty good shape to

Sophie. There were some scratches on the floor, but nothing she could see of interest.

John started dusting again. On the inside of the lip of the door that overlapped the other door he found a print. That was the only print he found in the cargo section of the van. It was slow and methodical work, but he was finally finished.

Then he took the luminal out of his van and sprayed the floor. When he hit it with the light, the cargo floor lit up bright yellow/green. "There was a lot of blood on this floor." He took specimens for DNA analysis and at least twenty photographs.

"We need to get the last driver's print before we leave."

"Alan, I think we need to know the name of the person who paid the rental bill," Sophie said.

"You're right," he said. They walked toward the rental office.

The girl behind the counter looked into the computer again and said, "The Angelique Company paid the bill with a credit card."

"Did you find the original paperwork for the rental?"

"No, I am afraid we tossed it," the girl answered.

Sophie called Harry Knight back. "Harry, what was the name of the owner of the big yacht on the end of "A" dock?"

"The slip rent was paid by credit card in the name of the Angelique Company," Harry replied.

Sophie asked the counter person, "Do you know who drove that van back here from the marina?"

"No, we don't keep a record of things like that. You'll have to ask the guys out back. They may know."

"Thanks anyway," Sophie said, as she went out the door.

There were two young guys out back cleaning out a recently returned car. One of them said that he was the last person to drive the van. He agreed to be printed once he heard the reason. John took his prints and he began to put his equipment away. "I'll let you know the DNA results as soon as I have them."

Alan also wanted a copy of the print they had found on the rear door if it didn't match the driver's prints. John readily agreed.

***

It was three o'clock before Sophie got home. It was the quietest time in their home, nap time, when parents get to breathe a sigh of relief. She looked around but couldn't find Pete in the house. She found him assembling his Austin Healy in the garage.

"Hi," Sophie said, walking into the garage.

"Hi, did you have a productive session detecting?" he asked, grinning.

"We sure did. We found where Janet was murdered and the vehicle in which her body was transported. And we also found a fingerprint, potentially, of the killer. We also know he was associated with the boat Angelique in some capacity from the rental car company records."

"Wow, I'm impressed."

"I just hope that the killer's prints are on file. I'm certain that killer is involved in some fashion with the Angelique."

"What is the Angelique?"

Patiently, Sophie explained, "The Angelique is or was that huge, dark blue yacht that was at the end of our dock."

"Oh, yea. Why do you think that?"

"Well," she began, "we found the van that transported her body, and it was rented by the Angelique. She was killed in the marina parking lot, and the Angelique left the day Janet's body was found."

"You're certain about all these facts?"

"The DNA tests won't be back for a couple of days, but I am fairly certain that's what they'll show."

"That helps a lot, but all it does is narrow it down to one of twenty guys."

"We'll get the fingerprints and find out which guy, that's simple enough."

"You know what he will say, of course, that lots of people drove the van, not just him."

"I see that problem arising. I'm going in and make myself some lunch. Would you like anything?"

He just grinned. "I meant to eat," Sophie said.

***

As Pete was climbing into bed, later that same evening, Sophie asked him, "Where would you go with a big boat if you didn't want to be found?"

"Do you mean something like the Angelique?" Sophie nodded. "Hide in plain sight is a pretty good rule."

"I mean specifically where would you go?"

"There are a lot of places you could go. Nantucket, Martha's Vineyard, Newport, anywhere along this coast. If you're thinking about trying to find that boat, you're looking for the proverbial needle in the hay stack."

"I guess I'll have to buy a big magnet," Sophie replied.

***

The next morning, when Sophie returned from taking Alexis to kindergarten, she called both Dianne and Carol. She and

Carol were going to Nantucket for lunch the following day, and she and Dianne were going to Martha's Vineyard the day after that. Sophie walked out to the garage where Pete was still working on the Austin Healy. She told him about her plans.

"I think you're wasting your time," Pete said. "What you're trying to do is almost impossible."

"It is my time after all. Besides, I'm never going to give up trying to find this murderer, not ever."

"Why don't you let the police do it? They're pretty good at this sort of thing, you know."

"I hired a criminologist who only takes two days to run DNA samples. It takes the police two months to do the same thing. By the time the police get around to looking for these guys, they'll probably be long gone."

"I don't know, Sophie. These guys are most likely long gone already. If I committed a murder in a foreign country, I wouldn't hang around."

"You would if you hadn't done what you set out to do."

"What do you think they are here to do?" Pete asked

"I don't know, but they rented two vans. Why would they do that?" Sophie asked.

"Who knows? There could be any one of a hundred different reasons."

"I gather you're not going to help me find this boat?"

"I didn't say that. You know I will always support you in whatever you do."

"Silently?" she asked with an innocent expression on her face.

"Probably not."

***

Sophie returned home the next day from her trip to Nantucket. Pete was looking into the pantry getting ready to start dinner for the children. "Did you have any luck today?" he asked her.

"No, but Carol and I just loved the island. It is really charming."

"Was that Carol's first trip to Nantucket?"

"Yes," Sophie answered.

"That's surprising since she grew up around here."

Sophie pitched in with the cooking and sat down and helped feed the children as well. When the cleanup was done, Sophie went into the office to check her email.

Pete walked into the office curious to know what was so important. "What's up?" he asked.

"I wanted to see if John Sheers had sent me his report," she said.

"And?"

"It came and all the blood samples match Janet's DNA."

"That's what you figured, isn't it?"

"Yes, but now it is official."

***

Sophie's trip to Martha's Vineyard likewise proved fruitless. They sailed on Saturday with Al, and they spent Sunday lounging around the house. Sunday night, once they were in bed, Sophie asked, "Pete, will you go with me tomorrow as I work my way down the coast looking for that boat?"

"Sure," he said, "but I think the place to start is in Rhode Island. It's closer and there's a lot of yachting activity there."

After a week of looking, Rhode Island proved unsuccessful as did the Connecticut coast as far down as Stamford. Pete said to Sophie on their way home from Stamford, "Sophie, I've enjoyed spending time with you, but this is impossible. I think it is time to give up."

"One more day and we'll be almost to New York City. Let's give it one more day."

"All right, but then it's over, right?"

Reluctantly, she agreed, although it occurred to her she could ask the New York triad for help again.

"Monday will be our last day."

It rained on Saturday, washing out their usual sail. The rain continued through Sunday.

Monday, however, broke clear and cool. They left for their last day of searching right after breakfast. It took them an hour and a half on the freeway to get to their starting point.

It was just after one o'clock when they decided to have lunch, and they stopped at a marina with a small restaurant. They seated themselves at a table overlooking the water. Pete was staring intently at the menu when Sophie said, "Hot dog!" Pete looked up. "That's it," Sophie said, pointing out the window at the boats.

"I think you're right," Pete replied. "What now? Call the cops?"

"I don't know."

They each ordered and debated the best course of action. Sophie wanted to set up twenty-four hour surveillance on the boat. Pete wanted to call the cops and head for home. "Leave it to the experts," he said. They sat for a while after paying the check. "Besides, you don't know for sure if the guy who murdered Janet is on the boat, or which one of the crew he is."

As they sat there debating, two of the crew walked up the dock. "Let's follow them and see where they go," Sophie suggested.

"Sophie, you are obsessing over this thing."

"Come on," Sophie said getting up from the table. She was halfway to the door when Pete, with a groan, got up to follow her.

The two crew men climbed into a dark green van. Pete and Sophie followed them into the town of Rye where they went to a rental car place. Pete and Sophie passed the place and made a U-turn through the parking lot of a strip center. They parked about fifty yards up the street. Ten minutes later, one of the crew men left in the dark green van. Thirty seconds later the second crew man followed driving a white van. Pete followed the second van, but they both vans went back to the marina parking lot.

"That's exactly what they did the night Janet was killed," Sophie said.

"Well, it is a little strange," Pete said.

"I want to watch them until we know what they are doing," Sophie said.

"Sophie, that could be all night, you know."

"I don't care."

"At the risk of pointing out the obvious, we are unarmed. I am confident that if they are up to something, they will be armed. And we know that they are willing to commit murder."

"That does present a small problem," Sophie acknowledged. "Call Mike and Jack."

"And tell them what?"

"We're on to something. It's too vague to bring the police in on, yet, but it needs to be checked out."

Pete called Mike on the land line in his house. Mike answered on the third ring. Pete laid the whole situation out for him.

"How do you want me to proceed?"

"What I would like to do is call Jack and Carol and get them on board. Then take your kids to my house. I'm going to call my mother and get her over there to take charge. The kids will have

Toy and Chou there guarding them. My mother, the amah, the au pair, and Mai Ling will be taking care of the kids. The blue van the CIA gave us is behind the garage. Have Carol drive, and Dianne can run the electronics. You and Jack take the white van, then come to this address."

"I'll do my best. It is going to take a little while to get everything organized," Mike said.

"If they operate the same way they did in Mystic, I don't think anything will go down until later tonight. Give me a call when you leave Mystic."

An hour and forty-five minutes passed before they heard from Mike. "We're moving," was all he said on the cell phone.

"They are on their way," Pete said to Sophie. "You've got about an hour and a half in which to formulate your plan."

"What plan?" she queried.

"I'm reasonably confident they'll want to know the immediate plan for tonight and then the plan for tomorrow."

"What do you suggest? What is so important about tomorrow?"

"I think everyone is prepared for a night vigil, but suppose nothing happens tonight, then what?"

"I guess we'll have to call that creep at the CIA and let him bring whoever is supposed to be in charge of such things. You're right; we cannot stay here indefinitely. What do you suggest?"

"That creep at the CIA, as you so crudely put it, is not a bad idea. The CIA never operated on American soil but since 9/11 all the lines are blurred. We have to go with who we know. There are other options too."

"Like what for instance?"

"One, maintain a one-person surveillance and keep the general and his guys on standby. Two, pass the whole thing over to General Lane which is probably the best idea. Or three, we could just kill them all and be done with it."

"How would you go about killing them all?"

"I think there's some semtex in the blue van. We could send them to nirvana, jet propelled, so to speak."

His last remark drew an annoyed look from Sophie. "Let me give it some thought," she said.

"I think the best approach is to pass everything we know to the CIA," Sophie said after five minutes, "but I think whatever they are doing is going to go down tonight. My guess is that Janet saw something in that parking lot she wasn't supposed to, and that's why they killed her. The killing caused them to lay low for a while, but this appears to be a continuation of their plan, whatever it may be."

"Why do you say that this is a continuation of the same plan?"

"They rented one van as soon as they arrived in Mystic. The afternoon before Janet was murdered they rented a second van. Then they leave the next morning. The mileage on the second van indicates that they drove it to the marina parking lot only."

"Pretty good guess I'd say. While we're waiting for the others to arrive, I suggest that we reconnoiter the area."

"What are we looking for?" Sophie asked.

"We need to find a place where we can watch those vans and not be seen, and where we can change the lookout without him being seen."

Two hours and twenty minutes later, the others arrived. They met in the parking lot in front of the marina.

"Sorry it took so long to get here. Between rush hour traffic in New Haven, Bridgeport, and road construction, it took a lot longer than it should have," Mike said.

"Let's get something to eat, and we'll bring you up to date," Pete said. When they entered the restaurant there was only one table occupied, and it was in the far corner of the room. They found a table where they could eat and watch the boat.

They chatted idly until the waitress finished taking their orders.

"Mike," Pete asked, "did you get a chance to look at the weapons locker in the blue van?"

"There are four Barrett's and half a dozen forty cal. Sig Sauer's with silencers."

"Everyone should have a pistol close at hand. You, Jack, and I will each take a Barrett," Pete said.

"I think we have to decide how we're going to allocate the surveillance tonight. I suggest we do it in pairs, that way no one will inadvertently fall asleep. The teams should be the same as the vehicle pairings. Dianne and Carol should take the first shift, Mike and Jack the second, Sophie and I will take the third shift. What do you think?"

"That sounds good to me," Jack said. The women remained silent, knowing that their husbands had done similar operations on many previous occasions.

"When we were driving in I didn't see a good location from which to conduct a decent surveillance," Mike said.

"Unfortunately, there isn't one. The street you came in on is a dead end. There is a small abandoned strip center fifty yards up, on the other side of the street. I suggest we park the white van on the end of the strip center and the other vehicles behind the strip center. It's not the optimum spot, but you can see the front half of one of the vans."

"I guess it'll have to do," Jack said.

"Dianne, we're going to have to get a GPS bug on each of their vans."

"I have two in my purse as we speak," Dianne replied.

That impressed Pete, forward thinking always did. "Good, did you test the equipment on the way down?"

"I put a bug on the white van and tracked it here. Everything is working fine. There is one thing that worries me though," Dianne said.

"What's that?" Pete asked.

"I am not sure how long the batteries are going to last. They're almost four years old, and I don't know if they were new when we got them."

"Not much we can do about that now," Pete said. "There is one last thing we need to discuss; what do we do if nothing happens tonight?"

"I've given this matter some thought, and I think there are three choices: one, we do nothing; two, we come back tomorrow night and do this all over again; or three, we call the CIA and let them take it from here."

Carol opened the discussion saying, "I don't think we can all keep coming back here indefinitely, we have families. I'm in favor of turning this over to the CIA."

"Maybe we can get the CIA to send us a couple of people to take up the slack if the ladies stay home," Jack suggested.

"If my husband is going, so am I," Dianne said.

"That goes double for me," Sophie added.

"I think we should table this discussion until breakfast tomorrow morning," Pete said.

They paid the bill and went to their respective vehicles. As they passed the two rental vans, they placed GPS tracking bugs in the front wheel well of each one.

***

It was five in the morning before the lights illuminated on one of the vans. The lights on the second van followed shortly thereafter. Pete shook Sophie. "They're moving," he said, simply. He climbed out of the white van and walked back to the blue. He tapped on the side of the blue, saying, "Let's go ladies they're on the move," then tapped on the rear window of the Escalade. Jack and Mike came awake instantly and got out through the rear door. Pete climbed into the Escalade and started the engine. Sophie opened the passenger door of the Escalade and climbed in as Mike and Jack walked to the white van. Pete had the car in gear when Sophie finally got her seat belt fastened. Pete dialed Dianne on his cell phone, and when she answered he said, "Conference in Mike and Jack. Have you got them on your screen?"

"Yea, the two vans turned right two blocks ahead," Dianne answered. "Standby for the conference call."

Pete pulled out with Mike and Jack following. "We're up," was all Jack said.

Carol followed the other two vehicles a few hundred yards back, as instructed. "They are turning on I95 south bound," Dianne said.

They followed the two vans about a mile back. Usually there would be at least two or three cars between them. After twenty minutes, Pete broke the silence on the conference call saying, "Looks like they're going over the GW Bridge."

As they were crossing the George Washington Bridge, Sophie said to Pete. "I'll have my head examined if I ever spend the night sleeping on the floor of a van again." He smiled and affectionately patted the plastic portion of her leg. The vans got off at the exit for the Newark Airport, and Dianne directed the tail vehicles perfectly.

Mike and Jack followed one van to the south end of the airport, where it entered the employee parking lot.

Dianne directed Pete and Sophie to the north end of the airport. The van they were following went into an old parking lot that was now used only by the personnel working in the maintenance hangers.

"What are your guys doing?" Pete asked Mike.

"I can't really tell," Mike said, "they went into the employee parking and that takes a sticker to enter, but I think I see a place where we can get eyes on them." Five minutes later Mike came back to Pete on the still active conference call, "We found a place over by the freight ramp, and we can see them now. They backed into a parking place and are cutting a hole in the chain link fence."

"My guys backed into a parking place as well. Hang on, one of them just got out of the rear door. He looks to be doing the same thing."

"This guy just got back into the van and shut the door," Mike said.

"Same thing here," Pete advised him.

After an hour had passed, Pete asked, "What the hell are they doing?"

"I haven't got a clue," Mike said in response.

Another hour and fifteen minutes passed with no sign of activity in either van. "Pete," Mike said, "they just opened the rear doors."

"My guys are doing the same thing," Pete said in response. He observed, "They are probably using cell phones, too."

"HOLY SHIT!" Mike hollered into the phone, "They've got a stinger in there!"

"SHOOT!" Pete said.

As Pete opened his door, he noticed Sophie reaching for the door handle on her side of the car. "You stay here," he said.

"No."

Pete walked around the front of the Escalade and just as he reached the now standing Sophie, they heard an enormous explosion. The explosion was loud enough that it would attract the attention of everyone on the airport grounds. "Stay here," he said with all the command authority he could muster.

"NO!"

Pete took the Sig Sauer and shot Sophie in her peg leg about nine inches above the ground.

"YOU BASTARD," she screamed as Pete caught her. Fortunately, a jumbo jet had just started its take off and her scream was not heard.

"Start the engine when you see me coming back."

Pete walked the sixty yards to the suspect van as quickly as he dared without drawing attention to himself, holding the pistol in his right hand close to his leg. As Pete stepped around the open rear door of the van, he saw one man with a stinger missile resting on his shoulder. The other man was stooped over taking a second stinger from its shipping crate.

"Hi fellows," he said. They both looked up at him as he shot the first one in the forehead and the second man through the right eye. He put a second shot into each of their heads, and he tucked the pistol into his pants and covered it with his shirt tail, for the walk back to the car.

Sophie had started the car, and as he opened the door she screamed, "You asshole."

"Not now," he said, calmly, backing out of their parking place. "I just killed two men. This is a very confusing airport, and we have to fight rush hour traffic. When we are north of the toll booth in Mamaroneck, you can holler all you want."

He started to put the car in drive, and he saw the nine-inch piece of Sophie's leg lying on the ground. Pete put the car in park, hopped out and retrieved the piece. He handed it to Sophie saying, "Here's a souvenir, many happy remembrances of the day."

Sophie just glared at him, and he knew a volcanic explosion was coming. He grabbed the cell, "Anyone there." When no one answered, he redialed Dianne. When she answered, he said, "Head for the parking lot we met in last night. Take seventy-eight to the Garden State Parkway or the New Jersey Turnpike to get out of here. Pass it along."

"Roger," she replied.

As soon as Pete and Sophie passed the Mamaroneck toll plaza, Sophie said, frostily, "I'm listening, asshole." Pete had thought the hour and half it took them to get there would have cooled her down. Unfortunately, he was wrong.

"Sometimes, you simply do not do what you are told. Most of time it really doesn't make a difference."

"Do what I am told!" she exploded. "Listen, you fucking shithead, not you or anyone else tells me what to do!"

"That was an unfortunate choice of words. What I meant to say was that you can be very stubborn, but rational thought always prevails once you understand the reasoning behind something."

"I'll let that go for a moment, but what reasons did you have for telling me to stay in the car?"

"Several actually: one, you cannot walk quietly, two, you cannot run, three, I don't know how well you shoot, four, there are four little people in Mystic that need you. They can get along without a father, but they must have a mother. Five, I knew I could do the job myself, six, I wasn't sure I could do the job if I had to protect you as well."

"You almost found out how well I can shoot!"

"I understand you wanted to be sure nothing happened to me. I truly appreciate your feelings, and I am frankly delighted you feel that way."

He could see Sophie mulling over what he had said. It took them another forty minutes to return to the marina parking lot. One look told him the large yacht had already left. Pete called Dianne, and when she answered he said, "Just return to base. Advise the others."

"Roger that." She hung up.

As they drove toward home, Sophie reflected on Pete's reasoning. She always said that no man was going to tell her what to do. But as she thought about it, she realized Pete told her what to do all the time and she complied docilely. Upon further reflection, she realized he only told her to do something when it concerned the family or her safety. She liked having someone care about her and the children. It made her feel as if she had an extra layer of security.

The trip home took two hours and fifteen minutes. Normally, it was an hour and a half. Sophie and Pete arrived first, and Pete parked in front of the garage.

"You haven't said a word for the last few hours. Am I forgiven?" Pete asked.

"I think so," Sophie answered.

"When will you know for sure?"

"I don't know. It could be several years." Sophie turned in her seat to get the remnants of her shattered peg leg through the door and she said over her shoulder, "You know you're going to have to carry me, don't you?"

"Having you in my arms is always a pleasure," Pete replied. He came around the car as Sophie waited, and when he picked her up, he tried to kiss her. She turned her head away.

"You're not that forgiven, yet."

Mike and Jack were the next to arrive. "What was the explosion?" Pete asked.

"We talked about that on the way here and the best we can figure is the shot I took hit the rocket's warhead. The second warhead blew a couple of milliseconds later, and then the gas tank went," Jack said.

Just as he finished explaining his theory, Dianne and Carol arrived. They both looked extremely upset. They went inside, collected their children, and returned in a minimum of time.

"Let's get back together Thursday evening to debrief. We should have a pretty good handle on what the authorities know then, thanks to CNN," Pete suggested.

19

The White House

It was two o'clock in the afternoon, seated at the conference table in the situation room were: Jon Kiley, Director of the CIA; General Lane, the Assistant Director of the CIA; Tom Perry, the Director of the FBI; Carlos Herrera, the Assistant Director of the FBI; Barry Daniels the National Security Director; and Ed Whelan, the Assistant Secretary of Homeland Security. They all stood as the President of the United States walked into the room.

"Gentlemen, I'm sure you all know why I have called this meeting," the president said. "I would like a complete briefing on what transpired at Newark Airport Tuesday morning. Tom, why don't you lead us off?"

The director of the FBI, Tom Perry gave the president a detailed account of the FBI's investigative efforts at the south end of the airport. Then he said, "Carlos, would you detail what we found at the north end of the airport?" Looking at the president the director explained further, "The bodies at the north end of the airport were not discovered until late yesterday afternoon."

"What took so long to find them?" the president asked.

"To be perfectly frank sir, we were unaware of them until we were advised by the Port Authority Police."

"What brought the bodies to the attention of the Port Authority Police?"

"A security guard noticed their van Wednesday morning. He didn't think any more about it until he was going home later that afternoon."

"Why was a security guard there in the first place?" the president wanted to know.

"His job is security at the maintenance hangers located about one hundred fifty yards to the west," Carlos responded. Carlos went on to detail everything that was known about the second set of bodies. He finished by saying, "Information is still coming in on that scene, sir."

"What do we know about these guys?" the president asked.

"The preliminary reports indicate that they are Middle Eastern," Carlos said.

"Why do you say that?"

"Their dental work, sir. We will have a better idea once we have run their DNA."

"Let me be sure I have this correct, at this point we have no idea who they are or where they came from?"

"Sadly, that sums things up," said the Secretary of Homeland Security.

At that point an aid came into the situation room unannounced. "Excuse me, sir, but I have a message for General Lane that I am told relates to this meeting and is very important." The president simply nodded.

"Oh shit!" General Lane mumbled to himself, as he read the message.

The President overheard him and asked, "Would you care to share that, 'Oh shit' with us?"

"Mr. President, do you remember visiting an ex-Delta named Pete Smith in the hospital in San Francisco?" the general asked.

"Yes. Get to the point."

"Well, Pete Smith recently asked me to run a print through our system for him. As a favor, I did it, and it came back unknown. It appears that the system records all unknown prints and saves who ran them."

"So apparently Pete Smith had a fingerprint belonging to a terrorist long before we knew this terrorist existed. Where does Pete Smith live now?" the President wanted to know.

"Mystic, Connecticut."

"General Lane, did you come by helo?"

"Yes, sir," the General answered.

"Good, get in that helo and go to Mystic, Connecticut. Ask Pete Smith where he got that print, and take Carlos with you," the president ordered. "I want you to do it in person so he can't get evade the question."

General Lane and Carlos Herrera promptly left the room. In the helo, they reviewed the crime scene information and the Assistant Director of the FBI laid out their plans on resolving all the gaps in their understanding of what had transpired.

After fifteen minutes, the president said, "All right gentlemen, I think I am aware of all the relevant facts thus far available. Please keep me informed as the investigation progresses. Thank you for coming."

The president walked toward the oval office. He stopped at his secretary's desk. "Has Marine One landed yet?" he asked.

"Yes, sir. I believe it has," his secretary replied.

"Would you tell whoever you tell such things to, that I want to go to Mystic, Connecticut? I would like to leave in five minutes. Please let the first lady know I will join her at Camp David later this evening. You will need to make suitable arrangements for her travel."

"Sir," sputtered the Secret Service agent following the president, "you can't do that. There is no security in place. We need time to prepare."

The president's glare silenced him. The president entered his office and after a quick glance at his calendar, left his office. "You can reschedule this afternoon's appointments for tomorrow morning after eleven, at Camp David." With that he left for Marine One.

20

Pete was out in the garage working on his current restoration project. He worried about how the events at Newark Airport would play out even though he knew deep down in his heart he had done the right thing. Those two guys were prepared to kill a lot of people, but, and it was a big but, he had still killed two guys. As he reflected on that, he realized a few years ago he would not have been concerned at all. His life had taken a new course since then, however. Now what he wanted most was the pleasure of participating in the raising of his children and the companionship of his wife.

Jack, Carol, Mike, and Dianne were coming over to review the events of the past few days. They intended to feed the children, put them to bed, and order pizza, before debriefing each other.

Mike walked into the garage at four forty-five. Pete was in the middle of reassembling the front end of the Austin Healy. "Hi, Mike, you're just in time to give me a hand with this thing."

"Sure," Mike said, sitting down beside Pete on the floor. "Pete, we came over early because I was hoping to speak to you alone. I'm worried. Do you think there are going to be any consequences over killing those guys?"

"Right now, nobody has any idea we were involved, at least according to CNN. I've racked my brain, but I can't think of any way they can connect us to the events at Newark Airport."

"What happened to the guns?"

"They'll never see the light of day, trust me on that," Pete said.

"That was the one thing that really worried me. The other thing is to impress upon the girls to keep their mouths shut."

Jack walked into the garage at that point. He overheard what Mike said. "You're right Mike. That's how most people get caught," Jack said. Looking to Pete he asked, "What happened to the guns?"

"Gone," was Pete's simple reply.

"I think that's about the only way they can connect us to the shooting."

"We had pretty much concluded the same thing," Mike said.

Mike's words had barely left his mouth when a school bus, painted Navy grey, pulled up on the street in front of Pete's house. Navy Seals, armed to the teeth, started pouring out of the bus. An officer directed their deployment, and they started to surround the house. "I think I spoke too soon," Mike said.

"What the hell is going on?" Jack asked.

"I think we missed the start of World War Three," Pete said. "Let me go out there and ask," Pete finished.

Pete started walking toward the front of the house, when he saw Sophie come out the side door. "What's going on?" Sophie asked.

"Stay here, I'm going to go ask," Pete said. He walked to the officer who was obviously in charge. "Lieutenant, I own this house. Would you please tell me what is going on here?"

"Sir, my orders are to secure the perimeter of this house."

"Who gave you those orders, if you don't mind my asking?"

The lieutenant hesitated for a moment before answering, "Centcom."

"Who specifically at Centcom?"

"Lieutenant General McHenry, sir. Centcom himself, sir."

Pete walked back to where Sophie stood with an expectant look on her face. "He doesn't know what's going on either. I have a feeling you should feed the kids, order the pizza; that's easiest." He started to turn away, but turned back toward Sophie and said, "Order a couple dozen pizzas. We might as well feed these guys as well, but be sure our pizzas come in the first delivery."

As he was walking back to the garage, he noticed a Coast Guard boat maintaining station on the river in front of his house.

"The lieutenant doesn't know why he was told to deploy his men here or in that fashion," Pete said before being asked.

Before anyone could issue a retort, Al Rocca pulled up on the street. They watched, as the lieutenant scrutinized his identification very carefully.

"I'm kind of curious as to how we're going to get our pizza," Pete observed.

"Gentlemen," Al said joining them in the garage.

"What brings you to our humble abode this fine afternoon?"

"About two o'clock this afternoon the FBI called me. They wanted to know where we had gotten a fingerprint we ran awhile back. I told them, quite candidly, that I was unaware we had run any prints recently. They told me to ask around and see what I could find out. Before I could get back to my office, they were on the phone again. It turns out Alan Baker had run the print. They wanted to speak to him, but he's on vacation. Where, they wanted to know. I told them I didn't know but I thought I could find out. Before I could walk down the hall, they were on the phone again. This time they stayed on hold while I asked around. Apparently, he took his kids to Disney World. Fifteen minutes later they were on the phone again wanting to know what hotel. I'm to ask around again to save them from deploying fifty agents from all over the state to Orlando, but when they called back the next time. I told them no one knew.

"When I finally had a moment to think about it, it occurred to me that Sophie might know where the print came from."

Before anyone could respond, a white, nondescript little car pulled up in front of the house and parked on the street. As they watched, the lieutenant checked the IDs of the two men in the car, and Al asked, "What the hell is going on around here?"

"I don't know and neither does the lieutenant in charge, but that guy might," Pete said indicating the man on the left.

"That's General Lane, I don't know the other guy," Mike said by way of explanation.

The lieutenant let them pass at that point.

"Who are they?" Al asked.

"General Lane used to command Delta Force, and now he is the Assistant Director of the CIA," Mike answered, by way of explanation. "The other guy I don't know."

"General, how are you?" Pete asked when he and the other man had reached the garage.

"I'm fine, thank you Mike. Are you doing alright?" The general asked Mike.

"You don't know Jack Carter, do you? And this is Al Rocca, the local police chief here," Pete said.

After shaking hands, the General said, "This is Carlos Herrera, Carlos is the number two man in the FBI." They all shook hands with Carlos. Sophie, who had seen the general arrive, entered the garage.

"Sophie, how are you?" the general asked.

"Rice bowl full," she answered, noncommittally.

Chou and Toy arrived at that point and Sophie said to them, "The general was just leaving. Toy, Chou, would you show him to the curb, please."

Toy and Chou each took a step forward. Pete held up his hand in the universal stop position and said, "Not now." Sophie glared at him for what seemed to Pete like an hour, but in reality was only ten seconds, and he knew he hadn't heard the last about this. Waving his hand at the military personnel, he asked, "Is it you we have to thank for all this?"

"No. I'm as surprised by this, as you are."

Two more SUVs arrived in front of Pete's house, and two men wearing suits got out of the first car. One of the men went to the front of their car. The other man went to the rear of the second car, and the lieutenant, in charge of the military detail, started to walk toward the cars, but he stopped dead in his tracks when the President of the United States got out of the rear seat on the passenger side. The president saw the congregation in the garage and came toward them, walking into the garage. He looked at Pete and said, "It's nice to see you standing up."

"Thank you, sir. Let me introduce you to everyone."

With the introductions complete, the president walked over to the two cobras. "These are magnificent," he said.

"They are beauties, aren't they?" Pete acknowledged.

As the neighbors gathered in front of the house, the president asked, "Do you think we might go somewhere a little less public?"

"Certainly, sir," Pete answered. He led the way into the house and took them into the dining room. The table only seated eight, but a couple of extra chairs were brought in from the kitchen. The two secret service agents stood catty corner to one another as did Toy and Chou.

Once everyone was seated and further introductions had been made, the president said, "I would like to hear the whole story of the fingerprint you had General Lane run for you."

"Ahh… Mr. President, I think I speak for the entire group, when I say that we are somewhat concerned about whatever exposure we may, or may not have," Pete said.

"Effective right now, each of you in this room have a presidential pardon for any and all crimes you may or may not have committed up to this point in time. That should clear up any concerns you may have.

"Please start at the very beginning and be very detailed."

"It all started the last Sunday in August," Pete began, and he went on to detail the events of Sunday morning.

Sophie picked it up from there, and when she got to the part about polygraphing the neighbor, the president asked, "How did you get this guy to agree to take a polygraph?"

"Well," Sophie said, her face reddening, "He tried to slam the door in my face, so I stuck my leg in the door to stop it from latching. Toy charged the door and it hit him in the forehead, as he lay on the floor, I explained to him that I was leaving with the truth. Toy and Chou were going to get that from him one way or the other."

Just then the doorbell rang. When Pete answered the door, the lieutenant stood on the door step, "Did you order pizza?" he asked.

"Yes, send the kid up." Pete started to turn to announce the pizza but one of the Secret Service agents stood so close that it became difficult.

"I am going to have to inspect each box before you take them into the dining room," the agent said.

Pete paid the teenage delivery boy, adding a generous tip. "Don't forget we want a dozen more as soon as you can get them out of the oven, but deliver them while they are hot, two trips if necessary." The young man left at top speed, anticipating another large tip.

While Pete was paying for the pizzas, Sophie, Dianne and Carol had been passing out plates, silverware, and napkins. Sophie took two of the pizzas into the kitchen for Soo Ling to give to the kids for their dinner.

Once everyone had a slice or two in front of them, Sophie picked up the narrative again.

Before she was halfway through her narrative, the pizza delivery boy arrived with a dozen more pizzas. The lieutenant rang the doorbell again and Pete, with a secret service agent following, went to the door. "Tell him to stay where he is. I'll be right out."

Pete retrieved a card table from the basement and took it out to the side of the Navy bus, and set it up. "How much do I owe you?" The boy told him. It took all of his remaining cash to settle the bill. "Lieutenant, these are for you and your men."

"Thank you, sir," the lieutenant responded.

"Sir, is it true that the president is in your house?" the delivery boy asked.

After a moment's hesitation, Pete answered, "Yes."

"Do you think he would autograph a pizza box for me?"

"I don't know, let's go ask him."

The secret service agent was not happy with Pete bringing the delivery boy into the house. "Mr. President, this young man would like you to autograph an empty pizza box for him."

The president, a consummate politician wrote on the lid of the pizza box, "Great Pizza" and signed his name. The delivery boy managed to stammer "Thank you, sir," before leaving. Pete knew that young fellow had a tale he would be telling for the rest of his life. Pete smiled at the thought.

Sophie continued her narrative. She detailed the search for the Angelique. She described the conflicts over the best course of action. From there, Dianne detailed how they followed the terrorists to Newark Airport using the old CIA van.

Mike described seeing the Stinger in the terrorist's hands and Pete yelling, "'Shoot!' Clearly their intention was to shoot down an airplane that had just departed and shoot through the hole in the fence at an airplane that had just landed."

"What caused the explosion?" the president asked.

"I'm not really sure, Mr. President," Jack said. "I am not sure if the bullet hit the chain link fence and deflected, or if the terrorist moved the stinger after I pulled the trigger. I aimed center of mass. The secondary explosion was clearly the gas tank."

Pete detailed how he had walked down and shot the other two. He omitted shooting off nine inches of Sophie's peg leg. He went to say they had gone back for the Angelique, but it had left.

Sophie piped up saying, "Don't worry Mr. President, I will find the Angelique, and resolve this matter completely and to everyone's satisfaction."

"That's quite a statement and, on behalf of the country, I thank you."

Shortly thereafter, the president left. Walking to the car the president told General Lane and Carlos Herrera he wanted them to ride with him.

The car pulled away, and once they were moving the president said to the others, "There are several things I want you to do; the most important is to give that group any aid or information they request, remembering, of course that deniability is an essential ingredient of clandestine operations. That van the CIA left with them is apparently four years old. Is there a more current one with better technology?"

"Yes, sir," General Lane answered.

"Good, get them a new one. Do you have a school on how to run that equipment?"

"Yes, sir. There is a training course for it," General Lane replied.

"Send those ladies through it. What we just learned in there is top secret. You are to share this information with no one, not even your respective directors. If there are any problems with that, refer them to me. Carlos, I want you to take charge of the investigation and steer it away from these people so they can get to work. I want each of you to do an outline for a press briefing I can give on national TV tomorrow night. Please bring those outlines to Camp David by one o'clock."

"Yes, sir," they both replied.

21

*F*riday evening Sophie and Pete were feeding the kids; the children insisting, of course, that they didn't need any help from mom and dad. The children all raced off after dinner to watch the Cartoon Network.

Pete loaded the dishwasher and, once things were cleaned up, he said, "The president is giving a news conference tonight. I'd like to watch that and put our dinner off a little while, if you don't mind."

"I was going to suggest the same thing," Sophie replied to his request.

During the entire news conference, the president continually referred to "government operatives," never once mentioning Sophie or Pete or any of the others.

"Let's go out for dinner," Sophie suggested.

"Good suggestion," Pete answered.

After they had ordered, Pete asked Sophie, "What did you think of the news conference?"

"It made me uneasy. He didn't do a very good job of explaining his visit to our house, and I am somewhat concerned that someone is going to realize that we are the 'government operatives' involved," she answered, making quotation marks in the air with her fingers.

"I dialed in on that as well," Pete said.

"What do you make of that?" Sophie queried.

"I don't think the news media will ever figure it out. They don't spend much time investigating when a story has gone cold, but some people in the government bureaucracy may. It will dawn on them that they were ordered to stand down immediately after the President's visit here."

"What do you see as consequences for us?"

"That is difficult to predict. I don't think anything is going to happen as a result, except of course, your notoriety is going to increase, especially locally."

"Changing the subject for a moment if I may, I have not seen Toy all day."

"I sent him to New York," Sophie answered.

"Why?" Pete wanted to know.

"I want to speak to the head of the triad in Chinatown," She replied.

"I repeat, why?"

"I want him to put the word out that I want to find the Angelique."

"So you're not done with this yet?"

"No," she went on to explain, "we may have gotten one of the people who participated in killing Janet, but we didn't get the person who set the whole thing up."

"Why don't you just let the CIA do it?" Pete asked.

"I don't trust that general."

"When are you planning to go to New York?"

"Monday, I need to shop for winter clothes. I thought I would ask Dianne and Carol if they would like to go with me."

"Are you taking the train?" Pete asked.

"I thought I'd have Toy take us in the limo," Sophie said.

"If you take the limo, and you want to miss the traffic, you won't arrive before ten thirty, and you'll have to leave by about three to miss the traffic coming home, which doesn't leave much time for shopping when you consider lunch."

"I hadn't thought about that. I'll talk to the others," Sophie said.

"Whatever you do, I want you to take Toy and Chou with you."

Their meal arrived then and the conversation drifted aimlessly from the children, to the house, to their boat.

"When is the boat coming out of the water for the winter?" Sophie asked.

"Either tomorrow or Monday, I'm not sure, Pete said.

"I am really going to miss sailing, especially Saturdays with Al."

"Maybe we could have him and his lady friend over for dinner," Pete suggested.

"That's a good idea. I didn't know he had a girlfriend," Sophie said, somewhat indignantly.

"Apparently, they just started dating, and 'girlfriend' might be too strong a word," Pete said as they were leaving the restaurant.

***

It was about eight-twenty Monday evening when Pete saw a car pull into their driveway. He looked out the window and confirmed his guess that Sophie had returned from New York. He thought briefly about going back to the office in order to avoid carrying the numerous packages into the house, but he decided against it. After changing his mind, Pete opened the front door to go lend a hand. Sophie was halfway to the door and he stood on the stoop waiting for her. "How was the shopping?" he asked.

"Great," Sophie slurred.

"Looks like you found the bar car on the way home," he said.

"We made our own bar car," she said lurching toward him with the intention of giving him a kiss.

Sophie normally drank sparingly. She would have a beer or two after sailing and occasionally a glass or glass and a half of wine with dinner. "Why don't you let me help you?" he said, picking her up and carrying her toward the stairs. He set her down on the bed and asked, "How did you create your own bar car?"

"Well," she began, "we found a wine store near the train station, and I bought you two bottles of Chateau Rothschild and a nice wine opener. Dianne and Carol did the same thing. We hoped it would sort of smooth over how much money we spent."

"Where is the wine now?" Pete asked, already having a pretty idea.

"In my tummy," Sophie said, collapsing backwards onto the bed.

"Thought so," Pete said, although he wasn't sure she heard him. He undressed the now prostrate Sophie. Her clothes were the easy part. He knew there was some sort of a trick to removing her leg, but he wasn't sure he knew it. He thought about just giving it a good yank, but after a few seconds of examination he figured it out. There was a small valve on the side which when opened released the vacuum that held it in place. It came off easily after that. With a minor amount of maneuvering, he got Sophie under the covers. He wasn't at all mad, thinking she's entitled once in a while to blow off steam with her friends. Besides, if he said anything, it would be the pot calling the kettle black. He went back downstairs to watch TV.

The next morning Pete awoke at his usual time of six-thirty. He dressed and went downstairs. There were enough packages in the living room to fill Santa's sleigh.

The kids were in the family room watching TV, as usual, so he went in the kitchen, and started breakfast. After breakfast, the younger kids returned to the family room under the supervision of the amah. He took Alexis, their oldest, to kindergarten.

When he returned, he found Sophie in the kitchen pouring herself a cup of coffee. "Ah, sleeping beauty," he said. "And how are we feeling this morning?"

A noncommittal grunt preceded a mumbled, "Okay." She sat down at the kitchen table, "I think I owe you an apology," she said.

"You don't," Pete responded quickly, "You're entitled once in a while."

"That was only the second time in my life I have ever been that drunk," Sophie said.

"I noticed a huge pile of shopping bags and packages in the living room. Did you leave anything in New York or did you buy it all?"

"I don't think it's all mine. Dianne, Carol, and I decided it would be easier if they just came over today so we could sort things out sober. I guess Toy and Chou put everything in the living room. You have to see the things I bought. We made the right decision to go to New York."

"How much did you spend?" Pete asked.

"A lot."

"How much?" he repeated.

"A whole lot," was the reply.

"Did Dianne and Carol spend a lot as well?"

"Yes, but I told them how to deal with it." Sophie said. She realized her mistake even before Pete had opened his mouth to ask the question she knew was coming. I have to learn to bite my tongue when I have a hangover, she thought.

"So how do you deal with it?"

"You don't want to know," she said, hoping he would drop the subject.

He didn't. "I'm all ears waiting to know how a wife is supposed to deal with overspending."

"Well, when your husband asks, 'How much did it cost?' You say, 'It was expensive.' If he continues you say, 'Very expensive.' If he keeps going you say, 'Don't ask.' But if he won't let it drop, and wait for the credit card bill, you're stuck. You tell the truth, all else having failed."

"I guess, it works pretty well, having just been a victim of the 'Sophie technique' myself. I still remain in the dark, as to how much you spent. Now I want to know, how much did you spend?"

"No, you don't," she said smiling.

"Sophie, I want a number now!"

"I'm not sure exactly."

"Quit stalling," he said, rapidly growing exasperated with her delaying tactic.

"To be honest, I'm not sure exactly."

"A number please, and my patience is wearing thin."

"About $600,000," she said. And added by way of explanation, "We went to Tiffany's."

"Good Lord," he groaned.

"But you should see what I bought."

"Can't wait," he said rising and headed for the office.

***

Sophie picked Alexis up at kindergarten at noon. She had just finished getting Alexis out of her car seat when two men dressed in expensive looking suits walked up the driveway.

"May I help you?" Sophie asked.

"Mrs. Smith?" the younger man asked. Sophie guessed his age at thirty-five.

"Yes."

"I am Jeff Gould. I am with Brackett and Company advertising. This," he said, indicating the older man, "is William Peck, marketing director for Cadillac."

"What can I do for you?" Sophie asked, politely, but clearly getting ready to turn toward the house.

"We would like you to become the spokesperson for Cadillac. I see you already drive a Cadillac," Jeff Gould said.

"We're going to sell it, so I doubt you want me to advertise your product," Sophie replied.

"Why?" asked William Peck.

"It is too difficult to get into the way back. We have four children and the last car seat has to go in the third row. It's very difficult to reach."

"Would you give me a week to see what we can do about that problem?"

"Sure, but I am not saying I'll do anything in regard to marketing for you."

"That is understood, but just having you drive one of our cars is good PR by itself," William Peck said.

"Thank you for stopping by," Sophie said.

"We'll be in touch, and it was a pleasure to meet you," said Jeff Gould.

As they left, Mike and Dianne pulled into the driveway.

Sophie waited by the front steps while Mike and Dianne got out of their car. "Hi, guys," Sophie greeted them, much brighter than she felt.

"How are you feeling?" Dianne asked, as they entered the house.

"Still a little rocky on my pins," Sophie answered in hushed tones.

"Who were those guys in the driveway?" Dianne asked, as they entered the living room.

"What guys?" Pete, who had overheard them, wanted to know.

"They want me to do advertising for Cadillac." Sophie and Dianne continued into the kitchen while Mike and Pete opted to sit down in the living room.

Mike looked at Pete and said, "Do you know what a shopping trip to New York costs?"

"Generally," Pete said. The doorbell rang, and Pete hollered toward the kitchen, "I'll get it."

Jack and Carol arrived with their two kids to pick up Carol's packages. Carol looked a little rough. Pete thought he could actually see Carol's temples pulsating. Their children sped toward the family room. "Sophie and Dianne are in the kitchen," Pete told Carol. Jack joined Mike and Pete in the living room.

"Carol was drunk as a skunk when she got home last night. How were yours?" Jack asked Pete and Mike.

"Dianne was shit-faced," Mike said.

"Sophie was wiped slick as well," Pete volunteered.

"Have either of you had a hard look at the price of a little jaunt to New York for winter clothes?" Jack asked.

"All I got out of Dianne was very expensive," Mike said.

"Carol bought three pairs of shoes at eighteen hundred a pop," Jack said.

Their wives overheard Jack's remark as they started to sort out the results of the shopping spree.

"Will you guys quit being so cheap!" Sophie said. "Women, in case you didn't know it, like to feel good about the way they look, and you guys can afford it, so get over it." Then she turned to Pete and said, pointing her index finger at him, "You are a prime offender."

"Feeling good about how you look is fine, but would you feel just as good in say three hundred dollar shoes?" Jack asked.

"NO!" they answered in unison.

They sorted through all the boxes, dividing into separate stacks whose was whose. Soon everyone left, Sophie went upstairs to the bedroom for a nap, and Pete headed out to the garage.

***

Later that evening, Pete and Sophie lay in bed watching TV, and Pete said to Sophie, "You never did tell me if you went to Chinatown yesterday."

"I did go and I met with Ching Fa. He is the head of the local triad. I told him I wanted to find the Angelique and he said he would ask around."

"Any idea how long it will be before he has an answer for you?"

"Not really," Sophie replied. "Oh, I meant to tell you that John Chen called me this afternoon. The CIA wants me to go Asia."

"Why do they want you to go?"

"To show the world I'm still involved, I think."

"I told them I would check with you and let them know in a day or two."

"What are you going to do?" Pete asked, recognizing Sophie's stall.

"I really haven't decided."

"Well then, what's your inclination?"

"I think I may go, but missing you and the kids is the limiting factor. If you say no, I won't go. What do you think I should do?"

"Do what you want, but I'm going to miss you as well.

"Sophie, do you remember the discussion we had when you ordered three boats?"

"Yes."

"Do you think that buying several hundred thousand dollars' worth of jewelry that you will never wear falls into the category a frivolous waste of money?"

"Maybe, probably."

"Good. How about toning it down a little then?"

"Okay."

***

Two days later Sophie said to Pete while they were eating dinner, "I decided to go to Asia for the CIA, but I told them that this will be the last time. Happily we're not leaving until after the first of the year."

"Okay, how long do you think you will be gone?" Pete asked.

"I'm not sure. I would think at least three weeks, maybe a month. Dianne wants to go too. What do you think about that?" Sophie asked.

"I think that's between Mike and Dianne, but do you think you'll like having someone with you all the time?"

Sophie said, "She won't be with me all the time. She said she wants to do some sightseeing and shopping."

"She'd better not say the word shopping to Mike after your last little jaunt into New York. Are you going to take your plane?"

"It's our plane, and yes, I thought I would. Why?"

"Suppose I wanted to go to Paris to see Giselle, how would I get there?" Pete asked innocently.

"By clipper ship, around the horn, and you are not funny."

Pete let the subject drop.

***

It was one week to the day when William Peck, Jeff Gould and their entourage returned. Curiosity drove Pete outside to watch what the people from Cadillac were doing to the Escalade. They removed all the seats behind the passenger and driver's seat and they installed four individual seats, a new rug, welded reinforcing under the floor. Sophie came out two or three times to watch their progress.

When they were finished, Sophie declared it a big improvement.

"Have you given any more thought to becoming the spokesperson for Cadillac?" Jeff Gould asked.

"I have, but I want to know what it pays," Sophie replied.

"There are two ways we do this," Jeff Gould replied. "We either pay you a flat fee or a residual based on how much we run the commercials and use the print ads."

"How many days would it take to do what you want?" Sophie wanted to know.

"Probably no more than five," Jeff answered.

"I'll do it, but I want a million dollars flat fee plus the residuals."

"I don't know about that. That's awfully rich," William Peck said.

"I not finished yet. I want the money divided equally between St. Jude's and the Shriner's hospitals. Also, I want it sent anonymously," Sophie finished.

"This is going to require approval at a higher pay grade then mine," William Peck responded.

"I'm leaving for Asia soon, and will be gone about a month, so there's no rush. The holidays will soon be upon us, so I wouldn't be interested in doing anything until after the first of the year."

"We will be in touch," Jeff Gould said.

Pete followed Sophie back into the house. He said, "That was pretty cool. If you had done that for the money I'd have been really pissed. That was just great. I can't tell you how proud I am of you at this moment.

"You sure surprised those guys, too."

22

The holidays came and went, and in mid-January, Sophie left for Florida to shoot the first of the commercials for Cadillac. She returned home Friday evening, saying, "I think we should move to Florida. I've decided I don't like being cold."

Pete's response was predictable, "It will start to warm up in another month or two. Besides you're going to Asia soon. It's warm there, isn't it?"

"The CIA postponed the trip for some reason."

The next Monday the phone rang early and Sophie answered it. Pete listened to her side of the conversation, but was unable to get a sense of what was being said. Sophie concluded by saying, "I'll call you back if I cannot manage that."

"What was that all about?" Pete wanted to know.

"The CIA wants to give us a new surveillance van and a course on how to use all its features next Monday. They want Dianne and Carol to attend the class as well."

"That's interesting. I wonder what prompted their largess. That sounds a little out of character for them," Pete mused. While Sophie was taking Alexis to kindergarten, Pete called General Lane. "What's the deal with the new van?" he wanted to know.

"It was the president's idea," General Lane told him.

"Did he say why he thought it was a good idea?" Pete queried.

"I believe he feels you may be useful to the country in the future and wants you to be adequately equipped in any event." After exchanging pleasantries they hung up.

When Sophie returned from taking Alexis to kindergarten, she called both Dianne and Carol. The idea exited Dianne. Carol, however, was somewhat reticent. She really did not want Jack getting involved with any more antiterrorist operations. Sophie fully understood Carol's reasoning; she didn't want her husband in harm's way either. Carol finally agreed after Sophie reminded her it was better to know what they were doing than not to know. That way you could say no on the spot.

As Pete lay in bed later that evening, he wondered why he and Sophie always seemed to have their most serious discussions in bed. Then he realized it was privacy. Their household was always a whirl of activity between the amah, the au pair, Toy, Chou, a cleaning lady now three times a week, and four kids. He put that thought aside as Sophie came out of the bathroom.

Sophie climbed into bed with her leg on, indicating she wanted to make love that evening, but Pete asked her, "Who do you intend to take to Washington with you?"

"Dianne and Carol," she answered simply.

"I meant Chou or Toy," he retorted.

"Neither."

"If you're going, one of them is going too."

"We're going to be on a secure CIA facility. We won't need any additional protection."

"The only thing you can say for sure is you may not need any additional protection, but if one of them is not going then neither are you."

"How are you going to stop me?" Sophie asked, her independent streak raising its head.

"I'll hide your peg leg, if it's necessary," Pete replied.

"You bastard! You would, too!"

"Damn right I would, if it meant keeping you safe."

"You have just threatened to use my handicap against me to get your own way. Do you intend to shoot me in the peg leg again?" Pete said nothing in reply. Sophie realized that he said all he was going to say. She continued, "All right, why do you think I need protection?"

"You are walking into a nest of trained killers. If you think I'm not going to be concerned about it, then you're crazy."

"Bah!" But she was secretly pleased that her husband cared enough about her to think about a bodyguard. She wasn't sure, but it seemed this being cared for thing had its limitations. It annoyed her no end that she was vulnerable to such an extent, being immobilized. "Okay, I'll take Toy," she finally conceded.

***

The following Wednesday afternoon Sophie called Pete from the plane and said, "We'll be landing in about an hour and a half. Will you call Jack and Mike? They can pick up their wives at our house."

"Sure."

Mike arrived first at Pete and Sophie's house carrying five pizza boxes and Mike Jr. Five minutes later Jack arrived with his kids and another five pizzas.

Pete opened the door, and said, "That makes fifteen pizzas. I ordered five and Mike brought five as well."

Over Pete's shoulder Mike hollered from the living room, "I guess we're going to have enough."

Jack started laughing and hollered back, "Yea, enough to feed the Italian army."

The women arrived thirty minutes later. They had taken the Rolls Royce and left it at the airport in Providence and Sophie was driving. Everyone went out front to greet them, seven kids plus husbands. "Where's Toy?" Pete asked as they walked toward the house.

"He's driving the new van back, but don't worry. He put us on the plane and I took a chance driving home."

***

The next morning, when Sophie returned from driving Alexis to kindergarten, Pete was in the office paying some bills. When Sophie walked in, Pete mentioned casually, "One of the boats you ordered arrived Monday."

"Really!" Sophie picked up her purse which she had just set down. "Let's go see it."

"There's nothing to see. I ordered some work done and I doubt that they've even started, yet."

"Come on, I want to see."

"Can it wait?" Pete asked.

"No!"

"Not even an hour?"

"Not even a minute. Let's go,"

"It will be there tomorrow, you know," Pete said.

Sophie just glared at him. Forty minutes later they pulled into the parking lot for the boatyard Sophie had selected. "What did you think about the yard when you were here the other day?" Sophie asked.

"The yard itself seems to have all the equipment and facilities that we need. The manager has raced sailboats himself and understands our needs."

As they walked through the yard Pete said to Sophie, "Be careful, these places can be very dangerous." His admonition drew an annoyed look from Sophie, who remained silent. They found their boat in one of the work sheds. A young guy had already started sanding one side of the keel.

"Why is he doing that?" Sophie asked.

"You want the keel perfectly smooth. Look at the other side," Pete said, walking around the trailer. They walked around the boat, and Pete climbed over the trailer to be able to touch the keel. Sophie had some difficulty getting over the trailer's frame, but she managed. "Just run your hand fore and aft on the keel."

She did and said, "Wow, that's not very smooth, is it? You can feel the dips easily." They clamored out from under the boat as the yard manager arrived.

As he walked up to them Pete said, "Sophie, this is Tom McLauflin, the yard manager. Tom, this is my wife, Sophie."

"A pleasure," Tom said, offering Sophie his hand and they shook.

"Can we see inside?" Sophie asked Tom.

"Sure, let me get some stairs," Tom replied, turning to look for portable stairs. He returned two minutes later with a set of aluminum stairs with wheels on the front legs, but the rear legs sat firmly on the ground.

Tom positioned the stairs by the boat. Sophie climbed up only high enough to be able to see the interior. Pete followed her up the stairs with the intention of catching her if she slipped. The stairs, with two people on them, were wobbly at best. There really wasn't much to see. She came back down. "How long until you're finished with the hull work?" she asked Tom.

"About two weeks and then we should be able to step the mast and see what needs to be done to put her in racing trim," he replied.

When they were back in the car and headed home, Sophie said, "I didn't realize there was so much to be done to get a new boat ready to race."

"That's always the case," Pete answered. They rode the rest of the way silence, but Pete could see Sophie's gears going.

***

Two weeks later, she and Dianne left on the postponed Asian trip. They were supposed to be gone three weeks, but it stretched into five weeks. Finally, Sophie was on her way home.

The children wanted to go meet mom at the airport and Mai Ling wanted to welcome her husband home, as well. Pete thought, "Why not?" The logistics were going to be a little complicated, but the solution was to take two cars. Pete drove the limo with the children, and Mai Ling drove the Escalade. Sophie had called from the airplane when they were two hours from landing. Her plane landed right on time, and they were permitted to drive out onto the ramp area once the airplane stopped. As the stairs were being lowered, Pete unbuckled the kids.

While waiting at the bottom of the stairs, the first thing Pete noticed was Sophie wore the neck rings, again.

"We're all very happy to have you back," Pete said. The kids all wanted to be picked up and hugged, and Sophie was only too happy to oblige.

"I'm probably happier to be home than you are to have me home," Sophie said, walking to the car. "It was a long trip and I am certainly glad it's over."

Sophie started to organize the kids into their car seats. Pete walked over to Chou, and said, "Chou, I'm sorry we couldn't bring your family, too, but we don't own a bus." After a short pause he added, "Yet."

Chou drove the limo with Sophie, Dianne, Pete, and the kids while Mai Ling and Toy drove the Escalade with the luggage. Sophie fussed over each of the children in turn.

Pete was concerned about the neck rings. He had once made a comment that he thought neck rings were sexy and Sophie had had them put on, but they did permanent damage to the wearer's body. The weight of the rings caused the rib cage to compress making the wearer's neck look longer. He thought, I've saved her from her sense of vanity before, and she knows the hazards, but if that's what she wants, so be it. Then he felt compelled to comment, "I see you had the neck rings put back on again."

"Yes, and this time they're staying."

"You sure you know what you're doing?" Pete asked. "You know that in ten years you are going to look like a stork?"

"Perhaps," she said noncommittally. "You might find some other surprises as well."

"Oh, Gawd," Pete mumbled. "Is that a new ivory leg you are wearing?"

"Yes."

"How did you get it through customs?"

"CIA made arrangements for us to clear customs at the Air Force base in Hawaii. Walk in the park."

Mike and his son were waiting patiently at Sophie and Pete's house when they arrived. Dianne gave them each a big hug, and they all went into the kitchen. Pete offered Mike a beer, which he accepted. The ladies passed.

"So, how was the trip?" Mike asked.

"Great," Dianne answered. "When you travel with Sophie, everywhere you go you're treated like royalty."

Pete arched an eyebrow at that observation. Dianne, Mike, and their son left shortly thereafter. The kids had departed the kitchen for the family room and the big screen TV, leaving Pete and Sophie alone in the kitchen.

"So what exactly did you do for the CIA?" Pete asked.

"Just showed the flag, so to speak," Sophie replied.

***

Later that evening, Pete could hardly wait for Sophie to come out of the bathroom ready for bed. He felt like a five year old on Christmas morning. Sophie came out completely naked, as he knew she would. She was indeed sporting new tattoos. She lifted her right arm to show him the large, red parrot with a blue tail tattooed on her right side, extending from just below her arm pit to her hip. Flowers draped over her shoulder went about half way down the bird. On her tummy was a pool of light blue water with a rock rising up the right side of her tummy. A mermaid was seated on the rock with a waterfall cascading behind the mermaid.

"What do you think?" she asked.

"Very nice," Pete said.

"That's kind of a lukewarm response, if I ever heard one."

"I think we need to take them for a test drive first," Pete said as she slipped into bed. Pete reached down to Sophie's peg leg and unscrewed the ivory portion.

He screwed in a two-inch piece which would level her hips when she was on her knees. "Are you sure you know what you are doing?" Sophie asked.

She got a leering grin in response. He pulled her closer and slid down a bit. His left hand found the lower portion of her tummy. His middle finger searched for her clitoris. As he gently stroked her clitoris, his tongue caressed her right nipple. Sophie's back arched involuntarily. "Hurry up!" she moaned. Pete entered her slowly and when he was two-thirds of the way in he pulled back and slowly entered her again. Sophie reached back and grabbed him by the buttocks and pulled him fully into her. Sophie had a small climax almost immediately. Pete rolled her over on her tummy and entered her from the rear pulling her up on her knees. Time seemed to stand still during the rapture of their mutual pleasure. Sophie climaxed again. This time she collapsed on her stomach.

Pete rolled off her. He pulled her on top himself, saying, "Roll over." She did, and sat up astride him. She took his penis in her hand and guided it into her. As she started to move rhythmically, Pete reached over and from under his pillow he pulled out a battery-powered vibrator. When he touched her clitoris with the vibrator, she let out a low moan of ecstasy. They both climaxed together.

They lay on top of the sheets both drenched in sweat. Finally, Pete said, "The new tattoos seem to work pretty good."

"Until I met you, I thought I hated sex," Sophie said. "Now I can't get enough. For the last month every time I got into bed, I thought about you."

He held her close, not responding, thinking that he could not get enough of her either. They drifted off to sleep still entwined in each other's arms.

It was the beginning of March before Pete asked, "What have you heard from the triad about the location of the Angelique?"

"Nothing, but I'm sure I will hear something soon," Sophie answered.

***

It wasn't until early April Sophie came to Pete and said, "I finally heard from the triad."

"What did they say?"

"Ching Fu will give me all the information at a meeting in New York on Friday. So I need to go to Atlantic City tomorrow."

"Why there? I thought you said that this guy was in New York."

"I need some untraceable cash. I can cash a check in the casino there for almost any amount."

It was not lost on Pete that Sophie had neglected to say how much cash she needed. He let it go in the name of domestic tranquility, saying only, "Take Toy and Chou with you."

Sophie retuned Friday afternoon, Pete kissed her hello and asked, "What did you learn?"

"When the boat left here, it went to Bermuda. The name was changed to the 'Scimitar' and it continued on to the Mediterranean. It spent the winter in Capri, but it left yesterday. They'll call with a current location as soon as they have it. It took so long to find because they changed the name."

***

Four days later, Sophie walked into the office where Pete was working on the computer and said, "It's time to get packed. The Scimitar is in Monaco."

"Just like that?"

"Yes," Sophie replied.

"How do you know the owner is there?"

"I don't, but sooner or later, he'll be on it."

"And, if I may be so bold as to ask, how do you plan to deal with four kids if we are away for possibly several months?"

"Between your Mom, the amah, the au pair, and Mai Ling, I'm sure everything will be just fine."

"Kids need moms," Pete replied simply.

"Do you have a proposal? I don't know why, but I sense one coming."

"Why don't I go over there and check things out? I'll call you when the owner shows up."

"That's okay, but you have to take either Toy or Chou with you."

"No. I'm not leaving here unless I'm positive that you and the children are very well protected." She started to speak, but he held up his hand and said, "No arguments." Sophie had learned to recognize when her husband would not change his mind. Annoyingly, this was one of those times.

"Well, let's give Jack and Mike a call and see if they would like to take a European vacation," Sophie suggested.

Sophie extended an invitation to the other couple to come over for an evening of Chinese food and beer. Mike and Dianne and their son arrived shortly before Jack and Carol and their two children. The ladies fed the children, who promptly disappeared to the family room to watch cartoons. Sophie ordered another delivery for the adults as everyone pitched in to clean up the mess made by seven young kids eating.

A dozen cartons were open in the center of the dining room table. Pete brought up the subject of the Angelique, and told them the boat, renamed the Scimitar, now lay in Monaco.

"Obviously, you would like to finish what we started earlier," Mike observed.

"Yes, any suggestions how it could be done?" Pete asked.

"Not without seeing the set up," Mike replied.

"I won't let Pete go alone, and he won't go if Toy and Chou aren't here," Sophie said.

"I understand his reasoning, and frankly, I agree with it," Mike said.

"I'll go with you," Jack volunteered. His statement drew a glaring look from Carol. After seeing the expression on his wife's face, Jack asked Pete, "You are just going to check this thing out, aren't you?"

"Yes, as Mike pointed out there's not much we can do without seeing the set up. There're no assurances that the owner is involved in this either."

"Why do you say that?" Carol asked.

"We are relatively certain the boat transported the stingers, but we don't know if the captain did it without the owner being aware. The owners of yachts of that size are rarely on them. We don't want to take someone down unless we know for sure that they participated," Pete replied.

"If you guys are going to try and do a twenty-four/seven surveillance on this boat, I should probably go with you, an Arabic speaker will probably come in handy," Mike volunteered. No sooner were the words out of his mouth than Dianne shot daggers at him. "Don't give me that look! You just spent a month and a half in Asia."

If Pete assessed the situation correctly, both Jack and Mike would go after lengthy discussions with their wives later that evening.

"What kind of equipment do you think we'll need?" Pete asked.

"A directional mic and some kind of recording equipment," Jack suggested.

"And a good digital camera with a good telephoto lens," Mike added.

"I think we should probably take some night vision binoculars with us as well," Pete said.

The good news was that the equipment that they had suggested was truly for surveillance; this eased their wives' fears of them being involved in something dangerous. "Does the van the CIA gave you guys have that type of equipment in it, or do we have to hunt it up?" Pete asked.

"We have all that and then some," Dianne responded.

"Let's get back together at say ten tomorrow morning and you ladies can show us how to work all this stuff," Pete said. Then he added, "And any suggestion you can make will be greatly appreciated."

At ten o'clock the next morning they reassembled. Dianne pulled the van out from behind the garage and took the lead showing the men the capabilities of the van. The guys assembled the equipment they wanted to take with them, as Carol made a list of the equipment they were taking, with the idea of replacing anything lost. They went into the house leaving the van in the driveway. Sophie made coffee, and everyone helped themselves to a cup.

As they stood around the kitchen, Carol asked, "When do you guys think you'll be leaving?"

Sophie remained silent; she wanted them to go now. Nothing was going to deter her from seeking justice for her friend. Pete knew exactly what his wife was thinking. When she focused on something, her intensity always surprised and amazed him, but after five years of marriage it shouldn't have.

They decided to leave the next evening at six o'clock. That way they would arrive in Nice at about eight in the morning. They could rent a car and drive the thirty minutes to Monaco.

"I'll make your hotel reservations," Sophie said.

"Sophie, let me do that," Pete said. "We need some small pension-type hotel. The last thing we want to do is call attention to ourselves by staying at some five-star hotel. In fact, now that I think about it, we probably ought to stay at three different hotels."

"I hope the rooms will be ready when we get there. Sitting around a lobby is the last thing I want to do after being up all night," Jack said.

"The plane has sleeping cabins on it," Sophie said.

"Oh, yea. Lost my head there for a moment, Madame Gin Sling," Jack replied, bowing from the waist. Sophie grinned as everyone else laughed. Jack's irreverence was one of the things she liked about him. You could always count on him to say exactly what was on his mind, and on his sense of humor, too.

After some further discussion, everyone decided to meet at the plane and Pete agreed to bring all the equipment they had selected. Sophie and Pete walked out with the others. With, "See you tomorrows," the other two couples departed.

"I have a question for you," Sophie said as they walked back toward the house.

"Oh," Pete responded noncommittally.

"Do you think opposites attract?"

"I don't know, why?" Pete answered.

"Well, look at us for example. You are mister white bread, Ivy League education, Army officer, white Anglo-Saxon protestant, and I am a half-caste, Asian, former hooker, with no education."

"Mike is a retired Army Sergeant Major, who earned a college degree going nights over the course of twelve years. Dianne, I think, is a high school dropout, and ex-stripper, which is one notch above a hooker.

"Carol is another white bread college graduate, former teacher. Jack is a rough and tumble marine, who was working as a carpenter when he met Carol.

"None of us are similar to our spouses, yet everyone seems very happy," Sophie mused.

"I've actually given this phenomenon some thought. I think everyone falls in love twice with their spouse; there's the physical attraction when you meet, and once you get sex out of the way, then you fall in love with the brain. By brain I mean who the person really is: their personality, outlook on life, sense of humor, and intelligence. That sort of thing."

"Interesting theory," Sophie said. A minute or so after they had entered the house Sophie continued, "So you are or are not interested in me only for sex?"

"My dear, you are one of nature's rarest of creatures. Not only do I find you to be extremely intelligent, but I also think you are the world's sexiest woman, in spite of the tattoos and neck rings."

"I ought to call you the artful dodger, because you just dodged a bullet on that one."

"You, however, did not!" Pete said picking her up and starting for the bedroom.

"The children," Sophie exclaimed.

"The door, my dear, has a lock on it," Pete said increasing his speed toward the stairs. Sophie smiled, wanting him at that moment as much as he evidently wanted her.

23

Sophie, Dianne, and Carol watched as the plane carrying their husbands broke ground on its way to France.

"Well, at least they aren't going to be in any danger," Carol said, almost to assuage her own feelings, as they walked back to the parking lot.

On board the plane, as soon as the seat belt sign was turned off, Mike moved over to where Pete was sitting. "What kind of ordinance did you bring?" Mike asked.

"Three silenced Glock Nines, the Barret that Jack sited in a while ago, and twenty pounds of C4 with various detonators," Pete answered.

Jack, who had overheard the question asked, "How did you manage that on the plane? I saw Carol hawking everything we unloaded."

"Yesterday afternoon when Sophie thought I was at the mall, I came up here and put it on board."

The flight attendant came over and asked, "Would you like anything to drink?"

They declined.

"We have a choice of prime rib or swordfish for dinner whenever you are ready."

"We'll let you know. Thank you," Pete said to the flight attendant.

They arrived in Nice at eight o'clock the next morning. It was nine o'clock before they had cleared customs and rented a car. The drive to Monaco took a little longer than expected, as they were catching the tail end of the rush hour traffic. Sophie, contrary to the earlier decision, had booked them into the same four-star hotel, explaining she had been unable to find two 'decent' hotels with rooms available. They checked in and agreed to meet in ten minutes in the restaurant for a cup of coffee.

"Well, what's the game plan?" Jack asked once they were all seated.

"I think we should take a stroll down by the waterfront and see if we can find the boat and a decent place where we can set up surveillance," Pete answered.

"That may be somewhat difficult. I don't think I have ever seen any place so densely packed with buildings and people," Mike observed.

"They use every square inch of their ground here, don't they?" Pete said.

"What's the attraction here?" Jack asked.

"No income tax," Pete answered.

"Sounds like Paradise," Jack said in response.

They walked leisurely down the hill to the quay and then along the promenade toward one end of the small harbor. Far from the center of the harbor they found the Scimitar. The Scimitar was docked with its stern to the quay, as were all the other boats. It had an elaborate ramp that extended from under the main deck sloping down to the quay. There was nothing but restaurants in the area.

"Sophie was right again! There's the boat," Jack noted.

"Yea, but there really doesn't look to be any place where we can set up any kind of surveillance," Mike said. "Maybe high up on the hill on the opposite side of the harbor if we can find a place."

"Let's walk down to that café and see if we can see the boat from there. That might be our best bet," Pete said.

Once seated in the closest café, Jack said, "You can't see squat from here." They could barely see the transom of the boat.

"Not quite the way I would have phrased it, but an accurate description," Pete said.

"We need to get on the internet and see if we can find an apartment for rent in one of those buildings that overlooks the port; otherwise, we might as well be back in Mystic," Mike said.

"You're right," Pete said. "Let's go back to the hotel and get to work on that. Mike, why don't you and Jack start the internet search while I call Sophie. She seems to be able to find anything."

Pete signaled the waitress for the check.

"Hang on a second," Jack said. They watched as two crewman came down the ramp to the dock. Each crewman went to a different corner of the boat and started to untie the dock lines. "Looks like they're getting ready to leave," Jack continued.

"I believe you're right," Mike said. Then he added, "What now?"

"Let's see what direction they turn when they leave, then we'll get in the car and see if we can follow them from shore," Pete said.

"What happens when it gets dark?" Jack wanted to know.

"I guess we'll just have to take a guess at their destination by their course, Pete said.

"That sounds a little sketchy to me," Jack said.

"It is, but if you have a better idea, I'm all ears," Pete replied.

"Unfortunately, I don't," Jack admitted.

They watched as the boat cleared the mouth of the breakwater that formed the harbor and then turned westward. "Let's go get the car and see what we can see," Pete said.

There was a road that ran mostly along the edge of the sea, but occasionally the road wandered inland. They would drive for fifteen minutes and then pull into one of the viewpoints to observe the boat. It came around a point and into a small bay as they watched, then turned into the wind and dropped its anchor.

They decided to go back to Monaco and retrieve their baggage. Jack drove while Pete sat in the back seat.

Pete called Sophie, and when she answered he said, without preliminaries, "They moved. The boat is now anchored in a small bay called Rade de Villefranche-sur-Mer. Can you find us a hotel overlooking that bay?"

"Hang on, I need to look at a map," she replied. When she came back on the line she said, "You don't need a hotel. Go to this address. Just a minute while I find it." Two minutes later, she came back and read Pete an address. Then she went on to tell him, "Madame Gerard will be expecting you."

"What is this place?" Pete asked.

"Don't worry about it. It's a nice place." Then Sophie hung up. There was clearly more here than met the eye.

They got lucky and found a parking place close to the hotel. Once back in the car after checking out, Pete plugged the address Sophie had given him into the GPS.

"What is this place?" Jack asked.

"I don't know. Sophie says it's a nice place. You now have all the information that I have," Pete answered. The address turned out to be on Cape Ferrat.

"Nice neighborhood," Jack observed.

"Gorgeous," Mike agreed.

An older, grey-haired woman in her mid-fifties came out to greet them when they pulled into the driveway. As they got out of the car, she introduced herself, in heavily accented English. "I am Madame Gerard."

"I am Pete Smith, this is Jack Carter, and this is Mike Jarwarski."

"Let me show you to your rooms. Giselle will bring your luggage up for you."

"That's all right; we'll take it up later ourselves. Some of it is quite heavy and has sensitive equipment in it."

"As you wish. If you will follow me, sir."

"The master suite is at the end of this hallway. I thought we would put your guests in these two rooms if that is acceptable to you, sir? They both have ocean views."

"That's fine," Pete replied, somewhat awed by the decoration. The view from his room was spectacular, looking out on the bay and across to Villefranche. There was a large king size bed, night tables on each side of the bed, a chaise lounge, and two dressers. The furniture was a cream-colored provincial style. The room was painted in a very pale blue, white trim, and gold leaf accents. Whoever had decorated this room had extremely good taste. It was simply gorgeous.

Pete wandered downstairs to recoup his luggage and bring it to his room. Once he had organized his room, he went back downstairs and took a seat in the living room to enjoy the view and scope out the Scimitar. Mike and Jack joined him a few minutes later. No sooner were they seated than Madame Gerard came into the room and asked them if they would like anything.

"Just a beer for me," Pete answered. Madame looked at Mike and Jack inquisitively.

"The same," they replied together.

"This place is just spectacular," Jack said.

Madame Gerard returned before Pete could respond. "Who owns this place?" Pete asked.

With a shocked look on her face, she said, "You do, sir." Shaking her head, Madame Gerard left the room.

"Nice digs there, Peter," Mike said, as Pete was reaching for his cell phone.

When Sophie answered Pete said, "Do we own this place, dear?" in an extremely sarcastic tone.

"I bought it for my father, but he decided he liked living in Paris better. I thought it might be a nice place to go on vacation with the kids. So I haven't put it back on the market."

"How much did it cost?" Pete asked.

"It was expensive," Sophie answered.

"I am familiar with the Sophie technique. I want to know how much it cost."

"28,000,000 Euros."

"Are you out of your mind?" Pete howled.

"Listen, we have an income of almost a half a billion dollars a year. That was a drop in the bucket. I'm getting tired of you being so cheap. Get in the swing of things, and buy yourself a couple of Ferraris." Click.

An expression of indignation and outrage crossed Pete's face as he stared at the cell phone in disbelief with his eyes crossing. That brought peals of laughter from Mike and Jack.

"What did she say?" Jack choked out.

"I'm supposed to buy myself a couple of Ferraris. Christ Almighty!"

That brought more laughter from the others. Their laughter was infectious and pretty soon Pete was laughing, too.

"Ah, yes," Jack said rising, to get another beer, "The problems of being married to the world's richest woman. She is apt to forget she bought you a beautiful villa on the French Rivera." Reaching the end of the living room he turned, and asked, "What color Ferraris are you going to buy?"

Pete just rolled his eyes. Mike, however, couldn't stop laughing.

Jack returned thirty seconds later, followed by the maid carrying a tray of three beers. She set a fresh beer in front of each of them and asked, "What time would you like dinner?"

"How about an hour?" Pete replied, looking at the others who nodded their assent.

"Mrs. Smith ordered filet mignon, but would you rather have something else?" the maid asked. Pete shook his head no after looking at the others.

"Let's go out on the patio and take a look at that boat," Pete said to the others when the maid had left. They carried their beers outside and sat down at an umbrella-covered table. "Jack, do you think you could hit Mr. Big from here?" Pete asked.

"The distance is about thirteen hundred yards. If he were standing on dry land, the distance would be no problem, but he is not. If I take the shot and a wave hits the boat, all we have accomplished is to alert them."

"That's a problem. You're right, of course," Pete observed.

"The hull is probably aluminum. That means we can't use a standard limpet mine and timer, even assuming we knew when they were going to go out again," Mike said.

"I'll bet the general has something that would work just fine," Pete said.

As they watched, a speed boat with four members of the crew left the boat and went to a dock in Villefranche. The crew left the boat, heading into town.

"We ought to find out what they are doing in town," Jack said.

"I bet they are just going in to party," Mike said.

"You're probably right, but we need to know exactly what they're doing," Pete said. "I know I don't need to say this, but I will anyway; be careful what you say in front of the staff. They don't need to know what we're doing."

***

When Sophie hung up the phone she was somewhat annoyed at her husband's attitude, although the fact that he didn't want anything showed he was content. She just wished he would enjoy the fruits of what they had earned a little more. Then an idea hit her and she went into their little office. She found his car magazine, which was really nothing but classified ads. After a little searching, she found the section on Ferraris. There were six advertised for sale, and she called all of them. Two of them had been sold, so she bought the other four, arranging payment by bank transfer. Then she called an auto transporter company. The transport company agreed to pick up the cars and deliver them to their house. Next she bought canvas covers for the cars. She decided he could discover them behind the garage, but she knew that she needed to rent a storage barn, sooner or later.

***

"That was the best meal I have ever eaten," Jack said, pushing back from the table.

"It was really excellent," Mike added. Then he went on, "In spite of the Smith family's jet, I'm feeling a little jet lagged, so I think I'll head up to bed."

"I'm going to do the same thing," Pete said.

Jack followed the other two up the stairs.

***

The next morning, Pete went downstairs in search of food. Entering the dining room on his way to the kitchen, he found the staff had set out breakfast pastries and coffee on the dining room sideboard. Pete poured himself a cup of coffee and put two croissants on a plate. He walked out to the pool area and sat down at the same table they had used the previous evening. Mike joined him twenty minutes later, and Jack followed shortly thereafter, a cup of coffee and a plate piled high with pastries.

"Did either of you happen to look at the boat last night?" Pete asked.

"Yea," Mike said. Jack just nodded with his mouth full of pastry.

As soon as he swallowed Jack asked. "What's the deal with all the lights?"

"They're security lights, and there are two crewmen on deck continuously monitoring them. It makes it impossible to get under the boat at night without being seen," Pete answered.

"Well, it would appear that we're going to have a very difficult time getting to this guy, should we decide to take him down," Mike observed.

"I wonder if General Lane can get us one of those scuba rigs that doesn't leave bubbles?"

"Worth a phone call to find out," Mike said.

"I don't know how to scuba dive; do either of you?" Jack asked.

They both confessed they did not.

"Carol does, but I don't think asking her is a very good idea," Jack offered.

"I agree with that completely," Mike said as Pete nodded his concurrence.

"So what's the plan for today?" Jack asked.

"Watch the boat, then about four o'clock, we'll take the rental car back. We can use the house car to follow the rental car. Then we'll head over to where they docked their speed boat last night and follow them. For now, we'll take two hour shifts, me first, then Mike, and then you, Jack. I'll give the general a call and see what he can come up with," Pete said.

***

Returning the rental car took a lot longer than they planned. The rush hour traffic in Nice was horrendous. "What did you guys see today of interest watching the boat?" Pete asked.

"Nothing, just crew members doing their routine maintenance," Mike said.

"It was the same for me, but I did try the directional mic. When the boat swings nose into the wind, you get nothing, most of the time it's unusable," Jack added.

They found a parking place and walked into the center of the older portion of Villefranche. Narrow passageways gave the feeling of almost being in a maze. The passageways were lined with restaurants, cafes, and small boutiques.

"This is really quite charming," Pete observed.

"It is, isn't it?" Mike agreed.

They made their way to the waterfront just as the crewmen from the Scimitar were walking from their speedboat into the center of the old portion of town. They followed about forty yards back. Two of the crewmen went into an Italian restaurant, while the others continued down the passageway to a Chinese restaurant.

They opted to go into a crowded Italian restaurant. They were seated at a table as far from the crew members as possible.

"This is unsatisfactory, we can't hear shit from here," Jack observed, with his usual bluntness.

"You're right. I wonder if that van we just got from the CIA has some sort of really small directional mic in it. Let me call Sophie and ask," Pete said rising from the table to go outside.

When he returned to the table, he said, "Sophie said they have some pens that should do the job. You click the pen as if you are extending the point and aim that end at the subject. It will record two hours of conversation. When you get to a quiet spot, you download it and listen to what was said. She said they also have a program that will translate the conversation into English, although that program doesn't work too well. She is FedExing those this afternoon. We should probably have them the day after tomorrow," Pete reported.

24

Sophie walked into the restaurant where she was meeting Carol and Dianne for lunch. She loved this particular restaurant. Done in a nautical motif, it overlooked the Mystic harbor with lots of windows, and a grey and white color scheme. She saw she was the last to arrive, Carol and Dianne were already seated at a window table.

"Sorry to be late," she said, sitting down.

"You're not, we only just arrived," Carol told her.

When the waitress had taken their drink orders, Carol said, "I heard from Jack last night."

"What did he have to say?" Dianne asked.

"He said they were all fine and that they were waiting on some equipment the general was rounding up for them. He didn't know when they would be home."

Sophie abruptly sat back and upright in her chair, a strange look crossing her face. "What's the matter?" Dianne asked.

"Shit. Shit, shit, shit," Sophie said startling both Carol and Dianne.

"What is it?" Dianne asked.

"I FedExed some listening equipment to Pete yesterday afternoon. You don't suppose they're going to try and take this guy down, do you?" Sophie asked.

"They said it was just recon. They wouldn't lie to us, would they?" Carol countered.

"They would in a heartbeat, if it kept us from worrying. We would never know if everything went just fine. Come on, there's one way to find out for sure," Sophie said, as she dug a twenty dollar bill out of her purse and put it on the table to pay for their drinks. "Let's go to my house."

Instead of parking in front of the house, as she usually did, she continued to the garage. One of the garage doors was already open, and Dianne and Carol followed her into the garage. They walked toward Pete's work area. Sophie noticed that Pete had almost finished his current restoration project. Against one wall were three old gym lockers. "Dianne, you're the tallest, can you reach that shelf and feel along the front edge and see if there's a key?" Sophie asked. "Pete showed me where he kept the key, but I wasn't really paying attention," she went on to explain.

"Nothing," Dianne said.

"Try that one," Sophie said pointing to a shelf on the other side of the gym lockers.

"Bingo," Dianne said and handed the key to Sophie. Sophie opened the locker on the left side.

"Remember there were four of those rifles and six pistols when we got back from Newark? Pete got rid of the pistol he used and the rifle Jack used so there should be five pistols and three rifles, but there are two rifles and two pistols," Sophie going through the math for the benefit of the others. She opened the middle locker next. "There should be twenty pounds of plastic explosive in here." But the locker was empty. "That lying, scheming, miserable, egotistical, son of a bitch!" Sophie said.

"What do you think they're doing with all that stuff?" Carol asked.

"Don't be naïve. There are going to attack that boat," Dianne said.

Sophie went back out to her car, and the others followed, curious to know what she was going to do. She reached into the car, grabbed her purse, and set it on the hood. She took her cell phone out, and after thumbing some buttons, held it to her ear. "Tom, Sophie Smith. I want you and Scott to fly the plane to Providence now. Be prepared to fly back to Nice at six tomorrow evening. She listened for a few seconds then said, "Good, I'll see you then."

"If you're going, so am I," Dianne said.

"Do you think your mother-in-law can handle seven kids? That's a lot to take on, don't you think?" Carol asked.

"I'm not sure. Let me call her, but between Soo Ling, the au Pair, Toy, Chou, and Chou's wife, she should be fine," Sophie replied.

25

"This place is gorgeous. Who owns it?" Carol asked, as the taxi pulled into the driveway of the villa on Cap Ferrat.

"Pete and I," Sophie answered. "I bought it for my father, but he decided he liked Paris better. He has a neighborhood bar where he goes to drink with all his pals so I think that's the attraction of Paris for him," Sophie added by way of further explanation.

As Sophie used her key to open the door, Dianne was taking charge of getting the second cab driver to unload all the luggage. Madame Gerard heard the commotion in the entry hall and came to investigate.

"Bon jour, Mrs. Smith, if you just leave your luggage there I will have it taken upstairs," she said.

"It is nice to see you, Madame Gerard. You don't need to worry about the luggage. Do you know where my husband is?"

"All the gentlemen are on the terrace taking their breakfast."

Sophie led the others through the villa toward the terrace. As they walked out of the villa they saw their husbands sitting at the table with the Cinzano umbrella.

"Well, if it isn't Colonel RAT!" Sophie said.

"Along with Sargent Major RAT!" Dianne said.

"And Lance Corporal RAT!" Carol added.

"Ladies," Pete said rising, "to what do we owe this unexpected pleasure?"

"You know damn well why we're here. You lied to us! You took guns and explosives with you, so it's obvious you guys intend to go after that boat. You told us you intended to just check things out."

Mike and Jack had also risen by this time. "Please sit down. Let's talk about this calmly," Pete said.

"Calmly, my ass!" Sophie hissed.

When everyone was seated, Pete said, "First of all, Jack and Mike didn't know anything about the guns and other ordinance until we were in route. Secondly, I wouldn't get anywhere near a guy as dangerous as this one without access to a gun." Carol and Dianne were somewhat mollified by Pete's declaration.

Sophie was not, however. "What about this special equipment you have the general hunting up for you?" Sophie wanted to know.

Pete laid out the problem of the security lighting and their inability to get near the boat. He concluded by saying, "We're just about to go through the recording we got last night in a restaurant where two of the crew were eating."

"There are breakfast pastries in the dining room, if you're interested," Jack said.

"I think I'll see what is available," Dianne responded, and Sophie and Carol followed Dianne into the dining room.

"If you ladies go upstairs and take a short nap, no more than two hours, the effects of jet lag will be minimized," Pete said when they finished eating. They all elected to take his advice, although Sophie wanted to know the plan for the day before she went upstairs.

"There isn't one. We're going to listen to last night's recordings and decide from there how to proceed," Pete told her. That drew a suspicious look from Sophie, but she said nothing.

***

They went into the small village on Cap Ferrat for lunch. Over lunch Pete laid out the plan for the rest of the afternoon. "About five o'clock, Mike and Dianne, and Jack and Carol will go over to Villefranche and shadow whoever comes ashore. Sophie and I will eat in the villa tonight."

"Why aren't we going over to Villefranche?" Sophie wanted to know.

"I am sure there are crew members on that boat who saw you in Mystic. You are distinct. There are not many Asian ladies who use a peg leg."

"That sounds boring," Sophie said.

"Boring?" Pete said. "Well, I guess the magic has gone out of this marriage."

I think it will be up to me to interject a little excitement into this evening, Sophie thought.

"The villa is really lovely," Carol interjected, trying to change the subject.

"I think I am going to soak up some rays by the pool this afternoon," Dianne said.

"I'll join you," Sophie said.

Carol looked at Pete and after a moment's reflection, said, "From what you said earlier, I gather you want to get under that boat. I've been meaning to tell you your idea of getting under the boat isn't going to work."

"Why not?" Pete asked.

"Several reasons," Carol said. "It would be almost impossible to swim that distance under water in accurate direction given the tides and current. Secondly, after being down that long, you would need some decompression time. There is no oxygen bottle big enough to do the job. Finally, all that assumes you can figure out how to get into the water without being seen."

"I guess we start working on plan B then," Pete said.

***

The others left the villa about five o'clock, leaving Sophie and Pete alone.

"What time are we eating?" Sophie asked.

"How does seven sound to you?"

"Just fine."

Sophie was in the bathroom working on her makeup when Pete stuck his head in the bathroom door and asked, "How much longer until you're ready?"

"About five minutes," Sophie answered.

"I'll go downstairs and open a bottle of wine while you finish getting ready," Pete said

"Okay."

Pete had opened a bottle of red wine and poured two glasses, when Sophie entered the dining room where he was seated. She wore an electric blue, Asian-style dress with the high collar and a slit up the side, and a blue, four inch, high heel on her right foot. The peg leg she had chosen for the evening was dark hardwood inlaid with silver. Her hair was piled on top of her head, and she looked gorgeous.

The staff had set the table with two places opposite one another, but Sophie sat at the end of the table and moved the place setting in front of her, to be closer to Pete.

Once seated, she reached into a small clutch purse and pulled out her gold cigarette case, a Dunhill lighter, and her cigarette holder. Slowly she fitted a cigarette into the holder, and pushed the lighter toward Pete. He picked it up and lit her cigarette. The realization of what she had in mind for later in the evening made him grin, but he said nothing.

Sophie sipped the wine in front of her. "Very good," she noted.

They skipped dessert, opting instead for the bedroom. Pete had taken off his shirt when Sophie asked, "Can you help me with this zipper?" as she struggled with the back of her dress. The dress fell away to reveal a black lace bra and a garter belt. "What are you waiting for?" she asked.

Pete's pants hit the floor as fast as gravity would take them. He picked her up and carried her to the bed.

"Just a minute," Sophie said. She opened the drawer by the bedside table and took out the two inch piece of wood that screwed into her leg in order to level her hips. "Here," she said, handing it to him, "Install this would you?" As Pete finished, she handed him the battery-powered vibrator. "I think you know what to do with this!"

They slept late the next morning exhausted by their evening's romp.

Mike spent the next morning listening to the recordings from the previous evening. Jack and Carol had recorded the captain and the engineer. The captain, sometime during the day, had spoken with the sheik, who owned the boat. The sheik had laid out the tentative plan for the captain. Mike went looking for Pete after he had listened to the recording three times to be sure he had a good translation.

He found Pete seated at the table with the Cinzano umbrella. "Bingo," Mike said, as he walked up to the table.

"Oh?" Pete said raising one eyebrow.

"Yea, they're leaving tomorrow after the owner arrives. They are going to St. Tropez, and the captain told the engineer that they would be crossing the Atlantic again. He wanted maximum fuel aboard when they leave the French coast."

"We need to let everyone else know and brainstorm how we're going to proceed," Pete said.

When everyone was seated at the table, Pete opened by saying, "Mike, why don't you share with the others what you got from last night's recordings?"

"Apparently, they are leaving sometime tomorrow. The owner is supposed to come aboard, and then they are sailing for St. Tropez. They didn't say how long they would be in St Tropez, but ultimately they're going to cross the Atlantic."

"Do we know their final destination?" Jack asked.

"No," Mike answered.

"After giving this a little thought, I think we go to St. Tropez. The problem is, we'll be so far away that the directional mic will be useless. Does anyone have any suggestions?" Pete asked.

"Shit," Sophie mumbled.

"What?" Pete asked.

"You promise you won't get mad?" Sophie asked.

"No."

"Then I guess we'll have to use your lousy plan, whatever it may be," Sophie responded.

"All right, I won't get mad."

"We can use our boat and anchor it close to their boat," Sophie said.

"Our boat is in a yard in Mystic, our other boats are in Old Saybrook in a boatyard."

"We have another boat, and it's in Cannes. We need a tender for our racing campaign, so I bought one. I just forgot to mention it to you. Then she added, "I like going first class."

"Forgot!"

"All right, I have been looking for the right moment to tell you about it. You can be awfully ornery at times, you know?"

Pete looked up and shook his head as Mike and Jack chuckled. Carol and Dianne looked on sympathetically.

"We going to need at least two cars to get us and our stuff to Cannes," Jack said, changing the subject.

"The crew has a car. I'll have one of the crew members bring it here, and we can follow the crew member back," Sophie said.

***

Two hours later they arrived in Cannes. Pete rode with the crew member while the others went in the villa car.

Pete took one look at Sophie's tender, and steam starting coming out of his ears. Sophie looked at Pete and knew he was beyond mad and all the way to furious. She was thankful that the others were there, because she knew Pete wouldn't say anything in front of them, and she hoped he would calm down a little before they were alone.

The boat was moored with its stern to the dock. A ramp, apparently housed under the main deck, extended to the dock for easy access. The name on the transom said Delta King.

"I'm Captain Steve Jenkins," he said, with an English accent. He wore a white shirt with four strips on his epaulettes, indicating his status, and dark blue slacks.

"Pete Smith," Pete said extending his hand. "These are our friends, Mike Jarwarski, his wife Dianne, Jack Carter, his wife Carol, and of course my wife Sophie."

"It is a pleasure to meet all of you. You can leave your luggage where it is and I'll have it taken aboard."

They went up the ramp to the main deck which had numerous deck chairs. Crossing the rear portion of the main deck, they entered the main salon. It was paneled in a dark hard wood with a rug at least two inches thick. Pete felt like he was floating as he walked across it. At the far end of the main salon was a bar on one side with five stools in front of it. A dining room table that could seat ten people was opposite the bar. Pete followed the captain down a set of stairs at the end of the main salon. The stairs led to a somewhat narrow passageway. Doors to several staterooms opened onto the passageway.

"This is the master stateroom," the captain said, opening the door at the forward end of the passageway.

The master stateroom was sumptuous; paneled in the same dark hard wood and very tastefully furnished with a pair of chairs separated by a small table, king size bed, night tables with cut crystal lamps and it had a private bath. As Pete stood in the room shaking his head, Sophie entered.

"Are you mad?" she wanted to know. When he didn't respond, she continued, "I did exactly what you said. You told me not to buy a two hundred foot, fifty million dollar boat, and I didn't."

"What did this thing cost?"

"It is one hundred eighty-eight feet and cost forty-five point five million."

Pete threw his hands into the air and walked out of the room. Sophie wisely did not follow.

Pete went up to the main deck. No sooner was he seated than a young female crew member asked him if he would like something to drink.

"Beer," he answered.

"Is Heineken all right, sir?" she asked.

"Just fine."

"May I have one of those, too?" Mike asked the young girl as she handed Pete his beer.

"Certainly, sir," she said.

"What's got your goat?" Mike asked Pete.

"This boat," Pete said.

"Why is that?"

"I'm worried we're going to raise four spoiled brats, whose only interest in life will be self-gratification. Any time not spent in that pursuit will be spent trying to get money out of their mother so they can continue that pursuit."

"Pete, you and I were raised in working-class households. I understand your concern. I think you can control that if you start early by making the kids start earning their own money. Give them a small allowance, then if they want something, let them save for it. They will learn how to save and that they create their own happiness.

"The other problem you're faced with is what you are trying to do denies Sophie the fruits of her own labors."

"Thanks for the advice; I'm going to have to give this serious thought."

A couple of minutes later Sophie came up on deck.

She walked over to Pete and sat on his lap. "Am I still persona non grata?" she asked.

"Not for the moment, but when we get home we are going to have a serious talk," Pete replied.

Sophie rolled her eyes up and said, "Oh goody, something to look forward to." Both Pete and Mike chuckled.

"What's so funny?" Dianne asked, as she and Carol joined them.

"My dear darling wife," Pete said. "By the way, what is the name of this boat?" he asked Sophie.

"I named it after you," Sophie said.

"The SS Pete?" Jack offered.

"No, the Delta King, get it?" Sophie replied.

Pete just groaned. After looking around he went on, changing the subject, "I know this is obvious but we have to be careful what we say in front of the crew. We don't want them knowing what we're doing here."

"When do you think we should leave here?" Jack asked.

"Probably tomorrow," Pete answered. "We don't know when the Scimitar is arriving in St. Tropez. I would like to anchor close enough so we can use the directional mic. That means we need to arrive after they do."

"Good idea," Mike added.

The always practical Jack suggested, "What say we go get some lunch?"

Jack's remark was greeted with nods from everyone.

"I want to go to the Hotel Carlton. I've seen it in so many movies, that I would like to see it in person, and I'll probably never have the opportunity again," Dianne said.

"Why not?" Pete said rising. As he did so he took Sophie by the waist and stood her up. "We need some transportation."

"Let's see if we can all fit in the crew's car," Sophie said. "I'll see if I can find the key."

Later that evening in their stateroom, Pete said to Sophie, "Do you remember the conversation we had about spending money foolishly?"

"Yes."

"This a perfect example. You spent forty-five million on a boat we'll use may be ten times, if that, next summer."

"I think we'll get more use out of it than that. I plan to send it to Florida so your parents can stay on it when they take their vacation next winter. And then on to the islands so we can get out of the cold for a little bit next winter."

Pete threw up his hands. "You could have saved a few bucks and bought a couple of hotels."

****

They arrived in St. Tropez at one o'clock the next afternoon and found the Scimitar already anchored. Pete guided the captain toward an area where he hoped they would be able to use the listening equipment. The captain was curious why Pete wanted to drop the anchor where he did. Prudently, he remained silent.

Pete and Mike tested the directional mic once the anchor was firmly set and found it worked well. They could hear any conversation on deck very clearly. They kept a loose visual surveillance on the boat for the rest of the day, but nothing seemed to happen.

They decided to do the same thing that evening that they had done in Villefranche. About five o'clock, a crew member took Mike, Dianne, Carol, and Jack ashore in the shore boat. They were going to follow the crew members if they came ashore and record their conversations for later review.

Sophie and Pete remained aboard. They ate in the dining room area of the main salon. After dinner they went up to the top deck of the boat with the remainder of the bottle of wine they had started with their meal. It was the first time either one of them had been on the top deck, which had a small bar, lounge chairs, and a hot tub.

"When did you buy the villa and this boat?" Pete asked Sophie.

"My father and I came down here in July. I wanted to do something for him, but that did not work out so well."

A crewmember brought them another bottle of wine after about an hour. Shortly thereafter, Pete stripped and got in the hot tub, saying, "Coming?"

Sophie never hesitated. She stripped while sitting on the edge of the hot tub. When naked she swung around and slid into the tub joining her husband. It was an evening to remember, making love under the stars.

***

Sophie and Pete were on the aft deck nibbling on croissants with their coffee and juice when Dianne and Mike joined them.

"What happened last night?" Pete asked Mike.

"Same thing as Villefranche, they ate and the younger crewmembers went to a disco. They struck out."

Jack came onto the back deck with a cup of coffee in his hand. "I've been thinking," he said. "How are we going to deal with these guys? We cannot get near the boat. Are we going to after the boss man on dry land or what?"

"All good questions," Pete replied, "but, the bigger question is why are they going to the United States? It doesn't make sense. They have to realize that the American authorities would have figured out by now that the guys with the stingers came from that boat. The only explanation is that they are up to something that makes it worth the risk."

"Yea, but what?" Jack asked.

"I don't know," Pete answered, "but more importantly, what are we going to do about it?" he continued.

"Why not just call that general you know, and lay the problem out for him and be done with it?" Carol asked.

"When they changed the name of the boat, they probably changed the ownership as well, so the boat can go into the United States with new owners and no one is any the wiser that it's the same operation," Sophie offered.

"How would that work?" Pete queried.

"You register the boat in the name of a corporation which has been formed in a jurisdiction that allows bearer shares."

"I don't get it," Dianne said.

Sophie explained, "In most countries a corporation is required to maintain a list of its shareholders, but some countries allow the shares to be issued to bearer, meaning whomever has the shares in hand is the owner. In other words, the same person could own two corporations and transfer the boat between them. No one would ever know the same person owned the boat after the transfer."

"Got it," Dianne said.

"That still leaves us with the same problem; how are going to get to these guys?" Jack wondered.

"I have an idea for that," Sophie said.

Pete motioned with his hand for her to continue.

Sophie went on, "Do you remember telling me, 'the first thing you do when you get on a boat is figure out where the life jackets are?' Well, I'll bet their shore launch has life jackets under the seats just like this one does. When they go into town tonight, we slip onto their boat and look at their life jackets. Tomorrow we buy some identical life jackets and stuff them full of explosive. Then you can wire up a sat phone trigger, et voila."

"And hope no one dials a wrong number," Jack added.

"That might work," Mike said.

Then Carol, who had been mostly silent up to that point, asked, "Who has the sat phone number?"

"Only General Lane, he gave me the sat phone, so I better give him a call and find out," Pete said.

"What's the battery life on a sat phone?" Jack asked.

"It's a couple of weeks at least. Those things are designed to be used in remote areas where electricity is not available, but when I call the general, I'll ask him," Pete said.

"How do we get on that boat without anyone getting wise?" Mike asked.

"The dingy dock is away from the center of town, over by where the ferries dock. We'll wait until they've tied up and gone into town, then we'll tie up next to their boat. When everyone leaves their boat, one of us will step onto their boat and look at their life jackets," Pete said.

"Seems simple enough," Jack said.

"Carol, you should be the one to climb onto their boat, since you're the shortest and least likely to be seen," Pete said.

"I think I'm going to go listen to the recordings we got last night," Mike said, rising.

"There was nothing of any interest on the recordings we made last night," Mike told Pete later that afternoon.

"When you go into town, see if you can rent a car," Pete said. He went on to explain, "Tomorrow someone is going to have to go to Nice to pick up a package from the general, then we have to go find the identical life jackets."

"They probably have all the stuff you need to rig the life jackets here on the boat," Mike said.

"The less the crew knows the better," Pete answered.

"You're right," Mike agreed.

***

That evening the others again went into town to dine, while Pete and Sophie remained on the boat. They enjoyed a repeat performance in the hot tub.

"I don't think I can do this again," Sophie said, catching her breath.

"Why not?"

"A heart attack is a very real possibility. I have never, ever experienced anything like the climax I had tonight," she said, still gasping.

Pete said nothing, but he felt exactly the same way. What a wife! Not only was she beautiful and smart; she could tie him in knots in bed. What a combo, killer combo, actually. He wasn't sure how life could get any sweeter.

***

The next morning when Pete came up to breakfast, Mike and Jack were already seated at the table. "How did it go last night?" Pete asked.

"We stole one of the life jackets," Jack said, in a low whisper to ensure a crew member didn't overhear.

"Good, where is it? I called the general last night after you left. I'm not sure we have enough C4 to get the job done. I'm meeting a guy in Nice at one-thirty today to pick up another twenty-five pounds. On the way back I'll find a ship chandler and buy some matching life jackets."

"That sounds like a good plan. The life jacket is still in the boat. Do you want some company on your way to Nice?" Mike asked.

"Love some," Pete replied, "but you'd better stay and man the directional mic, in case they say something worth hearing. When I spoke to the general yesterday, I also asked him to send us a satellite detonator."

"I'll go with you," Jack said.

"How did you and Sophie enjoy your evening?" Mike asked.

"We've used the hot tub after dinner the last couple of nights. I highly recommend it," Pete answered.

Carol joined them, and then Dianne shortly thereafter. Pete advised them of their intended course of action, seeking their input. They decided to stay on the boat with the intention of lying in the sun.

"Where's Sophie this morning?" Carol asked.

"She was still sacked out the last time I saw her," Pete said. "Could one of you run Jack and me into St. Tropez? We need to get on the road."

Pete and Jack returned to the boat around five-thirty. It took Pete an hour to remove most of the stuffing from the life jackets and refill them with C4. He placed the detonator in the last one. The next problem was how to switch the lifejackets without the crew seeing them.

The resolution was easier than he first thought. As the others were leaving for dinner that evening, he handed Mike a trash bag. The crew simply thought they were taking trash to the dumpster near the dingy dock.

Pete waited up for the others to return that evening. "How did it go?" he asked when they returned from dinner.

"Like clockwork," Mike answered.

"Good," Pete said, "Now we just have to find the right moment to blow the boat, but that is probably a subject for further discussion tomorrow. Why don't you guys give it some thought tonight?"

The next morning, when they were all seated at the table for breakfast, Pete asked, "Well, what do you all think about the timing to detonate the boat?"

"Carol and I talked about it last night. The only thing that makes sense is for someone to stay here until the boss man shows up and then boom," Jack said.

"The same thought occurred to me as well," Pete said. "I guess you all can head for home, and I'll stay and wait for the right moment.

"And how do we make sure the boss man was involved in the attempt at Newark Airport? I really don't want to take down someone innocent."

"I think I'd better stay with you," Mike said, "you don't speak Arabic, and as you said, we need to make sure that the boss man is involved."

"These guys don't seem to worry about innocent lives, so why should we?" Jack asked.

"Because we are not animals," Pete answered,

"If you're staying, so am I," Sophie said.

"We can talk about that later," Pete said, attempting to deflect Sophie's obvious intention. Sophie accepted the proposition that her staying was going to be the subject of a difficult discussion and best conducted in private, but she had no intention of letting her husband go into harm's way without her supervision. She knew he would take chances himself before letting anyone else take a risk, so she was staying, period. She admired his sense of duty but hated him for it at the same time. He jeopardized their life together and that she didn't like at all. If anything happened to him, she doubted she would survive the broken heart.

Later that afternoon in their cabin, Sophie stood up to emphasize her point, and repeated, "If you are staying, so am I."

Pete crossed the cabin and kissed her saying, "I'm worried about the children. My mother loves those kids dearly, but she is sixty-eight years old and doesn't have the stamina she once had. The children need someone looking out for them who is one hundred percent alert. My mother has to be wearing down by now."

Pete had just played the only card which had the possibility of dissuading Sophie. "I hate it when you do that."

"What?"

"Make the children the issue and not the danger to yourself."

"There is no danger. When I push the button their boat will not even be in sight. I don't want the crew to know anything, the less they see the better."

It all sounded reasonable to Sophie, but she was full of foreboding. "If you promise me you aren't going to do anything foolish, and I mean anything dangerous, I'll leave."

Holding her in his arms, Pete kissed her again. "You're doing the right thing."

"Promise!"

"Okay, I promise," Pete said. After a short pause, Pete added, "I am going to miss you an awful lot, you know." He kissed her again.

Sophie still had reservations, but instead of expressing them, said, "I guess I had better start packing if you're throwing me out tomorrow."

"I am hardly throwing you out. You are returning to the bosom of your family and to the people who love you and need you the most."

"Blarney Stone, again!"

"Moi?" Pete said in his most innocent tone of voice. Sophie refused to react, which indicated that she was quite upset.

26

The next morning one of the crew members took everyone ashore, and Pete drove them to the airport in Cannes, which was the closest airport that would handle an aircraft the size of Sophie's. Mike remained behind to monitor the directional listening mic.

When they got to the airport, Sophie said, "I want you to call me every day."

"Okay," Pete replied.

"You miss one day and I'll be back the next day."

"Okay, you made your point."

"And you'd better not be lying to me, either, or minimizing things."

"I would never do something like that."

"Yes you would if you thought it would keep me from worrying. You've done it before. I hate it!"

"Sweetheart, I shall be completely candid with you, or as candid as I can be," Pete cooed. They kissed one last time at the bottom of the steps leading up to the plane.

As the plane broke ground, a thought passed through Sophie's mind. "What did as candid as I can be, mean?" She had been distracted, and let it slide by without question. When she spoke to him tomorrow she intended to ask.

It was two o'clock when Pete returned to the boat, and he found Mike in his cabin with the porthole open listening to the directional mic. "Anything going on?" he asked Mike.

"Some guy we haven't seen before showed up about eleven o'clock. He went down below. The few crew conversations I've overheard gave me no indication of who, or rather what, he is."

"Sounds like we just keep watching and listening and see what develops," Pete said.

"Guess so," Mike replied.

At four-thirty Mike and Pete watched as the shore boat left the Scimitar. It returned twenty minutes later with one passenger who was greeted by the new arrival from earlier in the day. The two men embraced and kissed each other on both cheeks as is the custom in much of the world when old friends meet. Five minutes later both men climbed to the upper deck seeking privacy. The conditions were just right so Mike was able to listen to every word. They also had a digital recorder running. After fifteen minutes, the two men descended to the main deck. Mike took as many pictures of both men as he was able using the telephoto lens.

"Well, what did they say?" Pete asked.

"This is a beaut," Mike said. "They're making a rendezvous at sea and are being passed a lead box weighing five hundred pounds, apparently supplied by the Iranians. Then they are going to the Azores to refuel and head for the States. Once off the coast, one of them is sneaking ashore to carry out the plans for an attack on a shopping mall, made by some guy named Amer. The mall attack is to be coordinated with a suicide attack on the New York subway system, which they think will close the subway system for three hundred years."

"Sounds like they are being passed the makings for a dirty bomb."

"Yep, that's what I think as well," Mike said. Then he went on to say, "The attack on the mall is to be coordinated with the attack on the subway system in order to overtax the emergency responders, so the government will be forced to hire more people than they need and thereby strain the overall resources."

"Do we know what mall they intend to attack?" Pete asked.

"No, but it's close to New York," Mike answered.

"We'd better email the recording to General Lane, this really falls into his bailiwick. He can forward it to whomever he thinks appropriate," Pete said.

"I've emailed it, but you probably ought to follow up with a phone call," Mike said.

"My very thoughts," Pete said. "I'm going to do that right now," Pete added, standing to go to his stateroom and get the sat phone.

"General, we emailed you a tape of a conversation we recorded earlier today. I think it is really important you get a good translation and put it in the hands of your best analysts ASAP."

"Okay. Hang on a second… OK, I have your email, and I'll pass it along on a priority basis."

"Good enough," Pete said. After hanging up with the general, Pete went looking for the captain.

No sooner had he hung up the phone than Mike came up and showed him a print of the photo he had taken earlier in the day. "I think this is the guy we saw in Laos, Hermosillo, and Paris."

Pete looked at the print and said, "I think you're right. This guy is really bad news. I think that resolves the question of an innocent owner."

Then Pete went looking for the captain, he asked him if they had enough fuel to reach the Azores nonstop.

"Yes, sir," the captain replied.

"Have you been through the Azores before?" Pete asked the Captain.

"Yes sir, many times," the captain answered.

"Is there one major port or are there many?" Pete wanted to know.

"Well sir, there are several usable ports, but most people go to Ponta Delgada. It is the largest city and as such has the most services available."

"Let's plan on departing for the Azores in about an hour. We'll be continuing on from there to the United States."

"Very good, sir, but, it may take us a little longer before we can depart for the Azores. I am not sure about the state of the larder. We may have to restock provisions before we can depart. I'll check and let you know, sir," the captain replied.

"As soon as you know how long before we can depart, please let me know," Pete said.

"Very good, sir," the captain replied.

Pete and the captain departed in different directions, the captain to check with the chef and Pete to look for Mike. Pete found Mike wearing earphones listening to the recording again. Pete had to tap Mike on the shoulder to get his attention, and Mike took the earphones off as he looked up. Pete said, "I think we should head for the Azores so we can get there before the Scimitar arrives. We can stay there two days after the Scimitar leaves, and then we push the button and fly home. I'm sure Sophie will send the plane for us."

"Those are pretty much my thoughts as well," Mike said.

As Mike finished speaking, the sat phone rang. Pete thought it was probably Sophie. "Hello," he said picking up the phone.

"Pete, where did you get the recording you sent me?" General Lane said without any preliminaries.

"We made it," Pete responded knowing his answer to be insufficient.

"Okay, you win. Take your time and tell me the long-winded version."

"You remember the Angelique, the boat we were looking for? Well, Sophie's contacts found it in Monaco, renamed the Scimitar. We followed it to St. Tropez. We anchored Sophie's yacht near enough that we could use a directional mic. Today two bigwigs came aboard, at different times. Those are the guys talking on the recording."

"We are taking this very seriously, especially since the attempted attack at Newark Airport originated from that boat. Our analysts think that the lead box contains nuclear waste from the Iranian nuclear reactor. Those guys are right; a dirty bomb will contaminate the subway system for centuries."

"You don't need to worry about the nuclear waste. It will never reach the States. We're going to sink their boat before it gets there."

"How?" the general asked.

"We planned to take them down long before we heard about their plan to bomb the subway system. We managed to get forty-five pounds of C4, the satellite detonator, and the satellite phone detonator into the life jackets on board their shore boat."

"When do you plan to sink the thing?"

"We think we ought to wait until they have made their rendezvous at sea, and have the nuclear waste on board. We know they'ill be stopping in the Azores for fuel, two days after they leave there, boom. I am extremely concerned about what happens to the nuclear waste. The boat should be in deep enough water to minimize the danger the cargo presents. I don't want to poison the sea."

"I'll check with the experts and get back to you on that," the general said.

"What do you intend to do about the attack on the mall?" Pete asked.

"I don't know, we are still looking at that. The problem would be simple if we knew which mall, but we don't," the general responded. "How do you plan to keep them unaware that they are being followed?" the general wanted to know.

"By getting to the Azores ahead of them. That way they will believe they are following us. We are also going to stay on in the Azores for two days after they depart in case they have anyone watching for anything suspicious," Pete answered.

"I'll be back in touch with you as soon as the brain trust has reviewed all the information you have supplied us and coordinated it with all other resources," the general said.

"You're going to have to use the sat phone; we're leaving here as soon as we can. I look forward to hearing from you."

Pete had no sooner hung up than the captain knocked on his door. When Pete opened the door the captain said, "We can leave here as soon as you like. We have enough food on board to reach the Azores without a problem. We can call ahead and have more provisions waiting for us on the fuel dock in Ponta Delgado. All I need to do is clear outbound with the Port Authority here."

"Great, I would like to leave as soon as you are able."

"Very good, sir," the captain said turning to leave.

Pete followed the captain up the companionway looking for Mike. Mike was in the main salon with his ear phones on again. "I spoke to the general and thus far he is on board with our plan to head for the Azores. I told the captain to get under way as soon as possible," Pete told Mike.

"Have you called Sophie yet?" Mike asked.

"No. I must admit that's a phone call I am not looking forward, too."

"Why not?"

"Sophie isn't going to like that we haven't left yet," Pete said.

"Why don't I call Dianne and let her tell Sophie, might soften the blow a little."

"Good idea, but don't mention General Lane to her. Sophie reacts to his name like a bull to a red flag."

27

"Hello," Pete said answering the sat phone. "What's this shit that you're going to the Azores?" Sophie asked in a most abrupt tone.

"What, no hello?" Pete replied.

"Cut the crap, I want to know what is going on right now!"

"I have no idea what you are talking about."

"I was mad before, but I am really getting pissed now."

"Relax will you? We decided that we really needed to sink this thing in really deep water. We overheard a conversation where they said they were going to the States. Once they leave the Azores, they will be in water that is over two thousand feet deep. No one will ever be able to find that boat."

"I guess that makes some sense," Sophie said, somewhat mollified.

"Of course it does. Will you send the plane to Ponta Delgada in four or five days?"

"I guess so. I ought to make you swim home."

"Why?"

"Because I sense that you're up to something that you're not telling me, and I don't like it!"

"We're going to blow the boat. That's it, I'm telling you."

"Okay, for the moment I am going to let it rest, but if there is something you're not telling me… Well, let's not go into that now."

***

They were two days out of St. Tropez, when the general called again on the sat phone. Pete answered the phone saying, "Hello."

"Pete, it's General Lane. Can you get Mike and put this on the speaker."

"Hang on for minute. Mike is down below, I'll go find him," Pete replied.

Pete found Mike reading in his stateroom. "Can I come in?"

"Sure."

"Mike, it's the general, he wants to speak to us both," Pete said, closing the door to Mike's stateroom.

"Okay general, we're both here and you are on the speaker," Pete said.

"As I am sure you can imagine we have given this thing considerable thought. I want to advise you of our current thinking as it involves both of you. Mike, we would like you to fly to the States. Pete, we would like you to leave the Azores on the boat as soon as you have refueled. We are going to have a sub follow the Angelique, Scimitar now. It will blow the charges you have placed on board and verify that it sinks with all hands.

Meanwhile, we would like to use Sophie's yacht to make the pass down the Connecticut coast. When you receive the signal, what is the signal by the way? Anyway, we would like you, Pete, to take a dingy and follow the signal to Amer. We want you to keep in touch with Mike and Jack via secure radio, which will be supplied in Ponta Delgada. Pete, you will tell Mike and Jack where you're meeting Amer. Then you guys grab Amer. We need to know where he has his jihadists stashed. Use any method you deem necessary to get the information. We'll take it from there.

"You know what will happen if we grab the guy. He'll lawyer up and we'll lose a few hundred citizens," the general finished.

"That actually sounds like a pretty good plan," Mike said.

"The signal is a blinking light sending the letter A in Morse. Are you going to take out the trash?" Pete asked.

"I'll have a crew standing by in the neighborhood awaiting your call."

Mike nodded his approval at Pete. "All right, I'll be in touch when we leave Ponta Delgada."

***

The captain entered the port of Ponta Delgada slowly. As they approached the fuel dock, Pete saw a trunk from the catering company waiting, presumably for them.

28

It took eleven days to cross the Atlantic. In route, the general sent Pete a complete transcript of the recording they had made in St. Tropez. The general also sent a proposed plan for and suggested routing for Mike and Jack to follow as they paralleled the coast. The plan was simple. Mike and Jack would follow the coast line, while Pete waited to receive the signal from shore. He would advise Mike via secure radio. Amer would be squeezed between Pete coming from the sea and Mike and Jack coming from the land side. The general had also advised Pete that the Scimitar was no longer afloat.

Where they took Amer after they had him was something the CIA and the general did not want to know. Mike and Pete had talked about that problem. They decided to use Pete's garage, which left the problem of Mrs. Chou and her children. Pete talked to Chou on the telephone, and together they had solved the problem. Chou took his wife and kids to Disney World for a week's vacation.

When Pete told the captain they would clear customs in Nantucket, the captain replied that Nantucket was not a port of entry.

"The fix is in," Pete told the captain, and cautioned the captain about broadcasting anything he saw. Pete also told the captain to pass the word to the crew.

"Sir, I feel obligated to tell you there are severe penalties for not clearing Customs before touching the shore."

"Don't worry, I got you covered."

Coming into port, a coastguard launch came out toward the boat before they dropped the anchor, tying up to the stern. A Customs officer was in the launch. The Customs officer asked for the captain and all passports. He stamped the passports without leaving the coastguard launch.

When the captain returned to the main deck with the stamped passports, he said to Pete, "I would not have believed it if I hadn't seen it."

Pete just put the index finger of his right hand to his lips, "Shh."

Pete called the general to advise him all had gone well with Customs. As the phone was ringing, he heard the anchor chain coming up and felt the boat start to move. He stood up to look out the port hole, and saw they were moving toward the fuel dock.

The general answered saying, "Pete, the Scimitar left the Azores twelve hours after you left the Azores so that gives you twelve hours to get into position to cruise down the Connecticut coast."

"We are taking on fuel and then going to start toward the coast," Pete said.

"I have a phone number for you. Are you ready to copy?"

"Yes sir," Pete replied.

The general gave him the phone number and then said, "Just give them an address and they will take out your trash."

"Will do, general," Pete said hanging up.

Pete called Mike next and advised him they would be starting their run down the coast at eleven that night. Mike told him that they would be in position as per the general's plan.

"How did you deal with Dianne?" Pete asked.

"I did the only sensible thing. I lied. Jack and I are going to the Mohawk Casino tonight," Mike told him.

"I wish I could think of something as easy as that. Sophie is beside herself."

"I hope we'll see you tonight," Mike said hanging up.

Pete found the captain on the dock supervising the refueling operation. "How long do you think it will be until we can get underway?"

"We can go almost as soon as you wish. We've already up-loaded five thousand gallons," the captain answered.

"I need to show you what we are going to be doing tonight," Pete said.

"Let's go to the chart room. You can lay it out for me there."

Once they entered the chart room the captain turned and asked, "Sir, we are not doing anything illegal, are we?"

"Not at all," Pete said. "We need to be to be off Watch Hill, Rhode Island, at ten o'clock tonight, then we will proceed down the coastline as close as you can safely get to the coast. We'll be looking for a light blinking sending the letter A in Morse. When we see the signal, I'm going to leave the ship. You proceed to wherever my wife told you to go."

"You wife has said nothing to me about any of this, sir."

"After I leave the boat, captain, just go wherever you would like. Call my wife sometime the day after tomorrow and tell her where you are. But don't say anything about this portion of the voyage."

"Yes, sir."

Pete started to turn away but thought better of it. Turning back to the captain, he said, "If you should hear from my wife today, don't tell her where we are, or what we are doing. You are specifically authorized to lie if necessary."

"Yes, sir."

"Oh, and I am expecting a small inflatable dingy and outboard to be delivered this morning. When it shows up, will you let me know?"

"Certainly, sir," the captain replied.

The captain found Pete in the main salon five minutes later to tell him the dingy had arrived.

"Could you inflate it after we leave port?" Pete asked.

"Yes, sir."

"Will there be any problem launching it tonight?"

"None at all, sir."

At ten o'clock that night the boat was positioned just north of Watch Hill, Rhode Island. Pete used the radio to check in with Mike. He and Jack were in positon. Pete went below and changed into a black turtle neck and black jeans. The captain started southward, down the coast at five knots hugging the shore line, as close as he dared.

Pete kept in constant contact with Mike and Jack. They were twenty miles south of Mystic when Pete and the captain both spotted the blinking light simultaneously. The captain gave the helm to the first officer, and took Pete into the chart room. The chart of the Connecticut coast line was already on the table, and the captain pointed out their exact location.

Pete advised Mike on the radio of the precise location of the light. Mike said, "We can be there in four to five minutes."

The crew had launched the dingy while Pete was on the radio with Mike. Pete climbed in the dingy and headed toward the shore. He kept his speed down to allow Mike and Jack as much time as he could to get into position.

Pete got a radio call from Mike a half mile from shore. "We're close as we can get without knowing exactly where he is."

"Use the night vision binoculars to keep your eye on me," Pete whispered.

The light blinked again from shore. Pete adjusted his course so as to head directly toward it. Pete realized Amer had chosen the mouth of a small river as a landing spot. He was twenty feet from the river bank when he saw a man moving toward him. The nose of the dingy had just touched the bank when Amer realized the dingy occupant was not the person he expected.

Pete reached into his waistband and withdrew a twenty-two caliber pistol equipped with a silencer. Before Amer could react to the armed, unexpected man, Pete shot him in the leg. Thirty seconds after the shot, Mike and Jack appeared.

They immediately taped his hands behind his back and taped his mouth shut. They closed the wound on his right leg with crazy glue, which Mike had brought along with him. Pete took one of Amer's arms and Mike the other. They walked Amer up the river bank seven hundred yards to where Mike and Jack had left the white van.

Jack sat on the rear floor of the van with their prisoner, while Mike drove and Pete sat in the passenger seat.

"What did you say to Sophie to get the white van?" Pete asked Mike.

"I told her I needed to move something," Mike answered.

"Where are you going?" Pete asked, failing to recognize the route to Mystic.

"Oh, I forgot to tell you. We changed the plan a little. Sophie rented an old barn to store your project cars. She happened to mention it to me and Dianne last week and I got the address from her. Jack and I checked it out, and it's perfect. There are no other structures within two miles."

"I wish Sophie would quit bellyaching about my old cars."

"If that's all she complains about, consider yourself lucky."

"You don't know how loud and long she can complain."

Mike chuckled and ten minutes later they arrived at the old barn Sophie had rented. Pete hopped out and opened the door so

Mike could pull the van completely inside. Pete closed the barn doors after Mike entered.

In one far corner sat Pete's old MG. In the center of the barn sat a chair. They dragged Amer out of the van and taped him into the chair.

No sooner was he seated than Amer yelled, "I want a lawyer."

"Pal, you are way beyond a lawyer," Mike said to Amer.

"I'm not going to tell you anything."

Jack rolled a log three feet long and about fourteen inches across into the center of the barn. When just in front of Amer he stood the log on its end. Then, he went to the corner over by the MG and returned with an axe. Jack swung the axe and stuck it in the log.

Pete leaned in toward Amer and said, "When you get to Paradise, you are going to arrive without a hand and will for eternity be known as a thief."

"I want a lawyer!"

"The government might honor that request, but we are not the government. You will talk. The only question is how much pain you can take before you sing. But should you die during our little session here is over, we will bury you in a pigskin bag."

Amer struggled against the duct tape holding him in the chair. "You can't do this to me. I want a lawyer."

Pete took the hammer Mike handed him. "You can scream all you want. No one is going to hear you. Now, I want to know where you've stashed your would-be martyrs."

"I'll never tell you."

With that, Pete bent down on one knee and hit Amer as hard as he could on the little toe of his left foot with a two-pound hammer. Amer let out a horrible scream of pain.

When Amer stopped screaming, Pete asked him, "Ready to talk now?"

"No, I'll never tell you," Amer shrieked.

Pete bent over again, and hit the next two toes on Amer's left foot as hard as he could. Amer let out another scream.

"I'll talk, I'll talk," Amer screamed.

"Where are your men stashed?"

"Twenty-one Nile Street, Hartford," Amer gasped.

"How many men are there?"

"Three."

"How are they armed?"

"AK47's, nine millimeter pistols, and hand grenades," Amer answered Pete.

"Where do you have the various cars stashed?"

Amer recited all the locations and the make and model of each car.

Pete, Jack, and Mike walked over to the MG and, speaking in low tones, Mike said, "Suppose he is lying?"

"Why don't we give the general a call and let him figure out if this dirtbag is lying. We just leave him here. Once the general figures it out, he can take out the leftovers. If this guy is lying we can come back and go to work on him again," Jack suggested.

"That's a pretty good idea," Mike said.

"I agree," Pete said, pulling out his cell phone.

Pete gave the general all the information that Amer had furnished them, albeit, somewhat unwillingly.

When Pete had finished, the general asked, "Is this guy securely in place?"

"He'll be waiting right here for your guys to arrive," Pete said, hanging up.

Amer was still screaming about a lawyer when the three of them left the barn. This time Pete climbed behind the wheel. "Who goes where?" Pete asked.

"Jack picked me up, and we left his car at your house. Just go to your house, Jack can drop me at home."

"Okay," Pete replied.

Pete drove silently, deep in thought. He knew Sophie would have many questions, most of which he did not want to answer. That basically left him with only one option. He would not lie to his wife. He firmly believed that marriages survived and grew stronger with truth, but in this situation domestic tranquility required evasive answers.

The three friends shook hands in the driveway. Mike and Jack left just as the sun was rising. Pete entered his house through the side door. He tread lightly thinking that Sophie was probably asleep. As he slipped through the bedroom door, he saw immediately that Sophie was indeed asleep. He dropped his clothes beside the bed and eased his weight onto their mattress. He did not slide over to the side of the bed where he usually slept. He rolled over on his right side barely able to see all her black hair cascading over the next pillow through the lifting gloom. He closed his eyes just as her alarm rang. He faked being asleep, wanting to prolong the confrontation as long as possible.

He heard Sophie get up. As usual, she used her crutches to head into the bathroom. Exhausted, he fell asleep before she came out of the bathroom. He awoke three hours later. He took a shower before going downstairs to satisfy his hunger pangs. The three younger children were in the family room under the supervision of the amah watching TV. Pete went into the kitchen, and found a steak in the refrigerator. Moments later, the steak was sizzling in a frying pan.

Sophie came into the kitchen, when Pete was halfway through cooking the steak. She carried two bags of groceries into the kitchen. "You're up," she said, brightly.

"The boat got in late last night and I didn't want to wake you when I got into bed."

"You were certainly were quiet. I didn't hear a thing," Sophie said sitting down at the kitchen table. "So tell me what happened with the Scimitar?" Sophie asked.

"Well, I called the general, and brought him up to date. He offered to have a sub follow the Scimitar and report on the explosion. So we left St. Tropez as soon as we could. We went to the Azores, refueled and came straight on to the States. The last time we saw the Scimitar was in St. Tropez. We saw a guy we are certain was the owner. We had seen him in Laos and elsewhere. No doubt he was involved in Janet's murder. He went down with the ship."

"Why didn't you fly home from the Azores with Mike?"

"Mike wanted to get home, but I was enjoying the voyage so much I decided to stay."

"I'm glad you are home now," Sophie said, rising. She was secretly pleased he had enjoyed the new boat she had bought. She had been worried she was never going to hear the end of her buying a yacht without discussing it with him.

Pete breathed a sigh of relief as Sophie started to put away the groceries. He left his dirty dishes in the sink and headed for the garage. He spent twenty minutes taking stock of where he was in the restoration process. Then he sat down on a work stool, and got to work. At noon Pete went into the house to help with lunch.

When lunch was over, Pete went back to the garage and resumed work. Sophie went into the office to work on the computer. She checked on their investment portfolio and looked for new ways invest money.

Sophie was sifting through an investment site when a news flash came across the screen. The last terrorist captured in Hartford, Connecticut, had died. She immediately turned on CNN. They were reporting on an incident in Hartford where an FBI SWAT team had entered a house and a firefight ensued. Sophie leaned back in her chair and ran the events of the day through her mind. This morning she had thought it a bit odd that Pete had come into the bedroom when he did. How did he get home from where the boat docked? What time exactly did he get home? What time did the boat dock? How and where did they go through Customs at that time of the night? He had mentioned that damn general, again, and that general was worse than nuclear waste as far as she was concerned!

Then the thought occurred to her to look at the clothes Pete had been wearing. Sophie went upstairs and into Pete's closet. She found only one pair of dirty pants in his hamper. The left leg pant cuff had what looked like blood splatter on it. "Damn, double damn!!" she thought. "My husband was involved in another shoot out."

Sophie went back downstairs, went into the office and took a cigarette from the pack she had left on the desk. The more she thought about it the madder she got. As she walked toward the garage, she wasn't sure whether she was madder about Pete being involved in another firefight or lying.

She walked through the open garage door. She did not see Pete at first. "Peter J. Smith, where the hell are you?" she hollered.

Pete had his head in the trunk, installing a new battery. Pete stood up and realized from the look on Sophie's face that he was in trouble. Sophie's cigarette was not the only thing fuming in the garage that afternoon. "What's up?" Pete asked, in as innocent voice as he could muster.

"I want to know exactly what you were doing last night."

"Why? Nothing special," Pete said shrugging his shoulders.

"Do you think I'm stupid? You're lying to me and I don't like it."

Holding up his right hand, Pete said, "I swear I have never lied to you."

"The next thing you are going to tell me is that you know nothing about an FBI SWAT team take down of a terrorist cell this morning in Hartford.

"I don't know anything about it."

"Would you tell me how come there is blood on your pants?"

"What time did the SWAT team action go down?" he asked, deflecting her question.

"I don't know, other than it was this morning," Sophie said.

"Please remember that I was home in bed with you at six o'clock."

"I'll be back," Sophie said with uncharacteristic vehemence. Sophie's eyes hooded over as she looked at him suspiciously. "That better be the whole story. If I find out you're lying, I cannot tell you how pissed I am going to be."

"Sophie, I started by saying I have never told you a lie and that is still true. I don't think all the details are particularly important." He walked over and kissed her, long and hard.

***

Thirty minutes later, she came back into the garage. "Okay, you may be off the hook, but I want to know exactly how you got involved and how that miserable general got you involved. By the way, one of these days I am going to settle that general's hash once and for all!"

"I have no idea what you are talking about."

"You said you called the general. Why did you call him?" Sophie wanted to know.

"We recorded a conversation with the directional mic which we thought he should hear."

"What was the conversation about?"

"The guys on that boat were planning a terrorist attack somewhere in this area."

"And this conversation was about that planned attack?" Sophie asked.

"Yes."

"Humph," Sophie said. She turned and started back into the house, but turned back and asked, "Where is our boat?"

"I don't know."

"Why don't you know? You were there when it docked weren't you?" Sophie asked.

"No."

"What do you mean no?" she asked.

"Which part didn't you understand, the n or the o?" Pete replied smiling.

"Listen, Mr. Smarty Pants, I'm not in the mood. I want to know where you got off our boat," Sophie said continuing her interrogation.

"I got off at sea."

"What do you mean, you got off at sea?" Sophie asked. Then she demanded, "I want the whole story and no more evasions or double talk, and I want it now!"

"Well, the conversation we overheard laid out the plan for someone to come ashore by dingy. They were to be met by a guy named Amer, and Amer was to take this guy to wherever the attack on the mall was going to take place. So I used a dingy and went ashore. I snatched Amer by shooting him in the leg and took him to the barn you rented, where I extracted the location of his soon-to-be martyrs. I passed the address along to the general. That's all there is to it."

"Did you have help or do it alone?" Sophie demanded to know.

"Does it really matter who helped me?"

"Yes."

"Why?"

"Quit playing word games! I want the whole story!" Sophie said.

"Jack and Mike helped me."

"How did you work that out?"

"Well, as you know, Mike was with me until we got to the Azores. Mike knew the plan and when he got home he checked with Jack. Jack agreed to help. So as the boat came down the coastline we were in contact by radio. We did not know where Amer was located, but he was to signal the other yacht. He couldn't tell one 200 foot yacht from another a mile away at night. The plan was to catch Amer between Jack and Mike on shore and me coming in from the sea."

"Let me be sure I understand this. You came ashore in a dingy, at night, to meet an armed terrorist, hoping Mike and Jack would be able to find you?"

"Yea, that's basically it," he said, chuckling.

"Are you crazy?" Sophie hollered, as she kicked him in the shin with her peg leg.

"Ouch, that hurts!" Pete howled.

Sophie tried to kick him again, but missed. Pete, still smarting from the first kick, jumped backwards in the nick of time. "Will you quit that?" Pete yelled.

"What the hell is the matter with you? You have a wife and four children who need you. It's time you come to grips with the fact that you are no longer a commando and you have responsibilities to this family!" Sophie screamed as she turned on her heel and left.

Later on Pete walked into the kitchen to help Sophie with the children's dinner, and he found Sophie with her head in the freezer. Sophie's attitude was as frosty as the interior of the freezer she was looking into.

When the kids were fed and the kitchen cleaned up, Pete said to Sophie, "Let's go out on the back porch, I think we need to finish this discussion," Sophie said nothing, but left the kitchen heading for the back porch. Pete opened a bottle of red wine and poured two glasses. Then he joined Sophie on the porch.

"I poured you a glass of red wine," he said offering it to her. She took it saying nothing.

"Sophie, I think I need to tell you the whole story of what transpired over the last two weeks," Pete said, sitting down,

"So you did lie!" she spat.

"I did not; everything I said was true, but there is more to tell." He laid out the terrorists' entire plan, including the dirty bomb and the coordinated attack on the mall. He finished by saying, "You can tell absolutely no one."

"Looking back on this afternoon, I realize that perhaps I was a little harsh in my assessment of things. I can now see that you got caught up in events, but you didn't tell me the whole truth, and that's the same as lying."

"I answered every question you asked honestly. I can't help it if you don't ask the right questions, can I?"

Her eyes hooded over for the second time that day and she said, "If you think I'm going to condone evasion you are sadly mistaken, and I don't care how good the cause is."

"I have a question for you; if not telling all the facts about something is lying, what do you call forgetting to tell one's husband they spent eighty million dollars?"

"That's different," Sophie replied.

"How so?"

"I just spent money. You, however, sneaked ashore in a rubber boat looking for an armed terrorist at night, and you shot him! That's just plain crazy!"

"He wasn't armed."

"You didn't know that."

"Yes, I did," Pete said. "No one sneaking around trying to make a clandestine rendezvous would go armed because if you ran into a cop and you're armed, you'd go to jail. If you're unarmed, you go on your merry way."

"Then why did you shoot him?"

"I didn't feel like chasing some dirt bag around in the dark."

"Oh."

"I have a suggestion for you; why don't we just agree that we each overlooked something we probably should have told the other."

After a moment's hesitation and as Pete was rising to go refill his wine, Sophie said, "Okay." Then she said, "That means we get to keep the boat, right?"

As Pete stepped into the living room Sophie heard him mumble, "Me and my big mouth!"

The End

About the Author

*J*ay Alt grew up in Connecticut. He graduated from United States International University with a Bachelor's degree in English Literature in June of 1971. He attended Western State University, College of law, graduating in June of 1975. Jay was admitted to the California bar Association shortly thereafter.

After practicing law for five years, Jay decided to pursue a career in aviation. He worked as a flight engineer for UPS, and then subsequently moved to a major airline in May of 1987.

Jay and his wife of forty-five years divide their time between Virginia and the island of Bequia in the southern Caribbean.

KCM Publishing
a division of KCM Digital Media, LLC

www.ingramcontent.com/pod-product-compliance
Lightning Source LLC
Chambersburg PA
CBHW070742190726
48292CB00002B/380